PRAISE FOR THE NOVELS OF
ELIZABETH THORNTON

*The Marriage Trap*

"As multilayered as a wedding cake and just as
delectable . . . A memorable start to a new trilogy and a
fine introduction to Thornton's work."
—*Publishers Weekly*

*Shady Lady*

"Lively, brimming with marvelous dialogue, wit,
wisdom and a pair of delightful lovers, *Shady Lady* is a
joy. . . . A book to treasure!" —*Romantic Times*

"*Shady Lady* is an exhilarating Regency romantic
suspense. . . . Fans will gain plenty of pleasure from this
fine historical." —Harriet Klausner, Book Reviewer

*Almost a Princess*

"Well written on many levels as a murder mystery, a
historical romance, and a chronicle of women's rights—
or lack thereof—this book will appeal to fans of
Amanda Quick, Candace Camp, and Lisa Kleypas."
—*Booklist*

"A fabulous hero, a nicely brainy heroine, one red-hot
attraction and a believable plot makes for one great
bathtub read." —*Pittsburgh Post-Gazette*

## The Perfect Princess

"Steamy sex scenes, fiery repartee and strong characters set this romantic intrigue apart from the usual Regency fare." —*Publishers Weekly*

"An exciting historical romantic suspense that never slows down until the final page is completed." —*Midwest Book Review*

"Lots of action and a very neat twist at the end make this . . . a winning choice for libraries of all sizes." —*Booklist*

"Fast-paced, with a bit of intrigue and well-developed, passionate characters . . . *The Perfect Princess* is a joy to read!" —*Romantic Times*

## Princess Charming

"I buy Elizabeth Thornton books on her name alone. I know she'll deliver the goods, and that's what makes her one of my personal favorites. If you like plot, characterization, romance, and suspense all rolled together—buy Elizabeth Thornton!" —Linda Howard

"Delightfully entertaining." —*Philadelphia Inquirer*

"Ms. Thornton excels at writing a steamy passionate tale of love and *Princess Charming* gives you all that and more in this fast-paced historical romantic suspense." —*Romantic Times*

"True to her reputation for delivering excitement, mystery, and romance, Elizabeth Thornton crafts another breathtaking adventure set in the Regency period. *Princess Charming* is filled with delightful characterization, an intriguing plot, and sizzling sensuality. Once again, Ms. Thornton gives us a delightful mixture that satisfies even the most discriminating reader and keeps us begging for more."
—*Rendezvous*

## Strangers at Dawn

"An out-of-the-ordinary murder mystery set in the early 1800's with lots of suspects and a lovely romance."
—*Dallas Morning News*

"With her talent as a superb storyteller, Elizabeth Thornton skillfully blends suspense, murder and a powerful love story into a jewel of a book."
—*Romantic Times*

"Thornton has been a longtime favorite thanks to her well-told tales of intrigue peppered with sizzling romance, and *Strangers at Dawn* is among the best."
—*Oakland Press*

## Whisper His Name

"Thornton creates appealing characters and cleverly weaves in familiar Regency settings and customs."
—*Publishers Weekly*

"Ms. Thornton has delivered. This is a terrific book from cover to cover. The dynamic plot and characters will thrill and delight. Bravo!" —*Rendezvous*

## More Praise for Elizabeth Thornton

"This book is an absolute joy to read. I loved every minute of it! We are given humor, a murderer, sensuality, scintillating dialogue, and characters to cheer for. What more could you want?"
—*Rendezvous* on *You Only Love Twice*

"If you like mystery, murder and mayhem along with your romance, then *You Only Love Twice* will be your cup of tea." —*Romantic Times*

"This witty Regency romance/mystery will keep you up all night."
—*Atlanta Journal-Constitution* on *The Bride's Bodyguard*

"A rich, satisfying blend of suspense and passion."
—*Brazosport Facts* on *The Bride's Bodyguard*

"Cleverly plotted intrigue."
—*Publishers Weekly* on *The Bride's Bodyguard*

Nationally bestselling author Mary Balogh says, "I consider Elizabeth Thornton a major find."

*Rave Reviews* praises Elizabeth Thornton as "a major, major talent . . . a genre superstar."

*Publishers Weekly* raves: "Fast paced and full of surprises, Thornton's latest novel is an exciting story of romance, mystery, and adventure . . . a complex lot that exuberantly carries the reader. Thornton's firm control of her plot, her graceful prose, and her witty dialogue make *Dangerous to Kiss* a pleasure to read."

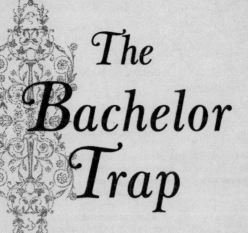

# The
# *Bachelor*
# *Trap*

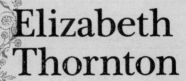

# Elizabeth
# Thornton

A DELL BOOK

THE BACHELOR TRAP
A Dell Book / May 2006

Published by
Bantam Dell
A Division of Random House, Inc.
New York, New York

This is a work of fiction. Names, characters, places, and incidents either are the product of the author's imagination or are used fictitiously. Any resemblance to actual persons, living or dead, events, or locales is entirely coincidental.

Dell is a registered trademark of Random House, Inc., and the colophon is a trademark of Random House, Inc.

ISBN-13: 978-0-553-58754-8
ISBN-10: 0-553-58754-4

Printed in the United States of America
Published simultaneously in Canada

www.bantamdell.com

OPM   10   9   8   7   6   5   4   3   2   1

*For my cousin, Lois Hobbs*
*A salute to all those memorable adventures we shared*
*when we were children*

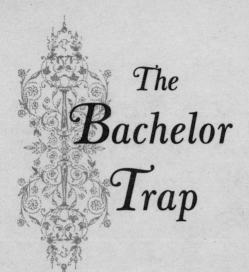

# The Bachelor Trap

# Prologue

## Longbury, October 1815

Edwina Gunn pushed through the back door of her cottage and quickly turned the key. There was a bar on the door and she slammed it home as well. Her heart was racing. She was breathing hard. She'd been asking too many questions, poking her nose in where it wasn't wanted. All she'd achieved was to rouse a sleeping tiger.

"Get a hold of yourself, Edwina," she told herself sternly. "You're sixty years old. At this rate, you'll give yourself an apoplexy! You're not a threat! You can't prove anything. And after all this time, he is bound to feel safe."

When she had control of her breathing, she crossed to the window and, standing well back so as not to be seen, looked out. Her cottage was just outside the estate, and all she could see beyond her own small patch of gardens and the outhouses were stands of yew trees, hawthorns, and oaks, the remnants of their winter foliage now bedraggled with the sudden downpour. There was nothing else to see.

She, too, was soaked through. She unfastened her coat and hung it on a hook beside the door. The fire in the grate had been banked by Mrs. Ludlow, her daily help, but Mrs. Ludlow had her own family to tend and always left in time to prepare their dinner.

She wouldn't get into the house tomorrow with the door barred. That couldn't be helped. She'd get up early herself and unbar the door, or Mrs. Ludlow could use the door knocker. That would get her up.

She was alone in the house and her nearest neighbors were up at the Priory.

This last thought prompted her to make sure that the front door and all the downstairs windows were locked. It was something she was in the habit of doing every night, though like most country people, she left her doors unlocked during the daylight hours. From now on, she was going to lock her doors during the day as well.

"Silly old woman," she chided herself. She'd probably run from a stray dog or one of the estate gamekeepers.

Feeling more like herself, she began to mount the stairs. It was a struggle and she had to use the handrail to haul herself up. She made up her mind, then, to move her bedchamber to the unused maid's room next to the kitchen. It was small but convenient for someone who couldn't manage the stairs. The very thought made her feel her age all the more keenly.

Once in her own room, she wrapped herself in a warm dressing robe, put on her wool slippers, then poked the fire to a cheery blaze. As she watched the flames licking around the small lumps of coal, she became lost in thought again.

She was thinking of Hannah, who would always remain young in her memory, Hannah who loved life and was fearless in how she lived it, Hannah who was the source of so much heartache.

Twenty years ago, she'd left this very house vowing never to return, and that was the last anyone had seen of her.

*Where are you, Hannah? What happened all those years ago?*

Had Edwina been a younger woman and in better health, she would have posted up to London and consulted with Brand. He was as close to her as any son, and what she had to say was better said face-to-face. But she hadn't been well enough to travel so she'd done the next best thing. She'd sent a letter to Brand's office in Frith Street, giving him a brief sketch of what she'd discovered. That was more than two weeks ago, but there had been no reply. She wasn't finding fault. All that meant was that Brand hadn't received her letter. He was a busy man and traveled around a great deal. The letter would catch up with him eventually.

There was another letter she had started many times, but had never sent to the one person who might well solve the mystery at one stroke: her niece, Marion. On that thought, she sat down at her escritoire and assembled her writing materials. After dipping her pen in the ink pot, she paused. This wasn't an easy letter to write. She hadn't seen Marion in nearly twenty years. Their correspondence had been sporadic, largely because she and her sister, Diana, who was Marion's mother, had had a falling out. Diana's tragic death from a tumor three years before, followed so closely by the death of Marion's father, had brought Edwina and her niece closer together.

She swallowed a lump in her throat. Not all her remorse and regret could make up for those wasted years. How could she and her sister have been so foolish?

She would not make the same mistake with Marion. But she hardly knew where to begin. After all, they did not know each other very well. If she started making unfounded accusations, Marion would think she was deranged.

She toyed with the idea of inviting Marion to come to Longbury for a visit, but soon discarded the notion. For one thing, Marion lived a good three days' journey from Longbury. For another, she had her hands full taking care of her two younger sisters. Nor did Edwina like the idea of bringing Marion into a situation that was fraught with danger.

If only Brand were here, he could advise her.

There was no harm, however, in corresponding with her niece. They could reminisce about the one and only time Marion had come for a visit. She must know what happened that night. She was there. Someone had seen her. Perhaps the memories were locked away in her mind and a little prompting would set them free.

She began to write. Not long after, she heard a floorboard creak. Her mouth went dry and she slowly got up. When the floorboard creaked again, she went to the fireplace and lifted the poker from its stand. In the corridor, she paused. All she could hear was her own heart beating painfully against her ribs. Nothing seemed amiss, nothing was stirring.

She walked haltingly to the top of the stairs and looked down. Nothing. Lowering the poker, she half turned to go back to her room and saw the face of her assailant before she felt the first blow.

*It's the wrong person* was her last terrified thought before the darkness engulfed her.

The following morning, Mrs. Ludlow arrived at her usual time and let herself into the cottage. She had a package under her arm, a nice shank of mutton that she'd picked up from the butcher that morning, enough to make a big pot of soup with meat to go with it, and perhaps a little left over for her own family. Miss Gunn was a generous soul.

After removing her coat and putting on her apron, she got the fire going. The kettle of water for Miss Gunn's morning cup of tea was soon whistling on the hob. When everything was ready, she set the tray and carried it into the front hall. A few steps in, she halted. Her employer was lying in a heap at the foot of the stairs, her sightless eyes staring up at the ceiling.

It was an hour before the constable got to the house. There was no doubt in his mind that the old lady had fallen down the stairs. Only one thing puzzled him. There were ink stains on her fingers, but no letter was found, nothing to show for those inky fingers.

In his view, it was a small thing and not worth bothering about.

# Chapter One

## London, May 1816

It was only a small thing, or so it seemed at the time, but in later years, Brand would laugh and say that from that moment on, his life changed irreversibly. That was the night Lady Marion Dane stubbed her toes.

She and her sister were his guests, making up a party in his box at the theater. They hadn't known each other long, only a month, but he knew far more about her than she realized. He and her late aunt, Edwina Gunn, had been friends, and from time to time Edwina had mentioned her sister's family who lived near Keswick in the Lake District. In the last few weeks, he'd made it his business to find out as much as he could about Lady Marion Dane.

She was the daughter of an earl, but she had never had a Season in London, had never been presented at Court or enjoyed the round of parties and outings that were taken for granted by other young women of her class. If her father had not died, she would still be in the Lake District, out of harm's way, and there would be no need for him to keep a watchful eye on her.

Though he'd taken a sketch of her background, he could not get her measure. She was an intensely private person and rarely showed emotion. But in the theater, when the lamps were dimmed and she thought herself safe from prying eyes, she gave herself up to every emotion that was portrayed on stage.

The play was *Much Ado About Nothing*, and he could tell from her face which characters appealed to her and which did not. She didn't waste much sympathy on Claudio, or his betrothed's father, and they were, one supposed, cast in the heroic mold. Benedick she tolerated, but the shrew, Beatrice, made her beam with admiration.

It was more entertaining to watch Marion's face than to watch the performance on stage.

The final curtain came down, the applause died away, and chairs were scraped back as people got up. Lady Marion was still sitting in her chair as though loath to leave. Her sister, Lady Emily—an indiscriminate flirt at eighteen—was making eyes at young Henry Cavendish; Brand's own good friend, Ash Denison, was stifling a yawn behind his hand. No affair such as this would be complete, for propriety's sake, without a chaperon or two, and doing the honors tonight were Ash's grandmother, the dowager countess, and her friend, Lady Bethune. The evening wasn't over yet. He had arranged for a late supper at the Clarendon Hotel where Marion's cousin, Fanny, and her husband, Reggie Wright, were due to join them.

Everyone was effusive in their praise of the performance, but it was Marion's words he wanted to hear. She looked up at him with unguarded eyes when he held her chair, her expression still alight with traces of amusement. Then she sighed and said, "Thank you for inviting us, Mr. Hamilton." She was using her formal voice and he found it mildly irritating. She went on, "In future, when I think of this performance, I shall remember the actress who played Beatrice. She was truly memorable."

She got up, a graceful woman in lavender silk with a cool smile that matched her cool stare, and fairish blond hair softly swept back from her face.

Some demon goaded him to say, "In future, when you think of this performance, I hope you will remember *me*."

The flash of unease in her gray eyes pleased him enormously. Since they'd met, she'd treated him with all the respect she would show an octogenarian. He wasn't a vain man, but he was a man. The temptation to make her acknowledge it was becoming harder and harder to resist.

Recovered now, she smiled vaguely and went to join her sister. He had to admire Marion's tactics: She diverted young Cavendish's interest to someone in another box, linked her arm through Emily's, and purposely steered the girl through the door. It was seamlessly done, but very effective.

Emily was an attractive little thing with huge, dark eyes, a cap of silky curls, and a smile that was, in his opinion, *too* alluring for her tender years. There was always a stream of young bucks vying for her attention. And vice versa. Marion had checked her sister tonight, but that didn't happen very often.

There was another sister, Phoebe, a child of ten whom he liked immensely. Though she was lame, she was up for anything. She was also a fount of knowledge on Marion's comings and goings.

He was calling her Marion in the privacy of his own thoughts. If he wasn't careful, he'd be doing it in public, then what would Lady Marion Dane, cool and collected earl's daughter, make of that?

"She makes an excellent chaperon, doesn't she?" Ash Denison, Brand's friend since their school days at Eton, spoke in an undertone. "All she needs is one of those lace caps to complete the picture. Then every man will know that she's a confirmed spinster and he had better keep his distance."

The thought of Marion in a lace cap such as dowagers wore soured Brand's mood. All the same, he could see that day coming. Though she was only seven and twenty, she seemed resigned to her single state. No. It was truer to say that she embraced it. All she wanted from a man, all she would allow, was a platonic friendship.

Did she know that she was setting herself up for a challenge? He let the thought turn in his mind.

"Careful, Brand," said Ash. "You're smiling again. If you're not careful, you'll be making a habit of it."

Brand turned to stare at his friend and made a face when he came under the scrutiny of Ash's quizzing glass. No one looking at Ash would have believed that he had spent the better part of his adult life fighting for king and country in the Spanish Campaign. Brand knew that those were brutal years, though Ash always made light of them. Now that the war was over, he seemed hell-bent on enjoying himself. He was a dandy and the darling of society.

Brand had neither the patience nor the inclination to make himself the darling of society. He knew how fickle society was. As the baseborn son of a duke, he'd met with prejudice in his time, but that was before he'd acquired a fleet of newspapers stretching from London to every major city in the south of England. Now he was respected and his friendship sought after—now that he could break the high and mighty with the stroke of his pen.

He knew what people said, that he was driven to prove himself. It was true. But he never forgot a friend or anyone who had been kind to him when he'd had nothing to offer in return. Edwina Gunn was one of those people. It was to repay his debt to her that he had taken Marion and her sisters under his wing.

Ash was waiting for him to say something. "The sight of a beautiful woman always makes me smile."

"I presume we are talking about Lady Marion? You haven't taken your eyes from her all evening."

This friendly taunt was met with silence.

"Is she beautiful?" Ash prodded.

"Not in the common way, but she has style."

"Mmm," Ash mused. "If she allowed me to have the dressing of her, I could make her the toast of the ton. I'd begin by cutting her hair to form a soft cap. We'd have to lower the bodices on her gowns, of course, and raise the hems. I think she would look her best in transparent gauzes. What do you think?"

Ash was known to have an eye for fashion, and many high-ranking ladies sought his advice. In Brand's view, their newfound glamour wasn't always an improvement.

"You know what they say." Brand moved to catch up with the rest of his party, and Ash quickened his step to keep up with him.

"What do they say?"

There was a crush of people at the top of the stairs and Brand felt a moment's anxiety. He relaxed when he saw Marion's fair hair glistening with gold under the lights of the chandeliers. Emily's dark cap of curls shimmered like silk. Then he lost sight of them in the crush.

"What do they say?" repeated Ash.

"One man's meat—"

The sentence was left hanging. A woman screamed. Some patrons cried out. In the next instant, Brand was sprinting for the stairs.

He shoved people out of his way as he thundered down those marble steps. He found her at the bottom, sitting on the floor, her head resting on her knees. Emily was with her.

"Stand back!" he flung at the group of people who had crowded round her. They gave way without a protest.

He knelt down and touched her shoulder with a shaking hand. "Marion?" he said urgently. "What happened? Say something!"

She looked up at him with tears of pain in her eyes. "I stubbed my toes," she said crossly. "There's no need to fuss."

Then she fainted.

Marion swam out of the haze that enveloped her. "Someone elbowed me in the back," she said plaintively.

A masculine voice asked, "Who would want to harm you, Marion?"

"David."

Just saying the word cleared her head. She lifted her lashes and blinked to clear the mist in front of her eyes. Emily's anxious face looked down at her. Then she registered Hamilton's presence and, finally, the painful throb in her toes.

She struggled to a sitting position. They were in Hamilton's carriage turning into the street that gave onto Hanover Square, where Cousin Fanny's house was located.

"You're taking me home?"

Hamilton nodded. "Apart from anything else, you gave yourself a nasty knock on the head. When we get to the house, I'll send for the doctor. I've already sent word to your cousins at the Clarendon."

"That isn't necessary! It will only worry Fanny and Reggie if I don't turn up. As I told you, all I did was stub my toes."

"You said David pushed you."

She felt a stab of alarm. "I said no such thing." Then, with an agility of mind that surprised even her, she added, "Who is David?"

When Hamilton looked at Emily, she shook her head. The subject of David was dropped, much to Marion's relief, but Hamilton hadn't finished yet. "Did you get a good look at the person who pushed you?"

"No. Everything happened so quickly. And I wasn't pushed, I was elbowed." Her toes were throbbing in earnest, so she managed no more than a weak smile. "That's the thing about London. It's a menace. People are always in a hurry. I'm forever dodging crowds of jostling shoppers, or carriages hurtling to unknown destinations as though it were a matter of life and death. The theater is no different. And do you know, old people are the worst? Lord Denison's grandmother uses her cane as though she is prodding cattle."

Her attempt at humor won a chuckle from Emily, though Mr. Hamilton remained stony-faced.

"You're right about that," said Emily. "I've seen her do it. But you're wrong about your fall. I'm not saying you were deliberately pushed, but someone fell heavily against you. Marion, our arms were linked and you were wrenched from my grasp. Luckily for you, there was a big man in front of you. He broke your fall."

"I can't remember." And that was the truth. At this

point, all she wanted was to get home so that Fanny's housekeeper could give her one of her magic powders to dull the pain in her toes. "I can't understand," she said, "how stubbed toes can hurt so much."

"Be thankful you didn't break your neck." That was Hamilton.

"Like poor Aunt Edwina." That was Emily. Suddenly aware of what she'd said, she went on hurriedly, "I'm sorry. It was a thoughtless thing to say at a time like this."

A pall of silence settled over them. Marion had to struggle to keep from showing how Emily's words had affected her. Guilt was a constant shadow on her mind. She'd hardly known this aunt who had left everything to her—Yew Cottage in Longbury, her goods and chattels, and the little money she had saved. All she had ever done for her aunt was write the occasional letter. It was the same with her mother, though she and Edwina were sisters. There had been a falling-out when Edwina and the youngest sister, Hannah, had come for a holiday to the Lake District, and the quarrel had never been mended, not properly. It was only glossed over.

Without Aunt Edwina's legacy, they would be in dire straits. When their father died, the title and estate passed to Cousin Morley, and she and her sisters had moved into the dower house. It wasn't long, however, before Cousin Morley took possession of that, too. He wanted it for his mother-in-law, who had outstayed her welcome at the Hall. They each had a small annuity from their father's estate, he pointed out. That should do them.

It seemed wrong to her that someone's tragic misfortune should be the saving of her little family.

Hamilton stirred. "So, when the Season is over, you're off to Longbury to start a new life?"

"That's the plan," answered Marion.

"What was wrong with the old life?"

Marion jumped in before Emily could open her mouth. One had to be careful about what one said in front of Brand Hamilton. He was a newspaperman and had the knack of making people say more than they wanted to.

"You know how it is," she said. "It passed away when my father died. Cousin Morley and his wife took over our home. It made things . . . awkward."

"All the same," he said, "you're bound to miss your friends. The Lake District covers a wide area. You could sell Edwina's cottage and set yourself up nicely in one of the scenic villages close to Keswick. That way, you could avoid Cousin Morley and keep up with your friends."

"Longbury has its own beauty," replied Marion, "and I'm sure we'll make new friends there." It sounded as though he didn't want her to go to Longbury.

"Oh? You remember the village, do you? And the woods and the downs?"

They'd had this conversation before, and his persistence in trying to jog her memory puzzled her. "Of course, but only vaguely. As I told you, I was only a child when my mother and I visited Longbury." The holiday was an attempt, she supposed, at a reconciliation between Edwina and Mama, but it hadn't worked. "But should we decide that it doesn't suit, or we start pining for the Lake District, we may take your advice."

"Marion, no!" interjected Emily. "Keswick is so isolated; Longbury is close to London." Suddenly moderating her tone, as though remembering her advanced years, she went on, "There is so much to do in London. You've said so yourself. And what about Cousin Fanny? We promised to be here over Christmas."

Marion flashed her sister an affectionate smile. An

eighteen-year-old girl could be forgiven for lusting after the glamour of life in town with its round of parties and balls, especially when there had been little to celebrate in the last few years. It seemed that they were hardly out of their mourning clothes when they were in them again. There had been no parties, no outings of any note, no laughter, and no joy. Cousin Fanny's invitation to take in the Season before going on to Longbury could not be resisted. Her sisters deserved a little excitement in their lives and something to look forward to.

Marion was aware that Hamilton thought she spoiled Emily, but she didn't care what he thought. He could not guess how harrowing these last few years had been, and she didn't want him to know. For one thing, she didn't know him that well, and for another, people who wallowed in their misfortunes soon found themselves without any friends. Her sisters had learned to smile again. That was what mattered.

She forced herself to forget the dull throb in her toes and find a convincing explanation for her desire to start a new life. "Family is important to us, Mr. Hamilton, and Cousin Fanny is the only family we have left now. We want to be close to each other. The Lake District is so far away that we've seen each other only once in the last ten years."

He inclined his head as though he understood. A moment passed and he observed idly, "I remember Edwina saying much the same thing. You were the only family left to her, but the journey was too arduous for an old woman to make."

Hearing a rebuke in the words, she gave him a keen look. His eyes reflected nothing but polite interest.

Sometimes she didn't know what to make of this man. He'd appeared on Fanny's doorstep the day after they arrived in London. It turned out that he and Reggie, Fanny's husband, were good friends; they attended the same clubs and shared an interest in politics. Reggie was the member of Parliament for a riding in north London. In fact, Reggie was hopeful of persuading Mr. Hamilton to become a candidate in the next by-election. Mr. Hamilton, he said, had risen from humble beginnings to become, at the age of thirty-three, the owner of a fleet of newspapers stretching from London to all the major cities in the south. Fanny was more explicit. Mr. Hamilton, she said, was the son of a duke but born on the wrong side of the blanket. Both she and Reggie agreed that with his ambition and influence, Mr. Hamilton could go far in politics.

There was, however, more to Hamilton's visits than friendship with her relatives. He'd called on them, he said, because he'd once lived in Longbury and had known their aunt quite well. She thought he must have known her aunt very well indeed, for he never referred to her as Miss Gunn, but by her Christian name, Edwina.

At any rate, he'd taken a proprietary interest in Edwina's nieces, and gone out of his way to make sure that they enjoyed their first Season in London. But there was no getting round the fact that he was a newspaperman. He was naturally curious, and that made her cautious.

When the carriage pulled up outside the house, Hamilton got out first, then turned back with outstretched arms. "I'll carry you," he said.

Marion balked at the thought of him putting his arms around her, not because she was missish but because she was fiercely independent and quite capable of taking care of herself. Then she remembered that she'd fainted and he must have carried her into the carriage. Too late now to assert herself.

"Marion," he said, gravely patient, "you're not wearing shoes. We had to remove them so that I could examine your toes."

"I have them right here," Emily piped up.

"Do you want to walk into the house in your stockinged feet?"

Her smile was a little tight, but she gave in gracefully. As he held her high against his chest, Emily ran to pull the bell. Since Hamilton was watching the door, Marion took a moment to study him. His features were too harshly carved to be truly classical, and his brilliant blue eyes were sometimes a little too intense for her comfort. Luxurious brown hair brushed his collar, and the thin silver scar that sliced one eyebrow lent an air of recklessness.

It was the scar that fascinated her. She knew that he'd come by it when he'd challenged a celebrated French swordsman to a duel. Hamilton was a shrewd man of business; he commanded respect and admiration. So why would a man like that risk everything in a duel?

"I hope you like what you see."

She'd been caught out staring. At the sound of his voice, she jerked her gaze from his scar. Never at a loss for words, she said coolly, "You were lucky not to have lost an eye."

White teeth gleamed in the lamplight. "True, but that is not what you were thinking, Marion."

The front door was opened by the butler, and Marion was saved the indignity of appearing speechless as Hamilton climbed the stairs.

# Chapter Two

Brand Hamilton took too much upon himself. This was Marion's thought as she assessed the distance between her bed and the dresser. On top of the dresser was her evening pochette, the one she'd had at the theater. She couldn't remember dropping it, though she supposed she must have when she fell. A maid had brought it in when the doctor arrived, and from that moment on, she could hardly keep her eyes from straying to it. The accident at the theater did not seem nearly so innocent now, and she could not understand why she had not suspected something sooner.

If she'd been allowed to take one of Mrs. Dyce's powders, she could have managed to cross the room. Fanny had even found a cane for her, now propped against the bed. But Mr. Hamilton had mentioned the dread word "concussion," and that was enough to persuade Dr. Mendes. Concussion and opiates did not mix.

"You've only stubbed your toes, woman. You don't

need laudanum for the pain." A very jovial fellow was Dr. Mendes. "You'll be as right as rain in the morning."

Easy to say, but her toes were still stinging and she really wanted to get to that dresser while everyone was downstairs, in Fanny's parlor, taking refreshments. The party at the Clarendon had simply moved to Hanover Square, at Fanny's request, when it became known that Marion's injuries were nothing more serious than a few bruised toes.

She thought about the fall at the theater for a long time, visualizing her first misstep. There was no doubt that she'd been pushed, but it hardly seemed credible that it was deliberate.

Incredible or not, she believed it. This wasn't the first mishap that had befallen her. Only the week before, when she was watching the fireworks display in Vauxhall Gardens, someone had come out of the shrubbery, pushed her down, and run off with her reticule. The reticule was returned the next day, intact. The gentleman who returned it had not left his name.

Just like this time.

She didn't think for one moment that anyone was trying to kill her. The mishaps were too minor for that. But someone was trying to scare her. If she could only get to her pochette, she would soon know whether she was right or merely allowing her imagination to run riot.

Gritting her teeth, she pushed back the covers and swung her legs over the edge of the bed. Now she could feel the other aches and pains she'd taken in the fall— scraped knees, knotted muscles in the small of her back, and an incipient throb behind her eyes. She was reaching for her cane when her bedroom door slowly swung open. Phoebe stood there, hesitating on the threshold, but when she saw Marion on her feet, her little face blossomed with a huge smile.

"I heard that you fell down the stairs at the theater," she said.

"I stubbed my toes, that's all. It doesn't hurt."

Marion spoke lightly. Phoebe had a fear of accidents. Three years before, when she was seven, she'd fallen from her horse and broken her leg. The bone had not set properly. As a result, when Phoebe walked, she limped awkwardly. Marion tried not to fuss over her sister because Phoebe hated to be treated as an invalid. But sometimes, when Marion thought herself unobserved, she would watch Phoebe and worry about her wan cheeks and how thin she had become.

It was late. She should send Phoebe back to her own room with a mild scolding. Instead, she sank back on the bed and patted the mattress, inviting Phoebe to join her.

"You're cold," she said, as Phoebe snuggled under the covers beside her.

She gazed down at a face that might have been her own when she was a girl of ten—gray eyes, stubborn chin, and pale, pale skin to match her flaxen hair. They'd both taken after their mother, while Emily had the dark good looks of their father. The difference between Phoebe and herself, thought Marion, was that at ten, she would have had a liberal sprinkling of freckles across her nose and cheeks. Phoebe spent too much time indoors with her nose in a book.

Marion hoped that would change when they got to Longbury. In the Lake District, with its spectacular hills and valleys, it was hard to get around. It also rained incessantly.

Marion resisted the temptation to kiss and hug her sister and made do with rubbing some warmth into her cold limbs. "I know why you're cold," said Marion. "You haven't come straight from your bed. You've been up to your old tricks again, eavesdropping on other people's conversations."

One of Phoebe's favorite pastimes was to hide behind the gallery banister and look down on the comings and goings of Fanny's guests.

"I wanted to know what had happened to you," protested Phoebe, "and when I heard Mr. Hamilton mention your name, I stopped to listen."

Marion opened her mouth to remonstrate and thought better of it. "Mr. Hamilton mentioned my name?" she asked innocently.

Phoebe nodded. "He said that you'd most likely broken a bone in your toe when you fell."

"Is that what he thought?" That would explain why the pain wouldn't go away.

"Yes, but the doctor said that there was nothing they could do for it and it would heal by itself eventually."

"Nothing they could do!" Marion was outraged. "They could have given me one of Mrs. Dyce's powders!"

"I thought you said it didn't hurt?"

Marion folded her arms across her breasts. Phoebe was adept at catching adults out in little white lies. "It hurt then," she allowed, "when I first came home. It doesn't hurt so much now."

Phoebe glanced at Marion, then she, too, folded her arms across her chest. Observing the gesture, Marion swallowed a smile. Her little sister's desire to be just like her was a passing fancy, or she hoped it was. Idols always turned out to be a disappointment.

"Was anything else . . ." She cleared her throat. "Was anything else said about me?"

"No. Not by name. But I heard Cousin Fanny say that

it would be a good thing if Mr. Hamilton found himself a wife."

Marion was astonished. "Fanny said that to Mr. Hamilton?"

"No, of course not. To Cousin Reggie, after he told her that he wouldn't be surprised if Mr. Hamilton became prime minister one of these days. Was she thinking of you, Marion?"

Marion gave a short laugh. "Hardly! What put that idea in your head?"

"Don't you like him, Marion? I know he likes you. And wouldn't it be grand if you married the prime minister? I could write it up in my family history and everyone would want to read it."

This is what came, thought Marion, of playing fast and loose with one of her own cardinal rules. Everyone was entitled to his or her privacy. She was no better than Phoebe, but at least Phoebe had the excuse that she was only a child.

She'd opened a Pandora's box and she'd better get the lid back on before murder and mayhem were let loose on the world.

"How is the family history coming along?"

Compiling a family history was Phoebe's latest hobby. There was always some new thing to occupy her mind, and whenever Phoebe's interest languished, her sisters thought of something new to occupy her. If she had been an active child, things would have been different. But she tired easily and spent much of her time indoors. She read well beyond her years, sewed, knitted, played the piano, sketched, and kept a diary. The family history had been Emily's idea, and Marion had reluctantly agreed to it, knowing that to forbid it would raise questions she had no wish to answer.

Phoebe gave a huge yawn. "There's not much in Aunt Edwina's letters, and she didn't write very often, did she?"

Marion didn't mention the estrangement between their mother and Aunt Edwina. "Maybe Mama didn't keep all of Aunt Edwina's letters, only the interesting ones."

"Yes, but that doesn't help me. All I know is that Grandfather and Grandmother Gunn left Brighton for Longbury after they were married, and that's where their children were born."

"Grandfather Gunn was a partner in the local attorney's office. It's his cottage Edwina inherited, and now us."

"I know *that*," said Phoebe. "I know about Mama and Aunt Edwina, but I don't know much about Hannah."

"Well, she died many years ago, long before you were born." She thought for a moment. "I do remember that she was kind to me."

"You *knew* her?"

Marion smiled. "I was seven years old when we visited Longbury, and Hannah must have been about twenty. She was a good many years younger than her sisters. She played with me, read me stories, and took me for long walks through the woods with her dog." Marion felt a little jolt. "I'd forgotten about the dog. Scruff—that was his name. He adored Hannah."

Phoebe said plaintively, "You never told me this before."

"It happened a long time ago. That's all I remember."

"What about Mama? She never spoke about Hannah. Didn't she like her?"

Marion put an arm around Phoebe's shoulders. "She didn't speak about her," she said, "because it made her sad. Papa was like that, don't you remember, after Mama died?"

Phoebe was bristling. "Well, I think that's nonsense! If I die, I want you to speak about me all the time. I don't want anyone to forget me."

"I promise," said Marion solemnly, "to talk about you so much that everyone will put their hands over their ears whenever they see me coming."

"I mean it!"

"So do I. I shall probably go into a decline and waste away to a shadow of my former self. Enough!" She held up a hand to silence Phoebe. "I must have a maggot in my brain, allowing you to stay up till this time of night. Don't think I don't know you do this on purpose, get me talking so I'll forget how late it is."

She pulled back the covers and pointed to the door. "Bed!"

Phoebe looked hopefully into her sister's face, seemed to recognize that the game was ended, and climbed out of bed.

Marion said, "Don't I get my good-night hug?"

Phoebe shifted from foot to foot. "Of course. But no kisses. I'm too old."

Marion had to smile. She wouldn't insult Phoebe by pooh-poohing the notion that she was too old to be kissed. A quick hug was all she got, then Phoebe limped to the door.

"And," Marion called after her, "no loitering on the gallery."

When the door closed, Marion sank back against the pillows. She was not convinced that Hannah had died all those years ago. From snatches of her parents' conversations that she'd overheard, she suspected that Hannah may have eloped. If so, it was a secret her parents had not wished to share with their children, a secret that belonged in the past, and she was happy to leave it there.

She doubted that Phoebe would discover the truth, but if she did, it was hardly earth-shattering.

That thought inexorably drew her eyes to the dresser and her pochette. Sighing, she got out of bed and tested her bruised toes. There was no swelling that she could detect, but the least pressure made her wince.

She reached for her cane and, using it to keep her balance, hopped on her good foot to the dresser. Just inside the pochette, tucked in beside her handkerchief, she found it.

*Silence is golden. You have been warned.*

She crumpled the note into her fist thinking that no one had ever misjudged a man as she had misjudged David.

"Really, Brand, I don't know how you can live like this." Ash Denison found the bottle on the sideboard and poured a neat measure of brandy into his glass. "It's not as though you're a pauper. You could live like a king if you wanted to. Why do you choose to live in these dreary rooms in St. James's when you could set yourself up nicely at the Albany or on Bond Street?"

"Too fashionable for my taste." Brand glanced around the sparsely furnished interior. "This serves my purpose, and I don't give out the address. If anyone wants to find me, he can apply to my office in Frith Street. You'd be surprised how many readers *do* want to find me, if only to spit in my face."

"What about beauty and elegance?" Ash took the leather chair on the other side of the hearth and gazed with ill-concealed distaste at the glass in his hand. "Where are the fine crystal glasses and decanters? The fine silver displayed on the sideboard? The velvet drapes?"

Ash's words evoked in Brand's mind a vision of the Priory, his father's splendid residence, in all its luxury and grandeur. He had lived there for a time, but he had never called it *home*. Home was the house where his mother's father had raised him. And after his grandfather died, home was something he stopped thinking about.

He took a sip of brandy, then said, "I don't need the so-called finer things in life to make me happy. A comfortable fire in the grate and comfortable chairs are enough for my needs. Don't worry, Ash. I don't entertain women here, if that's what you're thinking."

"Women?" Ash gave a hoot of laughter. "What women? You can't spare the time for them, you're so involved with your fleet of newspapers. And now that you're considering running for Parliament, you'll have less time than before. What about Julia? Where is she these days?"

"Julia," replied Brand indifferently, "has given me my marching orders."

Ash choked on a mouthful of brandy, sending droplets flying when his arm jerked. Not one of those drops landed on Ash's immaculately tailored coat and trousers. It was a trick Brand had envied since their school days. On the playing field, Ash always came out of a scrimmage looking as fresh as a daisy. It made him wonder how Ash had managed as a soldier.

Ash coughed to clear his throat. "So," he said at last, "that's the way of it. Your interest in Julia waned, and like the gentleman you are, you let *her* turn *you* off. This wouldn't have anything to do with Lady Marion, would it?"

Ignoring Brand's frowning stare, Ash went on merrily, "I saw your expression tonight when Lady Marion tumbled down those stairs. I thought *you* would faint, not Lady Marion."

"Cut the hyperbole. I was alarmed, that's all. However, I'm glad you raised the subject, because I invited you here to talk about Marion."

When Brand paused, getting his thoughts in order, Ash got the brandy bottle from the sideboard and topped up his friend's glass. This done, he went back to his seat and waited patiently for his friend to begin.

At length, Brand said, "I think you know how close I was to Marion's aunt?"

"Edwina Gunn? I know she was your teacher until your grandfather died. I know you kept up with her all through the years."

There was a lot more to it than that, but Brand always glossed over those turbulent years, so he merely said, "She wrote to me two weeks before she died. Unfortunately, she sent the letter to my office in Frith Street, where it got buried under a pile of letters from readers. The thing is, it did not reach me until after Edwina's death, so I had no chance to question her or clarify any of the points she had raised. And afterward, I didn't see the point in hanging on to it, so I threw it in the fire.

"It was a rambling letter about her youngest sister, Hannah. As far as anyone knows, Hannah eloped one night, about twenty years ago, with God only knows who. That's what everyone in Longbury believed, though Edwina never confirmed or denied it. I never heard her speak about Hannah, and I never asked about her. I was too young and too respectful to intrude upon a private grief."

"Did you know Hannah?"

"No. She was a governess in Brighton and only came home for the holidays—a week or two at most—when I was away at school. I may have met her, but I don't remember."

He became silent as his thoughts drifted back in time. Finally, he said, "Essentially, Edwina said that she suspected that someone had murdered Hannah, and that her niece, Marion, could identify the killer. One thing I do know: Hannah was visiting Edwina when Marion and her mother were there, and that's when Hannah is supposed to have disappeared."

Ash looked thunderstruck. "Would you mind," he said slowly, "repeating that?"

Brand did, amplifying his explanation. "In her letter, Edwina wrote that Hannah quarreled with her sisters one night and left the cottage vowing never to return. And no, Edwina did not tell me what the quarrel was about."

He sipped from his glass as he marshaled his thoughts. "As far as I know, Edwina never reported her sister as missing, so that leads me to suspect that she believed Hannah had run off, possibly with some man. Anyway, the years passed, and it was only recently that someone mentioned to Edwina that Marion was roaming the grounds the same night that Hannah disappeared. She didn't say who."

"How could they be sure it was the same night?"

"Edwina didn't say. However it was, this person put the thought in her mind that Hannah had met with foul play and Marion might well be a witness to it. You have to understand that Edwina's cottage is surrounded by woods and is close to the Priory and its extensive buildings and grounds. If Hannah was murdered, there were plenty of places to hide her body."

"That's a bit of a leap, isn't it? To go for twenty years, believing that your sister had run off, then suddenly decide that maybe she was murdered? It sounds to me that this is someone's idea of a joke, else why not come forward when Hannah disappeared?"

"You're not saying anything that I didn't say to myself when I read the letter. However, I was aware of another factor that added to my skepticism." He took a swallow of brandy, then went on, "When I was in Longbury for the funeral, I heard rumors. Edwina, it seems, had not been herself for some weeks. She was becoming forgetful and slipping into the past, becoming more and more childlike. You see what I was thinking?"

"That she was becoming senile." Ash sighed. "What did she want you to do?"

"To visit her so that she could talk to me face-to-face." He added with a touch of bitterness, "As I said, by the time I got the letter, it was too late. Anyway, I didn't receive the letter until long after I'd heard the rumors so I didn't take it seriously, or push myself to solve a mystery that was twenty years old. Marion, to my knowledge, was fixed in the Lake District. I thought of writing to her, but was loath to reveal that her aunt's mind was affected. So I did nothing."

"Until Lady Marion and her sisters arrived on your doorstep?"

Brand nodded, stretched out his long legs in front of the fire that was now blazing merrily, and slumped comfortably in his chair. "I didn't want to upset Marion or alarm her by telling her about Edwina's letter—what would be the point if it was all a figment of an old woman's imagination?—so I cultivated her acquaintance and tried to draw her out." He dragged his gaze from the blazing coals in the grate and looked directly at

Ash. "She doesn't know anything. In fact, she hardly remembers Longbury. She remembers her aunts Edwina
and Hannah, but not that Hannah disappeared while
she was there. When I asked her where Hannah was now,
all she could tell me was that Hannah had died young."

Ash sneered. "You mean Hannah's sisters tried to
hide her shame by fabricating an early death? I'll wager
she did elope with a married man and her family never
forgave her for it. Typical!"

Brand shrugged. "I thought that I had fulfilled my
obligation to Edwina and could leave it at that, but that
was before Marion was shoved down those stairs
tonight. And a week ago, she was attacked and robbed
by a footpad in Vauxhall Gardens. Oh, not that Marion
told me. I got that from Phoebe."

"Coincidences," scoffed Ash, "that could happen to
anyone."

"Thousands would agree with you," responded
Brand, "but I'm a newspaperman. I have an instinct
about these things. I think that Marion is in some kind
of trouble. What I don't know yet is whether it's related
to Longbury or to the Lake District."

He could almost hear Ash's quick mind adding
things up and filling in the blanks.

Finally, Ash chuckled. "And I say you're not telling
me everything. Either Lady Marion has confided in you,
or there has been a third incident that for some reason
you don't wish to mention."

"You're wrong on both counts." Brand drained his
glass and set it aside. "I repeat: I'm relying on instinct."

He was remembering the scared look in her eyes when
he'd bent over her at the foot of the stairs, and later, the
involuntary answer to his question as she came to herself in his carriage: *David.*

He hoped her troubles originated in the Lake District, because if Longbury was the source, it meant that he should have taken Edwina's letter seriously. It meant that he should not have accepted that her death was an accident so readily. It meant that if Marion returned to Longbury, she could be putting herself in danger.

It all seemed so far-fetched that, even now, he wasn't quite ready to believe it.

"At any rate," he said finally, "I've decided to do what Edwina wanted me to do, and that is solve the mystery of what happened to Hannah all those years ago."

"Do you think that's wise? You may stir up a hornet's nest."

"As I am well aware, but I intend to keep a close eye on Marion."

He looked up to find Ash staring at him speculatively.

"I was right!" said Ash. "You *are* taken with her! I should have known when you kept referring to her as Marion and not Lady Marion. Is that what you call her to her face?"

When Brand looked at him blankly, Ash grinned. "You're playing a dangerous game, my friend."

Brand tried, without success, to stare down the amusement in Ash's eyes. "I feel responsible for her."

Half joking, half in earnest, Ash went on, "Oh, that's how it starts, and before you know it, you get caught in the bachelor trap. Think of Jack."

Jack was a mutual friend and once, like them, a confirmed bachelor, but now happily married to the love of his life.

Ash got up. "A word of advice? Watch out for Mrs. Milford. The fair Julia may have the face of a goddess but she has the disposition of a demon. She won't take kindly to another female poaching on her preserves."

"I told you," retorted Brand, "she was the one who ended the affair."

"You don't think that matters to a woman like Julia? I'm surprised she hasn't come after you already with her fangs bared."

"She's in Paris."

"That explains it. She'll be back soon enough when she hears that another lady has displaced her in your affections."

"Will you sit down?" roared Brand. "And have done with your teasing! I didn't invite you here to play games. I invited you here because you're my friend and I need your help."

That got Ash's attention. He slowly sank into his chair. "Why do you need my help?"

"Haven't I made myself clear? I wouldn't be surprised if there *is* a third incident—you know, another of those coincidences that can happen to anyone? However, I can't be everywhere at once. I've agreed to seek my party's nomination for the by-election coming up. My time will be taken up with election business. Then there are my newspapers to consider. I have to instruct my second-in-command on what needs to be done in my absence."

"It sounds to me," said Ash, "that you have too many irons in the fire."

"Which is why I need your help."

"I'm listening."

Brand exhaled a long, slow breath. He said quietly, "I need someone to keep a close eye on Marion, at least until she gets settled in Longbury. Will you do it?"

Ash grinned. "My pleasure, old friend, my pleasure."

After seeing Ash out, Brand returned to his parlor where his manservant was clearing up. Manley was a grizzled, hefty gentleman in his early fifties, a former trooper in a cavalry regiment, who had fallen on hard times. He was a genius with horses but had been let go by his last employer for insubordination. In fact, he'd been let go by several employers for insubordination. There was no doubt about it, Manley did not know his place, but he'd had the good fortune to find the one employer who admired him for it.

Unfortunately, his talents were wasted because Brand did not keep a stable. He didn't see the necessity for it, but hired whatever he needed at the livery stable off Pall Mall. All that was about to change.

"Manley," he said, "we'll be going to Longbury in the next week or two. I have a stable there lying empty. Tomorrow, you and I are going to Tattersall's to look over the horseflesh and make a few purchases. I shall also require the services of coachmen, and the odd stableboy. I'd be obliged if you would take care of that for me. And Manley, only the best will do."

Apart from a slight working of his jaw, Manley showed no expression. "I think I can manage that, Mr. Hamilton," he said.

"Good. Oh, and I'll need household servants, too."

"Leave it to me, sir."

That obsequious *sir* told Brand just how pleased Manley was about setting up the stable in Longbury.

He turned away with a smile, but his smile faded when he noticed that the stuffing in one of the leather armchairs was poking through a seam. These chairs had once belonged to his grandfather. Ash would say that it was time to get rid of them, that they'd outlived their usefulness.

He turned back. "And Manley," he said, "I want you to find an upholsterer or a decorator or whatever. This place is downright shabby. I want everything refurbished, but don't replace anything."

"Yes, sir," replied Manley.

"And be careful with those glasses." The glasses had also belonged to his grandfather.

"Yes, sir."

With a courteous "Good night," Brand left the room.

# Chapter Three

Three days later found Marion in Cousin Fanny's dazzling ballroom, sitting with the chaperons, as the orchestra tuned their instruments for the next dance. With a will of their own, her eyes kept straying to the tall, broad-shouldered figure of Brand Hamilton. He was in conversation with Cousin Reggie, and she knew they would be debating some finer point in the latest bill before Parliament. She'd done a little eavesdropping of her own these last few days, and as far as she could tell, Mr. Hamilton's politics could be summed up as antimonarchy, antiestablishment, and just about anti-everything her father once championed.

Yet everyone said that he would go far in politics if he chose to take up the challenge. Strange.

Her reflections were interrupted when Lady Anne Boscobel's chaperon leaned toward her and whispered, "The orchestra is striking up for a waltz. It would be quite improper for a young girl such as Lady Emily to dance the waltz."

"Thank you for the warning, Miss Barnes." Marion's reply was cordial, but inwardly she was annoyed. Miss Barnes had set herself up as the arbiter of good manners and was always finding fault with some young girl or other. What was all the more galling was that Miss Barnes was always right.

Marion got up and had almost taken a step before she remembered to reach for her cane. She felt ridiculous having to use a cane for nothing more serious than a few stubbed toes. As long as she kept the weight off her foot, she felt hardly any pain, but the least pressure made her knee buckle, hence the cane.

The first step made her wince. At this rate, it would take her a week to reach Emily. She took another small step then stopped when she saw Brand Hamilton threading his way through the couples on the floor to Emily and her partner. He nodded in Marion's direction, showing her that he understood her predicament and he would take charge. He then led Emily from the floor, a laughing, flirtatious Emily, who was obviously enjoying all the masculine attention. Satisfied, Marion was just about to sit down again when she was joined by Fanny.

"I see we both had the same idea," said Fanny. "Thankfully, Brand is well aware, if Emily is not, that young, unmarried girls are thought to be fast if they dance the waltz before they are presented at Court. These silly rules are meant to try us."

What Cousin Fanny seemed to have forgotten was that Emily would not be presented at Court. They couldn't afford it.

Marion smiled at her cousin, knowing that she wasn't finding fault so much as commiserating with the trials that parents and guardians had to endure. Fanny was really her father's cousin, and her senior by a good many years. She and Reggie had two sons close to Emily's age who were presently away at university, so they expected young people to test the rules their elders laid down for them. Her most endearing quality in Marion's eyes, however, was that she possessed a deep well of affection for the three orphaned cousins she had not seen since Phoebe's birth.

"Handsome devil, isn't he?" said Fanny. She was watching Brand Hamilton.

Marion didn't pretend to misunderstand. "I suppose you could say that."

Fanny laughed. "Faint praise, indeed! I'm sure there are plenty of other ladies present who think as I do. If I were ten years younger, I'd give them a run for their money."

"If you looked any younger," replied Marion dryly, "you'd be giving girls as young as Emily a run for their money."

She was exaggerating, but there was a germ of truth in her words. Fanny's figure was firm and supple, her skin glowed with health, and there wasn't a trace of gray in her dark curls.

"Look," breathed out Fanny. "Elliot Coyne has just arrived."

Marion obediently looked. She saw a man in his mid-thirties, handsome without being too handsome, and very much at his ease.

"Who," said Marion, " is Elliot Coyne?"

"He's Brand's rival for the nomination for the seat that has become vacant."

He was joined almost at once by a tall, dark-haired young woman in her early twenties, dressed in floating muslins. They made a handsome couple.

Fanny went on, "And that is his betrothed, Lady Veronica, heiress to the Marquess of Hove. Elliot has done himself proud. Lady Veronica will make an excellent wife for a member of Parliament."

"Really?" Marion was truly interested. "How can you tell?"

Fanny chuckled. "Because she has the right bloodlines, and the right connections. She will be a real asset to him." She clicked her tongue. "Brand had better start looking to his laurels."

"Is it decided then? Is he running for the nomination?"

"Reggie is counting on it. It's not that we don't like Elliot, but he doesn't have Brand's drive. I must go and greet them."

With an airy smile, she left Marion's side and began to skirt the dance floor. As she reached the couple, she was joined by her husband. Reggie Wright was as fair as his wife was dark, and it was only on close examination that one could tell that his fair hair was liberally laced with silver. Marion liked him immensely. Like Fanny, he was warmhearted and took a keen interest in his three cousins by marriage.

Her expression softened as she watched them together. She couldn't help feeling a little envious. They seemed so content with their lot and content with each other. She doubted that Reggie had chosen Fanny to be his wife because she had the right bloodlines, or the right connections, or could advance his career. They had the kind of love that most couples could only dream about.

So where did that leave her?

Just where she wanted to be, she thought with a touch of defiance. In her cottage in Longbury with the people who meant most in the world to her, and she wouldn't have it any other way.

Though Marion stayed close to the dowagers, well back from the dance floor, she was anything but a wallflower. Lord Denison was never far away, and introduced her to a host of people whose names she forgot almost as soon as she heard them. She liked Ash Denison and enjoyed a mild flirtation with him, but she wasn't deceived. She knew that he wasn't seeking her company of his own accord, and suspected that Cousin Reggie had put him up to it.

Mr. Hamilton hadn't neglected her, either, but he rarely missed a dance. She supposed that a man with his eye on Parliament couldn't afford to miss any opportunity to make friends and win votes.

She couldn't make it to the dining room for supper, but Emily had promised to bring supper to her. Ash Denison was keeping her company when a ravishing redhead in a form-fitting scarlet gown swooped down like a hawk. The diamonds around her throat were magnificent, but did not lessen the impression of a beautiful, exotic bird of prey with gimlet eyes.

Lord Denison jumped to his feet. "Julia! This is a surprise!"

He sounded more shocked than surprised, and Marion almost pitied him, thinking that she wouldn't like to be in his shoes. She sensed a lovers' quarrel and was highly amused. Then she saw that those gimlet eyes were trained on her, and she automatically reached for her cane.

Denison said, "Lady Marion ... ah ... allow me to present Mrs. Milford, Mrs. Julia Milford."

Marion didn't try to get to her feet. She acknowledged the introduction with a slight inclination of her head. "How do you do, Mrs. Milford," she said. "As you see, I am slightly indisposed or I would greet you properly."

"Oh, pray don't apologize." Julia Milford showed off a perfect set of porcelains. "I heard about your accident." Her expression registered a mild sympathy. "It was to your right foot, was it not?"

"No. To my left."

Marion gazed down at her feet. She was wearing a pair of Fanny's satin pumps because they were the only shoes she could get into without feeling as though her toes were in a vise.

She lifted the hem of her gown to get a better look at her foot, and that's when Mrs. Milford did the unthinkable. Quite deliberately, she stepped on Marion's stubbed toes. Marion would have screamed if she could have found the breath, but the pain was so excruciating that she could do no more than gasp. Tears sprang to her eyes and rolled down her cheeks.

The pressure was removed when Ash grabbed the gimlet-eyed predator and hauled her off. "Behave yourself, Julia," he remonstrated, giving the woman a rough shake.

Whatever Mrs. Milford may have said was lost as Ash's angry words drowned her out. He had her firmly by the elbow and was propelling her to the door. If Marion had had the strength, she would have chased after them with the cane and whacked the stupid wretch. She couldn't remember being so angry.

Of course, she knew what had provoked Mrs. Milford's temper. The woman was insanely jealous—and it was all for nothing. Ash Denison wasn't attracted to her any more than she was attracted to him. And even if he was and she was, what of it? You couldn't go around attacking people. That vulture belonged in a cage.

She was beginning to catch her breath when Brand Hamilton approached, carrying two plates of food. The little tableau that followed made Marion forget about her sore toes. Julia Milford tore herself out of Ash's grasp and stalked over to Brand. He had the presence of mind to hand the plates of food to Ash before the termagant lashed out and caught him across the face with her open palm. The sound of that blow made Marion wince. She looked around the ballroom. Everyone's eyes were riveted on the trio in the middle of the dance floor.

Head held high, Mrs. Milford sailed out of the ballroom. Brand Hamilton retrieved his plates from his friend and strolled toward Marion.

Now she understood. The real object of Julia Milford's jealous rage wasn't Ash Denison, but Brand Hamilton. Obviously, the woman was a jilted mistress. Equally obvious was that Mrs. Milford regarded *her* as the other woman.

Other thoughts circled in her mind: Lady Veronica, who had the right bloodlines, the right connections, and who would be an asset to her husband's career. A man with Brand Hamilton's ambitions wouldn't tie himself to a shrew like Julia Milford in or out of marriage. He would choose for his wife someone who would be an asset to him, someone who would be accepted by the cream of society, someone like Lady Veronica— someone like *her*!

When he came up to her, he said, "You've got that look on your face again."

She was as cool as ice. "What look?"

"The one that conceals what you're really thinking.

Here, this is for you." He handed her a plate. "I told Emily I would deliver it to you. It seemed a shame to take her away from her friends."

When he took the chair beside her, she looked down at her plate. Lobster tarts, potato puffs, a medley of roasted vegetables, and thin-cut slices of ham and beefsteak. She was sorely tempted to dump them in his lap.

"I'm sorry about the scene with Mrs. Milford," he said. "What did she say to you?"

His careless apology grated. "She stood on my toes," she replied, mimicking his indifference, then she took a bite of a lobster tart and almost moaned with pleasure. Emily had chosen her favorites.

"Ouch!" he said, but he said it with a smile.

*Ouch?* That's all he could find to say? *Ouch?*

"Had I known she was here," he went on, "I would have steered her away from you. I thought she was in Paris."

She gave him a tepid smile. "I see how it is. With Mrs. Milford out of the way, you had a better chance of drumming up support for the nomination." She popped the rest of the lobster tart into her mouth and munched on it without tasting a thing.

She caught a flash of something in his eyes, annoyance or anger, then the look was gone and he gazed at her coolly. "What does that mean?"

"Come, Mr. Hamilton, I'm not naive. I hardly think a woman of Mrs. Milford's temperament would enhance your career." Her own temper began to sizzle when she remembered her stubbed toes. "On the other hand, to be seen with someone like me may well add to your credit."

He was concentrating on his plate, selecting something to eat. "Remember," he said, "it was Julia who stepped on your toes, not I. As for adding to my credit—how could that be?"

"Oh, think of Lady Veronica and Mr. Coyne." She tried to sound arch. "His credit has risen since he became engaged to her, or so I've been given to understand. And why shouldn't it? She has excellent bloodlines as well as connections. Alas for you, though, Lady Veronica is already taken."

He turned his head and looked at her curiously. "Marion," he said, "are you saying that you are available? Is this, in fact, a proposal of marriage?"

She drew in a deep breath and let it out slowly. "That is—well, I'm glad that one of us is amused."

"No, no. Your proposal has merit. You *would* be an asset to me if I seek the nomination. You're wellborn, a lady to the tips of your fingers, and people warm to you as they do not warm to me. On the other side of the balance sheet, I'm a rich man, and not tightfisted. You and your sisters would want for nothing. But I suppose you thought of that."

Through clenched teeth, she said, "I am not proposing, as you know very well."

He ignored her protest. "I'll have to give the matter some serious thought."

She'd been hoisted by her own petard. So much for crossing swords with a seasoned duelist.

The amusement in his eyes faded and he said seriously, "But first, I would want to know about David."

Her stomach fluttered in alarm. There was only one way to satisfy the curiosity of a man like this, and that was to tell him as much of the truth as she dared.

"David," she said calmly, "was the man I was engaged to when I was Emily's age. He said that I was the love of his life, but he jilted me at the altar. He'd found a new love, you see, that he couldn't live without."

"I'm sorry."

"Don't be. My heart didn't break. I didn't go into a decline. I got over him."

There was a long silence, then he said, "Yet it was *his* name that you mentioned when you came to yourself after your fall."

Her pulse skipped a beat. Why wouldn't he leave it alone? "Yes," she said, "I've wondered about that." She hoped she sounded convincing. "Perhaps, in my heart of hearts, I still love him a little."

He leaned toward her. "You're a fraud, Marion Dane. You're not pining for a lost love."

She clenched her teeth. "How would *you* know?"

"Because of this!"

Under her mystified gaze, he took her plate from her and set it on a side table along with his own, then he slipped an arm around her waist and kissed her. Right there, for anyone to see, he kissed her. She should have expected this reckless gesture from the telling scar on his brow.

She was too dignified to fight him, then too beguiled to do more than clutch at the lapels of his coat for support. It wasn't the kind of kiss she expected. He didn't make her submit; he wooed her with the gentlest pressure of his lips moving on hers.

When he pulled away, she blinked up at him. His eyes smiled into hers. "We've both wondered about that, haven't we? So, now we know."

He retrieved their plates and began to converse naturally and easily about setting up his stable and his latest acquisitions. Eventually, she was able to contribute coherently, and without too much embarrassment. All the same, she was conscious of the veiled glances cast in their direction.

By the time she went to bed, it was as bad as it could get. Rumors were flying thick and fast about the scene caused by Julia Milford and the kiss that had now turned into a torrid embrace.

Marion had just slipped into bed when Emily entered her chamber. "Is it true, Marion?" Her dark eyes were dancing. "Are you betrothed to Mr. Hamilton? That's what everyone is saying."

"Then everyone needs his head examined!" Marion snapped. And on the subject of Brand Hamilton, she refused to say another word.

She lay in the dark, eyes open, thoughts spinning inside her head. The kiss shouldn't have happened. She couldn't allow Brand Hamilton to matter. He thought he knew who and what she was, but he really didn't know her at all.

She'd known betrayal and heartache, but she'd learned to put them behind her. She wasn't a young girl now; she was a woman, a strong and capable woman with two sisters in her charge. There was no place for any man in her life, least of all someone like Brand Hamilton. She would do what she had always done; she would persevere.

She banished all thoughts of Hamilton and focused on an unpleasant though necessary appointment she had made for the following morning. Her errand would take her to Hatchard's bookshop on Piccadilly. And when she left Hatchard's, David would be out of her life forever.

On that happy thought, she drifted into sleep.

The watcher under the portico of St. George's Church in Hanover Square retreated into the shadows when the last carriage outside Reginald Wright's house pulled away from the door. The ball was over. All the guests were on their way home, and servants were already bolting the doors and windows before finding their own beds. Lady Marion Dane was securely locked up for the night and beyond his reach.

There would be other opportunities to get to her, he promised himself—if not here in London, then on the way to Longbury or in Longbury itself. City ways were not country ways. She would not be so well chaperoned in the country.

He did not hate her or dislike her. But he feared her and the harm she could do. If she kept her mouth shut, all would be well. It would be better for all concerned, however, if she never returned to Longbury.

He mulled over that thought as he struck out toward Brook Street and his waiting hackney.

# Chapter Four

Marion walked into the morning room and came to a sudden halt. Several days had passed since that infamous kiss in the ballroom, and this was the first time she had come face-to-face with the infamous man who had taken liberties with her. Mr. Hamilton was sitting at the table with his head bent over one of Phoebe's notebooks. He had yet to see her and she was tempted to tiptoe out. It was a childish impulse that she quickly suppressed. He was Reggie's friend. She couldn't avoid him forever.

Without looking up or turning around, he said, "Too late now, Marion, to make your escape. I know you're here." He rose to his feet, his eyes alight with amusement.

It was his amusement that rankled. He had the most expressive eyes of any man she knew. One look could make her blush, or tie her tongue in knots, or make her grind her teeth. He knew how to play her, and she was determined not to play his game.

"Mr. Hamilton," she said, bobbing him a curtsy. "Where are the others?"

The plan was to drive out to Richmond Park for a picnic. This was largely for Phoebe's benefit, to bring some roses to her pale cheeks. No one had mentioned that Hamilton was coming with them.

"They've gone ahead," he said. "You and Phoebe are driving with me. Phoebe will tell us when the carriage is at the door."

"And Fanny didn't think to mention it to me?" Marion asked faintly.

It was a long way to Richmond, and the thought of being with him for any length of time filled her with dismay. Besides, it would only add to the gossip about them. Fanny must know this. Was this her cousin's way of making a match between them? She'd get no joy there.

"Fanny is being diplomatic," he said. "She knows I have an apology to make. Will you hear me out?"

When she hesitated, he put his hands on the back of the chair next to his. "Why don't you sit down, Marion?"

It was more of a command than a suggestion. She was struck again by the dueling scar to his left eyebrow. It reminded her that there was a reckless side to his character and she had better watch her step. He stretched the rules of conduct between the sexes that she had been taught to follow, and that put her at a disadvantage.

She took the chair he held for her and watched him as he walked to the window. He moved like a fencer, she thought, gracefully, efficiently. She wondered if he knew how handsome and dashing he looked in his form-fitting dark coat and beige trousers.

He turned suddenly. "How are the toes?"

Her eyes dropped to his boots before she realized that

he was asking about her own stubbed toes. "They're better, thank you."

He took the chair next to hers. "I thought as much when Fanny told me that you'd gone to Hatchard's the day after her ball."

"I took the carriage," she quickly replied. Hatchard's? Why had he mentioned Hatchard's?

"Find anything interesting?"

"No. I didn't stay long. My toes started to act up again."

He nodded and smiled. "No other ill effects from your fall at the theater?"

He was bringing up all the things she didn't want to talk about. What did he know? Why was he so curious?

"None whatsoever." Her voice was crisp. "Mr. Hamilton, did I hear you aright? You said something about an apology?"

He shrugged negligently. "I'm coming to that. The last thing I wanted to do was cause you embarrassment. I'm sorry I kissed you in front of all those people."

It wasn't much of an apology, but he'd said the magic words, and she was happy to leave it at that.

She was on the point of rising when he said, "Why didn't you slap me?"

She sank back in her chair. Because she'd been beguiled. She'd thought about that kiss at odd moments throughout the day, every day and every night. The taste of him was still on her lips; the iron-hard muscles in his arms could still be felt by her fingertips. His gentleness, his passion, his . . .

Swallowing, she said, "Because you took me by surprise. It never occurred to me that a man with his eye fixed on a seat in Parliament would act so recklessly. What do your colleagues think?"

He grinned wickedly. "Oh, they applauded. They believed that I was staking my claim to an earl's daughter before someone else snatched you from under my nose—you know, that I was trying to improve my chances of winning my party's nomination. Others, however, thought I'd had a lucky escape. Most women would have demanded that I offer to marry them after that public display."

Now he was making fun of her. As coolly as she could manage, she said, "I should find Phoebe and see that she is warmly dressed."

He captured her wrist and held her in a loose clasp. All amusement was wiped from his face. "No one blames you for that kiss, Marion. Everyone knows that you're an innocent and too easily taken advantage of. The blame is mine."

Her voice was as dry as tinder. "But because you're a male, they make allowances for you. In fact, they expect you to sow your wild oats."

A laugh was startled out of him. "Marion, an innocent kiss in front of witnesses is hardly sowing my wild oats."

"It won't look so innocent if we're seen driving in your carriage with only Phoebe for a chaperon."

Before he could reply, the door opened and Phoebe entered. "Lady Bethune's carriage is here," she cried. "And Marion, it's an *open* carriage. Do hurry. Maybe we can catch up with the others."

Marion looked a question at Brand. "Lady Bethune?"

Lady Bethune was one of the ladies who had chaperoned them at the theater.

"And Ash's grandmother," he added. He offered her his arm. "A gentleman can't be too careful of his reputation." And with a broad smile, he ushered her from the room.

As was to be expected, Marion confined her conversation to the females in the carriage while Brand settled back to enjoy the spectacle of Marion studiously avoiding his eyes.

And he couldn't take his eyes off her.

He'd learned a lot more about her in the last week. Sensing that a proposal of marriage might be on the horizon, Fanny had been very frank when he'd led her to talk of Marion. Emily had been the favored child, Fanny told him, and when Diana had died, Marion stepped into her mother's shoes. Not that Diana had been a bad mother, but before she had married, Diana Gunn had been a paid companion, and Marion had borne the brunt of her mother's insecurities. After Marion's father inherited the title and they moved to Keswick, Diana raised Marion to the strictest standards of deportment so that no one could point a finger and say, "I told you so." Nine years later, when Emily came along, Diana had nothing to prove, and she allowed her younger daughters freedoms that Marion had never enjoyed.

As he saw it, the trouble with Marion was that, at seven and twenty, she saw herself as an old maid, and all her hopes and ambitions were pinned on her sisters. That's not how he saw her. In some way he had yet to fathom, he felt akin to her. There was more to him and more to her than they allowed the world to see.

He wasn't sure that the wisest thing he'd ever done was kiss her. But he'd done it anyway, and broken through her shell to find a fragility that had both stunned him and drawn him in. There was so much giving in her, and so much wanting, so much innocence and so much passion.

What made this woman so different? What made him so reckless when he was with her? Dueling with foils had lost its gloss. Marion was a bigger challenge.

He was becoming attuned to all her moods—the way her breathing altered and her lashes lowered when she felt uncomfortable. It was only when he looked into her eyes that he could tell what she was feeling.

They were going to Richmond at his suggestion. He'd heard from Fanny that Marion had stayed close to the house since the night of the ball, giving as an excuse her awkwardness with getting around with a cane. But that hadn't stopped her from going to Hatchard's. She'd stayed for only a few minutes. What had happened in that innocent outing to make her so skittish?

Had malicious tongues sent her hurrying home? He didn't mind what the gossips said about him, just as long as they left her alone. The last thing she should do is hide herself away as though she were guilty of something. She had to learn to snap her fingers at her detractors. Hence the trip to Richmond.

Thinking of Hatchard's and books had put another thought in his head, and when there was a lull in the conversation, he spoke to Phoebe. "While we were waiting for the carriage to arrive, I happened to look over one of your notebooks. The words 'Family History' were on the cover, but there wasn't much in it except a family tree."

"That's because," said Phoebe, "there's not much to tell about my family. We're all so boring."

Lady Bethune laughed. "Think yourself fortunate. Now, my family is thick with pirates and adventurers. We don't like to mention them in polite company."

"Really?" Phoebe beamed. "Well, that's famous! Papa was the only man in our family and, though I love him dearly, I could never make up a story about him."

"I wish I could say the same about my grandson," interjected Ash Denison's grandmother, and everyone laughed.

"If I were you," said Lady Bethune, "I'd be very careful about digging into family history. You never know what skeleton you may turn up. Every family has something to hide."

Lady Bethune, Brand thought, had put his own feelings into words, but he didn't think those words would put Phoebe off; just the opposite.

Marion said, "I'm sure Longbury has an interesting history, Phoebe. Maybe you could write about that."

Brand was thoughtful. After a moment's reflection, he dismissed the idea that Phoebe could be putting herself in danger by writing her family history. She wouldn't know the right questions to ask, and he knew that Marion would not allow her young sister to make a nuisance of herself.

It was Marion who was putting herself at risk by returning to Longbury, if there was a risk involved. He still hadn't made up his mind about that.

The sun beat down on them, the breeze was gentle and drenched with the scent of grass and trees; laughter filled the air. Marion was enjoying herself immensely. No one looked at her askance and Brand behaved like a perfect gentleman, dividing his time equally among everyone present. Ash Denison had brought his curricle, and he took all the ladies up, in ones and twos, for a brisk drive. Phoebe was in her element, and though nothing could persuade her to get on a horse's back, she enjoyed petting them and was ecstatic when it was her turn to drive with Lord Denison, though Emily was sharing the honor.

Emily was in her element as well. Ash Denison, the darling of society, had made her the object of his attentions—a heady experience for an eighteen-year-old girl. Marion paid no attention. Their visit to Cousin Fanny was drawing to a close. In a few days, they'd be setting off for Longbury. Emily was entitled to a little pleasure before they left the excitement of London for a quiet country life. No more Ash Denison and no more Brand Hamilton.

She watched Brand through half-lowered lashes. A small knot of regret lodged in her breast. She had allowed him to get too close to her, or rather, he had forced his way past her defenses. He had no idea that she was the last woman he should think of marrying.

Suddenly, her gaze was trapped in his hard stare, and he left Fanny and crossed to her. She cursed herself then for her lack of caution. She was sitting on a bench by herself, woolgathering, when she should have stayed close to her two formidable chaperons who had wandered off to the Lord only knew where.

He sat beside her. "I've come to say good-bye," he said. "That ought to scotch the gossip, especially as we've hardly said two words to each other all afternoon. When people see me leave, they'll think I'm a disappointed lover."

"You're going back to London?"

He gestured to a groom who had two horses in tow. "On horseback. I've said my good-byes to the others. And tomorrow, I leave for Brighton, so I may not see you for some time."

Marion knew that the trip to Brighton had to do with the by-election, but she had not realized that it was coming up so soon.

Brand got up and bowed over her hand. "Marion," he said in a soft undertone, "if you keep looking at me like that, I shall be tempted to kiss you again."

She snatched her hand away. Eyes snapping, she said, "Have a pleasant trip, Mr. Hamilton."

He laughed and turned away. She watched him until he and his groom had disappeared behind a forest of trees.

The appointed day of their departure seemed reluctant to dawn. A ferocious storm during the night had made little impression on the overcast skies. More rains threatened and candles had to be lit to stave off the gloom.

It wasn't a day to be traveling the King's Highway. That was Cousin Fanny's opinion. "Only think," she said, "what will happen if the rivers overflow their banks. Longbury may be cut off and you might have to put up at some ramshackle inn with a rough-and-ready set of people. I wish you would stay here, at least till the weather improves."

They were in Marion's bedchamber, packing her boxes. Marion's stubbed toes were no longer a problem and, as she spoke, she moved quickly around the room, picking up books and small personal items to pack in the last box. "I'm from the Lake District, remember? If I let a little rain put me off, I'd never go anywhere. And when we are settled, you must pay us a visit. Longbury isn't so far away."

This careless answer did not satisfy Fanny, and she

groped in her mind for words that would explain what she was feeling without giving offense.

Marion fastened the last strap, just as footmen arrived to carry her boxes downstairs. Linking her arm through Fanny's as they followed the footmen along the hallway, she said, "I want to thank you for making our time here so enjoyable. Longbury is going to seem very tame after London."

"Then why the haste to leave? The Season isn't over yet. Only be patient and I think you may be surprised at the result."

They were on the gallery overlooking the front hall. Fanny halted and looked Marion in the eye. "You must know," she said, "that I'm thinking of you and Mr. Hamilton. No. Don't try to stop me. I've screwed up my courage and mean to speak to you as though you were my own daughter."

She heaved a sigh, then went on quickly, "Surely you're not running away because of Julia Milford? Reggie tells me that affair is over. Marion, don't you know that there isn't a man alive who doesn't have a few regrets about his past?"

Laughter glinted in Marion's eyes. "Any man," she said, "who regrets Mrs. Milford must be a fool. No, listen to me, Fanny. I know what you think and you're wrong. Mr. Hamilton doesn't want to marry me. He has befriended me and my sisters because he was a close friend of my aunt."

"But he kissed you!"

"That makes no difference. He's running for Parliament, or he will be if he wins the nomination. He'll be in the public eye. You know me. I like a quiet life. I'd be a fish out of water in his circles."

"Don't be so modest! You'd be an asset to him."

The conversation was interrupted by Emily calling to them from the hall. "Marion, do hurry. The chaise is waiting for us and the postboys are becoming impatient."

"Coming," called Marion, and she hastened to obey.

Reggie was waiting for them at the foot of the stairs. He looked a question at his wife.

Fanny shook her head. "I can't persuade her to stay. They are used to this kind of weather in the Lake District."

"Stay!" exclaimed Phoebe, dismayed. "You promised we would leave for Longbury today, Marion."

Marion cast a critical eye over her youngest sister. She wasn't dressed as warmly as Marion would have liked, but she merely said, "I haven't changed my mind, but where is your traveling rug?"

"I put it in the chaise," said Emily, "and Cousin Reggie made sure the Bath chair was safely stowed."

At the mention of the Bath chair, Phoebe scowled.

"Remember," said Reggie, "there are many good posting houses on the way. Don't hesitate to break your journey if the weather worsens. Longbury will still be there tomorrow."

All that remained were the affectionate leave-takings and promises from Fanny and Reggie to visit as soon as Parliament was in recess. Then they were off.

"Why the long face?" Reggie asked Fanny when they turned back into the house.

"I was thinking of Brand," she said glumly, "hoping . . . oh, you know what, that he and Marion would make a match of it. But with him based in London and Marion in Longbury, nothing will come of it."

He wrapped his arm around her shoulders as they walked down the hall to the breakfast room. "Brand isn't returning to London, not right away. He's setting up his headquarters in Longbury in the house his grandfather left him. After all, it's in the riding we're contesting."

Fanny stopped in her tracks, an arrested expression on her face. "I don't think Marion knows that."

Reggie smiled. "She soon will."

Marion wiped the condensation from the coach window and looked out. The rain was unrelenting, they were a long way from Longbury and, though it was still light, every posting house they came to was choked with people hoping to find a bed for the night. The last posting house had turned them away. If the next posting house did not take them in, they might be forced to beg a bed in some kindly cottar's cottage.

The thought turned in her mind. Her mother had said those words the last time they made this trip.

*If the next posting house does not take us in, Penn, we must ask some kindly cottar's family for a bed for the night.*

Penn was her father's name, a shortened version of his title, Penrith. His Christian name was George, but no one ever called him that, not even her mother.

She shook her head. Her memory must be at fault. Only she and her mother had made the trip to Longbury. She couldn't remember where her father had been, but she knew that he and Aunt Edwina did not get along. He would not stay cooped up in a cottage with Mama's sister. Now where had that thought come from?

It wasn't her imagination. She did remember it. They were in the coach, and she was nestled in Papa's arms, just as Phoebe was nestled in hers. *Go to sleep, little elf,* Papa said, but she couldn't sleep. She could feel the tension in her parents, and sensed that nobody wanted to visit Aunt Edwina.

"Marion?"

She looked up to see Emily studying her. "What is it?"

"I've just remembered who David is. You were engaged to a David once, weren't you?"

Marion answered easily. "I was, until he discovered that my dowry was too small to keep him in the luxury to which he aspired."

Emily faltered a little, then went on resolutely, "Is he the reason you have never married? Are you still in love with him?"

Marion was startled. "What on earth put that idea in your head?"

Emily shrugged. "It was his name you said when you came out of your swoon."

"I did not swoon! I was dizzy, that's all."

"You haven't answered my question."

Marion clicked her tongue. "The answer is no. I'm not in love with David Kerr."

"What about Mr. Hamilton? He kissed you, didn't he?"

Marion was ready to throw a tantrum. "It was the kind of kiss Cousin Reggie might have given me. There was nothing to it. I swear I am not in love with anyone."

A slow smile curved Emily's lips. "I believe you, but I doubt the gossips will. They're saying that he turned off Mrs. Milford because she was an embarrassment to him, but you, an earl's daughter, would be a feather in his cap."

"You can't blame Mr. Hamilton for what people are saying."

Phoebe stirred. "I like Mr. Hamilton," she said.

Her sisters laughed. They talked of this and that.

Emily's lashes fluttered and she eventually dozed. Marion gazed out the window, her thoughts drifting.

*An earl's daughter would be a feather in his cap.* Well, this was one earl's daughter who was not tempted.

When the chaise turned off the thoroughfare to Brighton, her sense of relief was palpable.

# Chapter Five

Marion was jerked from sleep when the chaise shuddered violently, then lurched to one side. Books, periodicals, and odds and ends toppled to the floor. Emily screamed. Marion grabbed for Phoebe before she slid from the banquette. Phoebe struggled as she came awake, then subsided when she saw who held her.

Outside, horses were screaming and rearing in their traces as postboys tried to unhitch them. Marion's heart was pumping hard and fast. "Out!" she told Emily. "You go first and I'll hand Phoebe to you."

"It's pelting outside," protested Emily.

"Would you rather drown? *Out*, I said!"

Emily's eyes widened with fright as water bubbled up through the floor, and she hastened to do her sister's bidding. It was no easy task. The only door that would open was at such an angle that she had to push it open with her shoulder before clambering out of the coach.

Phoebe showed no fear but merely gritted her teeth as she put her weight on her weak leg and, with Emily pulling and Marion pushing, was finally hoisted through the door.

"Hurry!" called Emily. "The coach isn't safe. The wheel is broken and it's going to topple over."

The water was inches deep and rising fast. Marion could feel the weight of her skirts as they greedily sucked up the flood.

She called out, "I can manage. Look after Phoebe! Get her to safety."

Emily's hand was withdrawn and Marion climbed onto a banquette. She heard masculine voices close by and breathed out a sigh. In spite of what she'd said, she didn't think she could haul herself through the door without the postboys' help.

"Stand back!" A man's voice.

She recognized the voice. The coach swayed alarmingly as he climbed onto it. In the next instant, Ash Denison's face appeared above her. She was so shocked to see him that she could only stare.

"Give me your hand!" he commanded.

She automatically extended one arm then quickly withdrew it. "What are you doing here?"

"I've been checking every posting house on the road, hoping to find you high and dry. I missed you by minutes at the last one. They told me they'd turned you away."

"But . . . you've been following my chaise?"

"Let's leave the explanations till later, shall we? Give me your hand, Lady Marion."

She wasn't going anywhere without her reticule. This time, there would be no threatening notes for her to find. It was dark in the coach but she knew where she had left it. It was there, on the banquette.

"Now!" he commanded. "Before we're both swept away."

She grasped her reticule, gave one frightened yelp when the coach swayed, and reached for his hand. Inch by inch, he raised her through the gaping door, then he swept her into his arms.

They were perched on the side of the coach; the water seemed to be rising by the second. Either that, or the coach was sinking. She gave a terrified gasp and clutched her reticule to her breast.

"Watch your step," she cried.

With a reckless laugh, he jumped into the roiling water, making her teeth jar. She could see, now, how the accident had happened. They were halfway across a ford that the rain had turned into a torrent. The wheels of her chaise must have hit a submerged rock, and the chaise overturned.

Even before he reached the bank, he began issuing orders to the men who were standing by, among them her own postboys who were calming the horses from the chaise. There was a carriage there, his own, she presumed, and she recognized Manley, Brand Hamilton's manservant. He helped Phoebe into the carriage, then did the same for Emily.

Marion would have thanked Lord Denison profusely when he set her down, except that she wasn't given the chance. "Come along, Lady Marion," he said. "You're shivering with cold. Let's get you to a hot supper and a warm fire. Then I'll answer all your questions."

She hoped that her questions would be answered in the carriage, but Lord Denison elected to ride with Manley on the box. Strange, she thought. Why wasn't Manley with Brand Hamilton?

And why was she always suspicious when she should

have been thanking her lucky stars that they'd come
along when they had?

Lord Denison used Brand Hamilton's name at the next
posting house and it worked like magic. According to
Lord Denison, Brand was a popular figure in the area because he'd canvassed for a local man in the last election.
Though they were given only a small room in the attics,
Marion felt lucky to get anything. People were settling
in for the night in the taproom or on any spare bench
they could find.

Lord Denison spoke to her briefly before she and her
sisters went upstairs. He hadn't happened on them by
accident. "I knew," he said, "that you were due to leave
for Longbury today, and since I was going there myself, I
thought we might go together. I missed you by minutes
in Hanover Square, and became quite alarmed when the
weather turned desperate. But all's well that ends well,
and here we are."

"You're going to Longbury?" Marion asked.

"To help open up Brand's house. He'll be joining me
in a day or two, and Longbury is to be his base, at least
until the election is over."

Marion concealed her dismay as best she could. She
did not dislike Brand Hamilton. She just wished that
the riding he was contesting was on the other side of
England.

Denison left them in the lobby in Manley's care.

"I have to go back for the others and fetch your belongings," Denison said, "but everything is taken care
of, and Manley will look after you."

And Manley did, like, thought Marion, a seasoned,
grizzled sheepdog with a small flock of lost sheep. She

knew all about sheepdogs. The rocky soil of the Lake District could sustain only one crop: sheep. They roamed far and wide over the fells where no person could possibly follow, only the sheepdogs. They were not friendly like pets but they got the job done. Manley was like that.

He rounded them up—and a sorry lot they were—herded them up the stairs—patiently, where his injured lamb, Phoebe, was concerned—and penned them in their chamber. Finally, he warned them gruffly to stay where they were and he would have dinner sent up to them.

No sooner had the door closed on them than Phoebe exclaimed, "I like Mr. Manley, don't you?"

Her sisters laughed.

All smiles now, they surveyed their room. It was small with a low ceiling, a tiny dormer window, and a big feather bed taking up most of the space. Best of all, it was warm, with a cheery fire blazing in the grate, so warm that they removed their outer things then stood in front of the fire to dry off their damp skirts. It was the best they could do until their boxes arrived.

Not long after, a maid arrived with their dinner, hot mutton pie with dumplings, new potatoes, and carrots. Maybe it was because of the excellent dinner, or maybe because they were snug and dry, but as the meal progressed, Marion's mood mellowed considerably. Emily voiced the opinion that Lord Denison had treated them very handsomely, and Marion had to agree.

The maid returned to clear up after dinner and make up the trundle bed for Phoebe. Emily helped her roll it out while Marion looked around for her reticule so that she could give the maid a gratuity for all her trouble.

It wasn't on the bed among their coats and shawls. It

wasn't on the dresser. She stood there trying to get her bearings, casting her mind back to the last time she remembered her reticule. She'd set it down in the carriage when Ash Denison had conveyed them to the inn, then she'd forgotten all about it.

Abruptly turning to the maid, she said in a small, tight voice, "Did Lord Denison get in yet?"

The abrupt question seemed to startle the maid. "I don't rightly know, your ladyship. But Mr. Poole, the landlord, would know."

Marion knew that she wasn't behaving rationally, that she should ask the maid to find Manley for her, but she was gripped by a terrible sense of urgency. No one but she must touch that reticule.

She snatched her coat off the bed. "I left my reticule in the coach," she said. "I'm going to fetch it."

Then she ordered her sisters to stay where they were and slammed out of the room.

There was no sign of Manley, and among so many coaches in the courtyard, she could not pick out the one she wanted, so she went to the front desk and asked whether Lord Denison had arrived. The landlord directed her to the quarters for grooms and postboys above the stables.

"I had to move out two of Lord Lennox's grooms to make room for him," he said. "But it's no place for a lady. Why don't you go back to your room and I'll send someone to bring Lord Denison to you when I have a spare moment?"

She hadn't the patience to wait, not when there was a crush of people jostling her for the landlord's attention. Tempers were becoming frayed when they heard that there were no rooms to be had and they would have to bed down for the night in their coaches.

The courtyard was, by this time, lit by lanterns hanging from the walls. From snatches of conversation, she learned that the road to Brighton had been washed away, forcing travelers to go miles out of their way to find accommodation. This made little impression on her. All she wanted was her reticule.

One of the stable boys pointed to the door to Lord Denison's quarters. She could tell from the boy's expression that he was amazed to find a lady in this masculine preserve. She thanked the stable boy, put her head down, and mounted the stone steps to the narrow gallery overlooking the yard.

She was almost at the door when someone inside the room mentioned her name, not Lord Denison, but someone else. Brand Hamilton. Without conscious thought, she flattened herself against the wall. The small casement window was open and Lord Denison was standing beside it, blowing a stream of tobacco smoke to the outside.

"I'm surprised," said Denison, "that you thought it necessary to tear yourself away from your political cronies and come here when my messenger must have told you that I had everything in hand."

"I met your man when I came to the crossroads. Fortunately, he recognized me or I might have missed you altogether."

Another cloud of smoke streamed through the open window. "It was an accident, Brand, pure and simple."

There was the sound of water splashing, and she imagined Hamilton at the washstand, washing the dirt of the journey from his face and hands.

"You may be right," Hamilton replied. "But I know she is frightened of something or someone."

There was an interval of silence, then Lord Denison said, "It can't be connected to Longbury or she wouldn't be going there."

"True. I think she's running from a former suitor, but I can't be sure. Pass me the towel."

Damn and blast the man! How could he possibly know?

The same thought had evidently occurred to Denison. "How do you know that? Not about the suitor, but that she's frightened of him? Don't bother answering. I know what you're going to say. Your instincts as a newspaperman tell you so. And I suppose your instincts won't let you rest until you get to the bottom of this."

Nothing short of the threat of imminent discovery could have made her move away. Ears straining, she edged closer to the open window.

"It may come to that, but I'd rather she came to me by herself and told me what's troubling her."

"Why should she?"

There was a smile in Hamilton's voice. "Because she's learning to trust me."

Marion sucked air through her teeth. If she were a man, she would have him by the throat right now.

Denison said, "You do realize that, in the eyes of the world, you're practically engaged to the girl? Need I remind you of the scene with Julia Milford in Fanny's ballroom, not to mention the kiss that followed? If you continue to pay such marked attention to Lady Marion, everyone will wonder when the wedding is to be."

"Let them" was the curt reply.

Exasperated, Ash retorted, "What about Lady Marion? Doesn't she deserve to know what you're up to?"

Now for the moment of truth, thought Marion, and her fingers clenched into fists.

"Ash," said Brand, "would you mind smoking that blasted cheroot outside? The smoke in here is practically choking me."

Marion cursed under her breath. That was no answer, bur she dared not stay longer. Picking up her skirts, she slipped away, keeping to the shadows. Her pulse was racing and her resentment was edged with alarm. He was a newspaperman. He thought that gave him the right to ferret out everyone's secrets. Or maybe he wanted to make quite sure that the lady he took to wife wouldn't have any secrets in her past that could embarrass him when he became prime minister. Prime minister? Hah! She was beginning to sound like Phoebe. Her one consolation was that David wouldn't tell him anything, because she'd paid him handsomely for his silence.

She came face-to-face with Manley in the inn's lobby and wasn't surprised when he bared his teeth at her.

"I've been looking all over for you," he said.

"And I've been looking all over for my reticule." She recognized her boxes as her postboys carried them upstairs.

Manley dug in his pocket. "You left it in the coach," he said, and held it out to her.

She practically snatched it out of his hand. Everything was just as it should be. There was no threatening note tucked inside.

Her smile was brilliant. "Now you may snap at me as much as you like, Mr. Manley."

And she whirled herself around and went racing up the stairs.

Brand rose quietly, so as not to disturb Ash, shrugged into his coat, and went out onto the gallery for a breath of fresh air. Though lights still blazed from the inn's windows, the stable yard was fairly quiet. Only a few ostlers were on duty, and no carriages had entered the yard in the last little while. Postboys had brought the news that not only was Brighton cut off by the rising waters, but the road to Longbury had been washed away as well.

He couldn't sleep. His mind teemed with questions. He felt desperate to do something, anything, and he was stuck here in the middle of nowhere.

He'd examined the wheel of Marion's chaise and, as far as he could tell, it hadn't been tampered with. A submerged boulder had buckled the left wheel. His theory that Marion was deliberately being targeted was beginning to appear ridiculous. Or was that what he was supposed to think?

David Kerr. He'd got the name from Fanny, but she didn't know anything about him. Why wouldn't Marion confide in him?

At least he knew where she was and that she was safe. But he couldn't drop everything and go tearing up and down the English countryside looking for her, as he had done today, just because she might be stranded in some godforsaken place. And whose fault was that? No sane woman would have taken to the road in this kind of weather. Lucky for her, Ash was watching out for her.

What was he going to do with her?

His mouth curved in a smile that was ironic as well as humorous. Brand Hamilton, the baseborn son of a duke, and Lady Marion Dane, the highborn daughter of an earl? He was well aware that their mutual attraction appalled her as much as it appalled him. She thought that he wanted to marry her to further his political ambitions, that marriage to a blue-blood would add to his consequence. The opposite was true. With few exceptions, he felt nothing but contempt for the aristocracy and their assumption that a life of privilege was theirs by divine right.

Marion was an exception. Oh, she could act the grande dame when it suited her, those cool gray eyes chilling to ice. But that was a defense to keep him at arm's length. When she felt secure, as she did with her sisters and cousins, she was anything but aloof. Getting to know Marion was like peeling a rosebud, one petal at a time. One had to watch out for the thorns.

His grin faded. This wasn't a game. He had to be satisfied that there was no danger to Marion. He had things to do, places to go. He knew this terrain like the back of his hand. Flood waters or no, he could be in Longbury before dawn.

Marion wasn't going anywhere. Between them, Ash and Manley could look out for her.

On that thought, he turned into his chamber and wakened Ash.

The watcher cursed softly under his breath. Lady Marion had as many bodyguards watching over her as any princess of the realm. He would never get to her now. The note he was supposed to slip inside her reticule was burning a hole in his pocket.

He'd known that her chaise would eventually founder because he'd made sure that the wheel would buckle. What he hadn't known was when it would happen, or that Lord Denison would get to her first.

It seemed obvious to him that Brand Hamilton was taking a proprietary interest in Lady Marion and had enlisted his friend Denison to be her escort. The question he was asking himself was whether Hamilton suspected anything, or whether he was acting as any eager suitor would.

This was too close for comfort. The thing to do now was lie low and melt into the background.

Cold beads of sweat broke out on his brow. He felt chilled to the bone. It wasn't the thought of Lady Marion and what she might reveal that chilled him, but the thought of Brand Hamilton.

The last thing he wanted was to come face-to-face with that gentleman. He'd taken a chance at the theater, but it was a risk he wasn't prepared to take again.

A fresh horse was saddled and waiting for him in the stable. He mounted up, pulled his hat low over his face, and rode out, going back the way he had come.

# Chapter Six

Longbury was a small market town snugly nestled in a gap in the South Downs and owed its prosperity to the wool trade. Centuries before, it had also been home to a Benedictine monastery, but all that remained of the monks' presence was their Priory, now the stately home of the FitzAlans, the leading family in the area. Brand's family.

It stood on the summit of a hill, and though Brand had been riding for hours in a steady drizzle, and his eyes were heavy with fatigue, his gaze was inexorably drawn to the Priory's roof etched against the horizon. His grandfather's house, the Grange, was on the opposite side of the road, going down toward the river. In its time, the Grange had served as a granary, a farmhouse, and a vicarage before a prosperous wool merchant rebuilt it for his family's use. When the family's fortunes declined, most of the land was sold off and the main house and outbuildings passed from one owner to another until the property was acquired by the Hamiltons.

The Grange was an unassuming, two-story brick building set in extensive grounds, and a fitting though somewhat spartan residence for his Puritan grandfather.

Close to the house was a small stable block for which his grandfather had had little use except for sheltering his horse and buggy. Though it was barely first light, the grooms Manley had hired were hard at work, and Brand was glad to turn the care of his horse over to them. Then he stumbled to the house, threw off his sodden cloak in the vestibule, and climbed the stairs to his bed.

When Brand wakened, sunshine was streaming in his bedroom window. His first thought was that the rain had stopped. His second was that he should have remembered there were no soft feather beds in his grandfather's house, only mattresses that felt as though they were stuffed with bricks. In fact, they were stuffed with horsehair.

Yawning, groaning, he rolled from the bed and took a moment to stretch his aching muscles. He'd slept in his clothes and he wasn't sure whether the rank smell came from his horse, from the mattress, or from himself. Fortunately, he always kept plenty of his own garments in the dressers and closets, a countryman's clothes that were never in or out of fashion.

He noted that the fire had been lit and that gave him hope. Crossing to the bell rope, he gave it a hard yank. His hope was realized a few moments later when a towheaded boy of about twelve summers entered his chamber.

"And your name is—?" Brand inquired.

"Sam," replied the boy. "Sam Ludlow."

Brand remembered Sam's mother very well. She'd been Edwina's cook and maid-of-all-work. More to the point, she was one of the people he'd made this snap journey to interrogate. It was she who had found Edwina's body. Perhaps she knew more than she realized—if there was more to know.

"Any chance that I could have a bath this morning?" he asked the boy.

Sam smiled. "My mother told me you would say that, so the first thing she did when we arrived was light the fire under the boiler."

"Splendid," said Brand, rubbing his hands.

Less than an hour later, bathed and changed, Brand entered the kitchen feeling more like himself. Mrs. Ludlow was like most countrywomen: As soon as she heard her man's step at the door, she had his meal on the table.

"You'll have to eat in the kitchen, sir," she said, heaping a plate with scrambled eggs. "I haven't got round to setting fires in the other rooms."

"The kitchen is fine," Brand assured her. "And don't bother lighting fires. I'll be in and out a great deal."

He'd hardly sat down when the plate was set in front of him—cold mutton, kidney, and fluffy eggs. Next came the toast with a bowl of marmalade. He waited until she'd poured his coffee before he invited her to join him.

"To talk about your duties here," he said.

She smiled and shook her head. "I'm only helping out until your own people arrive. You see, I already have a job. I'll be working for Lady Marion up at the cottage."

"Ah. I should have known. All the same, do take a chair and keep me company for a little while."

She looked at him as though he'd taken leave of his senses. Servants did not keep company with their employers.

He gave her his most winsome grin. "I never got round to telling you how much Edwina appreciated all

you did for her. She never stopped singing your praises."
And that was the truth.

She relented, then, and took the chair he indicated,
her roughened hands loosely clasped in her lap. Her
Celtic ancestry showed in her dark coloring and fine
bones. He judged her to be in her early forties. Obviously, the boy got his looks from his father.

He remembered, then, that she was a widow. There
were other children besides Sam, younger children, who
were looked after by their grandmother while Mrs.
Ludlow worked to provide for them all. His respect for
the lady rose by several degrees.

She was looking at him expectantly.

Leading gently, he said, "How long were you with
Miss Gunn?"

"Not long. Five years, after I became a widow and my
mother came to live with us." A shadow of a smile
touched her lips. "Miss Gunn always remembered the
children's birthdays."

"That sounds like Edwina."

She nodded. "She was always so kind, so generous."

He let a moment of silence pass and chewed on the
cold mutton. "I had heard," he went on carefully, "that
she wasn't easy to get along with those last few weeks. I
mean, she was becoming forgetful and suspicious of her
friends." He stopped when he saw she was bristling.

There was no softness or respect in her voice now
when she spoke. "Have you never forgotten where you
left your spectacles or your keys, Mr. Hamilton? Do you
always remember everyone's name? She was no more
forgetful than the next person, but—" She bit down on
her lip as though belatedly remembering to whom she
was speaking.

"But?" Brand encouraged in the same gentle tone.

She breathed out a sigh. "She was troubled about the past, about her sister, Hannah. She wanted to know what had happened to her."

"Everyone believes she eloped."

"Miss Gunn said that that was a lie and she was going to prove it."

"Who told her it was a lie?"

"She wouldn't tell me, and I didn't press her. Well, it's not my place, is it? She was my employer."

"What did Miss Gunn think happened to Hannah?"

Her eyes flicked to the door as though hoping someone would enter and put a stop to the interview. Finally, she said, "She didn't say."

He didn't want to alarm her by firing off questions, but he hadn't learned anything he didn't already know, except that Mrs. Ludlow didn't believe Edwina was becoming forgetful or senile. She could be trying to protect an employer who had always treated her well, but Brand did not think that was likely. Her indignation on Edwina's behalf seemed genuine.

He swallowed a mouthful of coffee before going on carefully, "You haven't betrayed any confidences, Mrs. Ludlow. Edwina told me all this in one of her letters. And I would have to say she sounded as sane as you or I."

"She wrote to you?"

He nodded.

"When was this?"

"A few weeks before the accident. I was out of town and didn't receive her letter till after the funeral. Why do you ask?"

The interest died out of her eyes. "When I found her at the foot of the stairs, there were ink stains on her fingers, but neither the constable nor I found a letter or anything she might have written."

Now this was something new, and the first indication of something out of the ordinary. "Only one more question," he said. When she looked at him anxiously, he hesitated. He didn't want to frighten her off. He wanted to gain her trust so that she would confide in him. There would be other opportunities to speak with her.

Veering off in another direction, he said, "How do you get these eggs so fluffy?"

As he trudged up the steep incline to the house, Brand could not help reflecting on the irony of the situation. When he was old enough to strike out on his own, he'd left the Priory vowing never to return. Things hadn't worked out that way. Even in death, his father had managed to have the last word. By the terms of the duke's last will and testament, he had appointed Brand as sole trustee for his half brother and sister. Everyone expected him to refuse the trust or turn it over to his uncle, Lord Robert. This he would not do. Robert did not have the interest or the talent to manage Andrew's affairs, but Brand did, and he was determined to make his half brother worthy of his great estate.

When the butler opened the front door and ushered him into the Great Hall, Brand felt as though time had reversed itself. As a boy, he'd imagined Hartley to be about eighty years old. He hadn't changed a bit. Nor had the Great Hall. The same priceless tapestries adorned its walls, the same armored knight sat astride his stuffed destrier.

"You're looking well, sir," Hartley observed with a faint smile, then advised him that the ladies were breakfasting in the morning room.

"Only the ladies?" inquired Brand.

Hartley nodded. "Lord Robert and Lady Theodora, I

believe, are visiting friends in Windsor. There's a filly there that her ladyship has her eye on."

That sounded like Theodora. Horses and hunting were the loves of her life. She had no children to deflect her interest from her horsey pursuits, and no husband. Lord Robert might have accompanied his wife to Windsor, but once there they would go their separate ways.

"And His Grace?" inquired Brand, referring to Andrew.

Hartley's smile bunched his thin cheeks. "Oh, the young duke is with the estate agent, at the farm."

That was exactly what Brand wanted to hear. The FitzAlans' wealth depended on the land and its farms. It was imperative that the young duke be conversant with all aspects of how his estates were run. This was the lambing season, and the wool trade was important to the estate's fortunes. With the help of Mr. Terrance, the estate agent handpicked by Brand, Andrew's education had just begun.

"No need to announce me," he told Hartley, and he made his way across the flagstoned Great Hall to the west wing.

When he entered the morning room, he paused and took in the scene with a quick glance. The dowager countess, his grandmother, sat at the head of the table, looking as stately as he'd ever seen her in her fashions of a bygone era. Not for the duchess the high waists and flimsy gauzes of the modern miss. To her right was her longtime companion, Miss Cutter, whom he'd christened Miss Flutter from her habit of fluttering from one topic of conversation to another and leaving utter confusion in her wake. At the sideboard was his half sister, Clarice, in her late twenties, handsome, with the strong FitzAlan features and dark, intimidating brows, which she could use with formidable effect.

That formidable will was shared by all the FitzAlans, including himself, so when FitzAlans had a falling-out, those who were wise ran for cover.

His grandmother saw him first. "Well," she said, "don't stand there like a footman. Come in, come in."

Brand obediently crossed to the dowager and kissed the papery cheek she offered him. "Your Grace," he murmured with a respect that was tainted with irony. They both knew he was a republican at heart.

"You look more like your father every day," said the dowager.

Their eyes met. It amazed him that he was truly fond of this battle-ax who had given him such a hard time in his youth. Age, evidently, had softened him.

"Touché," he murmured, acknowledging the hit, and the dowager emitted a subdued chuckle.

Clarice seated herself. "So," she said, "the Prodigal has returned. To what do we owe the honor?"

"Good morning to you, too, Clarice," he responded pleasantly, then greeted Miss Cutter.

Miss Cutter, all in a flutter at Clarice's uncivil tone, quickly interjected, "Hardly a prodigal, Lady Clarice. Brand left the Priory and *made* his fortune, like that nice Mr. Lewis who has taken over the Sayers' place. Not that he is a local, but very civil for all that. They say that—"

The dowager took command. "Lotty," she said decisively, "would you ring the bell for Hartley and ask him to bring a fresh pot of tea?"

"There's still tea in the teapot," replied Miss Cutter.

"That will do fine," said Brand.

The dowager nodded. Her gaze shifted to Brand. "Now, what's this we hear about your entering politics? Sit down and tell me all about it."

Her Grace, as he well knew, had her own way of finding

things out, so he told her as succinctly as possible what his plans were. This kindled a tepid interest until he mentioned that he had opened up his grandfather's house and would be residing there until the election was over.

His grandmother had heard that the house was being opened up but not that he intended to reside there for any length of time. "What's wrong with the Priory?" she demanded with one of her piercing stares.

His teacup and saucer were put into his hand, and Brand spent a moment or two to set his thoughts in order as he went through the motions of stirring his tea. He didn't want to stay at the Priory because he liked to be master in his own house, and there were already too many masters here.

"I would not want to put you to the inconvenience, ma'am," he replied. "There may be gentlemen coming and going at all times of the day, taking their meals at irregular hours. I am not hosting a house party, but opening my house to my colleagues. We have an election to win."

"Oh, please," interrupted Clarice sharply, "spare us your excuses. You have never thought of the Priory as your home or us as your family. Why our father made you trustee of our funds is more than I can comprehend."

"That will do, Clarice," said the duchess in an awful voice.

Brand looked at his half sister and felt a twinge of annoyance, not at Clarice but at his father. The duke had tied up her funds in a trust. She and her dependents could live off the income, but the capital was reserved for the next generation. She could not rail against the old duke, but her trustee was fair game.

His brother-in-law was more easygoing. Oswald was a self-styled anthropologist, meaning that he loved to go digging in ruins and ancient mounds, looking for artifacts of bygone eras. Money wasn't important to him, and he would have been just as happy living in a tent as in his wife's palatial home. Brand liked Oswald very much.

He said gently, "I did not ask to be made your trustee, but since I am, you have only to ask and I'm sure I can find the funds to cover any reasonable request."

Eyes flashing, she demanded, "Who are you to judge what is reasonable?" She got to her feet. Bosom quivering, she declared, "This is such an insult to Oswald. Oh, yes, I know what you all think of him and you couldn't be more wrong." A note of triumph crept into her voice. "It may interest you to know that he is in London right now, negotiating the sale of one of his manuscripts. He expects to make a great deal of money on the sale."

The dowager said, "I didn't know poetry paid that well."

"It's a *history*, the life of Hannibal!" was her granddaughter's quick retort.

"Very nice, I'm sure."

Miss Cutter, ever the conciliator, rushed in to smooth things over. Her cheeks puffed up in a smile. "I'm sure it's not the money that counts. It's the sense of accomplishment. How many people can write a book?"

Brand carefully stirred his tea, then set the cup and saucer down.

"I think—" said Clarice, her breath catching. She shook her head. "Insufferable!" she finally got out, and stormed from the room.

There was an interval of silence, then the dowager sighed. "She's missing Oswald. I wish he would come home soon. It's very wearing on all of us. All the same, she has a point. Andrew takes control when he turns twenty-one. Clarice is twenty-seven now, and she will always be a supplicant."

Brand's patience was wearing thin. "Look," he said, "Clarice is not a pauper. She has more money than she knows what to do with. Oswald is the stumbling block. He doesn't want to live off his wife's money."

"I do admire a man with principles," said Miss Cutter warmly. "And love—"

When the duchess held up her hand, Miss Cutter obediently fell silent. "If he had principles," the dowager said in her commanding way, "he wouldn't have married Clarice in the first place. And don't speak to me of love. It's been the ruin of this family." Her eagle eye was fixed on Brand. "And that brings me to Lady Marion Dane. Is it true what they say? Are you engaged to the girl?"

The question came as no surprise. His grandmother had spies everywhere. "No," he said bluntly. "It's not true. I met her in London when she was staying with mutual friends. Since she and her sisters are Edwina's nieces, I felt the least I could do was show them the sights, especially as they are taking over Yew Cottage and we're going to be neighbors."

"Edwina Gunn!" said the dowager with asperity.

His grandmother had never approved or understood his close ties with his former teacher, and he had never bothered to explain it. Edwina had mothered him. The concept was foreign to the dowager. She did not believe in spoiling children.

Before the conversation could change direction, he said casually, "Edwina had another sister, didn't she? Hannah? Marion asked me about her"—and that was stretching the truth—"but I don't remember her at all. Did you know Hannah, Grandmother?"

"Not well," his grandmother replied. "She was a governess, was she not?"

"I remember her," said Miss Cutter. "She used to walk

her little dog in our park." Her brow puckered. "I heard that she was a headstrong girl and a great trial to Miss Gunn."

"In what way?"

Miss Cutter looked at him blankly. "I can't remember."

He swallowed a sigh. No use badgering Miss Cutter. He said gently, "What happened to Hannah? Where is she now?"

"I presume," said the dowager, "that she found a position somewhere else. She's probably happily married with a brood of children to her credit."

"No," said Miss Cutter, "she eloped. I'm sure I heard that she had eloped. Oh dear." Miss Cutter's face crumpled. "Or was that Mary Streatham? It happened so long ago. Have I become muddled again?"

"No," asserted the dowager firmly. "As we grow older, we have more to forget, that's all. Now, where were we before Brand arrived? Oh, yes. You were going to speak to Cook and tell her that there will only be three for luncheon, unless . . ." She looked a question at Brand.

"Thank you, but I have things to do at the Grange," he said. "But I'll hold you to that invitation for another day."

"You don't need an invitation," retorted the dowager, then she added with a complacent smile, "but do invite Lady Marion and her sisters. I should like to meet them. Go along, Lotty. Remember, only three for luncheon."

Miss Cutter excused herself and left the room.

As soon as the door closed, the dowager's smile slipped. She was silent for a moment or two, then said heavily, "There's no such thing as growing old gracefully, and don't let anyone tell you there is. Everything fades—looks, health, appetite—but the affliction we fear most is the loss of our mental faculties."

This little speech took Brand by surprise. He'd never seen his grandmother look so vulnerable. Old Ironsides, he and Clarice had called her when they were children. Everyone went in terror of her except her loyal and devoted companion.

"They tell me," he said finally, "that Edwina's mind had begun to wander, too."

All traces of vulnerability vanished and her expression was as resolute and intelligent as ever. "Rubbish," she declared. "When I spoke to her after church services, she was as argumentative as ever. If I said something was black, she was sure to say it was white. This isn't the first time you've quizzed me about Miss Gunn's state of mind. I told you at her funeral and I'll say it again: She was as sharp-tongued and as eccentric as ever she was. What's going on, Brand?"

"Nothing," he replied mildly, "nothing at all."

She pointed her finger at him. "And don't go harassing Lotty by asking her questions she can't answer. It only confuses her all the more."

"I wouldn't dream of it."

When Miss Cutter returned to the morning room, it was to find that Brand had left and the dowager was alone. When the dowager looked up, Miss Cutter's cheeks turned pink.

"Come and sit down, Lotty," said the dowager pleasantly, "and let's see what we can make of this."

Miss Cutter took her place at the table. "I wasn't muddled this time," she said earnestly. "I've thought about it and I really do remember that Hannah Gunn eloped."

"That's what I want to talk to you about." A moment

went by, then the dowager said, "Of course, if someone asks you about Hannah, you must say that you remember her, but there's no need to embellish your memories. That's the trouble when we get to our age. When we forget, our imagination fills in the blanks."

Miss Cutter looked chastened. "Not you," she said. "Your mind is as sharp as a needle. Everyone says so. And I don't *think* I make up stories. But . . . I know I get confused."

The dowager nodded sympathetically. "It's all right, Lotty. Don't worry about it. Just be careful. Think before you speak. I think Lady Marion may be trying to find Hannah, and we wouldn't want to raise false hopes, now would we?"

Now Miss Cutter looked really worried. "But I don't know *anything*," she cried.

"Of course, you don't. And neither do I."

They fell silent when a footman entered to clear the table. The dowager looked at her companion with a mixture of pity and affection. They'd been together since they were adolescent girls, first when Lotty came to live with the dowager's parents, and later, when the dowager married. They'd had little in common then, except that they were related by blood. Lotty had been a mousy sort of girl, afraid of her own shadow, while the dowager had been a little too headstrong for her parents' comfort. Now they jogged along, quietly devoted to each other, in a somewhat placid, uneventful existence.

Her Grace sighed. She hoped the past was not about to catch up with them and shatter their small world.

Brand spent a pleasant evening at the Fox and Hounds. At the end of the workday, that was where most of the locals gathered to exchange news and meet their neighbors before going home to their wives and families. Both the magistrate and constable were there, but they saw nothing sinister in the ink on Edwina's fingers. She might have written a letter and thrown it in the fire for any number of reasons. They had heard that Edwina had been acting strangely weeks before the accident, but neither had firsthand knowledge of it. Hannah's name raised only a mild response. No one, it appeared, had any clear memories of her.

As he undressed for bed, his thoughts turned to Edwina's letter and his skepticism when he'd first read it, a skepticism that was based on the rumors he'd heard about her declining mental faculties.

The reception after the funeral service had taken place at the vicarage; that was where Brand had first heard that Edwina was not quite herself. She'd become something of a recluse, and was suspicious of her neighbors. She still attended church services, but did not linger to talk to her friends or acquaintances.

All this he had heard from the vicar so, naturally, he had believed it, but others had embellished the tale when they'd offered him their condolences, women of the village whom he'd met in the local shops. The impression he got from them was that Edwina was becoming more and more senile.

That was when he should have broached the subject with Mrs. Ludlow, but she was tearful and there was no sense of urgency. It was still weeks before Edwina's letter reached him. He'd mentioned the rumors to his grandmother, and her response was much the same as it was today, that Edwina Gunn was as crusty as ever.

If anyone knew whether Edwina had become senile, it was Mrs. Ludlow. He'd take her word over anyone's. Not that he thought the vicar had lied. All he had described was a disturbed mind, and there was no doubt that Edwina was disturbed when she heard that Hannah might well have been murdered.

Then who started the rumors, and why? Was this a deliberate attempt on someone's part to discredit anything Edwina might have to say about the night Hannah disappeared? The rumors certainly had that effect on him.

That thought put him in mind of his grandmother again. He had the impression that she could have told him more about Hannah Gunn if she'd wanted to. What was she keeping from him?

The picture of Hannah that was forming in his mind was full of contradictions: She was the youngest of three sisters, a governess, headstrong, a trial to Edwina and admired by Marion. It was generally held in Longbury that she had eloped—or was that another rumor to throw everyone off the scent?

Then where was she?

When he blew out the candle and climbed into bed, his thoughts turned to Edwina and to how much he owed her. To a small, confused boy who found himself in a tug-of-war between two omnipotent beings, his father and his grandfather, her small cottage had offered a safe haven. All that Edwina asked in return was that he solve the mystery surrounding Hannah's disappearance.

Into the silence, he said, "I'll find her for you, Edwina, I swear it."

# Chapter Seven

The waters receded two days later, and Marion and her sisters set out for Longbury with Lord Denison acting as their escort. Marion could hardly refuse. Not only were they bound for the same place, but he had a well-equipped coach at his disposal—Brand Hamilton's, as it turned out. He had mentioned Brand's late-night visit to the posting house and subsequent departure before anyone was up as though it were of no importance, something vaguely connected to the election, and Marion did not dare argue the point with him. She could hardly let him know that she'd been spying on them.

They arrived at the village in the middle of the morning. They did not see much of Longbury because Edwina's cottage was on the outskirts, just off the main thoroughfare. The sun was shining, the air was fragrant with the scent of apple blossoms, and a hush had descended in the carriage as they looked out the windows, waiting expectantly for their first glimpse of the house.

Suddenly, they turned a corner into a small courtyard, and there it was.

"Yew Cottage! Why, it's lovely," said Phoebe, "and not nearly as small as I expected."

Her sisters agreed. It was a whitewashed two-story brick building with bow windows on the attached wings. A profusion of climbing plants clung tenaciously to a trellis on the walls. Marion's memory began to stir. One of those bay windows belonged to the front parlor, the other to the dining room. Hannah's bedchamber had been on the ground floor behind the parlor. They'd called it "the maid's room," though it had been a long, long time since it had been occupied by a maid, not since her grandparents had lived there. After they died, the Gunn sisters had learned to economize, just as she and her sisters had learned to do after the deaths of their parents.

There was a knocker on the front door as Marion remembered, a lion rampant, supposedly of Norman origin. She'd been fascinated by that knocker as a child, touching it reverently, imagining how many people had touched it before her.

As Emily and Phoebe walked to the front door, she turned aside to have a word with Lord Denison. She was sincere in her thanks, not only for his escort but also for the loan of Mr. Hamilton's carriage.

"Oh," said Denison, "you'll have the opportunity of thanking him in person. I'm sure he's here at the Grange. That was the plan, anyway. When he hears you have arrived, I don't doubt that he'll be calling on you the first chance he gets." And with a cheery wave, he got into the carriage and gave the order to move off.

Marion didn't have time to think about Ash Denison's parting shot. The door was opened by a dark-haired woman who introduced herself as Mrs. Ludlow, and they were ushered inside. It took her only a few minutes to decide that she liked Mrs. Ludlow. She was friendly in a quiet sort of way, was as neat as a new pin, and kept the house as neat as she kept herself. But it was the delicious aroma of freshly baked bread that established Mrs. Ludlow's reputation in Marion's mind. Already, the cottage felt like home.

As they toured the house, Marion was surprised at how much she remembered: the stone fireplace in the parlor; the solid oak furniture; the velvet drapes. She felt herself smiling. The layout of the house was all coming back to her. She could picture the vista of gardens and orchards from the upstairs windows; she knew where the outbuildings were and where the ruined refectory pulpit used to be and, beyond that, the Priory where the monks once lived. But her thoughts jarred and came to a sudden stop when they came to the oak-paneled staircase.

Emily said, "Is this where . . . ?"

Mrs. Ludlow nodded. "Yes, I found her," she said, and sniffed.

When Emily sniffed as well, Marion said decisively, "We'll talk about Aunt Edwina later, after we have unpacked. She wanted us to have her house and she wanted us to be happy in it. Just remember that."

Marion didn't want to be unfeeling, but neither did she want her sisters to mope about something they could not change. There had been too much death in their young lives already.

Her words had the effect she'd hoped for. Nodding and smiling, they trooped up the stairs.

Later, when her sisters were unpacking, Marion slipped downstairs into Hannah's room. It had a long sash window that overlooked the herb garden and let in plenty of sunlight, a pretty, girlish room done in muslins and chintz.

She felt a nagging uneasiness at the back of her mind now that she was touching Hannah's things—an empty cologne bottle on the dresser, a small cushion smelling faintly of lavender, paper and pens neatly laid out on the escritoire.

A memory came to her. They were quarreling, here, in Hannah's room, and she didn't like it. Hannah was yelling, then she stormed out of the house. Then there was silence.

What was the quarrel about?

Emily called to Marion from the stairs, and the memory faded as she went to answer her sister's summons.

Halfway through the afternoon, they took a rest from unpacking their boxes and had tea served in the front parlor. They were well pleased with the house and were able to speak about Aunt Edwina without becoming morbid or cast down. In fact, they were laughing and joking when Mrs. Ludlow announced that they had visitors.

When Marion got up, so did her sisters. They exchanged curious glances, wondering who would call on newcomers on the day of their arrival.

"Lady Clarice Brigden," announced Mrs. Ludlow, "and Miss Flora," and she stood aside to allow the visitors to enter.

Marion saw a dark-haired, fashionable young woman of her own age, taller than average, with strong features softened by her smile and blue eyes alight with mischief. It was the mischief that jogged Marion's memory. She knew Lady Clarice from before.

Fragments of memories rushed in. Secret chants and secret signs. Ghost hunting and midnight frolics.

She was startled. Could these memories be real?

Her gaze shifted to the child. Miss Flora was a leggy girl of about ten summers with a mop of fiery red curls, long-lashed green eyes, and a suspiciously demure smile.

The customary curtsies were exchanged and Marion invited her guests to be seated.

Lady Clarice ignored the invitation. Arms outstretched, laughing, she advanced on Marion. "You don't remember me, do you, Marion? Have you forgotten all the wild adventures we shared when you came to visit Miss Gunn?"

Marion laughed. "I've forgotten the wild adventures. But I haven't forgotten you. It's Clarice FitzAlan, isn't it?"

"Oh, that was before my marriage. Now I'm Clarice Brigden. And this is Flora, Theodora's niece. Flora has come for a little holiday." She paused, absorbing Marion's expression. "You remember Theodora? She is married to my uncle, Robert? You *do* remember Robert?"

Marion didn't but it seemed easier to nod vaguely, and she quickly introduced her own sisters. Refreshments were ordered, and Clarice took up the conversation again.

"They'll all be beating a path to your door! The FitzAlans, I mean, especially Grandmama. Ever since she heard your name was linked to Brand's, she has been burning with curiosity, but Brand won't tell her a thing. Well, we're all burning with curiosity. Is it true, Marion? Are you and Brand secretly engaged?"

More confused than annoyed, Marion said slowly, "Are you referring to Brand Hamilton?"

Clarice looked as confused as Marion felt. "Who else would I be referring to but my half brother? We had the same father, the Duke of Shelbourne. And his name, by the way, is Brand *FitzAlan* Hamilton, though he doesn't like to acknowledge the connection." Her lips thinned. "He's ashamed of us, I suppose. He thinks we're drones and parasites, not like him with our noses always to the grindstone. Poor Oswald—that's my husband—is ashamed to live off my money. He's a writer, by the way, and there's not much money in that. But what's the good of having money if I'm not allowed to spend it?"

When Marion stared at her blankly, she went on, "I'm doing it again, aren't I? That's what comes of living with Miss Cutter. Suffice it to say that Brand has control of the purse strings. Our father, in his wisdom, made him sole trustee of his estate."

Marion was torn between shock at Clarice's frankness with someone who was almost a stranger to her, and disbelief. No one had told her that Brand's father's estate was in Longbury. No one had told her that Brand was related to the FitzAlans or that his father was the Duke of Shelbourne.

She would never be rid of him.

She looked at Clarice and more memories stirred. It seemed inconceivable that she could have forgotten such an impetuous playmate. But she hadn't forgotten. It would be truer to say that she had misplaced Clarice in a miscellany of memories of holidays she'd spent in various places. What she remembered was that as children, Clarice FitzAlan had got them into one scrape after another. She was curious; she was adventurous; and, of course, she was fun to be with, especially for a girl like herself who had been raised to obey the rules. Clarice had seemed like a breath of ether. One whiff and a person was ready for anything. Marion couldn't remember exactly what they'd got up to, but she hadn't forgotten her mother's scolds and lectures. Clarice always got off scot-free.

Clarice said gently, "Marion, you haven't answered my question."

The rebuff was short and sharp. "Nor do I intend to."

Clarice's eyes lost none of their brightness. "I suppose you're waiting till he wins the nomination before you make the announcement. I can't think why. Grandmama says that Brand would stand a better chance of winning if he were engaged to the right sort of woman. Then people wouldn't care that he was baseborn."

That was the trouble with the daughter of a duke. She could say anything and no one from a lower order would dare contradict her or tell her to mind her own business— no one, perhaps, except the daughter of an earl.

As coolly as she could manage, Marion said, "What exactly has your brother told you about me?"

"Now, Marion," said Clarice, "don't make strange with me." To Emily, she added, "She was like this when we were girls. You know, prim and proper? It's just as well that my mother, or your Aunt Edwina for that matter, didn't know the half of what we got up to when they weren't around."

Phoebe seized on this. "What did you get up to?"

"I dare not tell you," replied Clarice irresistibly, winning a huge grin from Phoebe. "Now, where was I? Oh, yes, Brand. He hasn't told us a thing. In fact, he's as closed-mouthed as only he can be. This isn't the first time his name has been linked with a lady's," she chuckled, "not the first time by any means, but those others he dismissed in unflattering terms, which leads Grandmama to believe that his interest in you must be serious."

Marion was momentarily lost for words.

Emily was not. She'd been listening to the conversation with mounting vexation. In her opinion, Lady Clarice's manners were too free and easy to be tolerated, especially when there were young, innocent girls present, girls with flapping ears. "Phoebe," she said, fixing her sister with a hard stare, "why don't you show Flora the history you've been working on?" To Clarice, Emily added, "Phoebe is writing the history of our Gunn relations."

"Really?" Clarice's interest seemed genuine. After a moment's thought, she went on with a laugh, "I hope no one decides to write a history of the FitzAlans. The pages would catch fire."

"Phoebe!" repeated Emily, this time her voice more steely than before.

"I've hardly started the history," protested Phoebe. "There's nothing to show anyone except a few old letters and dates." Her sister's expression did not encourage her to argue the point. "Come along, Flora," she said in a resigned tone.

Flora obediently followed Phoebe out of the room.

On the other side of the door, Flora said, "Are you a cripple?"

Phoebe's breath stuck in her throat. She glared at the other girl, who was a good three inches taller than she. "No, I am not! I'm lame in one leg. That doesn't make me a cripple."

"Fine," said Flora. "Then we don't have to stay indoors, do we? We can go out and explore and have adventures."

*Explore? Adventures?* Those were heady words for Phoebe, but she was afraid that she might disappoint the other girl. "I'm not allowed to go far from the house," she allowed dubiously.

"Then we won't go far, only to the rock pond. If you're quick, you can catch frogs. There are scores of them."

"What about your mother? Shouldn't you ask her permission?"

"I don't have a mother," said Flora. "She died when I was very young. I'm here to visit my aunt, Theodora, and she never objects to anything I do."

"I wish Marion was like your aunt," said Phoebe with feeling. "Both my sisters can be Tartars when they want to be."

Flora laughed. "Well, are you game?"

The prospect was too good to resist. "I've never caught a frog before."

"I'll show you how."

"I should tell Marion where I'm going."

"It's only a short walk away. You'll still be in sight of the house."

That was good enough for Phoebe.

As they walked out the door, Flora said, "What's a family history?"

It was a bore, but Phoebe wanted to impress the other girl, so she made it sound exciting.

In the parlor, Clarice was reminiscing about old times. "You must remember the Priory ghost," she said to Marion.

Marion shook her head.

"You don't remember the night we hid in the refectory pulpit and lay in wait for our ghost to appear?"

"No. I'm afraid not."

At that point, Mrs. Ludlow entered and announced other visitors, Lady Theodora FitzAlan and Mr. Hamilton.

"Told you so," said Clarice to Marion in an undertone. "They'll all want to look you over."

The usual pleasantries were exchanged and when everyone was seated, Marion asked Mrs. Ludlow to bring more refreshments. Aware that all eyes were watching her closely, she forced herself to appear quite unaffected by Brand's presence. He seemed to be taking his cue from her. She thanked him for the use of his carriage. He replied in kind. Having cleared the first hurdle, Marion now turned her attention to the lady she did not know.

Lady Theodora was what Marion's father would have called a handsome woman. Marion judged her to be fortyish, tall and athletic, her black hair severely pulled back, her high cheekbones tanned by the sun. If her dress wasn't a riding habit, it was closely modeled on one. She looked as though she would feel more at home in the country than in town.

Lady Theodora said, "I won't pretend that I remember you, Marion. When you were last here, you were an infant in petticoats and I must have seemed like an old lady to you."

"Don't apologize, Theo," Clarice cut in. "I don't think Marion remembers you, either." On the next breath, she went on, "Robert not with you?"

"No. You know Robert. He met friends in Windsor and decided to stay on." To Marion, she added, "Lord Robert FitzAlan, my errant husband."

Marion sensed a nip in the air and groped in her mind for a neutral rejoinder.

Brand saved her the trouble by abruptly changing the subject. "That's a showy filly you brought home with you, Theo," he said. "Arabian, is she?"

"Half Arabian," Theodora replied, and went on to describe the finer points of the latest acquisition to her stable, all the while her eyes wandering over Marion as though, thought Marion, she was judging her finer points, too. Theodora then proceeded to ask Marion whether she and her sisters liked to ride.

Clarice interjected, "Be careful how you respond, Marion. You're in the presence of a devotee of all things horsey. No one can keep up with Theo."

Marion was becoming thoroughly annoyed. Since Lady Theodora and Brand had arrived, she and Emily had yet to get in one word. These FitzAlans, and she counted Brand in their number, were full of themselves.

Cutting across Clarice's next observation, she said, "We haven't done much riding of late, except in Hyde Park, and that hardly counts."

"Poor you," Theo commiserated.

As though her sister had been slighted, Emily said coolly, "Our father taught us to ride when we were infants. We are all comfortable around horses, but Marion . . . well, she is fearless."

"In that case," said Theodora, "perhaps you'd like to try out my new filly? Thunderbolt, I call her. She'll give you the ride of your life."

To say that Marion was dismayed did not reflect her feelings. She was aghast. It was easy to be a fearless rider when Papa chose only docile mounts for his darling daughters. And they weren't all comfortable around horses. Since her fall, Phoebe had never ridden again. What was Emily thinking to exaggerate her skill?

Brand was aware of her dilemma and did not hesitate to step in and rescue her. Rescuing Marion was becoming a habit he rather enjoyed. "Thunderbolt," he said humorously, "would give the devil the ride of his life. Tame your beast, Theo, before she does someone an injury."

His humorous rebuke did not give offense. Theodora said, "You know that I wouldn't dream of allowing anyone to ride Thunderbolt until John trains her." To Marion, she elaborated, "John Forrest is my trainer and man of business. Everything I learned about horses, I learned from him."

Brand said, "He'll have his hands full with Thunderbolt. I looked in on her before I came on here. I'd say she has a temper."

Theodora smiled. "If John says she can be trained, then I believe him. She'll give the FitzAlan stallions a run for their money. And when the time comes to breed her, believe me, I won't allow any of them near her."

The picture that came to Marion's mind wasn't of stallions but of FitzAlan men. A sideways glance at Theodora convinced her that this was a veiled jibe that everyone understood but no one, least of all Theodora, found funny.

The tea tray was brought in and when everyone was served, Brand remarked, "Did I hear you aright, Clarice? When I first entered, you said something about a Priory ghost?"

"First I've heard of such a thing," said Theodora.

"It was our secret," replied Clarice, "Marion's and mine. A childish escapade that terrified us at the time but seems amusing in retrospect."

Brand looked at Marion. "I'd like to hear what happened."

She shrugged helplessly. "I don't remember. Clarice was just about to relate the incident when you and Lady Theodora arrived."

"Clarice?" he said.

"There's not much to tell." Clarice looked at Marion as though for help, saw that none was forthcoming, and said, "We were half convinced that the ghost of one of the monks wandered the Priory grounds at night, or maybe the ghost of the abbot. I'd caught sight of him from my bedroom window, you see, carrying a lantern in his hand. To cut a long story short, Marion and I agreed to keep watch one night when everyone was asleep. So we hid in the refectory pulpit—"

"Refectory?" queried Emily.

"Where the monks used to take their meals. The pulpit is all that is left of it, and it was moved when the conservatory was built. It's about halfway down the hill between the Priory and Yew Cottage. But the pulpit is still intact and made an excellent hiding place for two small girls. So imagine us there, giggling and trembling at the same time, when out of the trees the monk appeared, or so we thought." She started chuckling as the memory came back to her. "We were stunned, we were terrified, and when some poor animal howled, we bolted like runaway horses, I to the Priory and Marion back here. Of course, there was no ghost." She looked at Marion. "We should have known. Our ghost had a lantern, don't you remember? What self-respecting ghost would need a lantern to see by?"

Marion nodded. "Yes, it's coming back to me."

Theodora said sharply, "You were lucky a smuggler or

one of the gamekeepers did not see you. You could have been shot."

Brand interposed in his easy way. "Oh, not so close to the house, Theo. The gamekeepers know better than to let off their guns anywhere near the Priory. I can't believe it was a smuggler, either, not when he was carrying a lantern. It would give his presence away."

Theodora gave a disbelieving laugh. "Smugglers are as bold as pirates in this neck of the woods. They fear no one. And why should they? No one wants to stop their trade, least of all the magistrate. Who else would supply us with fine French brandy if it were not for smugglers?"

A flicker of a smile touched Brand's lips. "What you mean," he said, "is that no one wants to pay the excise tax."

"Precisely."

Emily was staring at her sister. "How old were you and Clarice?" she asked.

"Seven, I think," responded Marion, "or maybe eight."

"And you went out when everyone was in bed?"

Clarice answered this time. "Your Aunt Edwina kept early hours, and my family wouldn't have noticed if I'd been gone for a week. We waited until it was dark, that's all, and we went out at night only once."

"I'm amazed," said Emily, still looking at Marion. "I can't imagine you creeping out of the house to go hunting for ghosts when everyone was asleep in bed. It's just not like you."

"Oh, she has her moments," observed Brand.

Marion smiled serenely. "Would anyone like more tea?"

As soon as she got back to the Priory, Theodora made for the stable block to check on Thunderbolt. Her husband's gelding was there; one of the grooms was currying it. She nodded to the groom as she passed the stall and crossed to the man who had her complete confidence in managing all her affairs.

John Forrest looked up and smiled when she joined him. He looked younger than his sixty years. He was spare and athletic, and his deeply tanned skin gave him a healthy glow.

"So," said Theodora, "Robert is home."

"This half hour," replied Forrest. "He went up to the house."

Theodora nodded, but inwardly she was irritated. Her husband was as careless with his cattle as a cuckoo bird with her nestlings. There would always be someone else to take over their care. In her opinion, the test of a real gentleman was that he put his horses first. She doubted that Robert would remember what to do with a curry comb even if she put a gun to his head. He was quite different when he found himself in a room full of beautiful women. No one had to give him lessons in flirting. No doubt, at this moment, he was in his favorite chair, a glass of brandy in his hand, reading Ovid, his favorite poet. She wasn't going to hold it against the gelding that his name was Ovid, too.

Ovid nuzzled her when she came up to him. Forrest snapped his fingers and one of the stable boys ran to get a slice of apple, which Theodora fed to the gelding, all the while murmuring words of endearment.

Thunderbolt poked her beautiful black head over her stall door and whinnied, drawing Theodora's attention away from the gelding. Laughing, Theodora went to pet her horse.

To Forrest, she said, "You seemed very cozy with the Earl of Brechin when we were looking over his stock. You're not thinking of leaving me, are you, John?"

His brows went up. "You know me better than that, milady. The earl is an interesting man to talk to. He knows, lives, and breathes horses. If he was a plain man like myself, I'd offer him a job."

She laughed, genuinely pleased with his answer.

"Besides," Forrest went on, "I'm too old to change my ways. I wouldn't fit in with a new master."

And that response made her eyes sting.

She looked at Forrest, and it occurred to her, not for the first time, that he was getting older and could not be with her forever.

The thought was too painful to contemplate and she pushed it to the back of her mind.

# Chapter Eight

Their first day in Longbury had tired them all out, so it came as no surprise when Phoebe went to bed without a fuss. It was a pleasant tiredness, Marion thought. The house felt like home. They now knew their neighbors, and Phoebe had found a friend.

Like Phoebe, Flora was an orphan. Half the year, she came to live with Theodora at the Priory, and the other half, she lived with another aunt outside London. According to Clarice, Theodora allowed the child to run wild while she was here.

It was an odd arrangement in Marion's opinion, but the girl seemed none the worse for it. Flora was a tomboy and just the kind of friend Phoebe needed to get her nose out of her books.

Marion and Emily spent the next little while quietly reading in front of the parlor fire. Emily was following the adventures of one of Mrs. Radcliffe's heroines and Marion tried to take an interest in the machinations of Jane Austen's Emma, but her mind kept wandering to other things—Clarice, the Priory ghost, and, for some odd reason, Hannah. Apart from her friendship with Clarice, Marion's memories remained vague.

Was it possible that Hannah had eloped? That's what she'd picked up from snatches of her parents' conversations. Entirely possible. The man, of course, would have been unsuitable, not up to Mama's or Edwina's expectations. Was that the quarrel she remembered? Poor Hannah. She must have been in desperate straits before she gave up everything—her home, her family, her place in society—to go off like that.

Maybe she thought it was worth it. Maybe she was desperately in love.

Before she could prevent it, a picture of Brand formed in her mind. He wasn't the kind of man to throw caution to the winds and elope with the woman he loved. He would think that that was the coward's way out. He would stand his ground. And the lady of his choice had better be prepared to stand with him. Marion had not known him long, but she understood that much about him.

Restless now, she set aside her book. "Ready for bed?" she asked Emily.

"More than ready. It has been an eventful day."

While Emily went upstairs, Marion went from room to room with a candle in her hand, making sure that every window and door was locked. She was just about to extinguish the lamp on the kitchen table when she heard a tapping on the back door. Her heart leaped to her throat.

"I know you're there, Marion." It was Brand's voice. "I saw your shadow pass in front of the window."

She opened the door with every intention of lecturing him for giving her a fright, but when she saw him standing there, his tall frame filling the doorway, his dark hair glistening with raindrops and a crooked smile on his lips, every rational thought went out of her head except one. It could be different with him, if only . . .

The smile left his face. "What is it, Marion? Why do you look like that?"

Immediately alert to her danger, she said coolly, "How could you tell it was my shadow? It could just as easily have been Emily's."

"Your profile. I'd know it anywhere."

His careless compliment warmed her heart, but only for a moment. She had to watch her step with this man. If she wasn't careful, she'd be telling him all her secrets.

She was becoming bored with the familiar litany. All the same, it was worth repeating.

She tried to sound matter-of-fact. "What brings you here at this time of night?"

"It's only ten o'clock. And you can drop the pose. I saw from your expression that something had upset you, and I want to know what it is."

Knowing that he would badger her until she gave him an answer, she said shortly, "I'm tired. That's all. It has been a long day. I was about to go to my bed."

When she glanced over her shoulder toward the door to the stairs, hinting him into leaving, he seized the opportunity of stepping over the threshold, forcing her to retreat a step or two.

"It's raining out there," he said ruefully. "We can talk more comfortably in here. Do you mind if I sit down?" He gestured to the table.

"Does it matter what I say?"

"No, because I know you don't always say what you mean." She stiffened, but he didn't give her time to respond. "Edwina," he said, "used to offer me a brandy when I dropped in on her of an evening, you know, just to talk things over and make sure she was all right."

His words blunted her wrath. Brand had every reason to expect Edwina's nieces to treat him with the utmost consideration. He'd been a good friend to her aunt. Lucky, lucky Edwina, she thought, and meant it.

"I'm sorry," she said, "we don't have any brandy."

"Oh, you'll find a bottle in the pantry, in a crock marked 'Barley.' It's contraband, of course, but that didn't bother Edwina. She thought it was her patriotic duty to support the smuggling trade, if only to provide a living for the smugglers' families."

In spite of herself, Marion smiled. "And I suppose you thought it was your patriotic duty to drink my aunt's brandy?"

"Hardly. Edwina's patriotism came in small doses. A thimbleful, to be exact. I'm hoping you'll do better than that."

She almost laughed, but she kept her lips pressed together as she crossed the room and entered the pantry. When she returned, she set the brandy bottle in front of him with a thump, along with a glass that could easily have served as a small vase.

"I do appreciate a woman with a sense of humor," he said.

She suppressed her own smile as she took the chair next to his. "You know this is highly irregular? There are no servants here, no one to chaperon us."

"There's Emily, and let's not forget Phoebe."

"But they are in their beds."

"Who is to know it? Tell you what, Marion: I won't tell anyone if you don't."

His ability to stand his ground was beginning to

annoy her. "You were about to tell me what brought you here at this ungodly hour."

He captured her hand in a move that was so unexpected she did not think of resisting. Eyes on hers, he brushed his thumb over her fingers, then her wrist.

"I can feel your pulse," he said. "It's beating hard and fast. Now, that tells me far more than your frowns and your shrewish words."

She snatched her hand away. She was careful to make her words cool and impersonal. "Last chance, Mr. Hamilton, or I show you the door. What brings you here?"

He took his time before replying, pouring himself a small measure of brandy, taking a sip as he watched her with a twinkle in his eyes.

"Two reasons," he said. "First to apologize for the behavior of my female relations this afternoon. They are atrociously outspoken. I'm surprised you didn't strangle them."

"Don't think I wasn't tempted! On the other hand, Clarice is like a confiding child. It's impossible not to like her."

He lifted a brow. "She doesn't confide in me. What did she tell you?"

Marion hesitated, then ventured cautiously, "That your father valued your judgment."

"Ah. She told you that he named me as trustee of his estate?"

She inclined her head.

"Don't read too much into it. The truth is that he didn't have much choice. It was either my uncle or me, and Robert is so open-handed that Clarice and Andrew would have bankrupted the estate before he turned around."

She was looking at him curiously.

"What?" he asked.

She shrugged. "You must have been very young for such a responsibility."

"I was twenty-six when my father died. Clarice was twenty and my brother, Andrew, was only eleven or so."

Now she was beginning to understand Clarice's straining at the bit. It could not be easy having a brother, who was not much older than she, controlling the purse strings.

"I'm surprised," she said, "that your father didn't name his attorney, or a close friend."

"He might have, but that would have meant I would have been free of him at last." His voice had taken on a hard edge. "He has a long reach, my father."

"We can all say that. But in your case . . . "

"Yes?"

She was sorry she had said so much. Shrugging helplessly, she went on, "You know him better than I. Could he have been trying to make amends?"

He swallowed a mouthful of brandy. "Some things are beyond mending. He turned his back on my mother before I was born. She wasn't a high-flier. She was a respectable, decent girl, but she had neither the fortune nor the bloodlines to tempt him. I won't bore you with the details. It's a familiar story. Suffice it to say that it was only when I became an orphan, when my grandfather died, that my father took an interest in me. And that was largely my grandmother's doing." As if suddenly realizing that his fingers had tightened around his glass, he deliberately relaxed them. His smile flickered momentarily. "The old buzzard knew I would not refuse to pay my debt to him."

"Your debt to him?"

He shrugged awkwardly. "He paid for my education.

He made sure my grandfather's house was not sold from under me when I was a boy. I always knew I had a home I could go to. Andrew was only eleven. I did not want him to grow up to be a typical aristocrat, thinking that he was entitled to his wealth and estates. He was an orphan as I had been. It seemed the least I could do was fill the void. He is my brother."

"Yes," she said, "Clarice mentioned that, too. You *are* a FitzAlan. Brand FitzAlan Hamilton is your name. Whose idea was that?"

Faint color ran under his skin. "It's a long story, but believe me, it was not of my doing."

She'd thought she'd gone too far, and color tinted her cheeks as well.

Brand dragged a hand through his hair. "You might say," he said, "that my father put his mark on me. He had the means and the will to take me away from my mother when I was born. My grandfather had no choice but to let my father have his way. I never used the FitzAlan name until I was brought to live at the Priory." A smile flickered and went out. "However, my grandmother never lets me forget that I'm a FitzAlan."

She sat back in her chair, gripped by an emotion she did not understand. For the first time, she didn't see him as capable and ambitious, sure of where he was going. He seemed like a lonely, solitary figure who rarely let his guard down, even with himself.

As she sat there, staring at the harsh lines of his face, everything inside her softened. She had heard the story of his life from others, but it had not made a lasting impression. In that moment, she felt as though a blindfold had been removed from her eyes. This truly remarkable man still carried the ghosts of his past inside him.

And, oh, how she wished she could be the one to lay them to rest.

She had to resist the impulse to reach out and take his hands in a comforting clasp. Anyway, she doubted that he would allow it. She could imagine him as a small boy, picking himself up after a fight, glaring, challenging, daring the world to do its worst. He would not accept a facile sympathy.

They were becoming too cozy, too intimate. She had enough sense to steer the conversation into safer waters.

"You said that you had two reasons for coming here. What is the second?"

He considered for a moment, hesitated, then nodded, as eager as she to change the subject. "Next Thursday afternoon," he said, "my grandmother is hosting a garden party at the Priory, an informal affair. You and your sisters are invited."

"A garden party?" she said carefully.

"She calls it a 'fête.' It's more like a fair." A knowing smile touched his lips. "I can't say that my grandmother won't take the opportunity of looking you over, but that's not the purpose of this event. It's one of the traditions of Longbury, and she holds it every year. There will be quite a crush, so it's quite possible that you and I may see each other only in passing."

A garden fête seemed harmless, and if there were plenty of people about, she could lose herself in the crowd without causing comment or speculation. Maybe she could avoid the dowager altogether.

And Brand.

"Thank you," she said. "We shall be there."

He studied her for a moment over the rim of his glass, drained his brandy, then set the glass down. There was an edge to his voice. "Smile, Marion. You might even enjoy yourself."

When he got up and walked to the door, she went after him.

"Brand," she cried, "what on earth has got into you?"

He opened the door and stepped onto the porch. She followed him out.

"Brand, what is it?"

He turned, his expression like ice. "Is it me or is it my family you want to avoid?"

She shook her head. "I just don't want people to get the wrong idea about us."

His expression did not change. "And what idea is that?"

She lifted her shoulders in a gesture of helplessness. "That there's something between us."

"Good God, woman, must you think that every man who pays you a little attention has designs on you?"

She let out a huffy breath. "I think no such thing!"

"You think just because I kissed you once, I want to marry you? Is that it? Marion, I've kissed scores of women in my time and have never been tempted to offer marriage."

The thought of him kissing scores of women made her jaw set. "I wouldn't marry you if you were the last man on earth!" She groaned inwardly. Surely she could come up with a better set-down than that hackneyed phrase? Before he could laugh at her, she went on quickly, "That's not the point. Everyone saw you kiss me. I don't want to be an object of gossip." She was floundering. "I have my reputation to think about."

Her words seemed to incense him. He reached out, grasped her chin, and held her face up to the porch lamp. "You think I'm not good enough for you, not good enough for an earl's daughter." He gave her a slight shake. "Is that it, Marion? In spite of all you've said, are you too proud to lower yourself to the level of a duke's bastard son?"

She could feel his fury in every harsh line of his body. It wasn't true. Oh, it wasn't true. She didn't want him to think the worst of her, but he had given her a way out. She had to take it.

Marion, pulling her shattered nerves together, said in a voice she hardly recognized as her own, "I'm sorry. I don't know what to say."

He removed his hand from her chin. "Good night, Lady Marion."

*Lady Marion.* She winced at the formality. On his lips, these words were an insult. This was hopeless. She couldn't let him think that she thought him beneath her. She felt cornered but not desperate enough to hurt him. And she had hurt him. She was sure of that.

She touched his sleeve but he shook off her hand. In the next instant, he was striding down the path. Marion stayed on the porch, hugging herself against the chill night air until he became lost in the shadows.

# Chapter Nine

The dowager's fête was open to all and sundry. Only her special guests were invited to the Priory for a late champagne supper, but no one felt deprived or left out. Every sort of entertainment was provided for the villagers' enjoyment—Morris and Maypole dancers; minstrels, jugglers, and acrobats; a horse show in the south pasture; and a baking contest in the marquee in the east pasture. Outside the monks' tithe barn, which had survived the centuries almost intact, servants were roasting whole pigs and sheep on spits, while inside, other servants and volunteers were setting out hearty fare to suit country appetites.

Though Marion and her sisters had lived in Longbury for little more than a week, it was surprising how many people they knew. Most of them they'd met after church services. They'd even had the honor of being introduced to the dowager duchess, a rather formidable lady with, if Clarice was to be believed, all-seeing, all-knowing eyes.

As a result, Marion had dressed for the occasion with particular care: a pretty muslin gown with embroidered vines on the hem and bodice, a straw hat with green ribbons, and, as a concession to the unpredictable English weather, sturdy shoes and an umbrella dangling from one arm. The finale would come at dusk, a military reenactment of some long-forgotten skirmish between Cavaliers and Roundheads. The weather could change between then and now, and Marion liked to be prepared.

From time to time, she caught sight of Brand. After initially acknowledging her presence with a slight bow, he did not spare her a glance, though they had not seen each other for several days. According to Mrs. Ludlow, Brand had been hard at work drumming up support for the party among the eligible voters in the smaller villages around Longbury. Lord Denison, meantime, who thought politics was humbug, had decamped for Brighton to pay his respects to the Prince Regent. At this time of year, Brighton was a magnet for pleasure-seekers, and the foremost pleasure-seeker of them all was the Prince Regent. She wondered if Brand would join Ash when the fête was over.

He had told her to smile and enjoy herself and that's what she was determined to do. Her sisters didn't need to be told. Emily had gone off laughing with some young people of her own age while the inseparable opposites, Phoebe and Flora, had apprenticed themselves to the Gypsies in the hope of learning how to tell fortunes.

Marion wasn't alone. Miss Cutter, the dowager's companion, had either taken a fancy to her or had slipped her leash to enjoy a few unfettered moments to herself. She was inclined to chatter, and Marion was finding it hard to follow her train of thought until Brand came into view. Then Miss Cutter became quite coherent as she kept Marion abreast of the lovely ladies who successively graced his arm.

"Mrs. Chandos," said Miss Cutter in Marion's ear. "She has had her eye on him for some time."

They were in the south pasture where the horse show was in progress. A series of jumps had been set out and when rider and horse completed the course successfully, the crowd broke into wild applause.

Marion's eyes trailed Brand and the willowy blonde. "I suppose she is a widow?"

Miss Cutter giggled. "A wealthy widow," she confided. "She inherited two fortunes, her father's and her late husband's. As you may imagine, there is no shortage of suitors, but until she is sure Brand is lost to her, she won't give up hope. You know, my dear, you really should announce your engagement and put the poor woman out of her misery."

Marion's only response to Miss Cutter's coy look was a neutral smile.

Mrs. Chandos did not last long. She was borne away by a tall, voluble gentleman who would not take no for an answer. Her place was taken by Miss Lacey, a redhead with a voluptuous figure and a lovely smile. Marion wondered whether she had freckles. Miss Byrd, another blonde, was slender and fragile; Miss Stead was Junoesque. And so it went on.

The last rider of the day waited for the signal to start: Andrew, the Duke of Shelbourne. He was a young man, no more than a boy really, but he sat astride his mount with the confidence of a seasoned cavalier. Horse and man made an arresting picture. They were both dark, both thoroughbreds.

From his detached position, Andrew moved his head slightly. Marion followed the path of his gaze. He was watching Brand. When Brand acknowledged the look with a slight nod, the young man quickly averted his head. He was unsmiling.

Miss Cutter said, "Handsome devil, isn't he? Andrew, I mean. In a year or two, he'll be a breaker of hearts. For the present, Brand keeps him on a tight leash." She sighed. "I suppose he doesn't want the boy to turn out like their father. He was a wild one, the old duke, but so were all the young men in those days."

Marion was thoughtful. That one glance between the young duke and Brand was telling. There was conflict there, but it was mostly on Andrew's part. All the same, he wanted Brand's approval. She sighed, thinking of herself and her sisters. A guardian's life was not always easy.

The flag dropped and Andrew and his mount cantered to the first barrier. He took it easily, and the next, then urged his mount over the water obstacle, curbed its momentum, and sailed effortlessly over the highest gate. By the time Andrew finished the course, the spectators were on their feet.

When the applause died away, Her Grace, the dowager duchess, came forward, leaning heavily on her cane, to hand out the ribbons. With her was Lady Theodora, and a dark-haired gentleman who moved with ease and grace. It came as no surprise when the blue ribbon went to Andrew.

"Who is the dark-haired gentleman with Lady Theodora?" Marion asked.

"Her husband, Lord Robert. He always comes down for the fête. We don't see much of him. Well, there's not much in Longbury to keep him here."

"There is his wife," Marion pointed out, her tone more severe than she meant it to be.

Miss Cutter merely shook her head.

Theodora raised her hand and beckoned someone over. Marion recognized the gentleman as John Forrest, who was in charge of the Priory stables. He looked to be in his late fifties, a fine figure of a man, who did not seem to enjoy being singled out. All that changed when Theodora spoke to him. He nodded and smiled and acknowledged the applause of the spectators with a small bow.

Miss Cutter said, "He's been with Theodora since she was a child. Everything she knows about horses she got from him."

Marion looked for Brand. He was still in the same spot, making no move to join the others in the field. All the same, she could tell that he was pleased with Andrew's success.

She felt suddenly irritated. He should have been one of the first to go forward and congratulate Andrew. It was obvious to her that it was Brand's approval Andrew wanted, not Theodora's or her estimable trainer's.

"Uh-oh," twittered Miss Cutter. "I see Her Grace is leaving the field. I know she'll want me by her side. Now what was it I started to say to you? Oh, yes, now I re-member." The haze in her pale eyes cleared to reveal a lively curiosity. "Never let the sun go down on your wrath. That's my advice to you, Marion."

"I beg your pardon?"

"You and Brand? Everyone can see you've had a spat. Phoebe told me—"

"Phoebe!" Marion was taken aback.

"Oh, dear, I've said too much."

"No, indeed! I think Phoebe has said too much!"

Marion checked her strong feelings. Miss Cutter was beginning to look alarmed, and really, she was a harm-less old biddy who had spoken without thinking. It was unkind to lose patience with her.

"Trust me, Miss Cutter," she said with a smile. "There is nothing between Mr. Hamilton and me."

Miss Cutter nodded and smiled. "Shall we see you at the Priory for Her Grace's champagne supper?"

"I wouldn't miss it for the world."

She waited until Miss Cutter had joined the dowager's party before she stalked off to find Phoebe.

Phoebe was in the grand marquee, resting on the benches that were set out for foot-weary visitors. She had enjoyed herself immensely. Flora was the best friend she had ever had. There was one small problem that took the gloss off her happiness. Flora could not sit still for two minutes together, and Phoebe needed to rest her weak leg.

Not that Flora was aware of it, because Phoebe had never told her. In Flora's eyes, she was just an ordinary girl, not an invalid who had to be coddled. The result was, Phoebe had become adept at finding things for them to do sitting down. Not for long, of course, because she liked to be up and doing, too, but just long enough to catch her breath and rest her leg.

Spying on the Gypsies had been her suggestion. That had proved to be a monumental bore because Madame Zelda, the fortune-teller, told all her customers the same fortune: A dark, handsome stranger was going to come into their lives. They knew this because after their own fortunes had been told—at sixpence apiece, no less!—she and Flora had loitered at the back of Madame Zelda's tent and eavesdropped.

And she'd so hoped that the dark, handsome stranger would turn out to be a stray dog that Marion would let her keep.

After that, they'd tramped around for a bit, enjoying

the music and the dancers, and had ended up here for a refreshing glass of lemonade. Flora had told her not to move, that she'd be back in a minute, and Phoebe had not argued the point. Now she felt rested and ready for anything.

She waved to Flora when she saw her at the entrance.

Flora was wearing a big straw hat to keep the sun off her face so that she wouldn't get any more freckles. It didn't seem to be working, and Phoebe didn't know why Flora bothered. She liked freckles.

As she sat down, Flora said, "Look what I found, Phoebe." She looked around furtively to make sure that no one was watching them, then opened a worn leather satchel and withdrew a small wooden box, which she set on the bench between them.

"What is it?" asked Phoebe, reaching for the box.

Flora put both hands on the flat of the box to prevent Phoebe opening it. "First, you must promise solemnly never to tell anyone about this box and what I'm going to show you."

"I swear on my honor," vowed Phoebe reverently.

Flora removed her hands and Phoebe opened the box. She found a gentleman's monogrammed handkerchief with the initials *R.L.F.,* a receipt for a gentleman's hat made out to Lord Robert FitzAlan, a button, and other bits and pieces that were not very interesting, except for a few notes and letters. They looked and smelled old, as did everything else in the box, and she wrinkled her nose as she spread open one of the notes.

"What does it say?" asked Flora in hushed tones.

Phoebe looked up at her friend. "Haven't you read it?"

When color started to run under Flora's delicate skin, Phoebe understood the reason not only for Flora's embarrassment but for showing her the letters as well.

Flora could not read.

"Lots of people can't read," said Phoebe emphatically, "especially girls. There's no shame in it. I'll teach you how if you like."

Flora was looking at the box. "I know my letters, but not all words sound the way they look."

"No, indeed," replied Phoebe. "And I'm not sure I know all the words here. Some of them are very long."

Brows knit together, she read slowly.

> *Dear Miss Gunn,*
> *Thank you for your kind expressions of sympathy.*
> *I remain your obedient servant,*
> *Robert FitzAlan*

She looked up. "Flora, this letter belongs to my Aunt Edwina. Where did you get it?"

"I was sure it was a love letter," said Flora.

"A love letter?" Phoebe was startled. "To Aunt Edwina from Lord Robert? Don't be daft!"

Flora's answer was to point to the lid of the box. The lettering was faint but still legible: *H.G.*

"Hannah," breathed out Phoebe. She looked at her friend. "This letter belongs to my family. Hannah was my aunt, too."

Flora quickly gathered her bits and pieces together, dropped them in the box, and slid the box inside the leather satchel. "Finders keepers," she declared.

"Not if you stole it from our cottage" came the quick retort.

Color surged into Flora's cheeks. "I am not a thief! I borrowed it, that's all."

"Then tell me where you found it."

"I will not."

Breathing hard, Phoebe said, "Lord Robert's letters belong to Marion now. She should decide what to do with them."

"So you can put them in your family history?" scoffed Flora.

"Maybe I shall!"

They glared at each other across the satchel.

"You," said Phoebe scathingly, "are the worst friend I have ever had."

"And you are no friend at all!"

With that, Flora picked up the satchel and stalked off.

Phoebe sat there stewing. She couldn't tell Marion about the box because she'd promised on her honor to keep it a secret. She couldn't understand why it had to be a secret unless Flora had stolen the box. Apart from the notes, there was nothing worth keeping. Come to think of it, the note they'd read was worthless, too.

No one in her right mind would save such rubbish, and she couldn't think why Flora had made such a fuss.

Some friend!

Her thoughts scattered when she saw Marion bearing down on her. Now what had she done?

Emily was having the time of her life. She hadn't expected to meet many people of her own age in Longbury, but she'd already made a few friends. That was the thing about church services. Even if the sermon was boring, people stood around after the service to talk and get to know each other, without waiting for proper, formal introductions.

Ginny Matthews was on one side of her, and Peter Matthews, Ginny's older brother, was on her other side. The vicar was their father and they knew everybody in

Longbury. They had just watched Lord Andrew, whom Emily had also met at church, win the ribbon for his faultless performance and were waiting to congratulate him.

Victor Malvern, the son of a local landowner, joined their group, and Emily's pulse started to beat a little faster. Victor was very handsome and seemed more worldly than her new friends. He was quite the dandy, and put her in mind of Ash Denison.

"Did you see Lord Andrew?" she asked Victor. "He looks as though he was born in the saddle, doesn't he?"

Victor's lip curled slightly. "Horses are all that poor little Lord Andy knows, that and sheep. Take him away from the Priory and what have we got?"

"What have we got?" asked Emily. Her pulse had stopped racing.

"A nobody, that's what. It turns my stomach to think that one of these days we'll all have to kowtow to him, you know, His Grace, the Duke of Shelbourne."

"Heavens," said Emily, "what did Andrew ever do to you?"

Peter Matthews remarked mildly, "Andrew is already the Duke of Shelbourne, Victor, and we ought to address him as 'Your Grace.' As for what Andrew did, he and Victor raced their horses across the downs, and Andrew won."

Victor's face flushed. "It wasn't a fair race. He took a shortcut. So he's a cheat as well as a nobody. Excuse me."

He sauntered off and joined two young men who also looked to be aspiring dandies. Whatever he said sent them off into hoots of laughter. They watched Andrew as he left the pasture, leading his horse, then, still laughing, they turned their backs on him.

Ginny sighed. "Victor is a beast, but Andrew is his own worst enemy. He doesn't put himself out to make friends. He rarely attends any assemblies, and when he does, he never asks anyone to dance. We're all in awe of him, really, because he *is* the duke. Some people think that he feels above our company."

"I think he's shy," said Emily. "And maybe he doesn't know how to dance." Privately, she thought that if she'd been lumbered with his family, she'd be like a fish out of water in society, too.

"I know that his father died when he was eleven," she went on. "What happened to his mother?"

Ginny answered. "Oh, she died when Andrew was an infant."

That explained a lot. Emily's heart went out to the young man. She looked at Ginny and Peter. "Come on! Let's show Andrew a little support."

He seemed startled when the three of them descended on him, then shyly pleased. Emily had the confidence to keep a conversation going, and there were few awkward pauses. She also knew how to draw someone out. By the time Andrew left to stable his horse, she had already decided that she liked this boy immensely.

He didn't make her heart flutter or her pulse race. They were the same age, but she considered herself a woman. Andrew was only a boy, though to be sure, he had the FitzAlan good looks. What he lacked was polish.

And friends.

He'd made a good beginning with Ginny and Peter. Emily was confident that the rest could be safely left up to her.

# Chapter Ten

Not everyone stayed for the finale. As at any country fair, the crowds swelled and diminished from hour to hour. Marion would have liked nothing better than to put her feet up in front of her own fire, if only for a short respite, but this was out of the question. As one of the dowager's guests, she felt obliged to stay to the end, especially when Her Grace sent a messenger to inform her that one of the household carriages would convey her and her sisters to the field. An honor, indeed, since most of the guests would be walking to the site or had prudently brought their own carriages.

Phoebe was subdued. In a careless moment, she had innocently remarked to no one in particular that Mr. Hamilton had not come near their cottage in a week, and a little buzz of gossip had taken on a life of its own. And now Marion wasn't letting her out of her sight.

Emily was in high spirits. She was looking forward to the battle between Cavaliers and Roundheads. It sounded romantic. She listened attentively as Clarice gave a disjointed account of what they could expect to see.

Finally, Clarice heaved a sigh. "I'm not the person to ask," she said. "History bores me. Now, if my Oswald were here, he could answer all your questions."

"History bores you?" said Phoebe, struck by the notion.

Marion quickly cut her off. "Do we have far to go, Clarice?"

"Not far. Just the other side of the Priory. But if it rains, and it always rains, those with carriages can wait it out in comfort."

The carriage duly arrived, an antique that looked as though it had been rescued from a museum. Was this Brand's doing? Marion wondered. Was this how he managed the estate, by pinching pennies? No wonder there was ill feeling in the family.

They arrived at the site and took up their positions on a little rise that gave them an excellent view. Here they were joined by Mr. Lewis, a newcomer to Longbury, whom Marion had met after church services on the previous Sunday. He was, she judged, not more than forty, spoke with an easy confidence, and was handsome enough to have attracted his share of feminine interest.

She gave her attention to the field. Brand was there, out in front, with a steel helmet, a plain jerkin, and a short cloak covering his shoulders. Evidently, he was to be the commander of the Roundheads. Lord Robert's dress, in true Cavalier style, was more gaudy. His bonnet had more feathers than a rooster's tail. The majority of the Cavaliers were magnificently mounted. The Roundheads, as they were derisively labeled, were all on foot. Marion did not think that was fair.

"Why are they standing around?" Phoebe asked. "Why aren't they fighting?"

"They're getting into position," replied Mr. Lewis. "See, Lord Robert is playing the part of King Charles, and Mr. Hamilton represents Oliver Cromwell. When the bonfire is lit, the action will begin."

"The Cavaliers look like fops," said Phoebe.

Clarice nodded. "They look ridiculous in all that finery, don't they? But just remember, Phoebe, we're on their side, so you must cheer for them." To Marion, she added, "We FitzAlans have always been royalists."

If there was one thing that could arouse Marion's sympathies, it was the plight of the underling. She knew whose side she was on.

Because the skies were becoming overcast (and it looked as though Clarice's prophecy might come true), they lit the bonfire early, much to the delight of the crowd. The drums rolled and the battle commenced. It was more like a ballet than a battle. No shots were fired, no pikes were lowered, and only the flats of swords were used so that no one could be accidentally run through. For all that, there was drama in the spectacle. Drums beat out a constant tattoo; Cavaliers and Roundheads screamed out bloodcurdling battle cries; horses charged and retreated; men fell upon each other as though they were in earnest. And all the while, the Cavaliers slowly retreated. When the king and his aides made their escape from the field and the Cavaliers charged the Roundheads to prevent the king's capture, the crowd went wild.

Marion's eyes were riveted on Brand and his troop of men. Unwavering, unrelenting, they came on. When the crowd began to jeer, Marion did the opposite. Phoebe looked at her sister, then followed suit. The bystanders close by stopped jeering and turned to stare. So did

Brand, and the sword thrust that he should have deflected easily caught him hard in the midsection and he sank to his knees. Marion was sick with fright until two of his comrades helped him to his feet.

That's when the ballet stopped and the fight began in earnest. Swords and pikes were thrown down, feathered bonnets were tossed aside, and men dismounted or were pulled from their horses. They went at each other with their fists as though they were caught up in a barroom brawl.

Their commanders could do nothing with them. Brand and Lord Robert strode up and down the field, pulling men off each other; Andrew, still on horseback, was driving runaway horses through a gate and into an enclosure with the aid of the Priory's stable hands; and the crowd cheered them on.

"This can't be how the battle was fought!" exclaimed Marion, turning to Mr. Lewis for confirmation.

He was no longer there. It seemed that the svelte Mrs. Chandos had purloined him when she wasn't looking.

Clarice answered the question. She had to raise her voice to make herself heard. "No, indeed! The Cavaliers are supposed to win this skirmish, but feelings run deep here, and it always ends the same way."

"Feelings run deep?" repeated Emily, shouting above the roar of the crowd.

"Yes," yelled Clarice. "Longbury was split into Cavaliers and Roundheads in King Charles's day and nothing has changed. Why do you think Brand's grandfather hated all us FitzAlans?"

"That is *pathetic*!" declared Marion.

"That's what Oswald says. Thankfully, the old quarrel is forgotten most of the time. It's only on occasions like this that it is revived."

*"Barbaric,"* declared Emily.

Phoebe piped up, "If it always ends like this, why don't they cancel it?"

"We've tried. The villagers won't allow it."

Out on the field, Brand was gnashing his teeth as he pulled men off each other. He felt ridiculous in his Roundhead getup, and didn't know why he allowed the locals to persuade him to take on the role his grandfather had once played. Family loyalty? Guilty conscience? Another debt he felt obliged to pay off? He felt like a little boy again, trying to win his grandfather's approval.

He knocked the blacksmith's apprentice off his feet, grabbed him by the scruff of the neck, and gave him a hard shake. "Go help Lord Andrew round up the horses or I'll have your guts for garters!"

He had to roar to be heard above the cheers, jeers, and catcalls of the crowd.

The boy gulped, nodded, and hastened away.

Brand shook his head as he surveyed the carnage. His men could not get it into their thick skulls that they were preordained to lose this battle. That's why it always ended in a brawl. No one wanted to be on the losing side, himself least of all.

Evidently, Ted Fields, the blacksmith, had taken umbrage at the way his apprentice had been manhandled. Sixteen stone of brawn and muscle came barreling down on Brand. He stood his ground (one of his talents) until the last moment, then shot out a foot and sent Fields sprawling in the mud. When the fallen man sat up, the pungent odor of horse dung filled the air.

"For God's sake, get yourself cleaned up, man," Brand said, his voice mirroring his look of revulsion.

The blacksmith laughed. "Didn't you know, Mr. Hamilton, sir? Horse shit is lucky."

"Tell that to your wife."

Fields grimaced. "Aye, right enough. I'd best get my-self cleaned up."

Big drops of rain began to fall. No one seemed to care. The unofficial battle still raged. There would be a few broken noses and black eyes, but no serious injuries. At the end of the day, everyone would get cleaned up and enjoy a pint of ale in the tithe barn or champagne at the Priory.

And to think he had given up Brighton for this. Had he not bowed to the call of duty, right this minute he and Ash would be sitting down to a civilized dinner in the Castle Hotel where Ash had taken rooms. This was Brand's usual reward to himself after a grueling day of tramping from farm to farm, calling on voters and drumming up support for the party.

Ash knew how to enjoy himself. He never lacked for a pretty woman on his arm or in his bed. He had legions of friends. He was easily amused.

That was the trouble. Brand was bored out of his mind with pretty women. They were two a penny, whereas Marion Dane . . .

Marion Dane. He still could not take her measure. She blew hot and cold. When she was hot, she was very, very good. But when she was cold, she was horrid.

He turned away with a smile, and right into the knot-ted fist of the butcher's boy. The blow winded him, but no more than that. Sixteen-year-old Billy, on the other hand, let out a howl of pain.

"I think I've broken my wrist," he cried.

"If you don't get off the field," Brand grunted, "I'll break your bloody neck!"

The weather changed so violently and suddenly that people were drenched in seconds. The rain came down in torrents. One good thing came of it. It stopped the brawl on the field. Everyone ran for cover.

"Come along," yelled Clarice. "Make for the carriages. We'll be safe from the storm there."

Marion unfurled her umbrella only to have to wrestle the wind for it. One ferocious gust tore it from her hand and whisked it away. It didn't go far.

"You go on," she shouted, "and I'll catch up to you."

She trotted after her umbrella, but each time she caught up to it, the wind picked it up and whisked it out of her reach. She was cursing under her breath by the time she gave up the chase, cursing and furious. Droplets of rain ran from the brim of her bonnet into her eyes. Her gown clung to her like a sticky spider's web. There was a stitch in her side. Her teeth were chattering. She didn't know whether she wanted to shake her fist at the wind or throw a tantrum.

A sudden shaft of lightning and its deafening roar almost panicked her. She did an about-turn and fell into Brand's arms. His face was as thunderous as the sky above.

"Looking for someone, Lady Marion?"

"You're not hurt?" she got out.

"Of course I'm not hurt. The swords we use couldn't cut butter."

As he spoke, he hoisted her into the nearest carriage. She was too spent and too grateful to object to his rough handling and black looks. It was dry in the carriage; that was all that mattered.

He followed her in, removed her bonnet and tossed it

onto the banquette beside his helmet, then draped his short cloak around her shoulders. His cloak was warm from the heat of his body, but not warm enough to stop her teeth chattering.

The coach began to move, but only at a snail's pace.

"Get this into you," he commanded. He had a silver flask in his hand.

"What is it?"

"Brandy."

Grim-faced, he stood over her and held the flask to her lips. She choked on the first swallow but that did not deter him. He kept the flask to her lips until she drank deeply.

He sat on the banquette beside her and stoppered the flask. "Feeling better?"

She nodded. At least she'd stopped shivering. She felt awkward, remembering their last encounter, and she wondered whether to apologize or let sleeping dogs lie. The flint in his eyes showed that he had not forgiven her.

"I suppose," she said, "I should get back to my friends."

"You won't find Mr. Lewis. He left when the rain started."

"Who?" For a moment she was stymied.

"You've forgotten him already? Now that surprises me. You seemed to be hanging on his every word."

A moment before, the last thing she'd wanted was to quarrel with him. Now she quivered in indignation. "Mr. Lewis," she said, "is a fund of knowledge. He was telling me about the battle and what would happen next."

"Balderdash! All you had to do was watch the field." He spoke slowly now, as though he were instructing an ignorant child. "That's why we reenact the battle, so people can see what happened."

Her nostrils pinched. "You call that a battle? It was

nothing but a barroom brawl. You were lucky the magistrate wasn't there, or the constable. They would have soon clapped you in irons."

"The magistrate," he replied tersely, "was one of the Cavaliers, and Constable Hinchley was my second-in-command."

That gave her pause for thought. "That doesn't make it right," she said finally. "It was still a disgusting display of masculine aggression."

He folded his arms across his chest. "What's really going on, Marion? Are you pouting because you lost your latest flirt?"

She showed him her teeth. "You're a fine one to talk. I couldn't turn around but there was another lady hanging on your arm. You're not very discriminating, are you? Blondes, redheads—they're all the same to you."

His lips began to twitch. "Don't forget the brunettes."

"How could I? There were three of them."

He put his hand over his heart. "Marion, you unman me. I didn't know you cared."

With a snort of derision, she reached for the door handle. He grasped her wrist, preventing her escape. He was still amused but not, she thought, gloating. She stopped struggling.

"Those ladies who were hanging on my arm," he said, "have husbands or fathers who wield influence. Their votes count. What do you think I've been doing this last week but visiting constituents to persuade them to vote for whoever wins my party's nomination? It's hard work. I'm not leading anyone on. I make it clear from the outset that all I'm interested in is winning votes."

"And only men can vote."

"Precisely."

"Mrs. Chandos doesn't have a husband or a father," she said, pointing out a flaw in his logic.

"Ah." He rubbed the bridge of his nose. "The barracuda. You may have noticed that my good friend, Tommy Ruddle, entered on cue and rescued me from her ferocious jaws?"

She remembered the voluble gentleman who wouldn't take no for an answer.

"That was your friend?"

"He was when he agreed to do me a favor. Whether he is still my friend remains to be seen. It's not easy to shake off a barracuda, and man-eaters are insatiable."

"Then you've nothing to worry about. Mr. Lewis rescued your friend from the barracuda."

"In that case, I shall try to think well of him."

A heartbeat of silence went by. "Marion," he said, "did I hear aright? Out on the field, were you cheering for the Roundheads?"

"No."

His expression hardened. "My mistake. I'm sorry I asked."

"I was cheering for *you*."

Their eyes locked.

A tightness in her throat made her voice hoarse. "Brand, I have an apology to make. I let you believe that I thought you were beneath me, that I was too good for you. I'm sorry. It's not true. I don't think that way at all."

His smile flickered and died. "I know," he murmured softly.

"How do you know?"

"Because I know you."

He picked up her hand and traced the lines on it with the pad of his thumb. When she gave an involuntary shiver, he looked up. "That doesn't mean you don't con-

fuse me. Sometimes your words say one thing and your
eyes say another. I believe what I read in your eyes."

When she didn't respond, he gave an odd little sigh
and lowered his lips to hers. "This is what your eyes are
telling me."

His kiss was as gentle and unthreatening as the first
time he'd kissed her, but her response was far different.
She wrapped her arms around him and held on tight. Her
heart ached with all the feelings she had forced herself to
suppress. She knew him so well. What she felt wasn't romantic love. He was no Prince Charming and she was no
starry-eyed debutante. But she cared. She wanted him to
know that, present or absent, she would always care.

Brand brushed his mouth against hers, hardly able
to believe the feelings she aroused in him. He was no
stranger to passion or to the pleasure he could give to
and take from a woman's body, but this was different.
This was Marion. He didn't want to tumble her in a
coach like some streetwalker he'd picked up in Vauxhall
Gardens. That wasn't his style. Marion deserved . . . He
was distracted by the tip of her tongue probing between
his lips, so he started over. Marion . . .

Oh, God, he couldn't argue against nature. She was
receptive, and he had wanted her for a long, long time,
long before Fanny had introduced them in her drawing
room, long before London, long before he knew of her
existence. It seemed as though he had been waiting for
her half his life.

When he cupped one breast and kissed her through
the thin fabric of her gown, a wave of heat swept
through her, making her go weak with need. She was
dazed by the power of that kiss. She willed her pounding
heart to slow down but it wouldn't obey. Her small
sound of protest turned into a helpless whimper.

That involuntary pleasure sound almost broke Brand's control. He was stunned by her response, stunned and exalted. He dragged her onto his lap and clamped his arms around her small, trembling body. He kissed her until they were both breathless. He kissed her until she was as reckless with passion as he. *More,* her kisses told him. *More,* her body told him as she pressed her soft breasts against the hard wall of his chest.

His cloak was in the way, so he tugged it from her shoulders. She responded by twining her arms around his neck and kissing his eyes, his cheeks, his throat. He laughed in sheer masculine exaltation.

"What are you feeling?" he whispered.

She felt as though she wanted to stay here forever, wrapped in his arms, in this small snug sanctuary, shut off from all her fears and troubles.

"I feel—free," she said, and smiled drowsily. "Brand, don't stop. Please don't stop."

He couldn't believe his ears. He couldn't believe that he'd allowed things to go so far. He had to stop.

When he took Lady Marion Dane to his bed, it would be with all the pomp and circumstance befitting a gently bred girl.

He looked out the window. Thank God, they had arrived at the Priory.

Suddenly, she found herself lifted and set down on the opposite banquette. Her bottom lip trembled. "Brand?"

He draped his cloak around her shoulders and grinned down at her. "We've arrived, Marion. Better tidy yourself before we meet the others." He shoved her bonnet on her head and eyed her dubiously. "I'm sure Clarice would be more than happy to lend you a gown." He kissed her swiftly. "Don't look so stricken. It was only a kiss."

With that, he opened the carriage door and jumped down. Marion looked out the window. The great portal of the Priory was lit up by a blaze of wall torches. There were people standing around on the steps, some in small groups, greeting each other before they entered the house.

She looked down at her gown. It was practically transparent, and clung to her in all the wrong places. She couldn't meet all these people looking like this.

Manley opened the carriage door. When he handed her down, his eyes widened momentarily then instantly blank. She wished the ground would open and swallow her up.

She saw a group of men surround Brand and clap him on the shoulder. Oh, God, what had she done? What should she do? What could she do?

Brand was calling her over. She was in no state to meet his friends. They would take one look at her and they would *know*!

Know what? It was only a kiss. Isn't that what he'd told her? Embarrassed, and just a little bit hurt, she turned her back on Brand and his friends and spoke to Manley. "Tell Mr. Hamilton I've gone home to change my gown."

"I'll take you in the carriage, my lady."

"No. The walk will do me good."

She did not wait to argue the point, but turned aside and made for the shrubbery at the edge of the turf. As soon as she was out of sight, she ran like a wild thing.

Brand had seen her go. "Marion!" he shouted. He left his friends and went to Manley. "What happened?" he asked.

"Lady Marion has gone home to change her clothes."

"Hell and damnation!" Anger and alarm roughened

Brand's voice. "Drive the coach to her house. I'll meet you there."

He sprinted after Marion, cursing under his breath. Why hadn't she taken the carriage? They were both too old to go romping through the woods. Why did she always have to make things difficult?

As she ran full tilt through the underbrush, it came to her that this wasn't the first time she'd come this way. She didn't hesitate or have to think about where she was going. This was where Clarice and she had played as children. Aunt Edwina's cottage was halfway down the hill.

She burst into a clearing and came to a sudden halt. The light was fading and she blinked rapidly as she tried to get her bearings. Of course—this was where she and Clarice had lain in wait for their ghost to appear. There was nothing here but broken-down walls and, towering above them, the stone pulpit. The broken-down walls, as she remembered, were all that was left of the abbot's house.

She ran on. Something was different. This wasn't how she remembered it. Something was missing.

What did it matter? She had more important things to worry about. What was she going to do about Brand? What could she say to him after the way she had behaved in the carriage?

When she dashed from the cover of the trees and saw the cottage nestled in its hedgerow of yews, she let out a sound that was halfway between a sob and a laugh. This was more like it. This was where she belonged.

She fetched the key from under the flowerpot near the back door, let herself in, and thought about what she should do next. She could almost hear her mother's voice reminding her that she should always remember that she was an earl's daughter and act like one.

She would change her clothes, pin a smile on her face, and attend the dowager's reception as though nothing had happened. And if Brand dared to mention what had happened in the carriage, she would deny, deny, deny . . .

Her foot was on the bottom step when she thought she heard someone moving around in what was now the breakfast room and where Phoebe did her lessons.

"Phoebe?" she called out. "Emily?"

There was no answer.

"Who is there?"

Silence.

She almost took fright but managed to check herself. She was overwrought. If she didn't get a grip on herself, she'd end up in Bedlam.

She debated one moment more; then, teeth clamped together, she marched to the door and threw it wide. The curtains had been drawn and the room was in darkness. She knew the window must be open because she could feel a draft of air blowing in.

She was stunned. She had locked all the windows before she went out. So, someone *had* broken into her house. Her housebreaker had chosen his moment with care, when he knew they would all be at the dowager's fête. She wondered how many other homes he'd broken into when everyone was at the fête. He'd get small pickings in her little cottage.

Indignant now, she hastened to close the window. Two steps into the room and she was brought up short. There was no time to scream. An arm clamped around her throat, cutting off her breath, and the cold muzzle of a pistol was pressed against her temple. Her assailant was behind her.

"Where are Hannah's letters?" a coarse masculine voice demanded.

Her throat worked, but no sound passed her lips. His arm was clamped so tightly around her throat, she was sure she would suffocate. She began to struggle.

He released the pressure on her throat to give her a shake. "Answer me!" he snarled.

She gulped in great draughts of air. "There are no letters," she choked out. Her heart was pounding so hard, she thought she might die of fright.

She felt rather than saw his hand raised to strike her, and pure animal instinct took over. She launched herself at him, grappling for the gun. Her strength was no match for his. With a mighty shove, he sent her toppling to the floor. That was when Brand came storming in. He paused for a moment on the threshold, clearly outlined with his back to the only light that entered that room.

"He has a gun," Marion yelled.

As Brand dived for the floor, a shot rang out. "Get behind me, Marion," he called out. "Give me a clear shot at him." He had a pistol in his hand.

That was enough for the intruder. He vaulted through the open window and ran off.

Marion quickly crossed to Brand and knelt in front of him. "You've been hit," she cried.

On a groan, he got out, "In my thigh."

She didn't waste time on words. She undid his neckcloth, made a pad with it, and told him to place it on the wound to staunch the bleeding.

"I can hardly see in this light," she said. "I'll get a candle lit."

Heart pounding with fear, she felt her way to the

mantelpiece, found a candle, and used the tinderbox to light it. Her fingers were shaking so hard that the small flame went out and she had to do it over. When she came back to Brand, he was sitting with his back against a dresser, his pistol in one hand and the other pressing his padded neckcloth against his thigh. His face was chalk white, but he didn't appear to be seriously hurt. The vice squeezing her heart seemed to ease a little.

She put the candle on top of the dresser and knelt beside him. "I'll get the brandy." Her voice was shaking as badly as her fingers. "I think we could both do with something to revive us."

He grasped her wrist. "You're not getting out of my sight. Manley must have heard that shot. He'll be here in a moment or two. Until he arrives, we stay together."

"But the thief is gone."

"You don't know that! In fact, the villain may be reloading his pistol at this very moment. Did you see him, Marion? Would you recognize him if you saw him again?"

She shook her head. "It was dark, and I was too frightened to notice anything but the gun in his hand. His voice was odd, hoarse, but I think that was deliberate so that I wouldn't recognize it if I heard it again."

Brand's voice was sharp. "What did he say?"

"He asked for Hannah's letters, but there aren't any. Why would anyone go to such lengths for a young woman's letters?"

"Because he thinks there may be something in them that incriminates him."

She sat back on her heels. "What's going on, Brand?"

He shifted slightly and groaned. "It's a long story. I'll explain everything later, once I get this wound looked after. Meanwhile, you and your sisters are not staying here. Manley will take us to the Priory, and that's where you'll stay until I look into this."

She stretched over him and picked up a small, round object that was lying on the floor.

"What is it?" asked Brand.

"A button." She passed it to him. "Did you lose a button?"

Brand shook his head. "It must have come from the coat of the man you were grappling with."

He cupped it in his hand while they both studied it. There was nothing out of the ordinary about it, a simple cloth-covered button in a nondescript gray that could easily match any man's jacket or coat.

"So, we're looking for a man's jacket that's missing a button," said Brand.

When they heard Manley calling from outside the cottage, he slipped the button into his pocket. "Let's hope we get lucky," he said.

Manley appeared at the door. "I heard a shot." He was out of breath.

"Did you see anyone?" Brand asked.

"No. What happened?"

Marion said, "Mr. Hamilton has been shot, Manley. Let's get him to the Priory and send for a doctor. I'll explain everything later."

Before they had got Brand inside the coach, he was issuing orders, telling them what had to be done. It was a break-in gone wrong, were his words to Marion. That was all she was to tell the magistrate. Meantime, she and her sisters were to stay at the Priory, and he would explain everything after the doctor had taken care of his wound.

# Chapter Eleven

Brand heaved a sigh of relief when Dr. Hardcastle arrived and took charge. The first thing the doctor did was clear everyone out of the room except for Manley and a footman with a wrestler's physique. As he set out his instruments and prepared to take the bullet out of Brand's thigh, he asked a few desultory questions about the attack, and made suitable clucking sounds, but Brand knew that that was to distract him from what was to come.

He groaned when Hardcastle probed gently around the wound. He couldn't wriggle because he was lying on a board on top of the bed. The board was the doctor's idea.

"You'll take a drop of laudanum?"

Brand accepted the glass the doctor offered, took one sip, then handed it back. He wanted a clear head when he spoke to Marion.

As he examined the wound, Hardcastle began to regale them with stories of the soldiers whose mangled limbs he'd amputated while cannonballs were flying overhead.

"Brave lads, every one of them," Hardcastle said.

He was in his sixties and had resided in Longbury as long as Brand could remember, but he talked of his years as an army doctor as though they'd happened yesterday.

"We had nothing to give them, no brandy or opium, but they bore all our ministrations with a smile. I remember one in particular . . . "

Brand had heard the same stories since he was a boy and could now recite them by heart. He was half convinced that the doctor did it on purpose so that his patients would think themselves lucky to get off so easily, and act accordingly.

As the good doctor rattled on, it occurred to Brand that if anyone knew the Gunn sisters, it would be a doctor who also happened to be one of Longbury's longtime residents. He waited for the first lull in Hardcastle's monologue before he asked about them.

"Dr. Hardcastle," he said, "do you remember Edwina Gunn and her sisters?"

"Of course I remember them. I knew all the Gunns, and I'm very happy to hear that Edwina's cottage has passed to her nieces." He picked up a pair of sharp-pointed tweezers and examined them closely. "Brace yourself, lad."

At a signal from the doctor, Manley placed his big hands on Brand's shoulders while the footman held his ankles.

"Wait!" Brand wasn't finished yet. "Where is Hannah now? Do you know?"

Hardcastle looked surprised. "She eloped, didn't she? That's what I always understood." He smiled into Brand's eyes. "Now then, be a brave little soldier. I'm afraid this is going to hurt."

*Hurt* wasn't the word for it. It was excruciating, so excruciating that Brand could do no more than suck great gulps of air into his lungs. He went as rigid as the board he was lying on. Manley was mangling his shoulders, while the wrestler seemed determined to crack his ankle bones, and a red-hot poker was boring a hole in his thigh.

"Good lad," said Hardcastle, beaming. "Now, that wasn't so bad, was it?"

Beads of sweat were running down Brand's cheeks into his ears. Tears of pain stung his eyes. But the worst was over. By slow degrees, he allowed himself to relax.

"No," he said weakly. "Not bad at all."

"And here is the little bugger that caused the damage." Hardcastle held up the tweezers with a bullet prized in its jaws. He studied it for a moment and frowned. "There's a chip missing. Manley, give him the laudanum. I'm afraid I have to go back in there and poke around a bit until I find it."

This time Brand drank every drop in the glass. Marion would have to wait.

It was a subdued group of people who waited in the drawing room for the doctor to come downstairs. No one had bothered to change. Lord Robert and Andrew were still in their Cavalier costumes, and the only difference in Marion's dress was that she was wearing borrowed slippers and a borrowed shawl. Emily had gone off more than an hour ago to put Phoebe to bed. She had yet to return, and Marion was wondering what was keeping her.

From time to time, they heard a step in the hall. Marion's heart would leap to her throat but it was never the doctor, only a servant passing. After one such occasion, Andrew got up and stalked to the window.

"Hardcastle knows what he is doing," he said. "He was once an army doctor." He turned to face the company. "And I've never heard of a wound to the thigh that was fatal."

Those were the words that had been drumming inside Marion's head for the last half hour, or words very like them. Her mind told her that Andrew was right, but there was a niggling fear that she could not quell.

Lord Robert responded to Andrew's comments. "In this case, far from fatal. You weren't there, Andrew, when his manservant helped him into the house. Brand was issuing orders as though he were a general, and the servants all scurried to do his bidding."

"That sounds like Brand," the dowager said. "What were his orders?"

"Let me see." Lord Robert gazed at the glass he'd been drinking from. "That Marion and her sisters were to take up residence here until he was satisfied that their cottage was secure. To get the magistrate onto finding the culprit—"

At mention of the magistrate, Andrew snorted. "Sir Basil is in no fit state to do anything. He's in a drunken stupor and is sleeping it off in one of the cellars. Not only that, the constable is with him."

"Yes, so we heard," replied Robert. "At any rate, we sent for the doctor and sent footmen and gardeners to secure Lady Marion's cottage until the authorities have a chance to look it over. I forget what else Brand told us to do, but he was far from ready to give up the ghost."

Andrew chuckled. Lady Theodora's expression softened and Clarice blew her nose. On the other side of the room, Miss Cutter came to herself after dozing off, and the dowager regarded Marion with an expression that held as much curiosity as sympathy.

Marion thought she understood. She wasn't a member of the family, but here she was in the dowager's drawing room, as though she had every right to be there.

She didn't care what they thought. She wasn't budging until she had heard from the doctor's own lips that Brand was out of danger.

Brows down, she returned the dowager's stare and was surprised to see a smile creep into those pale, aristocratic, all-seeing eyes.

As the silence lengthened, Marion studied Brand's family, and that's what they were, Brand's family. They weren't loveable or loving; they didn't know how to show their feelings, but she never doubted for a moment that they cared in their own eccentric, FitzAlan way. Just as Brand cared for them.

If this were her family, she would be sitting beside the dowager holding her hand. If she were Theodora, she would go to her husband and say something encouraging to wipe that anxious look from his face. As for Andrew, she would give him something to do to use up that restless energy that she could feel from halfway across the room.

When the door opened without warning, everyone straightened.

The doctor entered, a tall, stately gentleman with dark hair liberally laced with silver and an austere face softened in a smile.

When everyone saw the smile, a collective sigh went up. He walked straight to the dowager and bowed over her hand. "A trifling wound, Your Grace. I've given him a draft of laudanum, but he is still conscious. You may have a few minutes with him. No need to worry. He'll be out of bed in a few days."

The dowager swallowed a small constriction in her

throat. "Thank you, Dr. Hardcastle." She got up. "Will you give me your arm?"

"I'd like to go, too," interrupted Andrew quickly. "Someone should be there to take care of him in case he wakens during the night. Besides servants, I mean."

His grandmother smiled and nodded, and they turned to go.

"Wait," cried Marion. She was on her feet in an instant. "What about me?"

They were going to leave her to stew about Brand until he wakened in the morning. She could see it in their faces. She wasn't a member of the family. In spite of everything she and Brand had been through, in spite of him saving her life, she was only a guest in this house. Everyone else in that room had a better claim to go to him than she.

The thought made her bristle.

"What about you?" asked Miss Cutter, breaking the long silence.

The words formed on Marion's lips as though they had a will of their own. "I," she said clearly and without hesitation, "am Brand's betrothed."

It was the oddest thing. When she knelt by Brand's bed and saw with her own eyes that he was sleeping peacefully and that the color had returned to his cheeks, she turned into a watering pot. She, who never cried, was behaving with all the decorum of a frightened child.

"A trifling cold," she told the dowager gruffly as she blew her nose.

They did not stay long because the doctor wouldn't permit it, so she had no chance to question Brand or tell him that they were now betrothed.

For the sake of a few minutes at his bedside, she had perjured herself. How on earth was she going to explain this to Brand when he wakened?

She had a good reason for claiming to be his betrothed. She had wanted to see with her own eyes that he was all right. Then there was the mystery he had promised to explain to her. He could not expect her to play the shrinking violet after all that had happened tonight.

These were the thoughts that crowded her mind as she walked down the corridor to Emily's room. There were no candles lit, so she left the door open so that she could see her way to the bed. Curled up under the blankets, their arms around each other, were Emily and Phoebe.

Marion gave a watery sniff and collapsed into the nearest chair. She sat there for a long time, staring at her sisters, thinking, thinking, thinking. All she'd ever wanted was to keep them safe and happy. Now a third person had insinuated himself into her little circle and she had three people to worry about.

She gave another sniff. A few weeks ago, David Kerr had been her most pressing problem. Now she didn't know what to think. It hardly seemed likely that he was the man who had attacked her. She had paid him off; she had given him her mother's emeralds. That should have been the end of it. And the most telling piece of evidence in his favor was that he knew nothing of Hannah.

*Where are Hannah's letters?* She quaked, remembering how her breath had been cut off. She would never forget the sound of that menacing voice. That was not David's voice. This was something new, something that Brand understood and she did not.

She did not know how she could contain her impatience until he told her all he knew.

Sighing, she got up. If there had been room in her

sisters' bed, she would have crawled in beside them. She wondered if she would ever feel safe again.

Her own room was only a few steps down the corridor. She lit a candle from the embers in the fire and set it on the mantel. A footman had brought a trunk containing her clothes, and she was rummaging through it for a nightgown when someone knocked softly on the door.

"Marion?"

The dowager's voice. Marion quickly crossed to the door and opened it.

"Your Grace," she said, her voice scarcely audible.

"May I come in?

"Please do."

In spite of her cane, the dowager looked majestic as she entered and took the wing chair flanking the fireplace. Gesturing gracefully with one hand, she indicated that Marion was to take the chair opposite. Marion complied and sat with her back straight and her hands folded neatly in her lap. She tried not to feel intimidated, but the dowager would have been an intimidating lady even if she had not been a duchess.

Smiling faintly, the dowager said, "I could not go to bed without telling you how happy I am about you and Brand. I'm sure you know that my grandson is a good man. Not easy to live with, perhaps, and not easy to love, but a good man for all that. But, of course, you must know this."

Marion gave the other woman a narrow-eyed look. The dowager didn't sound like a doting grandmother, but who could tell with the FitzAlans? As pleasantly as she could manage, Marion replied vaguely, "I'm sure my sisters would say the same about me."

The dowager nodded. "I take your point. The people who are closest to us know all our weaknesses and faults. But I hope you will take *my* point." She leaned forward slightly, using her cane to balance her weight. "Bear with me, Marion. There are some things about my grandson I think you should know if ever you are truly going to understand him."

Marion held herself still. This was not the moment to interrupt Her Grace. The dowager didn't look majestic or aloof. She looked fragile, as though one wrong word could break her.

Breathing out slowly, the dowager began. "In spite of what you may have heard, Brand's father was not a bad man. He did not abandon Brand and his mother. It was old Mr. Hamilton who poisoned Brand's mind against his father. The truth of the matter is that my son fell deeply in love with Faith Hamilton when he was barely older than Andrew. He wanted to marry her when he came of age. It was settled between them. It was Faith's father, old Mr. Hamilton, who put his foot down. She was underage, and under her father's thumb, and even when she fell with child, her father would not relent. She did not have it in her to defy her father.

"She died when Brand was a few months old, from a broken heart, some say. Her heart wasn't the only heart that was broken. My son never got over her. But he felt betrayed, so he went a little wild."

When the dowager paused to gather her thoughts, Marion ventured to say, "I already guessed that it must have been something like that."

The dowager looked surprised. "What made you think so?"

Marion gave a tiny shrug. "Your son named Brand as sole trustee of his estate. He gave him a home, paid for his education. I think he must have loved Brand very much and, perhaps, felt guilty for the way things had turned out."

"He did feel guilty. Brand was his firstborn son. He was Faith's son. Brand should have succeeded him to the title and estates, and would have if it had not been for an embittered old man who despised our rank and wealth."

The dowager gave a wan smile. "Brand has fallen between two worlds, the Priory and the Grange."

"Cavaliers and Roundheads," Marion mused softly.

"Yes. But it's more than reliving old battles. Mr. Hamilton was a Puritan. In his eyes, the FitzAlans were a godless lot. He did not want his daughter or his grandson to be corrupted by us."

A long silence ensued. Finally, Marion said, "Why are you telling me all this?"

"Perhaps I'm hoping for too much." The dowager studied Marion for a long moment, then went on, "I don't think my grandson will ever be at peace with himself until he learns to bridge those two worlds. And more than that, I want him to know the truth about his father."

She held up her hand when Marion would have interrupted. "He doesn't listen to me. I don't suppose he'll listen to you. All the same, I felt I had to try, for my son's memory, and for Brand's sake, too. It doesn't do to carry so much bitterness inside you."

Marion felt as though she were seeing the dowager for the first time, not as the intimidating, all-knowing, all-seeing ogre she had imagined, but as a woman like herself, ageless, with the same fears and aspirations.

And she felt awful for deceiving her. She would never marry Brand, never marry, period.

She gazed down at the ringless finger of her left hand,

and when she looked up, her eyes were trapped in the dowager's intense stare. The words seemed to be dragged from her against her will. "Your Grace . . . we're not betrothed. I made that up so that I would be allowed to see Brand."

The truth did not seem to annoy the dowager. If anything, Marion's confession seemed to amuse her. "Of course you did. In your position, I would have done the same thing."

Marion bit down on her lip. Evidently, the dowager hadn't understood. "You don't understand. Brand hasn't asked me to marry him."

"Oh, he will. Of that I'm perfectly sure. All Brand needs is a little encouragement, and I think your declaration in front of the family may well do the trick."

When the dowager got up and walked to the door, Marion hastened after her to open it.

"But . . . but nothing has been settled."

The dowager smiled, patted Marion's cheek, and quit the room as gracefully as she had entered it.

Marion returned to her chair and sat there in frozen misery. There was so much to think about, so much to worry about. Fortunately, her mind was numb, so she couldn't think at all.

She left one candle burning when she climbed into bed, in case Phoebe got up in the middle of the night and came looking for her. She tossed, she turned, she pounded the pillows. Nothing helped. Tossing off the covers, she slid out of bed and padded along the corridor to Emily's room. It was a tight squeeze, but she managed to wriggle in beside her sisters. The warmth of their bodies pressed so closely to hers was vastly comforting. Even so, it was a long time before she slept.

Lady Theodora allowed her maid to undress her and put her to bed. "Leave the candles," she said.

The maid withdrew with a curtsy and a telling little smile. She would think, of course, that Lord Robert was going to pay his wife a conjugal visit. Theodora doubted that that would be the case tonight. His eyes had barely left Marion's face. He wouldn't be thinking of Marion, but the girl she resembled: Hannah.

She moved restlessly, despising herself for hoping that he would come to her. She should have more pride. She should have left this house a long time ago. She was still young. There was still time to make a new life for herself.

She checked her foolish thoughts. Life wasn't that simple. One made choices and suffered the consequences—wasn't that what her father told her the day that she married? Robert had turned out just as Papa predicted, and because she'd been so determined to marry him, she was too proud to let anyone know that they had been right and she was wrong.

She gave a start when the door opened. Her husband entered, wearing a dark maroon dressing robe tied loosely at the waist. He was, in her opinion, even more handsome than when they'd met and married. His boyish good looks had matured into a harsh beauty. He was smiling softly as he approached the bed.

He sat on the edge, raised her hand, and pressed his lips to her palm. "You are still the most beautiful woman I know," he said.

She took an uneven breath. "I didn't expect to see you tonight."

"Liar." He kissed her wrist. "I know when you're susceptible to me. I can feel it in my pores."

"Yes. You were always attuned to my moods." She twined her fingers through his hair. "Just as I have always been attuned to yours."

He made no answer, but looked at her with an expectant gravity.

She laughed softly. "Don't tell me you didn't notice the strong resemblance between Lady Marion and Hannah?"

His smile was not reflected in his eyes. "I barely knew Hannah."

"Don't lie to me, Robert. I saw how your eyes kept straying to Marion all night."

"A natural reaction. She had been attacked in her own home. I wanted to make sure that she was all right. And yes, I admired her. She came through a nerve-wracking experience without falling to pieces. That's all it was."

She closed her eyes and gritted her teeth. "Keep away from her! You can have your pick of any woman you want." She opened her eyes and stared fixedly into his face. "We don't want Marion to . . . "

"To what?" His voice was dangerously soft. "What are you saying?"

She moderated her tone. "Everyone knows that she will marry Brand. Just remember that."

"Yes, but that's not what you were going to say."

He rose easily, gracefully, and bowed over her hand, a formal gesture that was almost insulting. "It would seem," he said, "that I have misread the signs. I beg your pardon. It won't happen again."

She made no move to stop him as he quit her chamber.

# Chapter Twelve

The following morning, when Marion arrived at Brand's chamber, she found him groggy and unfit to do much more than acknowledge her presence.

"Is that my betrothed's voice I hear?" he crooned.

He asked the question without opening his eyes, but Marion caught the amused inflection in his voice, and she couldn't help smiling. He wasn't going to make things difficult for her.

She sat with him for a little while, but they were never alone, and he was too groggy to be coherent, so they didn't have the chance to have that heart-to-heart talk. It was not until the day after that that she had the opportunity of speaking to him alone. A maid delivered a note informing her that Mr. Hamilton was in the conservatory; would she care to join him?

He was waiting for her at the conservatory door.

"Are you sure you should be out of bed?" she asked as soon as she came up to him. He was walking with the aid of a cane, and there were signs of strain around his mouth.

"Quite sure. In fact, I'm obeying the doctor's orders. Having served in the army, Hardcastle doesn't believe in mollycoddling his patients. He expects us all to behave like good little soldiers, you know, get back to the action before the battle is lost."

When she laughed, he smiled. "Besides," he went on, "there are too many visitors coming and going in my room. We can talk without interruption here."

The conservatory, however, was no quieter than the house. Gardeners were moving in and out as they transplanted tender shrubs and other specimens to the flower beds outside. Lord Robert was there giving directions, but Brand and Marion slipped away before he could see them.

Marion said, "I didn't know that Lord Robert was interested in gardening."

Brand's tone was dry. "You might say that my uncle is passionate about all kinds of pretty flowers, so watch your step with him." He looked down at her. "I should hate to call him out."

Since he was smiling, she took it as a joke. "I'm desolate. He hasn't tried to flirt with me. All we talk about is you or the weather."

"Think yourself lucky because if he did flirt with you, Theodora would soon unsheathe her claws."

"Was theirs an arranged marriage?" she asked.

"No. According to our resident gossip, Miss Cutter, Theodora's family was against the match, but love carried the day. Lord Robert, you see, had a reputation as a young Lothario, but promised to reform." His smile was twisted. "He did not keep his promise much beyond the wedding day, and Theodora is not one to give second chances."

Beyond the conservatory, they looked down on the

herb garden, but Miss Cutter was there, fluttering like a butterfly, so Brand turned aside and led Marion to a stone bench that was sheltered on one side by a hedge. Far below them, the river meandered through field and pasture. It was a warm day and the bees were out in force, plundering the white spirea blossoms that grew in clumps at the sunny edges of a wilderness of shrubs.

It was hard to believe, in this sheltered little paradise, that someone had broken into her house and held a gun to her head.

Brand looked at her thoughtfully. "Cold?"

"No, frightened. While you have been convalescing, I've had plenty of time to think, but I never come up with any answers. Yesterday, I went with the constable to the cottage. Nothing was missing. Only the breakfast room where Phoebe keeps her books and notes was disturbed. The box with our family's letters was upended on the floor but, as far as I can determine, no letters were taken. It doesn't make sense."

"How did the thief get in?"

"He forced a downstairs window."

"What did you do with the letters?"

"They're at the Priory. I've read them all. There's nothing significant in any of them, and no letters to or from Hannah."

She waited for him to say something, but when he continued to stare into space, as though he were unaware of her presence, her patience ended.

"You said you would explain everything to me! Well, I'm not a mind reader. Start explaining. What do you know that I don't know?"

He shifted slightly and stretched one arm along the back of the bench. "Your aunt Edwina is the source of everything I know, so I'll begin by telling you of a letter she wrote to me shortly before she died."

In short, halting sentences, and with many interruptions from Marion as she tried to grasp his meaning, he told her about the delay in receiving Edwina's letter and his reluctance to take it seriously. He described the contents of the letter, and how Edwina had come to believe that Hannah had never left Longbury and that someone had murdered her. Finally, he explained that Edwina hoped Marion could tell her exactly what had happened the night Hannah disappeared.

Shocked, Marion sat back. She could hardly get her mind around his words. "Why would I know anything?"

He replied gently, "Because Hannah disappeared when you were here with your mother. You were out that night in the Priory grounds. Someone saw you."

"Who saw me?"

He took her hand and held it in a comforting clasp. "I don't know. Edwina was going to explain everything when I came down to see her. I wish we'd had that chat; then I might have taken her letter seriously. To put it bluntly, she seemed confused, but there was no getting around the fact that Hannah had disappeared twenty years before with not a word to anyone."

"And someone told Edwina I saw what happened to Hannah?"

"So Edwina said in her letter." He looked at her intently. "I'm sorry. I've shocked you. I didn't know how to break it gently."

"It's not that." She paused, then went on slowly, "I was thinking of the last time I saw Hannah. She used to enjoy walking in the Priory grounds with her little dog. I often went with her, but she didn't go out that day. I didn't mind because I knew I'd be going out later with Clarice, to lie in wait for our ghost."

She looked at him uncertainly. "If I had seen something that night, I would have run to the cottage for help. Clarice was there, too. Have you asked her if she saw anything?"

"No. Edwina didn't mention Clarice, only you. What happened, Marion? Do you remember anything of that night at all? In her letter, Edwina wrote that she quarreled with Hannah. Did you hear the quarrel?"

"Yes." She thought for a moment. "They were in Hannah's room—my mother, Aunt Edwina, and Hannah. I could hear Hannah crying. I think I was upstairs, waiting for everyone to go to bed so that I could slip away to be with Clarice. I hated quarreling. I was heartsick, and wished Mama and Edwina would leave Hannah alone. Then Hannah rushed out of the house and I heard the door slam."

"And that's the night you went out with Clarice?"

"I think so, but I'm not sure."

A moment went by, and he said, "Clarice mentioned hearing an animal howling. Did you hear it?"

She frowned in concentration. "I think so. Yes. I remember a dog barking, but can't be sure. I'm sorry."

"Don't force it. It may come back to you. Forget that for the moment. Tell me what happened when you were in the pulpit."

She looked down at her hands. "It's just as Clarice told you. We saw what we thought was the abbot's ghost, and ran home." She shook her head. "My memories are very vague. It happened a long time ago—and if Hannah was murdered, what happened to her body?"

"I don't know. She could have been pushed into the river or buried somewhere."

The thought made her shudder.

Some moments passed, then she said softly, "I'd like to think poor Aunt Edwina was confused when she wrote that letter, but I can't ignore the fact that you were shot by someone who broke into my house, looking for letters that don't exist." She looked up at him, her eyes deeply troubled. "It makes me wonder about Aunt Edwina. Tell me the truth, Brand. What do you think? Was Edwina's death an accident?"

He said as gently as he could manage, "I'd like to think it was an accident, but now"—he touched a hand to his thigh—"I think it's entirely possible that it wasn't."

He looked out over the fields and pastures to the meandering river below. "According to Mrs. Ludlow, Edwina was troubled about the past, about Hannah, and she was determined to find out what had happened to her. I think she started asking questions that someone didn't want to answer."

"But why twenty years after Hannah disappeared? What set Edwina off?"

"The only clue in her letter was the witness who saw you that night. I've thought about that witness till my brain is numb with speculation. He or she must have had a good reason to keep quiet all these years."

She shivered. "If I were that person, I'd be shaking in my shoes right now. The man who shot you wouldn't think twice about killing someone who knew too much."

After a short silence, he sighed and went on, "I blame myself for letting the matter slide, but the mystery was twenty years old and I didn't see the necessity for solving it quickly. You were fixed in the Lake District, or so I thought. I suppose I would have made the journey north to question you eventually, but you saved me the trouble. When I heard that you were coming to London for the

Season, I seized the chance of getting to know you, hoping that if you knew anything, you would confide in me." He shrugged. "Either you knew nothing, or you wouldn't confide in me. As time passed, and I came to believe that you were no threat to anyone, I relaxed my vigilance."

"Why didn't you tell me straight out in London about Edwina's letter? Why conceal your true purpose in befriending me and my family?"

"I told you. I wasn't sure that I could trust Edwina's judgment. Sometimes old people get strange fancies. I was sounding you out to see if you could shed light on what happened to Hannah."

A shard of glass seemed suddenly to pierce her heart, and she could hardly get her breath. Had she not been Edwina's niece, he would not have given her a second stare. The visits to the theater, the outings in his carriage, his charm, his kisses—they all had one purpose, and that was to find out how much she remembered about Hannah. He hadn't been courting her in hopes of ensnaring an earl's daughter. That thought had been put in her head by Cousin Fanny and Emily and Clarice, and others who had hinted that marriage to her would add to his prestige. He hadn't wanted to marry her at all. What a fool she had made of herself.

That put her in mind of their sham betrothal. Of course, the idea had come from her. He had never once hinted that he had marriage on his mind, just the reverse. She was the one who had brought it up.

There was no way to salvage her pride so she said abruptly, "I'm sorry I told your family that we were betrothed. I did it on impulse, because I couldn't see another way of being allowed near you, and I was desperate to know why someone wanted to break into my house."

"Don't apologize. It was a brilliant idea."

"It was?"

He nodded. "Now the gossips will have nothing to gossip about. We've taken the wind out of their sails."

"We have?"

"Think about it. People will expect us to spend all our time together. It's what engaged couples do. We have a mystery to solve. No one will think it odd when they see us together. They won't know what we're really up to. On the other hand"—he rubbed the bridge of his nose with his index finger—"a man can't be too careful." His eyes smiled into hers. "One false step and I could find myself married to you."

She shot him a withering look. "I have no more thought of marrying than I do of swimming the English Channel to France."

He laughed into her baleful eyes. "If we're going to convince the world that we're engaged, you'll have to watch your sharp tongue."

She searched her mind for the perfect snub and could only say coolly, "Luncheon must be ready. Shall we join the others?"

Brand slowed her furious pace by asking for her arm. "I'm not up to snuff yet," he said, grimacing and touching a hand to his injured leg.

She was instantly contrite. "I'm sorry! I wasn't thinking. Why don't you put your arm around my shoulders for support."

He accepted her suggestion with alacrity, not only because he needed the support, but also because he wanted to hold her. He kept thinking of what might have happened in her cottage had he not followed her, and a nameless dread settled in the pit of his stomach.

He would be the first to acknowledge that she did not lack courage, as she'd proved when she tried to wrestle the gun away from her assailant. But her bones were small and fragile, and a woman's strength was no match for a man's.

Their sham betrothal gave him the perfect excuse to put leading strings on her. He didn't want her to stray far from his side until they'd caught the thug who had broken into her house. It seemed to him, now, that the episodes at Vauxhall and the King's Theater were connected to the attack on her at the cottage, but he was reluctant to mention them. She had been through enough already, and he did not want to add to her worries.

"Marion," he said, "I don't want you to go back to your cottage until we're satisfied that you're no longer in danger. No one will think it unusual if you stay at the Priory for a few weeks."

She gave a shaky laugh. "That's exactly how I feel anyway. I've told Emily and Phoebe to stay away from the cottage as well. I keep thinking of what would have happened if one of them had surprised the intruder and no one was there to help them."

He withdrew his arm from her shoulders and turned her to face him. "If they are anything like their big sister, I'm sure he would have been glad to get away from them."

"He had a gun."

"He wanted the letters, that's all. He only shot at me because I had a gun, too, and he knew that I would use it."

He wasn't convinced by his own words, but he wanted to ease Marion's fears.

They walked on, but slowly, with Brand leaning on

Marion's arm for support. After a moment, he said, "Don't you have any letters from Hannah at all?"

"I haven't come across any. As I told you, all I have are a few letters that Edwina wrote to my mother, and I brought those with me from Keswick. They don't say very much."

"All the same, I'd like to read them."

"Fine."

They talked back and forth, speculating about this and that, then Marion said, "I think we should start our investigation with Hannah. Who were her friends? What were her plans? I know she was a governess in Brighton. Perhaps her last employer would know—if we can find her."

He flashed her a smile. "It seems that we've been thinking along the same lines. I know who her last employer was: Mrs. Love of Ship Street. And she still resides there."

She was thunderstruck. "How do you know this?"

"I got that piece of information from the good doctor. As it turns out, Hardcastle remembers Hannah and all the Gunns very well. He told me, in between doctoring me, about Mrs. Love. Hannah asked him to give her a character reference, you see."

"And Mrs. Love is still at the same address?"

"Apparently." He gave her a sideways glance. "He also told me that Edwina was so strict that Hannah didn't have much of a life. He accepted the rumor that Hannah had eloped because she was desperate to get out from under Edwina's thumb."

She let out a little sigh. "I think Edwina and my mother had much in common. They were both strong-minded, determined women."

"Like you?" he quizzed.

She looked up at him with an arrested expression. "Is that how you see me?"

"I meant it as a compliment. Only a strong-minded, determined lady," he went on, "would attack a man with a gun and try to take it away from him. You're a formidable woman, Lady Marion Dane."

Though she said not a word in reply, her cheeks bloomed. He felt oddly touched, surprised that such a careless remark should affect her like this. She was a lovely, intelligent, capable woman. Now, if only she could see him as a handsome, intelligent, capable man, they could stop sparring and . . . and what?

He couldn't imagine marriage, but he had a clear picture of taking Marion to his bed. He felt an entirely masculine and primitive satisfaction when he remembered how she had responded to his slightest touch, not to mention that he was finding it increasingly difficult to keep his hands to himself.

So where did that leave him?

Marion interrupted his train of thought. "Do you know, Brand, I'm puzzled about Hannah's little dog. Governesses don't usually have dogs, do they?"

"None that I know."

"Then who did it belong to and what became of it?"

"Perhaps Hardcastle knows."

"Or perhaps Mrs. Love. You *are* going to take me to Brighton to interview her? After all, I'm Hannah's niece. She might tell me more than she would tell you."

"I'll think about it."

Her look of outrage was his reward. He had every intention of taking her to Brighton with him. That's how leading strings worked. Where he went, she went, and vice versa. But he did enjoy sparring with her.

"I'm the one with the memories!" Her breath came

out in huffs and puffs. "Mrs. Love may say something that means something to me but nothing to you. I could be of immeasurable help in our investigation."

"That's true. But we don't want our villain to get wind of what we're doing. Whatever we do must appear innocent and unthreatening."

"I know *that*. I'm not a simpleton!"

He couldn't argue with that.

Brand made the formal announcement of their engagement over luncheon. Her sisters were thrilled. His family, as expected, received the announcement with their usual sangfroid, even the duchess, who Marion knew was pleased by the news.

Marion told herself that it was for the best. She need not feel guilty when the day came to announce that she and Brand were going their separate ways. There would be no tears, no dismay. She would be lucky if, a week after that, they remembered her name.

Emily rounded on Andrew as soon as they were alone. They were making for the stable block to look over his new curricle.

"What is the matter with your family?" she demanded. "Have they no feelings? Do they have ice in their veins? Don't they know how to be happy? Where was the champagne to toast the happy couple?"

He looked startled. "They were happy," he said. "We just don't show our feelings as easily as some families do."

"Why not? You're supposed to be Cavaliers, aren't you, and Cavaliers are supposed to be gallant and gay and . . . and larger than life?"

His lips curved. "You're the Cavalier, Emily."

She gave a self-conscious laugh. "You don't think I'm like this with everyone? I feel I can say what I like with you, Andrew. And I say that we should have done something special for Marion and Brand."

When they arrived at the stable block, they found Manley in conversation with Theodora's man of business. Mr. Forrest was proudly showing off his latest acquisitions, and Mr. Manley was obviously impressed.

Manley looked up when he saw Andrew and Emily.

Emily said, "Lord Andrew is taking me for a drive in his new curricle, Mr. Manley."

"Is he now? Well, it just so happens that I have nothing to do. I'll act as groom."

"That won't be necessary," replied Andrew, not coldly, but not warmly, either. "I can manage quite well on my own."

Manley's smile grew wider. "I'm sure you can, Your Grace. But I have my orders. I'll just set things up for you, shall I?"

When Andrew stiffened, Emily surreptitiously elbowed him in the ribs. "Thank you, Mr. Manley," she said. "We'll wait outside."

As they waited outside, Emily said, "There's no arguing with Manley. He has the instincts of a sheepdog and, I'm afraid, he sees me as one of his lambs. We'll just have to grin and bear it."

Andrew shook his head.

"What?" she demanded.

"He's only a servant."

"All the more reason for *you* to treat him like a prince!"

The curricle was brought out, and a pair of well-matched bays were soon harnessed to it. Andrew took the reins, Manley helped Emily into the curricle, then took his position in the rear. A flick of the reins and they were off.

Emily knew within a few minutes that Andrew was an accomplished whip, because when she glanced over her shoulder, she caught Manley smiling. After that, she settled back to enjoy herself. The curricle bowled rapidly down the drive and was soon traveling along the High Street.

"Look, Andrew," she said at one point. "There's Victor Malvern."

She waved to Victor in passing. Andrew tipped his hat. Victor's face went fiery red. There were others, however, who responded in kind and shouted out a greeting.

Emily was pleased because Andrew was finally coming into his own.

Andrew was pleased because Emily was pleased.

Almost a week went by before Brand was fit to make the journey to Brighton. In that time, he and Marion did a little discreet sleuthing. Several people remembered a white dog, but it had belonged to Theodora and its name was Snowball. A few of the residents remembered Hannah, but no one had known her well. They all seemed to share Dr. Hardcastle's view, that Edwina Gunn had kept such a close eye on her sister that poor Hannah was glad to take up a position in Brighton and escape Edwina's vigilance. As for Clarice, she added nothing to the story that she had already told Marion: that when their ghost appeared, and she heard an animal howling, she had run up the hill to the Priory while Marion went downhill to her aunt's cottage.

"I'm coming to think that there was only one dog," said Brand. "Theo's dog."

Marion nodded. "When I think of it, I have no memories of Scruff in Edwina's cottage. That's not to say," she went on quickly, "that he was not there. As I keep telling you, my memories are vague at best. What about Edwina's letters? Did they tell you anything new?"

"Only by omission. Hannah's name was never mentioned. I wonder why."

Marion sighed. They didn't seem to be getting anywhere. Mrs. Love was the only real lead they had, and Marion was impatient to meet the lady.

She learned that there was more to their trip than interviewing Mrs. Love. Brand was expected to put in an appearance at several key political functions leading up to the election and, as his fiancée, she would be expected to put in an appearance, too.

She made no protest. In the first place, an announcement of their engagement had already appeared in the local paper. In the second place, this was all part of Brand's plan to throw their villain off the scent. No one knew their real purpose in going to Brighton. Everyone thought they were going for the election.

It was a clever scheme and she was determined not to let Brand down.

That did not mean that she didn't give a thought to her sisters. But as Brand pointed out, they were no threat to anyone, since they had not even been born when Hannah disappeared. All the same, Andrew had agreed to watch over them, and the groundsmen had been instructed to keep a close watch on the cottage in case the thief returned.

# Chapter Thirteen

David Kerr stood well back from the curtained window of the Castle Hotel's dining room and watched as Mr. Hamilton handed Lady Marion into his coach. He continued to watch as the coach moved off. When it turned the corner into Marine Parade, he returned to his table and snapped his fingers to call a waiter over.

"Claret," he said, "and the best the house has to offer."

He smiled complacently, thinking that his luck was about to turn.

He had not come to Brighton with the object of finding Marion. When he'd left London, he'd assumed that she had practically bankrupted herself to pay him off, and money could not be got out of a stone. Though he'd seen her in town with Hamilton, it had never occurred to him that Hamilton's interest was serious. Why should it? He was one of the richest men in England. He could pick and choose his women, and Marion was as exciting as a wooden doll.

Leastways, that's how he used to think of her, when

he'd been engaged to her. Not that he would have married her. For one thing, her dowry was too small. For another, she wasn't the kind of woman who appealed to him. She was too well-bred, too much the dutiful daughter, too mousy. Even her looks were mousy. She was just a pawn he used to get to her father.

Life was full of surprises. When he'd tracked her down in London, he hardly recognized her. She'd learned how to dress and do her hair. But you couldn't change character. She was still just a pawn he could move at will.

When he'd read the announcement of her engagement in last week's *Gazette*, his jaw had dropped. He was wishing then that he'd asked her for more money to keep his mouth shut. The more he'd thought about it, however, the more he'd come to see that this engagement could work to his advantage. The money that had come to her from her aunt's estate was a pittance compared to the money that would come to her from her wealthy husband. He foresaw a happy future for himself, with a regular income—all courtesy of Marion.

The waiter brought the bottle of claret and poured a little into his glass. He sipped it slowly, tasting the flavor, rolling it around his tongue like the connoisseur he was. It was light and clean, the way claret should be. "Excellent," he said, and held out his glass for the waiter to fill.

He loved the claret, loved the Castle Hotel with its graceful, long windows and finely appointed rooms. Everything was of the best quality. Unfortunately, it was beyond his means, but he enjoyed loitering in the lobby or the taproom and occasionally sitting down to dinner. His own hotel was adequate but hardly in the same class. His trouble was that money slipped through his fingers. His only asset was his wits.

It helped that he looked like a typical English gentleman, conservative, pleasant to look upon rather than handsome, with the kind of face both men and women trusted. His manners were impeccable; he could turn a graceful compliment; he was a good listener. It was just as well that no one could read his mind or they would know that his quick intelligence was calculating the odds, deciding which gullible fool would be his next victim.

If only fate had decreed that he was to be a rich man, he wouldn't have had to resort to soliciting "gifts" and "loans" from his wealthier "friends." They called it "blackmail," but that was a criminal offence and he did not see himself as a criminal. He wasn't the one with something to hide.

He ordered a fillet of Torbay sole with all the trimmings, then he sat back in his chair, sipping his claret, contemplating how he could take advantage of this extraordinary stroke of luck that had come his way.

The first time around, it was her father who had paid him off, and a very tidy sum it was, too, enough to set him up nicely in the New World, or so he'd thought. In fact, that experience had turned out to be a disaster. Gentlemen in Upper Canada did not lead lives of leisure. They worked their plantations like farmers, shoulder to shoulder with their hired men. He, of course, hadn't known the first thing about farming and had lost his investment in short order.

The next few years, he'd lived on slim pickings, but always at the back of his mind was the thought that if worse came to worst, he could always return to England and squeeze another "gift" from Marion's father. It hadn't worked out that way, for when he finally got the money together to come home, much to his dismay, he discovered that the earl had died and Marion was practically a pauper. All he could squeeze out of her was a paltry sum of money.

Things had changed when he discovered that she'd inherited a legacy from an aunt. He had enough now to set himself up in Brighton at the peak of the Season, when London's smart set came in their droves to enjoy the sea air. Society in Brighton was more informal than in London. If he played his cards right, he'd thought then, he might snag an heiress or a rich widow.

That's what it had come down to, but the announcement of Marion's engagement had changed his plans. Why saddle himself with a wife when he had his own private treasure chest to supply all his wants?

Marion.

He'd known that Hamilton would be in Brighton for the start of the Whig conference. He'd read about it in the *Gazette*. All the party's bigwigs would be here, at least those that passed for bigwigs in the southern counties. It hadn't taken him long to discover that this was their hotel of choice. He'd hoped to make an impression on Hamilton and be invited to Longbury, where he could approach Marion openly as her fiancé's friend. She would know that one word from him would dash all her hopes. A man like Hamilton with a bright future in politics would not wish to tie himself to Lady Marion Dane.

Once again, his plans were foiled. Hamilton, evidently, wasn't the kind of man to be impressed by an honest face, or a nicely turned compliment, or an ability to listen well. He knew this because the night before, when Hamilton entered the taproom and ordered a tankard of beer, he'd tried to strike up a conversation with him. All he'd got for his friendly overture was a hard stare that warned him that the man did not suffer fools gladly. It seemed sheer lunacy to him that such a man would enter politics, unless he meant to *scare* his constituents into voting for him.

All was not lost, however, for Hamilton had brought Lady Marion to Brighton. Kerr had been in the hotel lobby when they'd arrived yesterday morning and had quickly turned aside so that Marion would not see him. There would be a time and place to make his presence known to her, a time when her formidable fiancé was otherwise engaged. Her chaperon, a maid, was not likely to deter him. He knew how to get around maids.

The waiter brought his dinner, succulent fillet of sole in a cream sauce, new potatoes à la Française, and an array of fresh vegetables. He enjoyed every bite and did not blink at the exorbitant bill that the waiter presented at the end of his meal.

Marion would be paying for it.

Ash Denison watched the fair-haired gentleman leave the dining room, then he called the waiter over for his bill. He was puzzled by the man's behavior. He'd been in the taproom the night before with Brand when the stranger had tried to insinuate himself into their conversation. He'd made a blunder, however, when he'd tried to flatter Brand. Brand hated toadying in all its forms, and he'd soon frightened the voluble stranger away. Now, today, this same stranger had watched Brand and Marion as they left the hotel to go to a political rally on Brighton's common.

What was he up to?

When the waiter presented his bill, he said, "That gentleman who just left the dining room? I seem to know him from somewhere."

The waiter looked through the open doors to the lobby, then turned back to Ash. "Do you mean Mr. Kerr, sir?"

"Is he the young, fair-haired gentleman?"

The waiter nodded. "Mr. David Kerr. He farms in Upper Canada, or he used to."

"No," said Ash, "that's not the gentleman I was thinking of."

He paid his bill, got up without haste, and sauntered into the hotel lobby. Kerr was just leaving. Keeping a discreet distance between them, Ash went after him.

Marion had never been particularly interested in politics, and after listening to the candidates who addressed the mob of men surrounding the speakers' platform, she doubted she ever would be. No one seemed to care that there was a vast world out there in sore need of a helping hand. The most pressing concern of these locals seemed to be bigger and better breakwaters to protect the shoreline. Breakwaters, bridges, and roads—those were the issues that got this lot going.

Like other ladies, she was watching the proceedings from inside one of the carriages that were stationed around the edges of the grassy common. She was in Brand's carriage, and with her was Mrs. Monteith, the wife of one of the party officials, and her two lovely daughters. There were no ladies on the common. Men would not tolerate it. They seemed to think that the presence of females would inhibit debate; either that, or make them mind their language and manners.

Mrs. Monteith seemed to understand Marion's lack of enthusiasm. Her bright, birdlike eyes glinted with humor. "This isn't the election," she said. "It's only a rehearsal, you know, for our hopeful candidates to practice their rhetoric. They'll improve in time. They all do. Look! It's Mr. Hamilton's turn. Now, *he* is a real orator."

Marion watched as Brand stepped onto the platform.

He seemed both confident and relaxed. Not so Marion. Her nerves were stretched taut as though *she* were the one who had to make the speech. She forgot to be nervous when she started to listen. Brand didn't make a speech. He spoke as though he were addressing every person in that crowd, even the ladies. He acknowledged the contribution of the other speakers and the importance of local issues; then he took his hearers one step further. He spoke of the need to bridge the gap between rich and poor so that no child in the land would ever go to bed cold and hungry.

He did not say one thing that Marion had not read in one or another of his newspapers. She already knew that he was for universal education and an end to child labor, but his spoken words seemed to carry more power. Her heart burned within her. He made her feel that anything was possible, if only people had the will to change things.

"He's brilliant, isn't he?" Her voice was hushed.

The Monteith ladies laughed. Mrs. Monteith said, "Of course he is. But there's more to it than that. Mr. Monteith says that it's his passion that makes Mr. Hamilton such a compelling speaker. He cares about those on the edges of society because he has been there himself." She patted Marion's hand. "Mr. Monteith and I are so glad that Brand has found someone to share his life. It's been a lonely life, as I'm sure you know."

*A lonely life.* The words touched a chord deep in Marion's psyche. The fear of exposure had made her keep others at a distance. With Brand, she guessed it was the fear of rejection. But that was in the past, leastways for him. Anyone with eyes could see that he was admired and respected. What more could he want?

As the Monteith ladies spoke among themselves, she let her thoughts drift. The lady who married Brand

Hamilton, she reflected, would have to be interested in what interested him. He wasn't exactly your typical English gentleman with nothing more pressing on his mind than cutting a fine figure in society or idling his hours away in a round of pleasure.

He had ambition. He wanted a seat in Parliament. His wife would have to be an asset to him.

The thought was depressing.

She had a clear vision of sitting down to breakfast with Brand and their brood of children—all blue-eyed imps in the image of their father—and there, for all the world to see, in that morning's paper, would be emblazoned the story of her life.

Just thinking about it gave her the shudders.

"Ah," said Mrs. Monteith, "here is Mr. Hamilton now."

Marion sat up straighter and pinned a smile to her face, just as Brand appeared at the carriage window.

"Well, how do you think that went?" His eyes were on Marion.

She didn't want to sound like a gushing schoolgirl when the Monteiths were hanging on her every word, but she didn't want to spoil his moment, either. "You were very persuasive," she said warmly.

" 'Brilliant,' she called you," added the younger girl with a titter, "but it's no less than we expected from your betrothed."

A smile lightened his face.

Mrs. Monteith quelled her daughter with a quick frown. "One more heedless remark like that, Sally, and you can keep you grandmother company tonight while we go to the theater."

"Mama! I didn't . . . I won't . . ."

"Enough!" To Brand, Mrs. Monteith said, "If you don't win the nomination, I shall become a Tory." Then to Marion, "Shall we see you at Lady Hove's reception tomorrow night?"

"I'm looking forward to it," Marion replied.

This was stretching the truth. Lady Hove was Lady Veronica's mother, and all the party's faithful would be there, looking over not only the candidates for the nomination, but their future brides as well. She had to make a good impression for Brand's sake.

The ladies left to go to their own carriage, but Brand did not join Marion.

"It's not over yet," he said, glancing over his shoulder. "At these events, the candidates are expected to fraternize with the locals, you know, stand them a round of drinks."

She looked over her shoulder to the cluster of buildings at the opposite end of the common. Sure enough, men were streaming into the Cat & Fiddle.

"That sounds like bribery to me," she said, but there was a smile in her voice.

"Hardly. I doubt if there are twenty men in that mob who are eligible to vote."

She was astonished. *"What?"*

"They don't earn enough money to qualify."

"That doesn't sound democratic to me!"

"It isn't." He shrugged. "When men become educated, they will demand the vote. That's when things will change. Meanwhile, all we are doing is making them receptive to our ideas."

"With *beer?*"

"No. By meeting them on their home ground; by listening to their point of view and arguing ours. What if we supply the beer? We should. These are working men. They haven't been invited to Lady Hove's reception, and they wouldn't thank you for an invitation." He looked over his shoulder. "Come to think of it, most of the gentlemen who will be sipping champagne at the reception would rather be relaxing in the Cat & Fiddle over a jar of beer."

Her eyes were scanning the common. "I don't see Lady Veronica or Mr. Coyne."

"This isn't their sort of do. As I told you, very few of these men are eligible to vote, and those who can are Tories anyway. Elliot has better things to do with his time."

"But not you?"

"No, I disagree with Elliot. I want to know what people are thinking and feeling. They may not have the vote, but they can influence *my* thinking, and I can speak for them if I'm elected to Parliament."

His eyes suddenly bored into hers. "I'm leaving you in Manley's care. If you set foot outside the hotel, he goes with you. Whatever he tells you to do, you'll do. Do you understand?"

This sudden change of subject caught her off guard. "Yes, but—"

"No buts." He looked up at the box. "Manley, take Lady Marion back to the hotel. You have my instructions."

"Yes, sir!"

As the coach moved off, Marion folded her arms across her breasts and let out a huff of breath. It was mortifying to be treated like a child. She had come of age when her mother died; she'd had to take care of her family. She'd weathered storms Brand couldn't dream about. But he should have known her mettle, should have remembered how she'd tried to wrestle the gun away from their assailant.

If she was so brave, why couldn't she tell Brand the truth about herself?

She dwelled on that thought all the way back to the hotel.

The fair-haired gentleman watched Marion's coach traverse the length of the common, then he entered the tavern. He'd hoped to approach Marion while everyone's attention was on the speakers, but there was no getting past the eagle eyes of the coachman who stood watch over her, nor the ladies who shared her coach. But that was only a small setback. What he had to do now was get himself invited to Lady Hove's reception. That shouldn't be too difficult. He was well turned out and conversable. And votes were hard to come by in this Tory riding. All he need do was introduce himself to a few key people, inquire about vacant properties in the area that he might rent, and the result would be inevitable.

He bumped into a gentleman who had a glass of beer in each hand, though not hard enough to spill the beer. "I know you!" he said, injecting a large dose of enthusiasm into his voice. "You're the gentleman who spoke so eloquently about rebuilding the breakwaters. That was well done. I'm David Kerr, by the way."

"Michael Graves. How do you do."

Another gentleman joined them. "Congratulations," he said, looking at Graves. "You did very well."

Graves beamed. "Thank you. I say, why don't you both join my table and I'll stand you a beer?"

"Thank you," said the newcomer. "I'm Denison, Ash Denison."

There were the obligatory bows all round, then the three gentlemen made for a corner table in the taproom.

# Chapter Fourteen

Brand had sent a footman to Mrs. Love's house requesting an interview, and the following morning, he received a favorable reply. Since he and Marion were not expected until the afternoon, he suggested that they spend some time at the *Gazette* offices to give Marion an idea of what went into the production of a newspaper.

"You own the *Gazette*, I suppose," she asked with a sideways glance.

"I do, the first paper I ever owned."

"Then of course I want to see it."

Her enthusiastic response had him grinning like a schoolboy.

Her head was spinning by the time the tour was over, and trying to remember the names of all Brand's employees was beyond her power. What struck her was that Brand seemed as comfortable with the humble laborers in dispatch who heaved bundles of the *Gazette* onto carts for distribution in Brighton and its surrounds as he was with the managing editor and his staff.

"This was my office when I was a reporter," he said.

They entered a room that wasn't much bigger than a closet. Brand spread his hand on the flat of the desk as though he were greeting an old friend. He seemed so much at home here that she wondered why he had ever thought of entering politics.

When he sat at the desk and picked up a pen, she said, "What will happen to your papers if you're elected to Parliament?"

"What do you mean?"

"Will you sell them?"

The question seemed to surprise him. "Not at all. Even if I'm elected to Parliament, I could be ousted in the next election. Then what would I do? I'm not ready to retire."

She could well believe it. "But supposing you had to make a choice, what would you do?"

He regarded her quizzically. "Now, what has brought this on?"

It was a good question. She looked at the battered desk and the cramped quarters that had once served as his office and she knew, she just knew, that she was one of the favored few to get this close to him.

She gave a tiny shrug. "Just an idle question."

He thought for a moment. "You're asking me which one gives me the most satisfaction. Well, that's an impossible question to answer. Ask me again when I've served a term as a member of Parliament.

"However," he went on, "my chances of making it to Parliament are very slim. I think I've mentioned that this is a Tory stronghold?"

"You don't sound as though your heart will be broken if you have to give up politics."

"It won't be." He got up. "But I hate losing."

She laughed. She felt lighthearted, as though a weight had been lifted from her shoulders. "What do you say," she asked, "to a picnic lunch on one of the benches overlooking the harbor before we go to see Mrs. Love?"

"Lead the way."

"I remember Hannah very well," said Mrs. Love. A pained expression dimmed her blue eyes. "What is it you wish to know?"

Brand replied easily, "We thought you could help us find her, that is, if she is still alive."

Marion added, "No one seems to know what happened to my aunt when she left your employ."

Conversation ceased when a maid entered with the tea tray, and as their hostess busied herself with cups and saucers, Marion quietly studied her. By Marion's reckoning, Mrs. Love had to be in her mid-fifties. She was pleasantly plump, with fair hair turning gracefully to silver, and a face made all the more attractive by laugh lines around her eyes. She wore a high-waisted white muslin gown trimmed with openwork embroidery, and a lacy shawl was draped carelessly around her shoulders.

It looked to Marion as though Mrs. Love would be an amiable employer. She was a welcoming sort of person, and had invited her and Brand into her home as though they were honored guests, though their warm reception might also be credited to Brand's acquaintance with Dr. Hardcastle.

"Thank you," she said, accepting the tea Mrs. Love offered.

Her attention now turned to her surroundings. It was an elegant room, but comfortable, much like its owner.

Everything was done in blue and gold with accents of white. There were, however, added touches that gave the room character—a basket of knitting tucked under an escritoire, a tambour frame with a needle in it, and that morning's *Gazette* folded neatly and resting at one end of the sofa that was occupied by their hostess.

Marion looked at Brand, waiting for him, as they had agreed beforehand, to take the lead. As he'd pointed out, as a newspaperman, he knew how to conduct an interview, when to press and when to hold back.

Brand was concentrating on managing his cup and saucer. He tried not to make a face as he sipped his tea. He didn't want to offend the lady, especially as it was obvious that she had been reading one of his newspapers when they were shown in.

One sip was all he could stomach before he put his cup and saucer down on the sofa table. "We were hoping you could tell us about Hannah's friends. Someone must know something."

Mrs. Love concentrated on stirring her tea. "I'd like to help you," she said, "but I have no idea where Hannah is. She did not write to me after she left here and I did not expect her to." She looked at Marion. "Hannah was not exactly an exemplary employee. Can't we leave it at that?"

Marion was startled. No one had ever hinted that Hannah had left Brighton under a cloud. Longbury, yes, but not Brighton.

"No, we can't," replied Brand. "You see, I made a deathbed promise to her sister, Edwina Gunn, that I would try to discover what happened to Hannah all those years ago, and I mean to keep my promise." He gentled his voice. "I'm afraid Edwina feared the worst."

"Feared the worst?" repeated Mrs. Love, her brow knit in perplexity.

"That Hannah had done away with herself."

His words jolted both ladies. Marion's cup rattled in its saucer. Mrs. Love's mouth fell open.

Coming to herself quickly, Mrs. Love said, "I don't believe that for a moment! Hannah may have been a disturbed girl—that is, too romantic and ingenuous for her own good—but she was not dispirited. She would never take her own life."

"Do you think it's possible that she eloped with someone?" Brand asked.

"Now, that is far more likely, given Hannah's romantical turn of mind."

Hands loosely clasped, Brand leaned forward in his chair. "You see our dilemma? Lady Marion and I don't know what to believe. Why don't you tell us about Hannah, about her work here as a governess. Who were her friends? Where did she go in her free time? And why did she leave here?"

Mrs. Love frowned into her teacup. "To blazes with this," she finally declared. She smiled at Brand. "Mr. Hamilton, there is a decanter of Madeira in the sideboard. I think we could all do with something a little stronger than tea, don't you? Would you mind doing the honors while I set my thoughts in order?"

Brand was happy to oblige.

"The children loved her from the moment she walked into the nursery. I used to think that Hannah had the imagination of a child." Mrs. Love paused to sip from her glass. "She could make up stories about anything and everything—a favorite toy, a piece of furniture. The butcher's boy wasn't the butcher's boy. He was a prince on whom a wicked witch had cast a spell. My husband wasn't impressed; he thought that Hannah was filling the girls' heads with nonsense. But he could not deny that they were making progress. Hannah had them write out their own stories, and they became voracious readers. Not only that, but they were happy. So I was happy, too."

As Mrs. Love spoke, Marion was transported back to that long-ago holiday in Longbury. That's how she remembered Hannah. A walk in the woods wasn't a walk. They were explorers in the jungles of the Amazon. It was like being out with Clarice.

Mrs. Love took another reviving sip of Madeira. "What we did not realize at the time was that Hannah's imagination did not stop with the children. How can I say this without making poor Hannah out to be a vixen? You asked about her friends. Mr. Love and I included her in all our parties and encouraged her to make friends of young girls the same age as she. They were nice girls, but Hannah did not go out of her way to please them. Her interest would fix on one young man after another. If he smiled at her, he was head over heels in love with her. If he asked her to dance, he had designs on her virtue. She was the heroine of all her make-believe stories, and I believed her."

"What did you do?" asked Brand.

"I stopped inviting those young men to my parties, and warned my friends about their conduct. I'm sorry to say that I did them a great wrong. Oh, I'm not saying that they were entirely innocent, but Hannah did lead them on."

Marion was shaking her head. "That doesn't sound like Hannah to me."

"Doesn't it?" Mrs. Love smiled faintly. "You were only

a child then, of course, and, as I said, my girls adored her. She could enter all their games. They're married now, with their own families, but they still remember Hannah fondly. They have no idea how it all ended."

"How did it end?" asked Brand.

Mrs. Love shook her head sadly. "One young man made an almighty scene right here in this room. He was desperately in love with Hannah and wanted to marry her, but Hannah would have none of him."

She visibly shuddered. "One or two disappointed lovers I could accept, but now I began to have my doubts, and when Mr. Robson showed us one of Hannah's letters, my doubts were resolved. Not only had she led this young man on, but she had made my husband and me out to be ogres! He thought he was rescuing her from a life of drudgery.

"She denied everything, said that the letter was a forgery and that Mr. Robson had mistaken her interest for something stronger."

She looked up at the portrait above the mantel. A gentleman in his prime stared stolidly back at her. "My late husband," she said, as though someone had asked her to identify the subject in the portrait. "I thought he was going to have an apoplexy. His face turned purple when he read her letter."

Another sigh escaped her and she looked at her guests. "Hannah was the only calm person in this room. She was dignified. One might almost say majestic."

After a silence, Brand ventured, "So you dismissed her?"

"It never came to that. She dismissed herself. I shall never forget her words. The great love of her life was waiting for her in Longbury. She had only accepted this position to test their love. And now she knew."

She looked at Marion. "I wrote to your aunt to apprise her of the situation. After all, Hannah was very young, and her sister was a good deal older. I wasn't trying to make trouble for Hannah, but I thought she needed close supervision."

Marion didn't know what to say. She didn't know what she believed. The picture of Hannah that she had carried in her mind all these years didn't fit the young woman Mrs. Love had described.

Brand said slowly, "Did Hannah tell you the name of the man she had left behind in Longbury?"

A look of surprise crossed Mrs. Love's face. "No. Quite frankly, by that point, I would not have believed anything she said. I thought then, and still think, that he was a figment of her imagination."

Marion's thoughts were on the Hannah she had known and admired as a child. "She had a dog," she said. "His name was Scruff. Do you know what happened to it?"

Mrs. Love shook her head. "She must have acquired the dog in Longbury." She leaned forward and spoke directly to Marion. "Apart from your aunt Edwina, we told no one about Hannah. As you may imagine, we had no wish to become embroiled in a scandal or cause gossip. We left it to your aunt to deal with her sister."

"Thank you," said Marion, not knowing what else to say.

Not long after, they rose to go.

"By the way," said Brand, "whatever happened to Mr. Robson?"

"Oh, he's happily married and living in the north of England. He had tears in his eyes that night. He said that he couldn't believe the change in Hannah, that he didn't know her at all. Well, that's how I felt, too. What my husband said doesn't bear repeating."

"And the letters Hannah wrote to Mr. Robson?"

"I sincerely hope he kept his promise and consigned them to the fire. Well, he would, wouldn't he? No man saves keepsakes from a woman who has made a fool of him."

After expressing their thanks for Mrs. Love's patience and frankness, Brand and Marion left the house.

As soon as the carriage moved off, Brand looked at his watch. "We have hours to go before the reception." He lowered the window and shouted to Manley on the box, "Show us the sights, Manley. This is Lady Marion's first visit to Brighton. Take us to the Pavilion."

Marion didn't care about seeing the sights. Her impatience showing, she said, "How much do you believe of what Mrs. Love told us?"

Brand sighed and took her hand in his. He knew that she wouldn't pull away or try to disengage from him. During the few days of his convalescence, she'd become accustomed to his touch. She would lend him her arm for support. Occasionally, she would go so far as to put her arm around his waist when they were out walking. Now that he had recovered from the gunshot wound, however, he was hard pressed to find excuses to touch her or have her touch him.

Her gloved hand rested trustingly in his, and he wondered what she would do if he peeled the glove from her fingers and kissed her open palm.

"Brand?" Her anxious eyes gazed into his. "Are you feeling all right? This hasn't been too much for you, has it?" She pulled off her glove and touched her fingers to his brow. "You don't feel feverish."

He thought he felt her fingers tremble and wondered

whether, like Hannah, he was allowing his imagination to run riot. Time would tell. He had a week with Marion to himself. No families running circles around them, no prowler stalking them, just he and Marion getting to know each other better.

Except, of course, that they had a mystery to solve, and he had a duty to turn up at party meetings to get to know his constituents.

"Brand?"

He gave himself a mental shake. After thinking about her question, he said seriously, "I believe that Mrs. Love is a decent, honest woman. She certainly believes what she told us."

"But Hannah's character? I can't believe she was a schemer or told so many lies."

"Maybe she didn't realize what she was doing." He squeezed her hand. "Listen to me, Marion. We can't always tell what goes on in someone's mind. We may think we know that person, but we don't. I knew a boy at school like that. He told the most vivid stories of his holidays with his father. Every summer, they went big-game hunting in Africa, and we all believed him. Turns out, his mother was a widow and lived very modestly in a village on the east coast of Scotland, and that's where Nigel spent his holidays."

"What happened to him? Did he run away when he was found out?"

"Lord, no! He said that his mother had lied because she was jealous of his father. The thing is, his imaginary life was so much better than his real life that I believe the two became confused in his mind."

She looked at him keenly. "Is that what you think about Hannah? That she was confused about what was real and what was not?"

He took a moment to consider her words. "I think," he said carefully, "that she liked to dramatize. You heard Mrs. Love. Hannah was romantical and ingenuous. Sometimes things got out of hand, as with Mr. Robson. She was playing a dangerous game."

She nodded and gazed down at their clasped hands. "That's what I think, too. Maybe Edwina knew as well. Maybe that's why she kept a close eye on Hannah, even before she got that letter from Mrs. Love."

She looked up at him. "Yet she was fun to be with."

"Yes, children would think so." He didn't add that some of the most depraved criminals he'd come across in his time as a newspaperman could have charmed the birds from the trees. "She was like a child herself," he said eventually. "We should pity her."

There was a tremor in her voice when she spoke. "Do you think that Hannah did away with herself? After all, she did go home to Longbury in disgrace."

His voice was very firm. "Absolutely not! In the first place, people who do away with themselves always leave a note, and in the second, this mystery is not finished yet, not when someone put a gun to your head and put a bullet in my thigh."

"Then why did you mention it to Mrs. Love? Suicide, I mean?"

"Because, in my experience, people become tight-lipped when the word 'murder' is mentioned, fearing they may incriminate some innocent person."

Admiration gleamed in her eyes. "That was clever," she said.

"Yes, wasn't it?"

She laughed, but her smile soon faded. "We're no farther ahead, are we, Brand?"

"Oh, I wouldn't say that. We know that there was

someone in Longbury whom Hannah regarded as the great love of her life."

"What if he was a figment of her imagination?"

He shook his head. "She didn't invent any of the other men in her life. According to Mrs. Love, she led them on. Perhaps the love of her life wasn't as forgiving as Mr. Robson. Let's hope that she wrote him letters, too, and he has kept them. Maybe those are the letters our thief was after."

After a moment, she said, "Perhaps she eloped with the great love of her life."

"Without leaving a note?" He fell silent as his mind slotted bits and pieces he had learned about Hannah into a semblance of order. "No," he said finally. "Hannah was playing to an audience. She would have left a note."

"Yes," she said slowly, "I think you're right about that, too. But how will we find him after all these years?"

"We'll do what every good newspaperman does. We'll ask questions, but we'll be very discreet. And I haven't given up hope of your memory returning. I'm not expecting you to put everything in its proper sequence, but some small thing may come back to you that will break the case. Now, can we forget about Hannah for a little while and enjoy the sights of Brighton?"

He lowered the window to give her a better view. It was a beautiful summer day with a warm breeze wafting in from the Channel. For the first little while, Marion could not draw her thoughts away from Hannah, but when they came into the square and she caught sight of the Pavilion, the Prince Regent's summer palace, she let out a breath. She had never seen anything like it. The huge dome of the stables, floating high above the prince's residence, seemed like something out of an Arabian fantasy.

She was intrigued by the shops, surprised by the droves of fashionable ladies and gentlemen who promenaded on Brighton's leafy streets, and awed by ladies who drove their high-wheeled phaetons like seasoned whipsters.

She turned to Brand with a smile. "It has the feel of London, only much freer and gayer."

"That's because the Prince Regent is in residence. When he returns to London, Brighton will become just another sleepy country town, much like Longbury."

"There are worse fates," she said tartly, as though he'd insulted Longbury, and she stuck her head out the window again.

Brand relaxed against the banquette. He had seen the sights before, many times, and he did not wish to see them again. His pleasure came from watching Marion. He was remembering what he had learned about her in London, that she had never been presented at Court or enjoyed the round of parties and balls that other young women of her class expected as their right. She had spent her whole life in a country backwater and, in the last few years, had devoted all her energies to raising her two motherless sisters.

Something, some small part of the picture, was missing. Marion, he had discovered, wasn't the shy retiring wallflower she seemed at first sight. If she'd wanted that Season in London—and what young woman wouldn't?—her cousin Fanny would have been delighted to sponsor her.

So, what was he missing? What was she keeping from him?

Thoughts of her former suitor were never far from his

mind. What had that bounder done to make her so wary of men? Had he seduced her, then discarded her? Why wouldn't she confide in him?

He straightened when Marion suddenly gasped and flung herself back against the banquette.

"Marion, what is it?" He got up and stood over her.

"My left eye," she cried. "There's a piece of grit in it, soot, I don't know what, but it hurts like the devil."

Tears were coursing down her cheeks as she scrubbed her eyes.

"Don't rub your eyes." His voice was stern. "Open them wide. I'll get it out. That's right. Relax."

"Easy for you to say," she grumbled, and sniffed.

He removed her bonnet, then put one knee on the banquette to steady himself, and with thumb and forefinger, he held her eye open. "I see it. Hold still." He used the fold of his handkerchief and delicately edged the speck of grit to the corner of her eye. One little dab dislodged it, and he smoothed it away. "There. I got it," he said.

She closed her eyes and breathed out a long sigh. "That feels wonderful." Smiling, she opened her eyes and looked up at him. "Thank you."

He was fascinated by the long sweep of her lashes, arrested by the smile in her eyes, lustrous eyes that had trapped his gaze so that he could not look away. He felt the change in her breathing; her lips parted.

"Brand?" she murmured.

She couldn't possibly know what she did to him when her eyes took on that fragile, appealing look. He knew he could bring her to passion. What he didn't know was whether it was the wisest thing he could do. He didn't want her to think of him as another David Kerr.

He braced himself with both hands on the banquette and lowered his head so that his lips hovered an inch from hers. "You're playing with fire again, Marion," he murmured.

With a supreme effort of will, he pushed himself away from the banquette and sat down beside her. He gave himself a moment to catch his breath. Arms folded across his chest, he turned his head to look at her. Strands of fair hair had slipped the confines of their pins and blew about her face in adorable abandon. Her face was flushed, and those lovely gray eyes, her best feature in his opinion, were staring at him as though she did not like him at all.

Oddly enough, his ability to fan her temper only added to her appeal. He'd never seen her lose her temper with anyone else.

Suppressing a grin, he said, "This is the second time you've made love to me in a moving coach. You're a dangerous woman, Lady Marion Dane. Next time—"

"Next time, I'll make sure that my chaperon is with me!"

His brows rose. "Will that make you behave?"

She surprised him by spreading her open hand on his thigh. His body quickened, then slowed when she increased the pressure. Her fingers were brushing against his wound, not enough to hurt him, but enough to make her point.

She smiled into his eyes. "I hope so, because if I lay my hands on you again, you are going to require the services of Dr. Hardcastle."

She removed her hand and looked around for her bonnet. As she tied the ribbons under her chin with quick, efficient fingers, he found himself smiling again, and it occurred to him that, around Marion, smiling was becoming a habit with him.

Now, where had he heard that?

Her brow went up, regal, commanding, putting him in his place. "You were going to show me the sights. Is this all there is?"

# Chapter Fifteen

Marion dressed for the reception with particular care.
Her white stockings were of the finest silk. Her new stays
nipped in her waist and pushed up her bosom to give
her the fashionable silhouette. She'd worn the gown
before, but only once, because it was a dress for special
occasions, and the sheer gauze over its lavender under-
dress was extremely flattering to her gray eyes and fair
hair.

But it was her new shoes that sent her into transports
of delight. They were lavender silk evening pumps, tied
with ribbons, with heels that added precious inches to
her height. Ash Denison had found them for her in a
shop on Ship Street when she told him that she hadn't a
thing to wear. That they pinched her toes and made walking difficult did not detract from her pleasure one bit.

It was the thought of Lady Veronica and all the other
beauties who had graced Brand's arm at his grandmother's fête that made her take such pains with her appearance. Mrs. Chandos would be there and, no doubt,

Miss Lacey, Miss Byrd, and Miss Stead as well. Marion was Brand's betrothed and, though it was only playacting, she meant to do him proud.

Playacting made her think of Hannah, and she sighed.

"I'm sorry, milady." Doris, her maid, put down the comb she'd been using to tease little curls and strands of hair to frame Marion's face. "Did I hurt you?"

"Not at all." Marion smiled into Doris's anxious eyes. "I was concentrating on breathing. Perhaps you could let out my stays a little?"

Doris, who could not have been more than eighteen, shook her head. "Not unless you wear a different gown. The waist is very small."

"Mmm," said Marion. "I'd forgotten that there is a price to pay for a woman's vanity."

"Shall I choose another gown?"

"Certainly not!" Marion rose and surveyed her reflection from every angle. Her eyes seemed to reflect some of the lavender of the gown; her skin seemed softer. The amethyst drop earrings, her only jewelry, were the perfect complement to the curls framing her face. And her waist was as tiny as a man's handspan.

"I'll have a tantrum if you try to take this gown away from me," she said.

Doris laughed. "You look lovely, milady. I'm sure that Mr. Hamilton won't be able to take his eyes off you all evening."

Marion didn't want to deflate her maid's enthusiasm, but she knew better. There would be no dancing at this reception, since its primary purpose wasn't pleasure. It was a political gathering of the faithful, and Brand would be right in the thick of it.

She was putting on her long white gloves when

someone knocked at the door. Doris ran to open it and Brand stepped into the room. He was looking at his watch. "We're running late," he said.

Marion gave a thin smile. "And you look very nice, too," she said.

In fact, he looked gorgeous in his dark fitted jacket, and the tiny scar below his brow gave him a decidedly rakish air.

When he looked at her, really looked at her, he didn't smile, didn't say a word. He looked as though he'd had the wind knocked out of him, and that was the best compliment of all.

"Doris," she said, "if you get bored, go downstairs to Mrs. Barton's suite." Mrs. Barton was the manager's wife. "She said that she gets lonely of an evening and could do with a bit of company."

"Thank you, milady. I may do that when I'm finished here."

"And don't wait up for me. I'm quite capable of seeing to myself."

Marion picked up her lavender pochette, draped a sheer gauze stole over her shoulders, and sailed from the room. Brand followed in her wake.

She teetered a little as she went down the stairs, but that was to be expected in her new shoes.

When Brand handed her into the carriage, there was a tiny furrow on his brow. "You look lovely," he said, "and I'm sure I'll be the envy of every man there. But you can hardly walk in those shoes. They're not practical. There's still time to change them."

So much for taking his breath away.

She turned her head and raised one imperious eyebrow. "I'll let you into a little secret, Brand. Women don't dress to please men but to impress other women.

Every lady at that reception tonight won't care a straw
that my shoes are impractical. She'll be dying to know
where I bought them."

"And where did you buy them?"

She shrugged. "I don't know. Ash got them for me.
He seems to know a lot about ladies' fashions."

Brand hunched down on the banquette. "Ash," he
said. "I might have known."

Hove Hall was on the east side of Brighton, toward the
village of Hove, and was approached through an avenue
of elms that formed a canopy above their heads. The
house was neoclassical in design, a larger and more opu-
lent version of Marion's home in the Lake District, the
one that had passed to her cousin on her father's death.
There was another difference. Her own home had gradually become shabby as her father's funds had dwindled.
It was obvious to Marion that there was no lack of
money here.

As they mounted the stone steps of the portico, they
heard the babble of voices above the strains of the orchestra. People were everywhere—on the staircase, in the
hall, in the grand salon—and liveried footmen in pow-
dered wigs moved among them, dispensing champagne
in long-stemmed glasses.

"If even half these people are Whigs," Marion said in
Brand's ear, "I'd be surprised if you don't wrest the seat
away from the Tories in the by-election."

"I only wish! No, these are mostly hangers-on or im-
posters; you know, they profess the true faith only as
long as the wine keeps flowing. When the wine dries up,
so do they."

"And that doesn't bother you?"

"I'm not paying for the wine."

"Cynic," she murmured, but her eyes were smiling.

He drew her hand through his arm. "Come along, I'll introduce you around." His voice turned serious. "Remember, not everyone here wants me to win the nomination. If they make insulting remarks, let them pass. That's the nature of politics."

She couldn't imagine Brand Hamilton allowing an insult to pass. He didn't have a temper, but he was a proud man. Or maybe it was just that he was sensitive. He didn't speak much about his life with his grandfather, but she knew it hadn't been easy. He was much more at ease talking about his newspapers or politics.

"Why so serious?"

She cleared the frown from her brow. "I don't think," she said playfully, "that you got that scar above your eye by allowing insults to pass."

He patted her hand. "That was in my dueling days. I'm all reformed now."

A voice halted their progress to the grand salon. "Brand!"

Mrs. Chandos, stunning in slinky red silk, smiled up at Brand, then turned the full volume of her smile on Marion. "Lady Marion," she acknowledged with a slight inclination of her head. "I've just heard the news. Had I known that this old bachelor"—she gestured to Brand— "was on the marriage mart, I would have snapped him up while I still had the chance."

It was a joke, so they all laughed, though the laughter on Marion's part was a little strained. Brand was still on the marriage mart, only Mrs. Chandos didn't know it.

Mrs. Chandos now looked around the crush of people. "There will be a few broken hearts here tonight, I shouldn't wonder."

"Amelia always exaggerates," said Brand, running his finger under his collar.

Marion merely smiled.

"Lady Marion Dane," said Mrs. Chandos reflectively. "Any relation to Morley Dane, who recently inherited his uncle's title?"

"Morley is my cousin. My father was his uncle."

Mrs. Chandos's smile died. "What a pity you weren't born a boy!"

"Not as far as I'm concerned." Brand swung one arm around Marion's shoulders and hugged her to his side. "You're forgetting, Amelia, Marion is betrothed to me."

"Silly me." She stifled a giggle. "What I meant was it's a pity that Lady Marion can't inherit the title and lands. No matter, she has the name. Lady Marion Dane—that means something."

Her babble of words was cut off when she was pounced on by a young gentleman who carried her off.

There was a silence, then Marion said, "Correct me if I'm wrong, but that gentleman's face seems familiar. Isn't he the one who rescued you from Mrs. Chandos at your grandmother's fête?"

Brand nodded. "Tommy Ruddle. He's always ready to oblige his friends. Besides, I think he is sweet on Amelia. I know she's a silly woman, but she isn't malicious. Her heart is in the right place."

"What does that mean?"

"She's a Whig, of course."

She laughed, as she was meant to, but at the back of her mind, she was thinking of Amelia's words.

Brand stayed with Marion for about half an hour, but it was just as she'd known it would be. He was soon in the thick of things, hailed by constituents or supporters who wanted a private word in his ear. She waved him away with the assurance that she was quite capable of fending for herself.

Her feet gave out before her smiles did. The ladies' cloakroom was upstairs. All she wanted was to find a quiet spot where she could remove her shoes and stretch her cramped toes. If there were other ladies there, they would understand only too well.

On the gallery, she came face-to-face with Lady Veronica. Marion had nothing against the girl except that she was a marquess's daughter and seemed very sure of herself: confident, aloof, and above the company. She hadn't seen Lady Veronica mingling.

The younger girl was standing at the balustrade sipping champagne. Marion searched her mind for something to say besides a bland inanity when Lady Veronica spoke.

"I'm green with envy," she said. "Where did you get those divine shoes?"

Marion's mouth dropped open. In that moment, she was completely won over. She lifted her skirts and looked down at her shoes. They were, indeed, divine.

She smiled ruefully. "I'll have blisters on my toes tomorrow."

"A small price to pay for perfection."

"Yes, isn't it?" Oddly enough, her shoes didn't pinch nearly as much as they had a few moments before. "Lord Denison found them for me. A shop on Ship Street. He knows what women like."

"I can see that."

Lady Veronica beckoned to a footman carrying a tray of drinks, and when he came up the stairs, she plucked a glass of champagne from it and offered it to Marion. "What shall we drink to?"

"To us," quipped Marion, "because . . . well . . . without us, where would our men be?"

It was a glib response off the top of her head, but it had a powerful effect on the other girl. Her bottom lip trembled. Her eyes bored into Marion's. "Easy for you to say. You don't suffer from nerves. I've been watching you for the last half hour. People really like you. I'm like a fish out of water. My father says that I'm no help to Elliot, that I'm a liability, in fact. He says that Elliot will lose the nomination because of me. But the more my father rants at me, the more I freeze."

Marion looked down at her shoes, wondering how the conversation had taken such a bizarre turn. She then looked at Lady Veronica's glass.

"Do you think I've had too much to drink?" asked Lady Veronica, divining Marion's thought. "Have I made a fool of myself?"

Marion shook her head. "I think your father has made a fool of himself. Of course you feel like a fish out of water. So do I. That's because we are new to this game. The more we practice, the more at home we'll feel."

"I saw you! You looked as though you were enjoying yourself."

"Look at me, Veronica," Marion said. "Can you tell that my feet are giving me hell?"

A laugh was startled out of Lady Veronica. "No. I take your point."

"Good." Marion set her glass on a side table. "Let's forget about my feet. Let's mingle with your father's guests and show them our mettle."

"Oh . . . I don't know. I'm not ready for that."

"We'll be together."

"You won't leave me?"

"I won't leave you," promised Marion.

She finally got to rest her sore feet during supper. Though she hadn't seen much of Brand, she felt relaxed and happy. The evening had gone off better than she expected. *She* had come off better than she expected. She could thank Lady Veronica for that. After her brave words about showing off their mettle, she'd had no choice but to be a good example.

Veronica's shyness had gradually melted, and now she and Ettie Monteith had gone off, arm in arm, to track down Ash Denison so that they could discover the name of the shop where he'd found Marion's divine shoes.

"You're smirking." Brand set a plate laden with savories on the table in front of her. "Either that or you've had too much champagne."

"I'm smirking," she said, "because, as I told you, my new shoes have made me the envy of every woman here." Her fingers hovered over her plate before she finally selected an artichoke tart. She took one nibble and made a small sound of pleasure before swallowing. "And now Lady Veronica and Mrs. Monteith's elder daughter have gone in search of Ash to find out where he bought my shoes."

She gave a cursory glance around the Long Gallery that served as the dining room on this occasion, but she could not make out Ash in that sea of faces.

Brand chuckled. "You won't find Ash here. Last I saw of him, he was being led by a very determined lady into the bowels of the conservatory."

"But there are no lights in the conservatory. Why would they go there?"

He raised his brows. "Use your imagination."

Enlightenment dawned. Ash had never shown the slightest interest in politics, yet he had accepted an invitation to Lord Hove's reception. Of course, there was a woman behind it! Everyone knew of Ash's reputation, and no one thought the less of him for it.

But this was a respectable do. There were no opera dancers or actresses here.

She leaned toward Brand and whispered, "Who is the lady?"

"I don't carry tales out of school." He gave her a lazy smile.

That smile got her dander up. "If she is a maid or an employee—"

"Don't be foolish. Ash would never take advantage of a defenseless girl, or any respectable girl for that matter. Didn't you hear me? The lady was leading him."

"She's married, then."

His eyes glinted down at her. "My lips are sealed."

She looked down at her plate and selected another tart. "Mrs. Milford is a widow, isn't she?"

"What?" He sounded startled.

"Mrs. Milford, you know, the lady who stood on my toes at Cousin Fanny's ball."

"I know who Julia Milford is!" Sighing, he reached for her hand. "She's a widow, but there have been plenty of others who weren't. They're not important. In fact, women have never played an important part in my life. Until now."

His thumb traced the lines of her palm, and she didn't know whether it was his warm touch or his words that made her breath catch. *Until now.*

His eyes captured hers. "I'm starting with a clean slate." He paused, then went on, "Can you say the same?"

She wanted to say yes, but she couldn't get the lie past her lips. "No," she said before her courage deserted her. "I don't think my slate will ever be clean."

"David?"

"Yes. David Kerr."

"What happened, Marion? Can't you tell me?"

She forced a smile. "We're not really engaged, Brand, so you have no right to ask me that question. And don't think I'm angling for a proposal of marriage. This is the wrong time and place to talk about it."

"And when will it be the right time?"

She couldn't hold his stare and looked away. "I don't know," she whispered. "Maybe . . . " She shook her head. "I don't know."

His face twisted and he dropped her hand. "Excuse me." He got up. "I think I need something stronger than champagne."

Before she understood his meaning, he pushed his chair out of the way and left her.

She watched him go with a hollow feeling inside her. Doing the right thing shouldn't make her feel so bad. Was it the right thing to do? She needed time to think.

She looked down at her plate and pushed it to the side. All her favorites were there, but she had lost her appetite.

"Marion?"

"Brand?" She looked up with a smile.

But it wasn't Brand who bowed over her hand. It was the man she hated and feared above all others, the man whom she'd last seen in Hatchard's book shop on Piccadilly when she'd given him her mother's emeralds, the only thing of value she had left to pay for his silence.

His lips were moving, but she couldn't hear his words for the roaring in her ears. Blood was pumping hard and fast to every pulse point in her body. She clutched at the table as her head began to swim.

"My, my," said that hateful voice, "I think you're surprised to see me."

His insufferable confidence had a steadying effect, and she breathed deeply to get command of herself. When she looked up at him, she made no attempt to conceal her hatred. He had enough sense to take a step away from the table.

"All I want," he said pleasantly, "is a word with you in private. Why don't we take a turn around the garden?"

A pleasant voice, a pleasant smile, a pleasing appearance—that was David. She wanted to spit on him.

She forced her knees to straighten as she got to her feet. He offered her his arm, but she shied away from it as though he had offered her a snake. Spine straight, she brushed by him without a word and made for the stairs.

Face like granite, Brand pushed past well-wishers in the inner hall, raising a few eyebrows in the process. This was the old Brand, grim-faced and unapproachable.

"Nerves, I shouldn't wonder," remarked one elderly sage to his neighbor. "The suspense of waiting for a final decision is bound to take its toll."

"I hope that's all it is," came the reply, "because I've already cast my vote for him."

Brand made straight for the library where he knew his host kept his best brandy. There were others of a like mind, the inner circle, who were smoking cheroots and making free with the selection of decanters on the sideboard.

He replied in a perfunctory way to their attempts to involve him in a conversation, and after pouring himself a generous measure of brandy, he excused himself and went through the French door to the terrace.

This is where Ash found him a few minutes later when he, too, came in search of something stronger than champagne. "Why the scowl?"

"Marion!" Brand said succinctly. He drained his glass. "Look, I'd better get back before she thinks I've deserted her."

"Ah, a lovers' tiff. I thought this was supposed to be a sham engagement?"

Brand was wishing he hadn't mentioned Marion's name. One thing was certain: He wasn't going to explain himself. Ash liked nothing better than to mock his friends who had fallen by the wayside, meaning that some woman or other had addled their brains to such a degree that they were willing to take that long, long walk to the altar. And maybe Ash was right. Maybe his wits were addled. One minute he was up and the next he was down. The specter of her lost love was always there between them.

He'd had enough of this. He'd wooed her with more restraint than a bloody saint could have shown. He knew damn well that she wasn't holding him off because she thought him beneath her. And he knew that if he pushed her he could have her in his bed. But David Kerr? How could he fight shadows?

He glanced at Ash to find his friend watching him with a speculative gleam in his eyes.

"I'd best get back," said Brand, and closed his lips firmly.

Ash grinned and put one hand on Brand's shoulder. "Too late. The lady has gone off with another gentleman. Don't scowl at me. It's quite innocent. They're walking in the garden. I passed them on my way here. He knew Marion in Keswick, I believe, though he has spent the last number of years farming in Canada."

"His name?"

The steel in Brand's voice wiped the grin from Ash's face. "David Kerr. Look, I checked him out after I met him at your hotel. He's exactly who and what he appears to be."

Whatever Brand was about to say was lost as his host clapped him on the shoulder. "The meeting is about to begin," said Lord Hove. "Come along, Brand. We're assembling in the library." He frowned at Brand's expression. "You did remember about the meeting?"

"Naturally," Brand replied.

Brand looked helplessly at Ash.

"I'll find Lady Marion," said Ash, correctly interpreting that look, "and make your apologies." When Brand still looked undecided, he added, "Leave everything to me."

# Chapter Sixteen

Her shock was beginning to wear off, and all the color that had drained out of her cheeks when she recognized David was surging back in full force. And with the return of her color came the determination to be done with him once and for all. She could not go on wondering where and when he would turn up, or what he would do. She'd been living in a fool's world to believe that this time she might be free and clear. He would never let her go.

He would have that private word with her as he had asked, but this time, it would be his last.

The gardens were lit by lanterns, hanging from poles set out at intervals along the paths and around the man-made lake. She had deliberately taken the lead, as if that small act of defiance made her more in command of the situation. She led him as far from the house as she could manage, away from prying eyes, but most of all, away from Brand.

At the edge of the lake, there was a dock with a boat tied to it. Here she turned to face the man she thought she had once loved. She'd thought him handsome then, considerate, gentlemanly, the epitome of a young girl's romantic fancies. Now she saw him as the devil incarnate.

He was out of breath and she was out of patience.

"Say what you have to say and have done with it," she said.

He shook his head. "Marion, Marion, is that any way to greet an old friend?"

She answered the question he hadn't asked. "You're out of luck this time, *old friend*." She threw the words back at him as an insult. "The cupboard is bare."

He smiled and scratched his chin. "I'm not asking you for money. I thought you might introduce me to your future husband, you know, persuade him to find me a lucrative position in one of his many enterprises."

Her hands fisted at her sides. She knew perfectly well that working for a living was the last thing on David's mind. He'd introduced Brand's name smoothly, obliquely, but she got his point. She was used to his roundabout way of coming at things. He would never admit to blackmail.

"I have no influence with Mr. Hamilton," she said.

His brow knit in perplexity, as though she'd spoken in a foreign tongue, then he smiled again, as a grown-up might smile at a rebellious child. "You underestimate yourself, Marion. I've kept my eyes and ears open all night. What I'm hearing is that marriage to an earl's daughter—to you, in fact—has considerably increased Mr. Hamilton's chances of winning the nomination."

He paused to adjust the cuff of one sleeve, then went on easily, "He has a rosy future ahead of him, and with you by his side, he should go far. It wouldn't surprise me if he were to become prime minister one day. Anyway, that's what I hear."

When she remained silent, his easy manner vanished, and his voice became razor sharp. "What do you think would happen to that rosy future if it became known that the lady he is engaged to marry has no claim to that title, and neither do her sisters because their parents never married?"

"They married!"

He gave a theatrical sigh. "If they did marry, prove it."

She stared doggedly up at him, saying nothing.

"You can't, can you? And if they did marry, they committed bigamy. Your father and mother set up house together when his first wife was still alive. You were seven years old when Lady Penrith died, Marion. The real Lady Penrith. That makes you—"

He looked around to make sure they were alone, then turned back with a sheepish grin. "I won't say the word. It would be ungentlemanly of me, but you know what I mean. Cheer up. Think of your good fortune. Once you are married to Hamilton, you'll have more money than you ever dreamed of. Think what you can do for your sisters. Isn't my silence worth something?"

Her breathing was hard and fast. "I already paid for your silence, not once, but twice. My mother's emeralds should have been enough for you."

"Marion, I got a pittance for them."

Her mind darted this way and that, but she knew there was no escape. Her father had paid this man for his silence, and when the money ran out, he'd come back for more. She had taken over where her father had left off. There was nothing left to give him, and even if there was, it would never be enough. There was only one way to be free of him.

Her hopes of a future with Brand didn't shatter so much as dissolve in a flood of unshed tears. She told herself that her hopes had been more like dreams anyway. At the back of her mind, there would always have been the dread that one day her parents' secret would be exposed, if not by David Kerr, then by someone else.

If there was one thing she had learned tonight, it was that Brand belonged in Parliament. That's where the laws of the land were made or changed. He was passionately committed to fighting the injustices that divided rich from poor, privileged from underprivileged. He didn't think in terms of a rosy future for himself. He wanted to serve to the best of his abilities.

Marriage to her would be a liability. Wasn't that the word Lady Veronica had used?

She felt a hand cup her shoulder and looked up. A smug smile had settled on David's lips.

"That's better," he said. "Now you're beginning to see reason. Trust me, Marion. You'll have Hamilton wrapped around your little finger in no time. The man is smitten with you. Everyone says so."

Each word pierced her heart like a splinter of glass. Each word made her realize just how much she was giving up. It wasn't wishful thinking on her part. Everything that was feminine in her nature knew that Brand cared for her as much as she cared for him. But all that meant to David was a weakness he could exploit for his own ends.

She had spent the last three years taking care of her family, doing everything in her power to keep them safe. And just when she thought she had succeeded, the past had caught up to her again.

It was too much to bear.

Her hand fisted and before she knew what she was

doing, she swung at him with all her might. Her blow struck him across the mouth and he reeled back with a howl of pain. He went too far, right to the edge of the dock. His flailing arms did not help him regain his balance, and in the next instant, he tumbled into the lake.

Marion nursed her sore hand, but the pain was forgotten when David's head appeared above the surface of the water.

"You're broken one of my teeth," he spluttered. "There was no call for violence."

His words brought her temper to the boil. "You can say that to me after the way you attacked me in London?"

He stopped spluttering. "What are you saying? I didn't attack you."

"Don't lie to me, David! Who else would set footpads on me in Vauxhall Gardens? Who else would push me down the stairs at the King's Theater? I might have broken my neck."

He was trying to hoist himself onto the dock, but the weight of the water in his clothes made his efforts useless. "That's absurd. If you broke your neck, you wouldn't be any good to me. Give me your hand and help me out of here before I drown."

"I'm more likely to give you my boot!" She inched away from him before he could grab her ankle. "You made sure there was somebody there to break my fall."

He blinked up at her. "What on earth are you talking about?"

His innocent look was almost convincing—almost, but not quite She crouched down so that she could see him better. "Let's not forget the notes you left."

"What notes?"

"'Silence is golden.' 'Let sleeping dogs lie.' Does that refresh your memory?"

"No. It does not! But if what you say is true, I'd say that someone is trying to scare you. Now will you give me your hand?"

"I don't care if you drown!"

When she straightened, he scowled. "Where are you going?"

"To tell Mr. Hamilton that I won't marry him."

"I don't believe you! No woman in her right mind would let Hamilton get away. Marion, come back here! I'll make you regret this! I swear I'll make you regret this!"

She could hear him cursing and swearing as she walked slowly back to the house. In spite of her brave words, Brand was the last person she wanted to see. Nor was she in the mood to make polite conversation with total strangers. All she wanted was a quiet place where she could nurse her wounds in private.

It was over. The truth would come out, and she need not fear David Kerr ever again.

The thought made her shudder.

As she neared the house, her steps slowed. She wasn't ready to face anyone yet. After glancing around, she veered off the path and made for a stone bench that was sheltered by the low-hanging branches of a laburnum tree. Here she sat, hugging herself to stop from shivering. After a while, it registered that supper must be over, because people were coming out of the house to view the gardens. She shrank back, hoping that no one would see her.

There was a lump in her throat she couldn't swallow. Her mind refused to think. Even her feelings were frozen.

A shadow blocked her light and she looked up to see Ash Denison.

"Where the devil have you been?" he began angrily, then his voice faded away. He peered down at her. "What's happened, Marion? You look as if you've seen a ghost."

Her lethargy would pass, she knew it would pass, but at that moment, all she wanted was to be left alone.

"I want to go home," she said. "I mean back to the hotel. Can you arrange it, Ash?"

His eyes gentled, as did his voice. "Let me get Brand. He's in a meeting right now, but I know he'll want to see for himself that you're all right."

"No," she said. "Let him be. It's only a headache. I'll feel better after a good night's sleep."

He gave her a searching look, then nodded. "You can go home in my carriage. I'll tell Brand about your headache."

"Thank you."

She felt a little disoriented on the walk to the drive where Ash's carriage was waiting, and missed the look Ash's coachman gave his master, but Ash was aware of it. Hawkins had expected to see another lady, not his best friend's betrothed.

Ash returned his coachman's freezing stare. As though he would stoop to trifling with a respectable lady, let alone his best friend's betrothed! His reputation as a rake was vastly exaggerated. He had some scruples.

A word in Hawkins's ear soon brought the coachman round, and he was all smiles when Ash handed Marion into the coach and shut the door.

"I'll tell Brand that you've gone home to nurse a headache," he said.

"Thank you."

He didn't want to leave her. She seemed ... withdrawn, beaten. What in hell's name had David Kerr said and done to put that look on her face?

In the same gentle voice, he said, "I'll come with you, just to make sure you get home safe and sound."

She gave a teary smile. "Thank you, Ash, but it isn't necessary. I'd feel obliged to make conversation with you." She touched a hand to her brow. "You do understand?"

Since he could not persuade her, he squeezed the hand that rested on the window frame. "I understand." To Hawkins he said, "I'll find my own way home. Make sure Lady Marion's maid is there to see to her mistress."

"Yes, my lord."

As soon as the carriage moved off, Ash retraced his steps to where he'd found Marion. When he'd first caught sight of her, she'd been coming from the direction of the lake. No one had been with her.

Then where was David Kerr?

He set off briskly, not really expecting to find Kerr, but as he neared the lake, he saw a group of gentlemen, all heaving and grunting, hauling another man out of a boat.

David Kerr.

Ash started forward and immediately took command. "My dear Mr. Kerr," he said, "I've warned Lord Hove to rope off this walk after dark. It's a dangerous spot. You might have drowned."

"The water is only four feet deep," one voice scoffed from behind Ash.

David Kerr blinked rapidly. "Lord Denison? Please tell these gentlemen that I have every right to be here. They seem to think I'm an interloper."

Ash cast a steely eye over the company. "Mr. Kerr is my friend," he said. "Need I say more?"

There were a few grumbles but the gentlemen backed off and one by one drifted away.

Ash went down on one knee. "My dear fellow, you're shivering." He spoke pleasantly, but his temper was anything but pleasant. He was sure David Kerr had put that hunted look on Marion's face, and he wanted to grab him by the throat and squeeze the truth out of him.

"Let's get you into dry clothes," he said, "then we'll talk."

The half-drowned man seemed to remember his dignity. He hauled himself up. "What I have to say," he said solemnly, "is for Mr. Hamilton's ears only."

"I'm glad to hear it because Mr. Hamilton, I know, has a few things he'd like to say to you, too. But first, let's get you into dry clothes."

Brand was too restless to give his full attention to the various speakers who rose, one after another, to endorse the candidate of their choice. There were six candidates for the nomination, but by the time the meeting had almost run its course, four had withdrawn from the race, leaving Elliot Coyne and himself still in the running. Lord Hove had the floor now, and as his voice droned on, Brand's thoughts dwelled on Marion, probing, weighing, trying to find the answer to why she would go off with a man who had jilted her.

He was jealous, of course, jealous and aggrieved. He'd thought Marion was his for the asking, but now he wasn't so sure, and he wondered if he really knew her at all.

He did not make friends easily, but that was largely by choice. For the most part, his friendships had been formed at school and university. He wasn't gregarious like Ash, nor did he want to be. He did not accept people at face value, but took his time to assess and weigh before he gave them his trust.

All that changed when Lady Marion Dane fixed him with one of her cool-eyed stares, and he'd realized that *he* was the one who was being assessed and weighed. The novelty had captivated him. Marion had captivated him. And the more she had kept him at arm's length, the more determined he had become to penetrate the veneer of reserve she used as a shield.

And he'd succeeded, with one major exception: David Kerr. Why was she so secretive about a man who should mean nothing to her? And what was he doing here?

He was still brooding on David Kerr when a round of applause drew him back to his surroundings. Everyone was looking at him, coming forward to congratulate him. While he'd been woolgathering, it seemed that Elliot Coyne had decided to throw his support behind him, and he'd won the nomination.

As soon as he could decently manage it, he made his escape. Ash was waiting for him at the foot of the stairs.

"I found her," Ash said at once, "and David Kerr as well. And no, they were not together, though there's no doubt in my mind that they quarreled. I sent Marion back to the hotel in my carriage, and yours is waiting for you. I'll walk you to it and tell you how things stand."

When they were clear of the house, Ash gave a concise account of what had happened while Brand was in the meeting, ending with, "There's something strange going on here. Marion seemed ... dejected ... beaten—I don't know how else to describe her, and Kerr ... " He shrugged as he groped for words, "Kerr is very much on his dignity, as though he is the injured party. Yet I sense that he's gloating about something. At any rate, he seemed to be relieved to hear that Marion had gone back to the hotel while you were still at the meeting. I think he wants to give you his version of events before she does. He's waiting for you in your carriage. I thought you could kill two birds with one stone, so to speak, you know, hear him out as you drive back to the hotel."

A thousand questions were circling in Brand's mind, but the one that made his temper blaze was what had David Kerr said or done to upset Marion.

He quickened his steps when the carriage came into view, but Ash's grasp on his arm brought him up short.

"Listen to me!" said Ash roughly. "If you go into that carriage ready to do battle, you'll never get a thing out of Kerr. Let your head rule you, not your heart. Think of Marion and what's best for her."

One jerk freed Brand's arm. "I am thinking of Marion, damn you!"

"No, you're not! You're thinking of the satisfaction you'll get if you beat Kerr to a pulp with your bare fists. Find out what he knows first, for God's sake."

Brand stood there, breathing hard and fast. Finally, he nodded. "You're right," he said. "I'll be as meek as a little lamb—then I'll kill him."

Ash laughed. Hands on his hips, he watched as his friend entered the carriage. There was no doubt in his mind that another bachelor friend had fallen by the wayside. If this went on, he'd be the last bachelor standing. What was so intriguing about marriage, he mused, that it could cause such havoc among his friends?

He liked Marion, really liked her. He could say the same about any number of women. But he liked the single life more.

He was whistling as he made his way back to the house, but he stopped when he saw Lady Griselda

Sneathe bearing down on him, her lovely features twisted in fury. He edged back when she came to stand in front of him.

Her shoulders rose and fell as she strove to master herself. "Do you know where I have been, Ash?"

He winced. He'd forgotten about her in the bustle of taking care of things for Brand. "In the conservatory?"

"Where you were supposed to come and fetch me when your carriage was ready! You promised to meet me there after supper."

"Ah. My carriage." He gave her a disarming smile, the one that never failed to seduce a woman from her righteous wrath. "I'm afraid I had to offer it to a lady in distress. You see, Griselda—"

His words were cut off when her hand lashed out and caught him across the face, jarring his teeth. "You . . . you faithless rake!" she declared, and she stalked off.

Ash nursed his sore jaw, thinking that it might be a long time before he could purse his lips to whistle.

Brand was glad of the gloom in the carriage, for it concealed the murderous rage that seethed inside him. He tried to hold on to Ash's advice: He must think only of what was best for Marion.

Ash was right about something else. David Kerr had the air of someone who had been wronged. *The injured party*, Ash called it.

"Let me see if I have this right," said Brand, modulating his voice to sound neutral. "You say that Marion attacked you?"

Kerr sighed. The faint light from one of the carriage lamps filtered inside to show that he held a folded handkerchief pressed to his lips. It also showed that he had changed into a footman's livery—Ash's doing, Brand supposed.

Another sigh from Kerr. "I should not have been surprised. We were engaged to be married once, you know, but I called it off because she is so unpredictable. Her temper is not to be trusted. There was no call to attack me. She broke one of my teeth—that's how vicious she is."

With as much patience as he could muster, Brand said, "There must have been a reason for the attack." He could not help adding, "I know it's not because you broke your engagement to her. Marion doesn't hold grudges. So what happened tonight?"

"I'll tell you what happened." Kerr's voice had lost some of its composure. "She accused me of setting footpads on her in Vauxhall Gardens, yes, and pushing her down a flight of stairs at the theater! When I denied it, she attacked me and pushed me over the edge of the dock."

Brand sat back and stared at the other man across the width of the coach. He had already made up his mind that the three attacks on Marion were all connected to the mystery surrounding Hannah. For the moment, he considered the possibility that Kerr was behind them all. That did not fit with how he'd summed up this man—a sniveling toad. The man in the cottage had not lacked for nerve. Besides, Kerr did not know about Hannah or her letters—or did he?

Kerr went on hotly, "She is far more likely to have set footpads on me than I on her."

"And why is that, Mr. Kerr?"

Kerr straightened and lifted his chin. "Because I know something that could ruin her if it ever got out." He exhaled a long breath. "That is why I wanted to talk to her tonight. When I learned that she was engaged to you, a man with a bright future in politics, I knew I could no longer hold my peace. If you marry Marion, you'll be ruined, too."

"Really?"

Kerr nodded.

"Well, don't stop there. What is it you know about Marion that could ruin her?"

Brand had no qualms about prying into Marion's affairs. Whatever touched her touched him. At least Kerr had got that right.

Kerr seemed uncertain now. He dabbed his brow with his folded handkerchief. "It pains me to tell you, Mr. Hamilton, that you have been misled. You see—" A brief paused ensued. "You see, Marion's parents were never legally married, so she and her sisters are, um, illegitimate."

This was not what Brand expected to hear and he could not conceal his astonishment.

Kerr smiled, gratified by the effect of his words. "It's true. And I can prove it. So, you see, neither Marion nor her sisters have any right to the title of Lady. They are mere Misses."

It was the complacent smile that brought Brand out of his stupor. He stretched his fingers taut to prevent him from using his fists to wipe the smile from Kerr's face. He had to keep calm if he wanted to get to the bottom of this.

"And Marion knows this, you say?"

Kerr bobbed his head then added quickly, "Not that I was the one to tell her. I think she has known for a long time. Perhaps her parents told her when I broke the engagement."

Brand allowed the glossed-over statement to stand,

but he was well aware that there was more to it than that.

"I'm disappointed in Marion," he said evenly. "She should have told me." And that was the truth.

"That's what I told her." Kerr bobbed his head. "I suppose she was afraid you would withdraw your offer. Marriage to a rich man such as you, Mr. Hamilton, must have been very tempting."

Brand was beginning to read between the lines. It was subtle, but it was there. He could be bought off if the price was right.

"You mentioned proof?" said Brand.

"Parish records, for one. You see, my father arranged the burial of Lord Penrith's real wife. Before he died, he was the vicar where she was domiciled. She died when Marion was seven years old. In the records, her name is given as Mrs. Rose Dane, neé Sellars. That is her real name, by the way, but she was Lady Penrith."

David Kerr was a vicar's son? His poor father must be turning in his grave. Trying to conceal his contempt, Brand said, "Where was this, and why didn't she live with her husband?"

"She was deranged and locked up in an infirmary. My father used to visit there in a pastoral role. He said that poor Mrs. Dane was so confused she imagined she was Lady Penrith."

"Where was this?"

"In the parish of Lonsdale, near Berwick. Oh, in case you're wondering, the infirmary was pulled down years ago and all the records passed to my father." His smile was almost apologetic. "And when my father died, they passed to me."

"Parish records can be falsified."

"There's more. I also have in my possession a letter

written to my father from Marion's father thanking him for the funeral service he performed for his dear departed cousin, Mrs. Rose Dane. The thing is, Lord Penrith had no female cousins by that name."

Brand made a small sound of disbelief. "How could you know that?"

That complacent smile settled on Kerr's lips once more. "I made it my business to find out."

"When you were engaged to Marion?"

"Naturally. A man is entitled, surely, to discover as much as he can about his prospective bride's relatives?"

As affable as his imperturbable companion, Brand said, "Mr. Kerr, the evidence you have is flimsy at best. I doubt it would raise an eyebrow."

"The letter was franked," Kerr went on quickly, "so Lord Penrith's signature is on the outside, and his crest is on the inside."

"I'm sure a clever lawyer could prove it was a forgery. Perhaps someone was out to discredit the earl." *Like you, you bastard!* Brand thought to himself.

He obviously hadn't shaken Kerr's confidence, because that complacent smile did not waver.

Kerr's voice lowered to a confidential whisper. "Show me the evidence that proves Lord Penrith married Marion's mother. There isn't any. Oh, I know that Marion says they married, but if they did, it was bigamy. I don't think the earl would be so foolish as to commit a criminal act, do you? No. Marion's mother was Lord Penrith's mistress, plain and simple."

Brand steepled his fingers and took a moment to frame his reply. "I think you know, Mr. Kerr, that I'm very attached to Marion. That her parents never married means nothing to me. It's common knowledge that my own origins are nothing to boast about. However, I will do whatever is necessary to save Marion and her sisters from embarrassment." He swallowed the bile in his throat. "Tell me what I must do to convince you to forget about Mrs. Rose Dane of the parish of Lonsdale."

Kerr drew himself up, proud to the backbone. "You see here," he said, "a gentleman who has fallen on hard times. If I don't pay off my debts, I may end up in a debtors' prison. My friends do what they can to help me, but my debts are quite extensive, so it's never enough. I hate to ask for help, but if you could see your way to giving me the money to pay off my debts, I would be most grateful."

"How grateful?"

"Marion's secret would be safe with me."

Brand's brows rose. "Come now, Mr. Kerr, that's not good enough. I did not get to my present position by buying a pig in a poke. First, I'd want to examine your evidence, then I'd expect you to hand it over in exchange for the money I'm to give you."

Kerr seemed taken aback, as though his honesty was in question. He shook his head. "I'm afraid I can't do that. You might say that the evidence is my insurance, in case anything happens to me. I'm not a fool. If anything were to happen to me, my sworn statement along with the evidence will be in the hands of my attorney, and he will know how to proceed."

Brand laughed. "Then all I can say is 'Do your worst!' I'll take Marion in her shift if she'll have me."

Kerr stared. "And what about your career in politics?"

"I've weathered worse storms. However, I'd still like to save Marion any embarrassment, but on my terms."

The haggling became serious after that, but on one thing Brand would not budge. He was buying the evidence as well as David Kerr's silence. At the back of his mind, however, he was devising ways to punish this man. There were huge gaps in his story that had yet to be told. Brand hadn't accused him of anything because Kerr was still in a position to hurt Marion.

Once the danger was over, however, retribution would follow. Meanwhile, all he wanted from Marion were some straight answers.

# Chapter Seventeen

Marion lay on top of her bed, fully clothed, listening to the constant gurgle of the rain as it spilled from the eaves and splashed off the roof of the hotel's front portico beneath her window. She was waiting for her maid to return with a jug of hot water for her ablutions and a glass of medicinal brandy to dull her senses.

The last thing she wanted was to dwell on her troubles, so she pictured the scene outside—roofs and windows slicked with rain; eaves dripping; carriages throwing up streams of water as they drove through puddles; horses neighing and tossing their heads; Brand combing his fingers through his damp hair—

She groaned. Now she understood the lure of brandy. Oblivion—that's what she wanted.

Since her ploy to evade thinking about her troubles wasn't working, she hauled herself up and got out of bed. The fire in the grate had not been lit because this was June, the beginning of summer, and only the elderly or the infirm did not lose face by lighting fires. Everyone else shivered in silence. The English liked to think that they were a hardy race.

That's how she liked to think of herself: hardy, capable, in command of every situation. And what a fraud she was! Oddly enough, the thought of telling Brand about her parents did not agitate her nearly as much as the thought of telling her sisters. He had suffered all his life from the stigma of his birth. He would understand. But her sisters would be stricken, their safe and comfortable life shattered. They would become objects of curiosity, objects of scorn and laughter.

She tried to rehearse in her mind what she would say to them, but all she'd come up with so far was that they had done no wrong so they had nothing to be ashamed of. It was easy to say, but when fingers started pointing— as they would—they would all share in their parents' disgrace.

Dear Lord, how could she have permitted them to have a Season in London? How could she have trusted David Kerr to keep his word? How could she have allowed herself to become engaged to Brand? Once, she and her sisters were provincial nobodies. Now the whole world knew about them. Their names and faces would be recognized wherever they went.

And it was all her fault.

She was starting to shiver again. She glared at the cold fireplace for a long moment, then, coming to a decision, took the candle from the mantelpiece and set it to the kindling. When the fire blazed to life, she gave a defiant nod. So, she was a weakling. There was no one there to see her.

On her way to the dresser to find her warm robe, she stumbled over her evening pumps and paused to pick them up. There wasn't a scratch on them. She gave a teary sniff, remembering how she'd felt when she'd put them on to go out with Brand. A great deal could happen in the space of a few hours.

A discreet knock on the door brought her head up. Finally, her maid had returned. Tossing the shoes on the bed, she went to let her in.

When she opened the door, however, it was not Doris who stood on the threshold, but Brand. For one wild moment, she thought he had stepped out of her imagination. His dark hair was windblown and glistening with raindrops. His jacket was open, his neckcloth askew. But it was his eyes that held hers, blue, blue eyes that were burning brightly with some strong emotion that held him in its grip.

He knew everything.

She wanted his respect and admiration, not his pity. A look from him, a word, would break the dam of her pent-up emotions. Tomorrow she would face him, but not tonight.

"You . . ." She cleared her throat. "You shouldn't be here. People will only think the worst."

"I met an old friend of yours tonight," he said. "David Kerr. So I already know the worst." He paused, then went on in the same pleasant tone, "I met your maid on the stairs and told her to get off to bed."

Smiling faintly, he stepped into the room and kicked the door shut. "What shall I do with these?"

He held a jug in one hand and a glass of brandy in the other. As she studied him warily, she realized that he was spoiling for a fight, and it was the last thing she expected. He must know what she had endured in the last hour—the dashed hopes, the anguish, the fear of imminent exposure. She'd expected comfort, sympathy, anything but this coolly commanding stranger asking her where he should put her brandy and jug of hot water.

She didn't want pity, but the injustice of his unfeeling manner began to grate. "I'll take the brandy," she said, as cool as ice, "and you may deposit the jug in the washbasin."

He handed her the glass and set the jug on the washstand. Having done that, he came back to her. With a smile that wasn't a smile, he said, "Drink the brandy."

Keeping a careful eye on him, she took a small sip, then another. The fiery liquid gave her nose a pleasant buzz and sent a welcoming heat to her chilled bones. She took another sip, then another, each more minuscule than the last, hoping to delay the inevitable moment when she would have to defend herself.

She couldn't drink any more. She wasn't used to strong spirits; one more sip would make her choke.

As though reading her mind, he took the glass from her and set it on the mantelpiece. "That will do for the moment," he said. "Feeling better?"

She nodded.

"Good." His smile vanished and his voice became strident. "Do you know what you have made me suffer, not only in the last few hours, but in the last number of weeks?"

In fact, it was during the last *half* hour that his emotions had made a complete turn, from outrage at David Kerr's presumption to a sense of betrayal at Marion's demonstrable lack of trust. He'd dropped Kerr off at his hotel, just as it started to rain, and had decided that the walk back to the Castle would give him time to reflect on what he should do next. His thoughts had ranged far and wide, but they always returned to the one inalterable conclusion: Marion had not trusted him enough.

"What *you* have suffered? Now just a moment—"

"David Kerr!" His voice had risen dramatically. He turned away from her and began to pace. "When you said his name at the theater, I thought you were afraid of him."

"I was—"

"But later, when you wouldn't confide in me, I wondered if you were still in love with him." He stopped pacing and pinned her with a stare. "You even told me so. Shall I ever forget your words? 'I shall always be half in love with David,' you said."

She gave a derisory snort, which only seemed to rile him more.

"How could I tell?" he demanded. "All I knew was that every time I got close to you, you pushed me away."

His anger was beginning to stir strong feelings in her, too. "For your own good!" she cried.

He laughed at that, but it was a mirthless laugh. "And I let you push me away, because I suspected that Kerr had seduced you, or worse, raped you."

She gave a strangled gasp.

He went on as though he had not heard her. "So, I held myself back in case I frightened you. I didn't want you to think that I was a brute, thinking only of my own pleasure. I took my lead from you. And what did it get me? A cold shoulder."

That gave her pause. In her own mind, she had responded to his kisses with more passion than she'd thought herself capable of.

Piqued, she retorted, "You took your lead from me? That will be the day!"

"Give me one instance when I have not!" He took a long, calming breath. "I thought . . . God knows what I thought. For all I knew, you might have had a secret baby that you were hiding away in the wilds of the Lake District."

Her jaw dropped. "A secret baby? A fine opinion you have of me!"

"Oh, I soon discarded that thought. You were Lady Marion Dane, with all the airs and graces that you were entitled to as an earl's daughter. I was sure your father would have put a bullet in Kerr's brain if he'd dishonored you."

She heard something in his voice that softened her. "I did not give myself airs and graces. I never thought that I was better than you or anyone else. I was reserved. I didn't want or need a best friend to share all my secrets, and if you've spoken with David, you'll know why."

"I should not have had to speak to David!"

He plucked her glass of brandy from its perch on the mantelpiece, drained it in one gulp, and set down the glass with a thump.

His voice was harsh. "You and I were friends, closer than friends. And who would know better than I how to advise you? Do you think you are the only one whose parents never married? You should have confided in me."

Had he said those words in a different tone of voice, she would have been more receptive. But he was attacking her, and she instinctively tipped up her chin. "I should have confided in you?"

"Damn right you should."

"As you confided in me?"

"What in blazes are you talking about?"

His frown did not intimidate her. She waved her index finger under his nose. "If I'm reserved, you're like a block of granite. Getting information from you is like squeezing a stone. If I had to write a book about you, I could do it in two or three sentences." She changed her voice as though she were reading from his biography. "'Mr. Hamilton, the baseborn son of a duke, was raised by his maternal grandfather in plain sight of the ducal mansion'—and who knows what to make of that?" She reverted to her singsong voice before he could interrupt. "'His father, the duke, paid for his son's education, ensuring that Mr. Hamilton would have a bright future in whatever endeavor he undertook. And let's not forget that he insisted that his son would carry the FitzAlan name. But father and son never reconciled. No one knows why.'"

She stopped and gave him a spare smile. "You see what I mean? I know a few facts about you, but you never elaborate."

"It's not my way."

"I understand. My point is that it's not my way, either."

His eyes were hard and intense. "Your instincts should have told you that you could trust me. You should have told me about Kerr."

She made a gesture of impatience with one hand. "I didn't see the point. I thought I had taken care of the problem and that I would never hear from him again."

That wasn't entirely true. She'd *hoped* she would never hear from him again.

He had that stubborn look on his face, and she didn't understand why she was trying to justify herself, except that his opinion mattered to her.

"Look," she said, "what if you were right about the secret baby? What if I came to you and told you that David was blackmailing me about that. What would you say or do?"

"That's a hypothetical question."

She pounced on that. "You see? You don't know what

you would say or do. Can you wonder that I was afraid to trust anyone?"

"Marion," he said softly, "I thought you knew me better than that. Of course I know what I would do. I'd claim the child as my own. We'd marry and give him a home." His hands cupped her shoulders. "That's if you'll have me." His eyes searched hers. "Is there a baby, Marion? Is that what you're trying to tell me?"

Her breath caught. As she looked into his eyes, her lips parted, but no words came. She couldn't find her voice. Her mind, however, was crystal clear. He meant every word.

And she was engulfed by remorse. What demon had made her spout that nonsense about his early years? He was more, far more than that lonely little boy growing to manhood in the shadow of two bitter adversaries. So he didn't bare his soul even to those who were closest to him. There was no need. He did not let his painful past drag him down, but it had shaped him into the man he was today. And she would not have him any other way.

Though her throat was tight, she forced herself to speak. "Till my dying day, I shall never forget that you said those words to me. Brand, there is no baby." She gave a teary chuckle. "You were right and I was wrong. I should have confided in you."

When he stared at her with the same serious expression, saying nothing, she reached up and touched a hand to his cheek. "There is no secret baby," she said softly. "I promise."

"Thank God for that."

It was his smile that was her undoing. She felt the sting of tears and a piercing sweetness spread through her. There was nothing this man would not do to protect her. Uncaring of consequences, she went on tiptoe and kissed him.

It was her kiss that was his undoing. Though the pressure of her lips was whisper soft, a tide of desire roared through him, making him tremble. He didn't know what to do with his hands. He didn't know what to do with his burgeoning sex. But he knew what he wanted to do, and the thought appalled him.

He'd never considered himself an impetuous lover but rather a model of restraint. And just when he most needed that restraint, it hovered tantalizingly out of reach. Seconds passed as he wrestled with his better nature. It was the thought of Marion that gave him the control he needed. She wasn't herself. It would be wrong to take her in a weak moment.

She pulled back a little to get a better look at him. "I think," she said, "one of us had better lock the door."

Did she know what she was saying, what she was implying? He looked deeply into her eyes, and what he saw there made him forget to breathe. She was completely, utterly his. This brave and lovely girl was his for the taking.

That was when he hesitated, and that was when Marion knew she could not let his scruples stand in the way of what she wanted with her whole heart. She didn't know what the morrow might bring. Shame. Heartache. The humiliation of pitying glances. Tomorrow she would ride out the storm. Tonight belonged to Brand.

She shook off his hands, padded to the door, and locked it. When she turned back, he was gazing at her with something like humor in his eyes, his arms folded across his chest.

The humor no longer worked on her, for she knew now that he used it as a last defense.

"Marion," he said with a smile, "I'm flattered. Honored, in fact, but I don't think you've thought this through."

"I have thought this through and I'm doing exactly what you told me I always do."

"Which is?"

"I'm taking the lead."

Slowly, sinuously, in a rustle of skirts, she moved toward him and stopped when they were toe to toe. "I'm done with talking," she said.

"Marion," he chided, and got no further.

With a small sound of impatience, she looped an arm around his neck and stifled his words with a searing kiss. He raised his arms weakly in a silent protest, but he was in the grip of powerful emotions. She was the only woman who had ever mattered to him, and she was soft and womanly and yielding. He didn't stand a chance.

Whatever she had learned from him, she put into practice now. Holding his head steady with both hands, she used the tip of her tongue to separate his lips. The small groan of pleasure at the back of his throat sent her pulse soaring. Fire danced along her skin.

Their kisses grew hotter, wetter, each more wanton than the last. She twined her arms around his neck. He wrapped his arms round her and crushed her to his hard length.

For the first time ever, Marion felt the proof of a man's desire pressed intimately against her body. She wasn't shocked. She was a country girl and was well aware of the mating habits of farm animals. But this was different. She was dismayed. In spite of her bold words about taking the lead, she didn't know what to do next.

Brand felt the change in her, but he didn't know if he could let her go. For weeks, he'd fantasized about taking her to bed and making love to her the way he wanted. He'd curbed his fantasies because Marion was a gently bred, refined young woman who, he thought, had to be handled with kid gloves. All the same, it was the passionate woman he'd discovered behind the well-bred façade that fascinated him.

There was more to his fascination with her than passion, but damned if he knew what it was, except that she had insinuated herself into his life so that he could not imagine not having her there to spar with, argue with, give him grief when he was in the wrong or withdrew into himself. And he was perfectly sure that it was the same for her.

They were two of a kind, both knocked about a bit, but still fighters for all that. Only, in the last little while, Marion had taken some harder knocks than anyone could have expected her to withstand.

Was she having second thoughts? He could easily seduce her, but that did not sit right with him, not here, not in a hotel room, in a strange bed, with no ring on her finger. When all these details were settled, then he'd have her. And he wouldn't have to wait long. If he procured a special license, they could be married by the end of the week.

He held her at arm's length. "I'll understand if you've changed your mind."

There was a suggestion of surprise in her voice. "I haven't changed my mind. It's just that my mind's a blank. Kissing is all I know." She averted her eyes and fingered his lapels. "If you don't take the lead, I suppose I shall remain a virgin for the rest of my life."

The corners of her lips turned up and she peeked up at him.

His good intentions quietly evaporated. He was only

a man after all, not a saint. He looped his arms over her shoulders and linked his fingers behind her neck. "A tragic fate that will never come to pass, not if I have anything to do with it."

She gave a gurgle of laughter.

"Let's begin," he said, "by divesting ourselves of these clumsy garments, shall we? They just get in the way."

Suiting action to words, he shrugged out of his jacket and tossed it on a chair, then did the same with his neckcloth. "Now, your turn."

She was wishing now that she'd allowed her maid to undress her for bed. It seemed wanton to take off all her clothes with him watching her. When she thought of each article of clothing she'd have to remove, her cheeks became warm. She almost groaned when she thought of her stays. How could she remove them? Even her maid found her stays hard to undo.

A fine time to turn shy! She had more gumption than that.

She gave him a clear, level look. "You'll have to help me with the buttons." And she turned to give him access to the row of buttons that marched down her back.

Her blushes were adorable, he thought, and made him all the more determined to go gently with her. As the edges of her gown parted, however, and first one shapely shoulder then the other was revealed, he couldn't resist brushing the pads of his fingers over her soft skin. It wasn't enough for him. He had to taste. Her flowery scent filled his mouth, his nostrils, his throat, his lungs, and settled in his loins. He gritted his teeth, struggling to remember her innocence.

Marion was having trouble breathing. Those languorous touches and open-mouthed kisses were having a curious effect on her insides. Her muscles were softening, her bones were melting, she could hardly hold up her head. In another minute, she would dissolve, and all that would be left of her would be a puddle of water at his feet.

Teeth still gritted, Brand labored to release every last button. When her gown slipped to her feet, much to his dismay, he discovered another barrier. She was encased in stays!

In very short order, having loosened the strings, he hauled her stays over her head and tossed them away. She was down to her chemise and drawers and her white silk stockings. Tantalizing.

He was mildly surprised when she moved away from him, but it was only to pick up her discarded garments and drape them over a chair.

After settling herself on the edge of the bed, she said, "Seems to me that you're no stranger to a woman's undergarments."

"What?"

He was still savoring the delectable picture of Marion in her underthings. The silk chemise was practically transparent, revealing her lush curves and subtle contours.

She tipped her chin in the air and that small gesture got his attention. "What did you say?" he asked cautiously.

"My maid has more trouble undoing my stays than you do."

He cocked his head to one side. "Marion, are you pouting?"

When she glared at him, he laughed and joined her on the bed. Lifting her hand, he brought it to his lips and pressed a kiss to her palm. "One of us had better have a little experience," he pointed out, "or it will be a case of the blind leading the blind."

Her chin dipped a little. "Only a little experience?"

This was one discussion he had no intention of embarking on. Against her lips, he murmured, "Less than a little. A pinch. A dash. A sprinkling . . . "

His weight carried her back against the mattress. He felt her smile when his lips touched hers, but the smile became tremulous when he palmed her breast. He shifted her in his arms so that she was open to him, a liberty he had taken only in his dreams. He had wanted her so long.

He propped himself on one elbow and looked down at her. Her skin was love-flushed, her eyes were glazed. Something fierce moved inside him, something entirely primitive in his nature.

He veiled that look when she gazed trustingly up at him. "Undress me," he said.

She reached for the buttons on his shirt and as she undid each one, her breathing became shallow, more audible. She didn't know why he smiled.

He dragged his shirt over his head and flung it on the floor, then stretched out beside her again. To his extreme satisfaction, she did not avert her eyes or turn shy, but splayed her fingers wide and touched them to his chest. His satisfaction turned to something else when she began to brush those fingers along his bare skin, from his waist to his shoulders and down the length of his flanks.

Marion was both entranced and curious. Muscles she had not known that he concealed under his fine clothes clenched and rippled beneath her touch. His chest rose and fell with each harsh breath. He was a powerful male animal whom she had miraculously tamed to her hand. The knowledge humbled her.

She reached for him. "Love me, Brand, love me."

"Oh, I will," he whispered hoarsely before covering her lips with his.

Through the fabric of her chemise and drawers he kissed her breasts, her navel, her belly, lingering over the hollow between her thighs. His caresses became more intimate and more desperate, and where he led, she followed, returning kiss for kiss, touch for touch. She was too steeped in sensation to care about modesty when he removed first her stockings, then her chemise and drawers, too caught up in the moment to wonder at her own boldness when she helped him remove his own clothes.

With soft moans and sighs, they came together, warm flesh sliding over warm flesh. He told her that she was made for this, made for him. She told him that he was going too slow for her. He took her at her word.

His breath was rasping painfully in his chest when he spread her thighs. Reminding himself for the hundredth time that she was a virgin and he had to be gentle, he entered her slowly, giving her time to adjust to his penetration.

She gasped, and went as taut as a bowstring. After a moment or two, her breath came out in a sighing moan and she relaxed beneath him. "That wasn't so bad," she said.

His one and only virgin, he promised himself. He couldn't go through this again. He reared back and thrust through the last barrier, fully embedding himself, and Marion's back came clean off the bed. Tears of pain stood on her lashes. Droplets of sweat beaded his brow. When she gave a fainthearted laugh, the knot of tension in his chest quietly dissolved.

"No more pain," he promised against her lips.

"You should have told me."

"How could I know? You're the only virgin . . ." He stopped, appalled.

She didn't take offence, quite the opposite. Pleasure bloomed in her cheeks and she wrapped her arms around him. "And you're my only lover, or you will be if you ever finish this."

Eyes locked, smiling, they moved together in perfect rhythm. Eyes glazed over, smiles slipped, their movements became faster, then frenzied. Her body began to shake. He buried his face in her hair. At the last, when she crested the peak and shattered into a thousand pieces, Brand was only a heartbeat behind her.

Stunned, weak as a kitten, she made a purring sound and collapsed against him. By the time Brand covered them with the bed quilt, she had drifted into sleep.

# Chapter Eighteen

It was still dark outside. The rain had stopped. Candlelight flickered behind her lashes. She came awake slowly, languorously, then with a start when she realized she wasn't wearing a stitch. Hauling herself up, she stared at the figure who sat at the small polished table sipping from a glass.

"So, you're awake," said Brand. "I fetched a bottle of wine from the taproom and two glasses to go with it." He got up and crossed to the bed. He was wearing his shirt and breeches, putting her, she felt, at a disadvantage. Clutching the quilt, she raised it modestly to cover her breasts.

A smile flickered in his eyes. "Put your robe on. We have a lot to talk about, but we'll do it over a glass of wine and away from the temptation of the bed."

She accepted the robe he held out while managing to preserve her modesty. "Thank you" was all she could think to say, because she felt awkward. She couldn't reconcile the wild woman who had seduced him in this very bed an hour or so ago with the reserved girl she knew.

Sighing, he covered her lips with his in a slow, persuasive kiss. When he pulled back, he was unsmiling, unsmiling and faintly unsure.

"Tell me you don't regret what happened between us," he said.

His uncertainty put her awkwardness to flight. She smiled into his eyes. "That," she said, "was the most wondrous experience of my life, so don't talk to me of regrets."

He kissed her again, this time long and deep. When she responded with equal vigor, he pulled back and arched a brow. "If we don't move away from this bed, before I know it, you'll be having your wicked way with me again. So put on your robe while I get the fire going."

As she slipped into her robe and tied it, she watched him at the fire. I love him, she thought. She wasn't surprised or awed, because she'd known it for a long time, but this was the first time she had dared to admit it to herself. He might not be a knight in shining armor, but he was the right man for her. She hoped she was the right woman for him.

A shadow covered her heart and she shrugged it off. Nothing was going to dim her happiness, not tonight.

She was at the table, sipping from her glass of wine, when he joined her. He looked like a big cat, self-satisfied and replete after feasting; she wondered if she looked like that, too.

"I forgot to tell you," he said. "I won my party's nomination. I'll be running in the by-election."

His words jarred her. "I thought you said that you had only an outside chance of winning the nomination."

"Seems that I was wrong. The other candidates withdrew their names. They couldn't garner enough support and did the gentlemanly thing without putting it to the vote."

Now she understood why he looked so replete. He had just won a major victory. She should feel happy for him, not all at sea. But this was something she had never expected. Elliot Coyne was the favorite to win.

Forcing a smile, she said, "That's splendid. What do you think your chances are of winning the by-election?"

"Fair to middling."

"And what does Lord Hove think?"

He swallowed a mouthful of wine and grinned. "Oh, he thinks that nothing can stop my momentum. I'm on a winning streak."

She made sure her smile was fixed. "Let's drink to that."

They clinked glasses and sipped.

Her mind was teeming with all the implications of Brand successfully winning the by-election, so that she missed his next words. She shrank into the folds of her robe as a chill settled over her. Her happiness had been short-lived.

Brand's warm hand covered hers. "No need to look like that. I should have told you at once that I've taken steps to ensure that he'll never try to blackmail you again."

"What?"

"David Kerr. That's why I came to your room tonight, to talk about Kerr. He thinks I'm buying the evidence that proves your father's first wife was still alive when your mother and father set up house together. I have other plans for David Kerr that need not concern you.

You're safe, Marion. You and your sisters are safe. That's all you need to know."

She sat back in her chair and stared at him with huge uncomprehending eyes. Now he had her full attention. "How can you be so sure? You don't know David as I do. Don't let his looks fool you. He's as devious as a snake. You may think you're getting the better of him, but he'll twist out of your grasp and strike when you least expect it."

He gave a short laugh. "He won't be in a position to strike at me or you. I'm going to defang him, Marion. All that needs to be decided is the when and the how. Meanwhile, we've made a bargain. I'm not just buying his silence. I'm buying the evidence he has to prove that your father and mother were not married."

She was incredulous. "You're *paying* him? What good will that do? He'll only come back for more."

"He can't blackmail me if I have the evidence he threatens to use against you."

"How can you be sure you'll have all the evidence?"

"It won't matter." He gave a rueful, half-mocking smile. "You see, Marion, I'm not as nice as you think I am. When I have to deal with scum, I can be the meanest bastard on earth, quite literally."

He expected his little joke to win a smile from her. Instead, she pulled her hand from his. "Marion, what have I said?"

"You're not thinking of calling him out?"

"No. That's against the law, and my colleagues might take a dim view of that. But I promise you that Kerr will get his just deserts."

It was a respite of sorts, but that's all it was. Even if he took care of David, it wouldn't be enough. If anyone ever decided to investigate the Dane sisters, the truth would come out.

Wasn't that what she'd been telling herself since she'd looked up to see David tonight? The truth would come out, and what would Brand's colleagues make of that?

He said softly, "Marion, it would help if I knew everything there is to know about your parents and how Kerr came to know they were vulnerable to his blackmail. Are you up to telling me?"

She knew that whether she was up to it or not, he would persevere until he had the whole story. She might as well get it over with.

"I hardly know where to begin."

He squeezed her hand. "Tell me when you first learned that your father ... wasn't married to your mother. Take your time."

She was silent for a long time, her eyes staring at the wine in her glass, then she began to speak. "My mother told me. I don't think she knew who I was. She was heavily sedated with morphine. It was near the end." She swallowed. "She said that she had done Lady Penrith a great wrong and an even greater wrong to her own daughters. She wanted me to forgive her." She looked up at him. "I can't remember all that she said, but I understood her drift. This went on for several days. Whenever my father came into the room, it had a calming effect. They truly loved each other."

She sighed. "I was too cowardly to raise the subject with my father. He had suffered enough, and I half believed, hoped, that my mother was delirious. I waited too long. My father suffered a stroke and I could not ask him then."

She made a small sound, grief or impatience with herself. "When he died, I went through all his papers, hoping to find records, marriage lines, anything to prove that my parents were married. There was nothing. I was relieved, then, that there were no sons in our family to inherit the title. Thank God for Cousin Morley! Can you imagine the straits my sisters and I would be in now if one of us was the earl? Doesn't Parliament investigate every claimant to a title?"

She looked into his eyes. "I thought we'd had a lucky escape, and that's when I opened a letter to my father from David Kerr. He hadn't known that my father was dead. But he left me in no doubt of what had transpired all those years ago when he broke our engagement. It was all there in the letter. His only interest in me had been to calculate how much money he could squeeze out of my father. But his funds had run out and he desperately needed more money.

"I can't believe now that I was ever in love with such a snake." She swallowed a mouthful of wine without being aware of it. "I was heartbroken when he left Keswick. It took me a long time to get over him. But that was as nothing to what I felt when he came back into my life demanding money for his silence. I was distraught. I didn't know what to do or where to turn. My parents, my father . . . " She shook her head. "We were still in mourning, and my sisters looked to me to take our parents' place. So I did what my father had done. Though we hardly had enough for our own needs, I paid him off."

Brand felt his hand fisting, and lowered it to his knee where she could not see it. He didn't want to interrupt her train of thought or let his anger distract her. One thing he knew for certain: When he was finished with David Kerr, Kerr would be sorry he'd ever heard the name Lady Marion Dane.

"What happened next, Marion?"

She looked at him blankly, as though she had forgotten he was there, so he repeated the question.

"Not long after that, Aunt Edwina died. I remember feeling guilty because her legacy saved us and gave me hope. So we went to London to take in the Season. Can you believe it? What a fool I was! I thought I was finished with David, but he turned up in London and asked for more money."

Fire came into her eyes and her voice was strong and hard. "I was going to call his bluff, then I was attacked in Vauxhall and afterward at the theater. What could I do? I was afraid he would turn on my sisters. So I agreed to meet him in Hatchard's bookshop, and I gave him the only thing of value I had left, my mother's emerald drop earrings and ring. I knew they were worth a great deal of money, but he told me tonight that he got a pittance for them."

He made a mental note. *Hatchard's.* That's why she'd been so reluctant to talk about it. There would be a reckoning, he promised himself.

"He denies that he had anything to do with those attacks on you," he said.

Her laugh was edged with sarcasm "Oh, he would. Then how do you explain the notes he left after each attack? 'Let sleeping dogs lie'? 'Silence is golden'? They had to come from David."

Brand did not debate the question of who was responsible for the notes. They would get to that later when they reviewed things point by point. "Tell me about your father's first wife," he said.

She replied bitterly, "You mean my father's *real* wife?" When he was silent, she lifted her shoulders and sighed. "No one in Keswick knew her, because my father didn't inherit the title until after he and my mother were supposedly married. Before that, we lived in Leeds. Everyone knew he'd been married before, but they thought he was a widower."

"Did you know he was married before? I mean, did you think he was a widower?"

"Yes. But we never spoke of his . . . his first wife. Most of what I know comes from Cousin Fanny, and she believes what she was told, that my father was a widower when he married my mother. 'Poor Rose,' she used to say, 'she had to be locked up for her own good.' I took that to mean that she was a danger to everyone around her."

When she paused, he said, "Kerr told me that you were seven years old when your father's first wife died."

"Was I? Oh, I suppose he got that from the date of her death in the parish records. All I remember is that I was born long before she died. What are you thinking?"

"I'm trying to put myself in your father's shoes. I could not put things right for you, but I'd make damn sure that any other children I had would be legitimate. I'd have married your mother if I were he. That's what any sane man would have done."

"Yes, I thought of that, too. But there's no proof. I told you, I went through all my father's papers. I went to the solicitor and asked whether my father had given him something to keep for me. There was nothing."

"Yet Kerr told me that you said your parents had married."

The hopeful look in her eyes died away. "That was bravado, wishful thinking, based on nothing more substantial than a gown my mother kept wrapped in tissue in its own box. She said it was her wedding gown and she hoped that her own daughters would wear it when they got married." She took a healthy gulp of wine. "My poor mother. It's sad, isn't it? I'm beginning to know what she must have suffered to keep up the charade, even with her own daughters."

And he was beginning to understand why Marion had had to forgo a Season in London and her presentation at Court. Her father had a lot to answer for. Yet he couldn't wish that the earl had waited until he was a widower before he met and married Marion's mother, because there would be no Marion.

That was a puzzle for philosophers to debate.

He said quietly, "I think you're wrong, Marion. I think your parents did marry. I don't know what happened to their marriage lines, but I think I know where they likely said their vows. I think it's close by. Oh, not in Longbury. Your mother's name was too well known there. In one of the other parishes, perhaps."

She pressed a hand to her brow. "I don't see how—"

"No. Hear me out. You were seven years old when your father became free to marry your mother. You were seven years old when you came to visit your aunt Edwina. Longbury is as far away from the Lake District as it's possible to get in England. They could marry, very quietly, and no one would be the wiser."

"You're forgetting one thing. My father didn't come to Longbury. He and my aunt didn't get along."

"Perhaps he stayed in Brighton." He threw up his hands when she started to protest. "All right. I may be far out on that point, but I still say they married. You were their only child. Your father had a title and an estate to pass on. He'd have wanted a son."

She responded snappishly, "If that was the case, then it serves him right that he had two more daughters!"

Her hand flew to her mouth and she shook her head. "What a fine picture you must have of my parents! They were good people. They were well respected in Keswick.

They didn't live lavishly and they always gave generously to anyone in trouble. We were a happy family. In spite of everything, we were a happy family." Her voice cracked. "I have no right to judge them."

He reached across the table and took her hand. "I know they were good people."

"How can you know?"

"Because I know you and your sisters. You wouldn't be the people you are without good parents to guide you. And that's why I'm convinced that your parents made amends the first chance they got."

"Then where are their marriage lines?"

"I don't know, but I know how I can trace them. Did you never apply to the various dioceses to see the Bishops' Transcripts?"

"What are those?"

"Parish records that clergy send to their bishops every year. You don't have to visit every church. All you have to know is the year the marriage took place and in which parish. A clerk can look up this information."

She sat back. "Can it be that easy?"

He rubbed his chin. "I didn't say it was easy. We have to apply to the right bishop and know the year the marriage took place. It may take some time. I'll send out express riders first thing in the morning."

It sounded like an impossible undertaking to her, but she concealed her disappointment because he was going to so much trouble on her behalf. She stirred herself to say, "What are you going to do about David Kerr?"

His smile was devilish. "Mr. Kerr is going to be hoisted by his own petard!"

"Hoisted by his own petard?"

"You know, blown up by his own keg of gunpowder."

"I know what it means. But how?"

"You will be happy to know that you gave me the idea. No. I won't tell you what it is until I have set things in motion. But first things first. I have to pay for this so-called evidence."

"I should warn you, it's genuine."

"I was sure it would be, but it's not here. When Kerr retrieves it from his solicitor, I'll arrange to meet him to finalize terms. That gives me time to arrange a small surprise for Mr. Kerr."

He topped up both their glasses, waited until she'd taken a sip, then went on, "Let's go back to something you mentioned earlier, those incidents where notes were left for you. Describe what happened at Vauxhall and at the theater."

She told him in a few sentences what he wished to know, but the notes that were left in her reticule were what interested him most.

"And you assumed Kerr was responsible," he said.

"Not personally, of course. He doesn't have the stomach to do his own dirty work. But he could have hired others to do it for him."

"I'm not so sure. I'm thinking it was the man who attacked us in Yew Cottage."

She stared at him, speechless for a long, long moment, then burst out, "That would mean that he followed me from London to Longbury, wouldn't it?"

"I don't know. It's just a thought. But of one thing I'm certain: David Kerr was not behind those attacks on you. He is a blackmailer, Marion, and blackmailers don't put their victims at risk. And if he hired others, then he would be putting himself at risk. They could turn around and blackmail him, or identify him if they were caught."

"But the notes?"

"I'm thinking about the notes, and what they tell me is that someone is afraid that you may remember what happened the night Hannah disappeared. He was giving you a warning, showing you how vulnerable you were if he ever decided you'd become too much of a threat to him."

"Why not kill me? Why spare me?"

He shook his head. "I have no idea. All the same, don't go off on your own to investigate. Let's play this out carefully."

She gave a short laugh. "Investigate what? Hannah's disappearance? I don't know anything, I don't remember anything, and, quite frankly, my own troubles are all I can think about right now, not solving a decades-old mystery."

He watched her as she got up and began to prowl. When she stopped with one hand on the mantelpiece and stared at the fire, he rose from the table and joined her on the hearth.

Turning her slowly to face him, he tipped up her chin and pressed a feather-light kiss to her lips. "Listen to me, Marion," he said. "I've dealt with bigger rogues than David Kerr. Read my newspapers. I've investigated and toppled corrupt ministers of the crown. I've sent mercenary landlords into bankruptcy and shut down the mines of owners who made their wealth on the backs of child laborers. I didn't do it by playing fair. I played by their rules. And if I had to, I'd do it again."

Since she seemed unconvinced, he cupped her shoulders and gave her a little shake. "David Kerr is a maggot, a parasite, and I'm going to crush him under my heel."

She found her voice. "I wish you would! The only thing that has stopped me from going after him with a gun is that I don't know how to use one."

"I'll teach you."

"That wouldn't be wise. They hang women for murder, too, then what would become of Emily and Phoebe?"

The lighthearted moment did not last. He gathered her close, and she was happy to stand there, absorbing his maleness, savoring his strength. She moved closer, burrowing into the warmth of his body. She had never felt so safe and cherished, but she knew it could not last. Even if he dealt with David, there would always be the fear that someone else would take David's place, someone who had known the one and only Lady Penrith. She would always be looking over her shoulder, wondering when the ax would fall. And it wouldn't fall only on her. Brand had far more to lose than she did.

He had worked hard to get where he was, overcoming so many obstacles. She didn't want to be another obstacle in his path.

She needed time to think things through.

He held her at arm's length. "What is it, Marion? Why do you look like that?"

"I'm tired. That's all."

"No. It's more than that." She tried to look away but his eyes held her fast. "I want to know what you're thinking, feeling."

He gave her a little shake, and that loosened her tongue. "I was wondering where it would all end. I've spent the last three years wondering where it would end. It's not only David. If you can stop him, well and good. But someone else could take his place. I was thinking that it may be time to start over somewhere else, where no one knows us."

He frowned at her. "Somewhere else?"

"Didn't you once suggest that I could sell Yew Cottage? No one will be surprised if I do, not after what happened there. We're all living at the Priory anyway. It's time we found another home. I shall have to explain things to Emily first, of course, but—"

"And what about us? You know my situation. If I'm elected to Parliament, I'll be spending half the year in London and the other half down here. Or did you take that into your calculations?"

That's what frightened her. She said quietly, "I have as much right to choose how I want to live as you do. I made you no promises and you made none to me."

"Christ!" He gestured violently to the bed. "What happened in that bed, then? Wasn't that a promise on your part? A promise on my part? I spilled my seed into you! Do you think I do that with every woman I take to bed? What in blazes was going on in your mind? Do you think I'm like my father? Do you think I'd take the risk of bringing a bastard child into the world?"

He dragged a hand through his hair and stalked to the table. When he turned back to her, his eyes were vivid with temper. "Three years you've endured the burden of knowing you were a love child. You'll note, I've softened my language now that I remember I'm in the presence of a lady. Well, let me tell you, I've had to endure it all my life. You say that you can tell my life history in three or four sentences. Very true. And that's because I refuse to inflict my pain on my friends. I got over it. I didn't take the coward's way out and run away. Face up to David Kerr! Best him at his own game! And if the truth gets out, ignore it."

As levelly as she could manage, she said, "What kind of life would I have if I married someone in the public eye? Not that you've bothered to ask me to marry you—"

"Consider yourself asked," he retorted.

She bowed her head, unable to meet his eyes. "I'd be in the public eye, too. Your enemies would always be sniffing around, trying to ferret out every scandalous tidbit that could ruin your career. I would never have any peace of mind. How could I face it if I was responsible for ruining your career?"

"Are you asking me to give up politics?"

Her eyes flew to his. "Of course not. It's where you should be. It's your passion."

"Oh, I know it. I wasn't sure that you did."

"Well, I do."

The silence drew out. He seemed baffled as he studied her. By degrees, the harsh lines around his mouth softened. "Don't tell me you're doing this for me?"

She did not return his smile. "I'm doing what I think is best for everyone."

"I see. In that case, let's not make any hasty decisions. Let's stick to our plan until the by-election is over."

"I won't do anything to hurt your chances."

"Oh, I didn't think you would."

He sounded cheerful. He walked to the door and paused. Turning to look at her, he said, "You won't do anything rash before consulting me first?"

"Of course not."

He nodded and went out.

He was smiling hugely when he met Ash at the top of the stairs. Ash said, "I'm glad you're still up. You should have told me you won the nomination! Congratulations."

"Thank you," said Brand. "Let's go to my room and crack open a bottle. There's something I want you to do for me."

"You know you only have to ask."

"It's about David Kerr."

As they walked down the corridor to Brand's room, Ash listened intently as Brand sketched out his plan of retribution for David Kerr.

# Chapter Nineteen

They arrived at the Priory three days later to a warm summer sun and the scents of lavender, rosemary, and sweet marjoram wafting over from the herb garden. The family was on the terrace, lounging in wicker chairs while footmen dispensed tea and cake. There was no sign of Emily or Phoebe, and the only gentleman present was a stranger to Marion.

Clarice was the first to see them. She jumped to her feet and made straight for Marion. Linking arms, she began to lead Marion to the stranger, who rose at their approach.

"This," said Clarice, beaming with satisfaction, "is my husband, Oswald. He arrived home yesterday."

From what Clarice had told her, Marion had already formed an impression of Oswald in her mind. Scholarly, she thought, because he had published a book on Hannibal; tall and handsome, because Clarice was tall and handsome; and as wise as Solomon, because his wife was always singing his praises. This funny little man with wiry dark hair, a big smile, and brown puppy eyes did not match her impression at all.

She couldn't help responding to that smile. She curtsied, he bowed, and the usual pleasantries were exchanged.

The dowager looked at Brand. "You're home early. We weren't expecting you until . . . well . . . the dinner hour."

Brand shrugged. "Blame Marion. She couldn't wait to get home to her sisters."

The dowager smiled at Marion. "Come and sit by me and tell me all about Brighton. What's the latest gossip?"

Marion was taken aback. Brand's family knew that he had gone to Brighton to seek the nomination. That's what the dowager should have asked her about. She looked at Brand.

He was lounging against the terrace wall. He refused the tea a footman offered, but accepted a slice of cake. "Where are the others?" he asked idly.

Was it her imagination, Marion wondered, or did everyone suddenly look guilty?

The dowager replied to Brand's question. "Phoebe and Flora are in the house, and Andrew went riding with Emily."

"Are you sure of that?" asked Miss Cutter. A speaking look from the dowager put her in a flutter. "I only ask because I thought I saw them in the herbarium." To Marion, she added, "You know young people—"

Theodora ruthlessly cut her off. "As for Robert, who can say? He comes and goes as he pleases."

This observation cast a pall on the company, which Clarice's husband only partially succeeded in dispelling. "I saw him on horseback earlier," he said easily, "not an hour ago. I think he was making for the downs, too."

The awkward moment passed and people began to talk among themselves. Marion glanced at Brand to find him staring at her with a look that spoke volumes. The trouble was, she had no idea what that speaking look was supposed to tell her. She looked away and responded automatically to something the dowager said, but her mind was still on Brand.

In the last few days, they'd rarely been alone. After winning the nomination, he'd become the man of the hour, and they'd both been obliged to attend functions where the ladies entertained themselves while their menfolk hammered out their strategy in the event that they won enough seats to form the government. She had entered into everything, giving the performance of her life, determined not to do or say anything that could rob Brand of his dream.

She was beginning to think that Lord Hove was right. Brand had the momentum and would carry the day. One part of her dreaded the thought of what that might mean, but another part, the best part of her, was bursting with pride.

Miss Cutter was rambling on about the herb garden, bemoaning the fact that worms had got into her rose hips, but no one was listening. Clarice and Oswald were talking in whispers like two besotted lovebirds, and the dowager and Theodora looked as though they were having words.

If this were her family, thought Marion wrathfully, she would disown them. Her family was far from perfect, but at least they knew how to celebrate one another's triumphs. Everyone here knew that Brand had gone to Brighton seeking the nomination, yet not one of them had asked him how he had fared.

That, as her father used to say, was soon remedied.

She drank the last of her tea except for the dregs, then quite deliberately dropped her cup on the paved terrace, where it shattered into tiny pieces. It had the desired effect. Conversations were abruptly broken off and all eyes turned to look at her.

"I beg your pardon," she said. "I'm not usually so careless." Then, before anyone could interrupt, "Your Grace, you asked about the latest gossip from Brighton. I'm surprised it hasn't reached your ears. Brand has won his party's nomination and goes forward to the by-election. You should be very proud of him."

A look of surprise crossed the dowager's face.

"Marion," said Brand, "they—"

"And," Marion went on, riding a wave of indignation, "he won it on his own merits, not because he is related to the FitzAlans."

"Ah, but he *is* a FitzAlan," replied the duchess, her eyes gleaming.

Miss Cutter added, "And FitzAlans stick together." She was serious.

So was Marion. "It may interest you to know that Lord Hove has marked Brand out for a position in the cabinet."

"Yes, dear," replied the dowager with a twinkle that had become irrepressible, "but that can only be when the Whigs have the majority in Parliament, and that may take a few years."

When Marion opened her mouth to reply, Brand cut her off. "Marion!" He lowered his voice. "They know I won the nomination. I don't know how they know, but they do."

Clarice let out a rich laugh and got up. "I told you this was hopeless. The girls are going to be so disappointed."

Marion looked at Brand but all she got from him was a helpless shrug. He didn't know any more than she did.

One by one, everyone got up. "Give me your arm, Marion," said the dowager. "I'm a little unsteady on my feet." Marion hastened to obey the command. "All will become clear to you when we enter the house." To Brand, the dowager said, "Hot-blooded wench, is she?"

"Grandmother," he remonstrated.

"No, no, I approve. She'll make a fine mother, but I don't see a wedding ring on her finger."

Brand's response was terse. "That's because we're not married."

"In my day, we didn't waste time" came the pert reply.

Clarice added mischievously, "The bishop will be here for dinner. You should talk to him, Brand."

Marion shot her friend a withering glare. She understood the reference to the bishop. Only he could issue a special license so that couples could marry quickly, without the banns being called in church. She wished she could glare at them all. She felt like a governess trying to keep order on a tribe of unruly children.

There was a step down into the house which the dowager carefully navigated, and only a few steps to the Great Hall.

"Well," said the dowager, "did we do right by the boy or did we not?"

Marion could only stare. The banisters in the gallery were festooned with ribbons of every color. An army of footmen were moving furniture and plants under the direction of Emily and Andrew. Housemaids were scrubbing and polishing every available surface. When the dowager pointed her in another direction, she turned her head. A banner was stretched across the other end of the gallery. The lettering was hardly skillful, but the message was legible and brought an odd constriction to Marion's throat.

## WE VOTE FOR BRAND AND MARION

The dowager said, "We had planned a small family dinner, but Emily and Andrew took over and this is the result. There is to be a reception tonight to which everyone is invited."

Clarice elaborated with a laugh. "You took us all by surprise when you arrived early. No one knew where to look or what to say."

She stopped when Phoebe and Flora came tearing into the hall, their arms full of fragrant red roses. They stopped when they saw Marion. Phoebe's face fell. "You're not supposed to be here," she wailed. "This was supposed to be a surprise!"

Marion exchanged a quick glance with Brand. He's touched, she thought. He's really touched. She had to look away because that constriction in her throat was beginning to burn and her eyes were beginning to sting.

What that man needed, she thought fiercely, was some serious spoiling. In Brighton, he'd been fêted by his colleagues, but that wasn't the same. As she'd told his grandmother, what he'd gained he'd won by his own merits. Spoiling was like love. Merit didn't come into it.

She stopped right there. Thoughts like these would turn her into a watering pot.

The girls were right in front of her now. Flora squinted up at her. "Are you sad, Lady Marion?"

Marion's tears instantly evaporated. "No," she said. "I am not."

Phoebe said, "She always cries when she's happy."

"I don't feel sad," said the dowager. "I feel like dancing a jig." Her eyes roamed the Great Hall and she nodded her approval. "What this house needs is more parties, more laughter, and more children, *many* more children. I've been living in a tomb these last years, only I didn't know it."

Marion laughed along with the others, but her eyes strayed involuntarily to Theodora. The older woman's smile was tight, her eyes were blank, but she held her head proudly.

Marion quickly averted her eyes, and when she looked again, there was no sign of Theodora.

Brand was feeling very mellow as he mingled with their guests. He'd always thought of the Priory as a monument to a bygone age. A tomb, his grandmother had called it. The only receptions held here that he could recall were all rooted in some stuffy tradition. Tonight, four young people—Emily, Phoebe, Flora, and Andrew—had stood tradition on its head, and the result was charming. It made him wonder what changes Marion would effect in his grandfather's house.

He was very sure of her now. Some might say that he was overconfident, but they didn't know Marion as he did. In fact, he knew her better than she knew herself. She thought she still had a choice, but he knew better. On the terrace earlier, when she had rushed to his defense like a troop of cavalry coming to the rescue, she had given herself away.

It was a new experience for him. He'd always fought his own battles, and still had the scars to prove it. Now he had a champion; he, Brand Hamilton, a warrior in gentleman's clothing, had a warrior in petticoats looking out for him.

She was also her sisters' champion, and therein lay the rub. She would never do anything to hurt her sisters, and he wouldn't ask her to. Ash was already in London taking care of one problem; he would speak to the bishop tonight and, with luck, take care of the other.

His eyes sought her out in the crush. She was with Emily, and they appeared to be having an earnest conversation. Emily was lovely, but it was Marion who held his gaze. Quality, that's what people saw when they looked at Marion. When he looked at her he saw lacy white stays that nipped in her waist, frilly drawers, and white silk stockings. In his mind's eye, he began to undress her. He was just about to remove one silk stocking when she turned her head and their eyes collided.

She gazed at him for one uncomprehending moment, then her hand fluttered to her throat and color crept into her cheeks. He lifted a glass of champagne from the tray of a passing footman and raised it in a silent tribute. When she gulped and turned her head away, he smiled.

They must be made for each other if she could read his mind with no words spoken. The message was clear. For the last two nights in Brighton, he'd been kept up to all hours on party business. On the long drive to Longbury in the carriage, the maid's presence had had a sobering effect. There was nothing to keep him from her tonight.

Except Marion, and he wasn't giving her a choice. He knew how to get around Marion.

The orchestra, a quartet of local musicians, tuned up for the first dance of the evening, a waltz. As the guests of honor, he and Marion had been asked by Andrew to take the opening turn around the floor. He deposited his glass on the nearest table and went to get her.

Marion was burningly aware of his approach, and she was cursing herself for starting this conversation with Emily. All she'd wanted was to casually put the seed in her sister's mind that her marriage to Brand might have to be postponed indefinitely. What she'd got in return was a motherly lecture on bridal nerves.

Emily's voice was both low and forceful. "It's your age," she said. "The longer you put it off, the more you come to fear it. It's the unknown we fear. Trust me. There's nothing to be afraid of." She chuckled. "Not that I speak from experience, but I've talked to some of my friends who have older married sisters. If you had an older sister, she could tell you. It's as easy as taking a bath." She suppressed the next chuckle. "Some of them say they prefer the bath. It doesn't take as long."

If Marion's cheeks were pink before, now they were red. One day, she would put Emily right about a few things, but not tonight. "Thank you," she said, "but I don't need an older sister with you to guide me. All the same, you've relieved my mind. I mean, of course, when you say that you're not speaking from experience."

Emily gurgled. "You're such a joker!"

She knew he had come up behind her before he said her name. It was uncanny how she could sense him. Her skin seemed to heat, her breathing began to hum, and odd images filled her mind. She banished the more fanciful and thought of a cold bath.

He whirled her away as the orchestra struck up. All eyes were on them, so they had to behave. Tonight, he had the look of Ash Denison about him, casual, devilishly handsome, and, of course, rakish.

"Read my mind," he said.

"What?"

"I'm testing a theory. Read my mind. Look into my eyes, Marion, and read my mind."

She knew where this came from. It was because he'd brought a blush to her cheeks from halfway around the room. He'd caught her out fantasizing about the night he'd loved her wildly, passionately, and she'd known that that was what he was thinking about, too.

He was doing it again, making her blush.

"I'll read your mind," she said, "if you'll read mine."

"Done!" he said.

Eyes locked, they whirled around the dance floor.

"Well," he said finally, "tell me what you see."

She replied with great dignity, "If you could read my mind, you wouldn't have to ask. Didn't you feel the slap I gave you?"

His shoulders began to shake. Her lips began to twitch, but not for long. She was hopelessly, helplessly in love with this man, and she couldn't see how it would end.

Across the floor, Andrew squared his shoulders and skirted the floor to Emily's side. As the highest-ranking gentleman present, he should have been the one to partner Marion for the first dance. The rules had been relaxed tonight because this was an impromptu reception arranged by the young people. His usual practice was to hide out in the stables and let his uncle Robert do the honors.

Emily was expecting him. Her eyes made a critical inspection, then she smiled up at him. "You're the handsomest gentleman present, and I'm the envy of every girl because you're chosen me to be your partner." She batted her lashes.

He groaned. "Don't tease me, Emily. This is hard enough as it is."

"I'm not teasing. It's the truth. Besides, I was flirting with you. Now it's your turn."

He'd rehearsed this part. "That gown is very becoming. It does wonderful things for your eyes."

"You're getting the hang of it. That was very good. Ready?"

When he extended one gloved hand, she gave him her gloved hand and he led her onto the floor. She counted for him, and on the next count of one, he swung her into the dance.

"If you must count," she said, "don't move your lips. Pretend you're reading a book."

"I always move my lips when I'm reading a book."

She beamed at him. "Andrew, that was a riposte. You're getting as good as Lord Denison."

He smiled at her praise. "You've been an excellent tutor."

"I have, haven't I? Except when it comes to small talk. We really must practice that."

"You begin." When she gave him a reproving look, he said quickly, "I'm still counting my steps."

"Very well." Brand and Marion whirled past them, and Emily forgot about making small talk. "Andrew," she said, "have you noticed a change in Brand? He still wants to marry Marion, doesn't he?"

"Are you joking? He's crazy about her."

Emily nodded. "That's what I thought. Then it must be bridal nerves."

"What is?"

Since Andrew was her best friend, she felt no hesitation in telling him about the odd conversation she'd had with her sister before the dancing began.

The reception, ball, party—Marion hardly knew what to call it—should have been long over, but no one seemed inclined to go home. Marion sat on the top step of the gallery, catching her breath, waiting for Brand to join her. They had things to discuss, he said, so she wasn't to wander off until he had a chance to talk to her.

David Kerr or Hannah, it had to be one or the other, and she couldn't seem to muster any interest. After that first dance with Brand, she'd made up her mind to live for the moment, at least for the duration of the party. She owed it to her sisters and all the kind people of Longbury who had turned out to wish her well tonight.

Socrates was wrong when he said that the unexamined life wasn't worth living. He didn't know her. Too much introspection could make a person go mad.

Phoebe and Flora began to climb the stairs toward her, their heads together, whispering. They stopped when they saw her. She knew at once that they were up to something, but she felt, in that odd mood that had taken hold of her, that they were entitled to live for the moment, too. Besides, it was a good sign that Phoebe was up to something. She'd been a lonely, timid child too long. Energetic, intrepid Flora was as good as a tonic.

She smiled benignly as they came up to her. "What have you two been up to?"

Flora answered. "We've just had supper."

That child had the most innocent eyes of any child Marion knew.

"Mmm," said Marion. She turned her attention to Phoebe. She was sporting a healthy tan and had mounted those stairs as though she'd been running up and down stairs all her life. There was a satchel under one arm.

"What's in the satchel?"

Phoebe shrugged. "Nothing that you would think is important. Just our treasures."

And that child had the most honest eyes of any child she knew.

"Don't stay up too late."

"We won't," said Phoebe.

Marion watched them troop off to Flora's room. As a treat, Phoebe had been allowed to share the room for one night, so Marion doubted that they'd get much sleep.

She sat there waiting for Brand, idly watching the company through the wrought-iron slats of the banister. She'd have to go down soon if only to say good-bye to their guests, so Brand would have to postpone that talk he wanted. He was at one of the windows, in conversation with the bishop. Lord Robert and Theodora were there, too, though they had barely looked at each other all evening. Anyone would have thought that John Forrest, her man of business, was Theodora's escort. Miss Cutter was talking to him, and the poor man looked very ill at ease. And who could blame him? Poor Miss Cutter was becoming more and more confused.

Marion got up and started down the stairs with some idea of rescuing Mr. Forrest, but Clarice's husband, bless his heart, got there before her. Oswald Brigden had that happy knack of putting people at their ease. Mr. Forrest's look of relief was almost comical.

Miss Cutter looked rather lost, so Marion crossed to her.

"I haven't had a chance to talk to you all evening," said Marion with a warm smile.

Miss Cutter fussed with the pearl pendant at her
throat. "Dear Lord, child, I don't expect it of you. You're
young. You should be with young people." She gave
Marion a sideways look. "You take after your aunt, so I
shouldn't be surprised. A kinder girl I have yet to meet."

Miss Cutter, Marion knew, was referring to Hannah.
They'd had this conversation before. When Hannah
came home to Yew Cottage for a holiday, she often
visited Miss Cutter at the Priory. Until that moment,
Marion had never doubted Hannah's visits were innocent. Now she was remembering what Mrs. Love had
told her, that Hannah had come home to Longbury that
last time to be with the great love of her life.

Could Hannah have confided in Miss Cutter? Could
Miss Cutter know something without knowing that it
was important? And how did one get any useful information from an old lady whose mind kept wandering?

She gave a start when a hand snaked around her
waist, but it was only Emily. A shawl was draped around
her shoulders.

Emily said, "Andrew and I . . . that is, a group of us are
going out stargazing. Andrew is quite an astronomer.
We won't go far."

"Who is going to chaperon you?"

Emily laughed. "Don't be silly. If we have chaperons,
it won't be any fun. Marion, you worry too much."

Peter Matthews and his sister, Ginny, joined them.
"Ready, Emily?" asked Ginny.

Emily said, "If my sister gives me permission."

Marion relaxed. She liked Peter Matthews and his sister and could not see the harm in stargazing if they were
to be there. "Go," she said, "and enjoy yourselves."

As Emily and her friends moved to the entrance
doors, Miss Cutter edged closer to Marion. "First you

and Brand, then Emily and Andrew," she said. "Mark my words."

Marion stared at the older woman. Andrew and Emily? The idea was laughable. Andrew was a boy. Emily was a woman. It was Ash Denison who got her sister in a flutter.

"Miss Cutter," she said, "Andrew and Emily are too young to form an attachment. They are friends, nothing more."

Miss Cutter nodded. "Friends," she said. "Yes, that would explain why they spend so much time together. But you're wrong about Andrew. He isn't a boy. He'll be nineteen in a few months. Her Grace is very proud of him." And with a complacent smile, she moved away.

Sometimes, thought Marion, Miss Cutter could sound as lucid as the next person. All the same, she knew her sister. Emily had taken Andrew under her wing. They were more like brother and sister. And they were never alone. They were always with a crowd of friends.

Poor Miss Cutter had got it wrong again.

She really must stop calling her "poor Miss Cutter."

She looked around for Brand, found him, and went to join him.

Guests began to leave, and the trickle soon became an exodus. The Great Hall had almost emptied when Manley entered. He made straight for Brand and spoke quietly in his ear. A moment or two later, Brand drew Marion aside and spoke to her.

"Manley has just told me," he said, "that a group of young people from the Priory, among them my brother and your sister, caused quite a stir tonight at the Rose and Crown."

"They were supposed to go stargazing," said Marion. "What were they doing at the Rose and Crown?"

"Stargazing?" Brand's brows shot up. "Is that what they call it these days?"

"Don't keep me in suspense. Tell me what happened."

"There was a brawl," he said. "The boys have been locked up in the roundhouse until someone pays the damages and stands bail for their good behavior."

"The roundhouse?" Marion went weak at the knees. "Don't tell me Emily is locked up in the roundhouse?"

"No. She is free to go, but she won't leave without Andrew. I'm going there now."

Marion was beginning to recover from her initial shock. "I'll come with you."

When she started forward, Brand grabbed her wrist and held her fast. "You'll do no such thing. What I have to say to Andrew is best said in private. I don't think my language is going to be suitable for a lady's ears. I'll send Emily home with Manley. You can deal with her. Make my apologies to my grandmother."

As he followed Manley out of the hall, she had the oddest feeling that, in spite of his words, he was quietly pleased.

# *Chapter Twenty*

The roundhouse was the only lockup in Longbury, and was reached through a cobbled courtyard just off the High Street. Hardened criminals were sent to Brighton, where there was a proper jail to house them and guards to subdue them if necessary. The roundhouse inmates rarely spent more than a night behind bars. Their offences were minor, and the men who guarded them little more than watchmen.

All the same, a night behind bars was not an experience anyone would want to repeat, as Brand could well remember.

Jennings, the watchman who greeted Brand, was well known to him. He was well on in years now, with a bald pate, but he still possessed the physique of a wrestler, an endowment that had deterred many a fractious inmate from putting him to the test.

Jennings said, "Well, Mr. Hamilton, sir, changed days, ain't it, with you here to bail out the duke and not the other way round?"

Brand didn't waste time on reminiscences. "True, Jennings. Where is Lady Emily?"

"Oh, not in the cells, sir, not a nice lady like that. She's with my missus in our quarters. I couldn't let her go, don't you see, because she resisted arrest, and Constable Hinchley wants me to teach her a lesson. No charges, sir, but she ought to know better than to interfere with a policeman who was only doing his duty."

Good God! This was worse than he thought. "Tell me what happened."

"A curricle race was what started the trouble," said Jennings, "right there in the middle of the High Street." He gestured vaguely. "Can you believe it? Decent folks was afraid for their lives. They got Constable Hinchley to go after the young bucks who had caused the trouble. He caught up to them outside the Rose and Crown, your Andrew and Sir Giles Malvern's boy and a crowd of their cronies. What started out as a celebration ended up as a brawl. Your Andrew beat the snuff out of the Malvern boy, and when Constable Hinchley tried to arrest him, Lady Emily got between them."

"Is she free to go?"

Jennings looked taken aback. "Course she is, a nice lady like that! My missus is very taken with her. But she had to be taught a lesson, don't you see?"

Brand did see, and he expressed his gratitude to Jennings in more eloquent words than he was in the habit of using. It always paid to stay on the right side of the law, or at least give the appearance of doing so. This was one of the cardinal rules he'd learned as a newspaperman.

"Now, tell me about Andrew," he said.

Jennings scratched his chin. "His case is different," he

said. "I've got Sir Giles and young Malvern in the office, and Sir Giles is pressing charges. He's waiting to see you."

"How badly hurt is the boy?"

"He's caterwauling like a cat in water, but I can't see no injuries. I think he's trying to make things look bad for young Andrew."

Brand thought for a moment. "Have you sent for a doctor?"

"No. His father said he'll take care of that when he gets the boy home."

"If he is pressing charges, I'll want my own doctor to have a look at the boy." Brand flashed his shark's smile. "Send for Dr. Hardcastle. And give him my name. That should bring him out."

"There's a doctor here on the High Street, just a few doors down."

"Hardcastle," said Brand. "If I'm paying the shot, I want my own doctor present. Oh, and be sure you let Sir Giles know."

Jennings nodded. "And Lady Emily?"

"Manley will take her home. Our carriage is outside. Do you think you could whisk her out of here with no one the wiser?"

"Leave it to me."

"Good man. Now I'll see Andrew."

The servants were extinguishing all the candles in the Great Hall when Marion climbed the stairs to her bed. Her mind was buzzing with speculation, but she was not unduly alarmed. The footman who had given her the candle to light her way whispered that Andrew's lark was nothing more serious than a curricle race and that Lady Emily was in good company with Ginny Matthews

and other of her friends. The constable might put a
fright in them, but no more than that.

Before going to her own room, she slipped into
Flora's chamber to check on the girls. It was in darkness,
so she held her candle high as she approached the big
tester bed. Her sister's hair was done in papers to give it
some curl, something new she had started this last week
in an effort to copy Flora's copious curls. Flora, on the
other hand, envied Phoebe her freckle-free skin and had
taken to dabbing lemon juice on her complexion every
night in an effort to fade the horrid spots. Marion could
smell the lemon juice.

All this Marion had heard from the little maid who
had become the girls' confidante and coconspirator.
Mattie put the papers in Phoebe's hair every night and
found the lemon juice for Flora's complexion.

Marion sighed, wondering, not for the first time, how
the girls would manage when it came time for them to
part. This method of rearing Flora, sharing her between
two aunts during the year, was, in her opinion, cruel and
selfish. It didn't give Flora the stability she needed.
Theodora left her ward's care to servants and strangers.
The child deserved better than that.

She knew she ought to pity Theodora as a neglected
wife, but she had never warmed to the woman. She was
cold and proud, and hadn't a motherly bone in her body
except when it came to her horses. As for Lord Robert,
he was distant, but not cold. Wearied, defeated—what
was it that gave her an odd sense of unease? There were
currents here that she did not understand.

The breeze from the open window riffled some papers on a small table and scattered them on the floor.
Marion went to retrieve them. When she saw the box on
the table, she guessed that these must be the girls' trea-

sures. Odd treasures, she thought as she turned the papers over in her hand. Her heart skipped a beat when she saw that some of the papers were letters to Hannah, and that they were signed by Lord Robert. A more careful perusal had her puzzled. There was nothing loverlike here. A bill of sale, a thank-you note, a recipe for doctoring a colicky horse, and harmless notes to various other people written in an offhand tone.

Marion now turned her attention to the box. It was typical of handcrafted boxes that were to be found in every household, inlaid woodwork and a snug-fitting lid. In her parlor at the cottage, she had a similar box in which she kept her needles and thread.

The light was not good, but she had no trouble making out the initials engraved on the lid. *H. G.* It seemed more than likely that it was Hannah's box. Some of the notes were addressed to Hannah, though not all of them. She opened the lid and went through the contents. The only thing of interest was a handkerchief with Lord Robert's initials.

She began to speculate, but no one theory that came to mind satisfied her. What she wanted were love letters, something that would show that Hannah was planning to elope with the great love of her life. Had someone removed other, warmer letters?

She glanced at the bed. Phoebe and Flora had much to explain, but not now. In the morning, she would demand to know how they had come by this box, and what was in it when they found it.

Clutching the box under one arm, she tiptoed to the door and quit the room. There would be great consternation in the morning when they found their box of treasures gone. Good. Those girls were becoming too independent for her comfort. A little discipline wouldn't come amiss.

She put the box on top of her dresser, then got herself ready for bed. Not that she had any intention of going to bed until she'd spoken to Brand and, hopefully, Emily as well. Trying to contain her impatience until they returned, she sat down with the box of treasures, but this time, she looked for a hidden compartment. Much to her disappointment, there wasn't one.

Restless now, she returned the box to her dresser and began to pace. When she heard wheels on the drive outside, she opened her door a crack and waited. It was Emily who eventually appeared in the corridor, entered her own room, and shut the door.

Marion took the candle from the mantelpiece and went after her.

Emily turned at her entrance and gave her a huge smile. "I thought you would be asleep," she said, "and I didn't want to waken you. Put your candle down and I'll tell you all about it."

This happy, confident girl was not what Marion expected, and she did not know whether she was relieved or vexed. It seemed that Flora and Phoebe were not the only two who needed a little discipline.

She put her candle down and sat beside Emily on the bed. "Well?" she prompted.

"Tonight," declared Emily as though she were playing a part on stage, "Andrew acquitted himself like the gentleman he is. He's a hero, Marion, oh, not in the Greek style, but one that we English can admire, you know, humble, honorable, and a man of action when the occasion demands. If he were a few years older," she went on gaily, "I might be tempted to set my cap at him."

Marion's growing alarm abated a little. "You're not in love with him?"

Emily scowled. "Don't be daft. He's only a boy. I'm a full-grown woman."

Marion prudently refrained from mentioning her conversation with Miss Cutter. "Emily," she said patiently, "don't keep me in suspense. Tell me what happened tonight."

"You can blame that insufferable Victor Malvern," Emily began hotly, then smiled. "Though, all things considered, maybe we should thank him. He came off the worst."

"Emily!" cried Marion impatiently.

Emily nodded. "There was a curricle race," she began.

When Brand entered Andrew's cell, the boy hauled himself up from his prison cot and gazed at Brand with eyes that were half wary, half rebellious.

"What have they done with Emily?" he demanded.

Brand was pleased to see that he had his priorities right. "Jennings's wife has been looking after her, and Manley is taking her home in the coach. There are no charges pending, so she was free to go."

Relief flared in Andrew's eyes then quickly faded.

When Brand lowered himself carefully to sit on the cot, Andrew moved over to give him room. They were shoulder to shoulder.

Andrew said moodily, "Is this where you lecture me on the sins of my father?"

"*Our* father," Brand corrected. "Were you drunk?"

Andrew straightened his spine. "I had one mouthful of beer before the fight started!"

In the same mild tone, Brand went on, "Were you tri-fling with innocent young girls?"

Andrew glared. "That's despicable!"

"Did you lose a fortune at the gaming tables?"

"I don't have a fortune to lose!"

"That never stopped our father. Not that I think you should get off scot-free. I want to hear what happened before I make up my mind about that. My point is, I know you are nothing like our father."

Andrew said, "You should have told me he was a drunkard before I heard it from boys at school."

Brand nodded. "I see that now. Frankly, I was hoping you would never find out. People have long memories."

Andrew's shoulders slumped. "I'm sorry I let you down."

This observation startled Brand. "Have you let me down?"

"I'm here, aren't I?"

Brand lapsed into a reflective silence for a moment or two then suddenly got up. "Come here, Andrew," he said, "and tell me what you see."

He walked to the back of the cell where the light from the wall sconces barely penetrated. Andrew dutifully peered at the brick wall. "There are letters here," he said, "carved into the brick."

"What do you see?"

"H, and I think it's a C."

"Ah, yes, that's Harry Cornell, a regular tearaway. He's in the navy now, and doing very well for himself. Try higher up."

Puzzled, Andrew did as he was bid. He muttered a few letters to himself then stopped. I see a B, an F, and an H."

"My initials," said Brand.

"I know." Andrew turned and looked at Brand speculatively. "The *F* stands for FitzAlan. That's your real name, isn't it? Brand FitzAlan?"

"You know too much," said Brand, but he was smiling.

Andrew laughed. "Grandmama told me that you insisted on adding your grandfather's surname to spite Father."

Brand's smile faded. "No. My grandfather did that. But that's not why I wanted you to see the initials. You're not the only FitzAlan who has spent time in the roundhouse. I'll say this for our father. He always came and bailed me out."

Andrew beamed at the letters on the wall, but his satisfaction was short-lived. When he looked at Brand, his eyes were troubled. "Sir Giles says he is going to bring charges against me."

"Well, that will depend on what happened tonight. Why don't you give me your side of events before I meet with Sir Giles."

It started out innocently enough. Young Malvern had challenged Andrew to a curricle race. Since Andrew knew Malvern to be a cheat and a bully, he had refused. Taunts were exchanged and Andrew finally agreed.

"Not to do so would have been tantamount to admitting I was no match for him and," he added tellingly, "I didn't want to lose face in front of Emily's friends."

*Emily's* friends, Brand noted, not *my* friends, and he felt the prick of his conscience. Had Andrew friends of his own? He did not know. He'd been too preoccupied with his own affairs to spare the boy much time.

"Go on," he said softly.

Andrew shrugged. "I won, and we all went off to the Rose and Crown to celebrate. The girls, of course, stayed inside the closed carriage and drank cordial, while waiters brought out tankards of beer for the men. That's when Malvern and his friends showed up. He challenged me again, said it wasn't a fair race, but I told him we had to get back to the Priory for the end of the ball."

He stopped, looked uncertainly at Brand, then averted his eyes. "Malvern said something no gentleman could tolerate, and I went at him with my fists."

Brand frowned. "He insulted Emily?"

"No."

"Ah. Then the insult was to me?"

Andrew did not reply to this. He let out a long breath. "Then everyone started shoving and pushing and before I knew it, a brawl had broken out."

"And that's when the constable turned up?"

Andrew nodded. "Constable Hinchley ordered everyone home except Malvern and me. Malvern swore I'd attacked him unprovoked. And I didn't want to repeat Malvern's insult, so I had no defense."

There was a silence as Brand considered this. He could not think of anything he'd done to deserve such loyalty.

"Tell me about Emily," he said gruffly.

Andrew grinned. "She jumped down from the carriage and started to argue with the constable, so he took her into custody, too. I had no idea she had such a temper. Nothing could shut her up, not even the threat of arrest."

It wasn't Emily's face that came to Brand's mind but Marion's.

His train of thought was interrupted by raised voices on the other side of the door. He thought he recognized Hardcastle's voice. The cell wasn't locked, so he pushed through the door and went to investigate. After a moment's hesitation, Andrew went after him.

They found them in the office, Sir Giles Malvern and Dr. Hardcastle. They were nose to nose. Young Malvern was sitting on a bench with a sly smile on his face. Jennings was off to the side, arms folded across his chest, beaming affably at the spectacle of two well-heeled members of the gentry squaring off for a fight.

Sir Giles's face was an angry red. "I say that my boy took a vicious beating and if you won't write that in your report, I want a second opinion."

Hardcastle's chin jutted dangerously. "And I say that your boy is a malingerer. I saw plenty of those in the war, so I recognize one when I see one. A few scratches and bruises?" He pinned young Malvern with a steely eye. "You should be ashamed of yourself, boy, for making such a fuss. I understand you want to make the army your career. I'd advise you to have second thoughts. There's no place for cowards in the army."

Sir Giles's breath rushed between his teeth. He made a turn, saw Brand, sneered, and pointed a shaking finger at him. "You put Hardcastle up to this! Well, you'll get your just deserts at the hustings. Don't think that marriage to an earl's daughter will elevate you to her level. You'll always be a bastard."

Hardcastle said, "Now we know where the boy gets it from."

Brand looked bored. Andrew scowled. Jennings flexed his muscular arms and took a threatening step toward Sir Giles.

"One more word like that," said Jennings, "and I shall arrest you for disturbing the king's peace."

Sir Giles eyed Jennings's brawny shoulders and his

lips flattened. "Come, Victor," he said. "We'll get our revenge on election day."

There was a long silence after father and son stormed out, then Hardcastle turned his bird-bright eyes on Andrew. He fisted his hands and moved them rapidly as a pugilist would in a fight.

"Did you give him the one-two in the solar plexus as I taught you?"

Andrew flushed and darted a guilty look at Brand, then quickly shifted his gaze to the doctor. "Yes, sir, just as you taught me."

"And he went down like a winded bellows?"

Andrew grinned. "He gasped for a full minute, like a fish out of water."

Brand was amazed. To the doctor, he said, "You've been teaching my brother how to fight?"

"Indeed, I have, and he is a natural, as I should know. I'm an avid follower of the sport. Never miss a prizefight if I can help it."

Brand looked at Andrew. "How long has this been going on?"

Andrew shifted restlessly. "Since the night Dr. Hardcastle took the bullet out of you. We got talking afterward, and one thing led to another."

The doctor said, "That's a nasty cut you've got on your face, Andrew. Let's have a look at it."

After leaving the roundhouse, they walked the short distance to the Rose and Crown. The damages didn't amount to much—the cost of repairing a broken window and replacing a few wooden chairs and benches that were left outside for patrons' convenience during the summer months. Andrew's curricle and horses were there, too, safely stowed in the inn's stables, and Brand had to pay for that, also. Trust a FitzAlan to think of his horses first! Brand thought ruefully.

Since Andrew was driving, Brand settled back and was soon lost in quiet reflection. He was thinking that instead of setting himself up as his brother's mentor, he should have been more of a friend to him, more of a *brother*, especially when they saw each other only in the holidays. He hadn't wanted his brother to turn out like their father, so he'd kept the boy busy, first with his studies, then with estate business. It would not have been true to say that he'd neglected Andrew, but his focus had been too narrow. He should have been the one to teach Andrew how to fight.

In spite of his own inadequacies, thought Brand, Andrew had turned out well. He was proud of the way he had handled himself tonight. No need to tell him what kind of vitriol Malvern had spewed out. He'd been used to it all his life. What he wasn't used to was a brother.

"Andrew," he began, and cleared his throat. "I was hoping you would stand up with me at my wedding, you know, as my groomsman."

There was a sound like a sharp intake of breath, then Andrew said, "What about Ash Denison? Don't you want him to stand up with you?"

"No. Ash comes out in hives when he gets too close to the altar. He can't stop weeping. He'd disrupt the service."

Andrew laughed.

"Besides," Brand went on, "you're my brother. That means a great deal to me."

This time, it was Andrew who cleared his throat. "I shall be honored."

Brand smiled. "That's settled, then."

"Is it? Settled, I mean? I did wonder after what Emily told me tonight, but anyone can see that you and Marion belong together."

In the process of yawning, Brand froze, then snapped his teeth together. "What did Emily tell you?"

Andrew chuckled. "That one or both of you were suffering from bridal nerves and if you did not get a hold of yourselves, there might not be a wedding."

"Interesting," drawled Brand. "Tell me more."

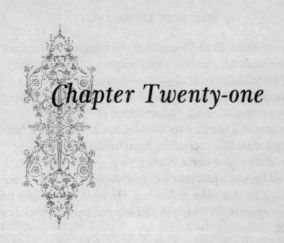

# Chapter Twenty-one

Marion heard the soft knock at her door and started up. "Who is it?" she called out.

A muffled voice replied, "Who else would it be at this time of night?"

The door wasn't locked, but she ran to open it anyway. "Brand," she said.

When he entered the room and locked the door, she had no doubt that he was in the grip of some powerful emotion.

Her heart leaped to her throat. "It's Andrew, isn't it? What happened, Brand?"

"It isn't Andrew." He advanced a step, then another. "He's home and none the worse for this adventure. I don't want to talk about Andrew. I don't want to talk about Emily. I want to talk about us."

There were times when Brand Hamilton could look quite debonair. This wasn't one of them. His face was set in harsh lines and his blue eyes were glittering like cold steel. She hovered on the brink of fear; then common sense returned. Brand Hamilton in a temper might scare the breeches off the high and mighty in both government and Court circles, but he did not scare her.

She stopped retreating and held her chin up. Eyes steady on his, she said, "What about us?"

He lowered his face to hers. "Since when does a hot-blooded miss like you suffer from bridal nerves?"

He didn't give her a chance to respond. His mouth covered hers in a kiss that was calculated to subdue every remnant of feminine resistance. He used his weight to pin her against the bedpost, and cupped her face with his hands.

"Now tell me about bridal nerves," he said, and he kissed her again.

She would have rebelled if she had not felt so guilty. Evidently, her muddled conversation with Emily had got back to him and his pride was hurt.

When he raised his head, she whispered, "Brand, you don't understand."

"Does this give you bridal nerves?" he asked fiercely, and he molded his hand to her breast. He didn't stop there and, in the space of single heartbeat, her knees began to buckle. She clutched his arms for support.

His voice lost none of its force. "Do I have to prove to you how ready you are for this?"

She shook her head.

"Then why in blazes are you having second thoughts? I thought everything was settled between us."

"I want what's best for everyone," she cried.

Air rushed out of his lungs and he rested his forehead on hers. "Do you want what is best for me?"

"You know I do."

"Then I'll show you what's best for me."

Keeping his gaze riveted to hers, he lowered her to the

bed, and came down beside her. Capturing her wrists in one hand, he held them above her head and used his other hand to sweep from her throat to her breasts, all the way to her loins.

Lips against hers, he whispered, "I wish I understood how your mind works. Since I don't, I'm going to tell you how my mind works. All I can think about is this— you, wanting me as much as I want you. Do you think I want to feel this way? You're not a distraction, you're an obsession. No, don't turn your head away. It's more than lust. I want a future with you. I want to have children with you. Compared to that, everything else is like ashes." He inhaled a ragged breath. "Now tell me that's what you *don't* want."

"That's unfair! I'm trying to be unselfish."

"And I'm trying not to lose my temper."

She gave a teary chuckle. He sighed. Their lips met and clung. Her yielding softened the fierceness inside him, but it did not deflect him from his purpose. She was his mate. The sooner she realized it, the easier it would be for both of them.

Slowly, piece by piece, he removed her nightclothes. There wasn't a part of her that did not feel the stroke of his fingers, the brush of his lips. He was awed by her beauty and lingered over the rosy tips of her breasts, the flare of her hips, the slight swell of her belly, and the soft mound that guarded the core of her femininity.

"You're so beautifully made," he told her, "so wonderfully female." His words became more ardent, more explicit, as she moaned and moved restlessly beneath his touch.

When he probed gently and found her wet for him, he had to grit his teeth to prevent himself from falling on her like a ravening wolf.

"Brand," she said softly.

He heard the uncertainty in her voice as well as the longing. It was the uncertainty more than anything that helped him gain his control. He came back to her and rained feather-light kisses on her eyes, her cheeks, her lips.

"I won't go on with this if you don't want me to," he said.

She stared up at him in disbelief. Her whole body was aching with unslaked desire. She was frantic with need. Couldn't he see it?

Her response was pure feminine instinct. She lifted her head and kissed him with all the love and passion that was buried deep inside her. She felt the leap of his heart against her breasts. Her breath caught.

He was everything she could hope for in the man she loved. There was no one like him, and there never would be, not for her.

He heard her struggling to catch her breath, felt her leap to passion. "Marion," he said wonderingly, "Marion."

Laughing now, he got off the bed and stripped out of his clothes. When he came back to her, he wasn't laughing. His mouth took hers again, ravenous, demanding, and when she answered that demand, he thought his heart would burst.

When he parted her legs and rose above her, his breath became harsh, uneven. "Marion, look at me," he commanded.

Her lashes fluttered and her love-dazed eyes stared up at him. "No more doubts or second thoughts," he said.

Slowly, giving her time to adjust to his body, he entered her. When he began to move, she arched beneath him. As his movements became more abandoned, she lavished kisses on his arms, his throat, his shoulders. A torrent of heat swept them to the edge. He felt her body contract beneath his, heard her wild cry of rapture. Only then did he take his own release. At the end, he cried out her name. Marion buried her head in his shoulder.

"I love you, Brand," she murmured, and her whole body went lax.

She was curled into him, eyes closed, her breath tickling his armpit. He lay on his back, hands linked behind his head, staring blindly at the canopy overhead.

*I love you.* He couldn't get his mind around the words.

When she stirred and sighed, he propped himself on one elbow and studied her face. In sleep, she looked no older than Emily, and he felt about the same age as Andrew. He didn't know anything about anything—not that he would have been aware of it at eighteen years old. Now that he was older and wiser, he realized how much he had to learn.

"Brand, what is it?"

His eyes met hers. "You're a passionate woman, Lady Marion Dane, and I'm a very lucky man."

He smiled into her eyes and smoothed back strands of fair hair that fell in unruly disorder around her face.

Her hand closed around his wrist, bringing his eyes back to hers. "Yes, but that's not what you were thinking."

"How do you know?"

"Because . . . you looked pensive, and that's not like you."

She dragged herself up to get a better look at him, and pulled the coverlet up to her chin. He had to follow her example or be smothered by the bedclothes.

"Well?" she prompted.

He shrugged. "You said you loved me. Did you mean it?"

Her heart stopped beating. She could make light of it and pretend that she couldn't be held responsible for what she said in the throes of passion. What stopped her was Brand. She had never seen him look so vulnerable. They couldn't both be vulnerable. One of them had to take a chance and this time, it seemed, the short straw had fallen to her.

"Yes, I meant it."

His fingers linked with hers and he brought her hand to his lips. As carelessly as he could manage, he said, "No one has ever said those words to me before."

She suppressed a smile. "Brand," she said, "mistresses aren't paid to love their protectors, but to sell them their favors."

He scowled. "What would you know about it?"

Her look was pure exasperation. "You and Emily seem to think that I'm a hothouse flower. I'm not. I don't need to be pampered. I'm not delicate at all. My mother put me wise to the ways of the world, and drawing-room gossip completed my education."

"Drawing-room gossip! You make it sound like a grand tour."

"You could say it's the female equivalent, and when Emily is a little older, I shall put her wise to the ways of the world, too."

She was wishing she hadn't introduced Emily's name into the conversation, because the endearingly uncertain look on his face vanished, and he was giving her one of his narrow-eyed stares, the one that searched her mind for all her secrets.

Before he could begin to question her, she said, "I did not tell Emily that I was having second thoughts. I was trying to prepare her for the possibility of us moving away from Longbury—you know, in the event of unseen things beyond our control oversetting our plans? Obviously, I botched it, but I'm surprised at Emily. She shouldn't have mentioned it to you."

"It wasn't Emily who told me, it was Andrew. And," he added moodily, "it sounds to me as though you *are* having second thoughts."

"Brand," she said, appealing to him. "Nothing was settled between us. You know it as well as I do. What if you can't silence David Kerr? What if you can't prove that my parents married before Emily was born? If it comes out, can't you see how this could ruin your chances of advancement? Can't you see that my sisters and I would be better off out of the public eye, and living quietly somewhere else?"

"It won't come to that. These things take time. Bishops are busy men. It may take them a while to look over their transcripts. Patience, Marion. They'll get back to us sooner or later."

"And what if they say that there is no record of my parents' marriage?"

He dismissed her misgivings out of hand. "Then we'll widen our scope to include other counties. I haven't changed my mind. I still believe that your father married your mother as soon as it was legally possible."

Her mouth set in disgruntled lines. "You're always so confident! Don't you ever have doubts about anything, like ordinary people?"

He brushed a careless kiss on her bare shoulder and smiled when she shivered. "You told me that you loved me. I'm not confident about that."

She was ready to take umbrage since he hadn't given

her the words in return, but something about his watchful expression changed the direction of her thoughts. What was it he wanted to hear?

"Perhaps I shouldn't have told you," she said, not challenging him, but feeling her way carefully. "If it makes you uneasy, I won't say it again."

"Make me uneasy?" He rested his head on the back of the bed and covered his eyes with his arm. "It's just the opposite. No one has ever said those words to me before. No one." He grinned at her. "Not even the occasional lady, the very occasional lady, I've had in my keeping."

"There must be someone. Your grandfather? Father? Grandmother?"

"No one."

He was amused, and though she returned his smile, she wasn't amused at all. He'd just enlarged on those three or four sentences that made up his biography and she ached to make it up to him.

Careful, Marion, she cautioned herself. Trying to make up to people for their misfortunes was one of her biggest failings. Some unscrupulous people took advantage.

"I'm sure your mother said those words to you," she said quietly.

"Yes, but she died when I was a few months old, so I have no memories of her."

"What about you? Haven't you said those words to anyone?"

His expression was arrested. "Never."

"Are you going to say them to me?"

The amusement faded from his face, and he turned to her with an expression that bordered on pain. "It's not our way. We FitzAlans are not a demonstrative lot."

She noted that he had put himself in the FitzAlan

camp. "That's not true," she said. "Look at Clarice. She's crazy about Oswald and doesn't care who knows it."

"Clarice is a female," he protested.

"Mmm." She folded her arms across her chest and gazed into space.

He nudged her shoulder. "Let me hear those words again."

With a hoot of laughter, she rolled on top of him. "I will if you will." She put her index finger to her mouth. "Watch my lips. It's easier than you think. *I . . . love . . . you.* Now it's your turn."

He rolled with her on the bed and came out on top. Eyes locked on hers, he said, *"Read . . . my . . . mind."*

When she glared up at him, he kissed the pout from her lips. "I need you so damn much," he said, and it was enough to win her over.

They were both smiling when their lips touched, but when their breath quickened, their smiles slipped away. At the end, she gave him the only words he wanted to hear. He would never let her go now.

When he heard her get out of bed, he lifted his lashes a fraction and watched her don her night robe. He could not remember a time when he'd felt so replete, so satisfied, and so at peace with the world. He was no stranger to the carnal delights of a woman's body, but this was different.

*I love you.*

A smile tugged the corners of his mouth. She wouldn't have given him those words if she hadn't meant them. She could be devious when she wanted to be, but in the things that really mattered, Marion was as transparent as glass.

Smoky glass . . .

Glass misted over . . .

Through a glass darkly . . .

His replete smile became a huge grin. Perhaps he would never entirely grasp how her mind worked, but what seemed difficult became simple when he took her to bed.

"Are you smiling, Brand, or is that a death grin?"

He opened his eyes. She was standing over him with a box in her arms. With one hand, he snagged the back of her leg and tugged. She squealed and promptly fell on the bed, but she was careful not to dislodge the contents of the box.

"This is important!" she hissed, holding the box up.

"So is this."

He took the box from her and dropped it on the floor, then he rose above her.

She shifted restlessly. "Why do you always stare at me with that intent look in your eyes?"

"I'm trying to read your mind."

She dimpled up at him. "And?"

He shook his head. "It's beyond me. You'll have to give me the words."

For a moment, she looked puzzled then her face softened and she touched a hand to his cheek. "I love you, Brand," she said softly.

He gazed at her with a curious gravity. "Prove it," he said.

"I'm waiting, in case you haven't noticed."

"Read . . . my . . . mind." He smiled into her eyes.

She made to get off the bed, but he pinned her with his weight and kissed her with an urgency that took her breath away. He brushed kisses over her face and lingered on her lips.

Their breathing became labored, their bodies flowed together. Frantic now, they raced for the edge and hurtled into that sweet oblivion.

It was some time before they got around to talking about the box. Brand had dressed to go back to his own room, and they were sitting at a small table in front of the curtained window.

"I don't know where the girls found it," said Marion, "but it must be Hannah's box. I don't know what to make of it. These bits and pieces are worthless. Now, if the box contained love letters, it would make more sense."

Brand examined the letters, especially those that were dated, and turned his attention to the small objects. Marion was right, they were worthless: a brass button, a monogrammed handkerchief that was yellowing with age, a penknife, and a pen.

He said reflectively, "Hannah was a magpie. It didn't matter what she collected, as long as it was connected to Robert." He looked at Marion. "From the date of some of these notes and receipts, we can trace when her obsession began."

"Her obsession," said Marion faintly.

He shrugged. "Call it what you will. She was lovestruck, that's all I meant. See here?" He pointed to a dated receipt for a gentleman's hat. "She was employed by Mrs. Love when she acquired this. That means she'd been collecting these items two years before she disappeared."

"Yes, but where are Robert's letters to her?"

"There's only one, thanking her for her expressions of sympathy. My notes to my tailor are warmer than this.

The other notes from Robert are to Miss Cutter and his valet."

"There must be more than this."

He sat back in his chair and shook his head. "I don't think there were other letters."

"Then why did someone break into my house and try to steal them? They wouldn't have been desperate to steal this rubbish."

He spread his hands. "I don't know."

Her brows came down. "Yes, but you're thinking plenty."

A smile flashed. "I'm speculating, that's all."

Her chin lifted. "I thought we were in this together?"

"I'm thinking of our conversation with Mrs. Love. Hannah, you may remember, wrote letters to some young man—"

"Mr. Robson," she supplied.

He nodded. "—who took her at her word and got nothing but grief for his trouble. If anyone wrote letters, I think it was Hannah." He gazed into space. "She had a taste for melodrama, and I think she got more drama than she bargained for."

They fell silent as they became absorbed in their own speculations. A moment or two later, Brand said, "Ask the girls where they found the box. That may help us."

"I will," she replied, "and I'll ask them if this was all that was in it when they found it. Are you going to talk to Robert about it?"

He looked surprised. "There's not nearly enough to go on. Besides, maybe Robert fell out of favor. Maybe someone else had taken Hannah's fancy."

She said quietly, "What about your father?"

"My father?" He was astonished. "Apart from the fact that he was practically twice Hannah's age, he would never have thought of eloping. His estates are here. Besides, my father is dead. This mystery is ongoing. Someone attacked you in Vauxhall Gardens and pushed you down the stairs at the theater. And let's not forget the thief we interrupted at your cottage."

She shivered. "I feel as though I've been cast adrift on the open sea without a compass."

He leaned across the table and kissed her quickly. "I'm your compass," he said. "Hang on to me and I'll bring you about."

He took the box with him when he left, promising to return it in the morning, and went through everything again before he went to bed. Odd thoughts came and went, but he made no effort to connect them, not yet.

He remembered Edwina's letter and how he'd thought the task of discovering who was involved with Hannah was monumental. He'd cast his net of suspicion wide to include Longbury and Brighton. Now, with Hannah's keepsakes coming to light, it seemed that he should have looked no farther than the Priory and its environs. There was nothing in that box to show that Hannah had wandered far from home.

A witness told Edwina that Marion was out the night Hannah disappeared. Who was the witness? What did Marion see? She'd adored Hannah. If she'd seen anyone hurt her, she would have run screaming to her mother for help.

He was more convinced than ever that Hannah had written letters to his uncle. The coldness of Robert's note was telling. He could hardly confront his uncle with his suspicions. So he'd received letters. Robert was a man of the world. He would know how to depress the attentions of a love-struck young woman.

Unless he'd fallen in love with her and was not so

easily got rid of as Mr. Robson. Stranger things had happened.

Then there were the attacks on Marion in London and the notes she'd attributed to David Kerr. Who was behind them? Who was away from the Priory at the crucial time?

At last he had something to go on.

When confronted with Hannah's box, the girls turned into watering pots. Flora had found it under a squeaky floorboard in the linen closet in Edwina's cottage when they were playing hide-and-seek. They swore they hadn't removed anything. They had tried to put it back where Flora found it, but they were always turned back by Mr. Manley or by groundsmen. So they'd made up their minds to hand it over to Marion, but she'd found it before they'd had the chance.

They couldn't see the urgency. If the box had been full of gold coins, that would have been different.

Having settled them to writing her an abject letter of apology for their misdemeanor, Marion went in search of Brand to tell him the little she had discovered.

# Chapter Twenty-two

The ritual of taking tea on the terrace was in progress, and Brand almost dropped his cup when he absently took the first sip. "Coffee?" he asked the footman. It was his favorite brew, but in his grandmother's house coffee was viewed on a par with medicinal brandy.

"Lady Marion said that you would prefer it" came the stilted reply. "If you prefer tea, sir, I shall get you a fresh cup."

To break with tradition at the Priory was frowned on by both the FitzAlans and their servants. "Thank you, but I prefer coffee," said Brand.

Marion was watching him. He lifted his porcelain cup in silent tribute. She nodded and smiled.

She was trying to win him over, he supposed, but to what purpose he had no idea. He had offered her marriage, and she refused to give him a yes or a no. This business about David Kerr and the damage he could do was beginning to wear thin. He didn't want her to come to him after he'd removed every obstacle. She said she loved him. If that were the case, she should come to him without counting the cost.

He didn't want to keep on telling her all this. That would only defeat his purpose. If she didn't come to him freely, without conditions, something precious would be lost. He could live with it, but it would be a compromise. The cynic in him expected no less. It was Marion, herself, who had shown him a different way, but she did not practice what she preached.

Meantime, he was playing hard to get, up to a point. He did not go to her room at night. If she wanted him, she had to come to his. He had thrown down the gauntlet, but so far she had not picked it up.

Theodora arrived, but without Robert, and that started him on a new train of thought. He'd been doing a little sleuthing, trying to find out who, with easy access to the Priory, had been away when Marion was attacked in London. Small help there! The Priory had been practically deserted at the crucial time. Lord Robert was still the only person who came close to being a suspect. He had the opportunity and he had the motive, though the motive hung by a thread. Was he in love with Hannah? Had he killed her in a violent rage when she played the same trick on him as she had played on Robson? Had he written love letters to Hannah and broken into the cottage to look for them the day of the fête?

Oswald got to his feet. He was looking over the terrace wall. "Isn't that Andrew and Lady Emily?" he said.

Brand turned to look. Hand in hand, Andrew and Emily came racing across the turf from the direction of the conservatory. Those on the terrace could see at once that something was far wrong.

Brand did not wait for Andrew and Emily to come on,

but put down his cup and went to meet them. Oswald was right behind him.

They were all on their feet now, Her Grace, Marion, Miss Cutter, Clarice, and Theodora, all watching the men on the turf. Andrew was pointing to the conservatory, but Emily came on. When she came up the stairs, she half crouched over, trying to get her breath.

When she straightened, she choked out, "There's been a terrible accident. In the conservatory. John Forrest. I'm afraid he's dead."

There was a shocked silence, then Theodora let out a keening cry and would have gone after the men had the dowager not prevented her.

"Let Brand and Oswald take care of John. If you go up there, they will be taking care of you. Is that what you want?"

Theodora stared at the dowager as though she disliked her intensely, then she shook off Her Grace's restraining hand and walked into the house.

A gardener directed Brand and Oswald to the body. Forrest wasn't in the conservatory itself, but in a shed for tools and other gardening supplies that was screened from view by thick shrubbery. The door was open and they could see Forrest lying facedown on the earthen floor.

The gardener had found the body and had run back to the conservatory to Andrew and Emily, whom he'd last seen admiring the flowers with a party of friends. The friends had gone home, but Emily and Andrew were still there.

"I felt for his pulse," said Andrew, "but I knew I

wouldn't find one. The back of his head has been crushed. Besides, he was cold. I knew he was dead."

There wasn't much light in that small shed. Brand sent the gardener to fetch a lantern, then crouched down and examined one of Forrest's hands. "It's warm in here," he said, "so that makes it difficult to say how long Forrest has been dead." Forrest's hand was cold and stiff. "At least ten hours, I would say."

Andrew said, "Where did you learn about such things?"

"As a reporter, covering murder trials and coroner's inquests."

The gardener returned with the lantern. Brand held it high and examined the body. The wound to the head had obviously taken some force. Blood and brain matter coated Forrest's graying hair. Brand looked around for a weapon.

"Well, what do we have here?" Brand reached for an iron bar that was half hidden by the door. There was blood on one end.

"We use that to lift paving stones," said the gardener.

"My God!" Andrew breathed out. "Who would want to murder Forrest?"

"That," said Brand, "is for the authorities to find out."

Brand sent Andrew to fetch the magistrate and doctor and left Oswald guarding the body, with instructions not to touch anything, while he had a look outside. Around the shed itself, there was nothing, no footprints and no scuff marks to show that Forrest's body had been dragged to the shed, no sign of a fight or a struggle. Forrest had walked into that shed all unsuspecting.

When Brand stepped out of the shrubbery surrounding the shed, he had an excellent view of the Priory and its grounds. On his left was the conservatory and, beyond that, across the turf, the Priory itself. In front of him, down the incline to Yew Cottage, was the great refectory pulpit, and to the right of that, the herb garden. The stable block, where one would expect to find Forrest, was on the other side of the Priory. To get to the shed, he would have had to pass in front of the Priory in full view of anyone who might be watching.

Unless he came at night.

Fear mingled with frustration made him curse. Nothing was simple. He hadn't a clue to what was going on. Why would anyone want to kill John Forrest?

Hannah, Edwina, Marion, and now Forrest. His instincts told him that they were all connected. What was truly alarming was the thought that there was a murderer at large. Where would he strike next?

He gazed across the sward to the stable block and John Forrest's cottage. Maybe he would find some answers there.

When he arrived at the cottage, he wasn't surprised to find that the door was locked. Forrest was more than Theodora's groom. He was her man of business. There would be accounts and ledgers and receipts to protect. There might even be bank drafts. A cautious man would want to protect his business from prying eyes and sticky fingers.

Forrest wouldn't complain about prying eyes now, or the lack of a key to gain entry to his cottage. Brand put his shoulder down and charged the door.

It took him only a few minutes to familiarize himself with the layout. There was a living room, a large office, and a small bedroom not much bigger than a closet. Any cooking would be done in the recessed fireplace, but the fireplace was so spotless that Brand doubted Theodora's groom had done more than boil water for tea. Either Cook sent his meals out to him or he ate at the house.

The whole place smelled of horses, much like his own place, Brand thought. The smell of horses and leather always reminded him of his grandfather. With his father, it was the smell of brandy and snuff. He shook his head, thinking that those two had been worlds apart in the way they lived their lives.

He wondered about John Forrest and how he'd lived his life. He knew that Theodora had brought him with her when she married his uncle, more than twenty years ago. The groom must be close to sixty, so he ruled out any romantic involvement. But they were close, far closer than employee and mistress. Father and daughter? he hazarded.

The cottage was as spotless as the fireplace. Brand made a brief search of the desk, but decided not to force the locks. Theodora might take exception to that. He was far more interested in the clothes in John Forrest's clothes press.

He almost missed it, the button that had been recently resewn onto one of Forrest's shabby jackets. It had left a tear when it was pulled off in the struggle with Marion. The tear had been neatly mended and the button reattached. Only one thing was different. Though the button matched the others, it was a shade smaller.

Brand removed the loose change from his pocket and combed through it. The button he held to the groom's jacket was an exact match.

His hand closed around the button as though he was squeezing the life out of John Forrest. *He* was the man who had attacked Marion and shot at him. He was the man who had attacked her in London. He'd had the opportunity. He was there with Theodora to look over stock for her stables. And Lord Robert was with them.

Could Forrest have been the great love of Hannah's life? Twenty years ago, he would have been forty. Everything added up except for one thing: Hannah had kept mementoes of Robert, not Forrest.

More complications to befuddle his mind.

He heard a step in the next room and quickly pocketed the button, then relaxed when he heard Theodora's voice.

"Brand, are you there?"

He put the jacket back where he'd found it and went to join her.

The tears in her eyes dried when she saw him. "Oswald told me you were here. I saw him at the conservatory, but he wouldn't let me see John or tell me anything." Her voice changed. "Bloody little upstart! Did he think I'd faint or become hysterical? I have a right to know!"

Anger only heightened her beauty, the sculpted bones, the huge eyes in her pale face, the determined set to her mouth. She would not be an easy woman to live with.

"Sit down," he said, "and I'll tell you what I know."

"Thank you."

He told her as much as he wanted her to know, but nothing of the button or his suspicions. "I came on here," he finally said, "because I thought whoever killed Mr. Forrest might have burglary in mind."

She squinted up at him. "Do you think whoever attacked you and Marion did this?"

He told her no lies. "At this point, I don't know what to think."

When she stared at her clasped hands, lost in thought, he said gently, "Theo, where is Robert?"

Her head jerked up. "Robert? You don't think he did this?" She shook her head. "Robert will be where he usually is, with some woman or other who has taken his fancy for a night or two. His favorite haunt is the Three Crows on Broad Street, but he's well known at all the watering holes in and around Longbury."

Something registered in her eyes and she suddenly got up. "You think Robert was jealous of John?" She gave a disbelieving laugh. "I could have twenty lovers and Robert wouldn't feel a twinge of jealousy. Besides, John was like a father to me. Robert knows that."

When she began to tremble, he said, "You shouldn't be alone. Let me take you back to the house to the others."

Her smile was bleak. "That's when I feel most alone," she said. "When I'm with the others."

Though no one was allowed to leave the house, the magistrate and constable were in no hurry to question them. All the servants, gardeners, and stable hands had been assembled in the Great Hall. Their statements were to be taken first while the family assembled in the library to await their turn. Meanwhile, Mrs. Ludlow had been sent for, and she was supervising Phoebe and Flora.

Dinner was delayed because there was no Cook to make it. She had still to be questioned. Oswald was amused.

"I'm of the opinion," he said, "that Sir Basil can't conceive of a FitzAlan committing a crime, no, nor anyone of his own class. It must be one of the servants. That's why this is taking so long."

No one shared his amusement. No one responded.

They sat there in sphinxlike silence, the picture of gloom and doom. The dowager in particular, in Marion's opinion, seemed dazed by it all. Brand had procured a glass of wine for her, and he nudged her arm gently, encouraging her to take a sip now and then.

A collective sigh went up when a footman entered and told them that the magistrate was ready to see them now. Their relief was short-lived, however, when the footman said that they were to be called in order, beginning with the gentlemen who had found the body.

After fifteen minutes, only Emily, Clarice, and Marion were left, so it was obvious that their interviews with the magistrate would not take long.

Emily said, "Why has no one returned to tell us what's going on?"

"I expect," responded Clarice, "Sir Basil wants to make sure that our alibis stand up without help from our friends and relations."

"Well, my alibi will stand up." There was an edge of irritation in Emily's voice. "And so will Andrew's. We spent the morning at the seaside with Ginny Matthews and ... oh ... there must have been half a dozen of us—having a picnic. We'd only just got back and were admiring the conservatory flowers when the gardener ran in and told Andrew about Mr. Forrest."

Marion said, "Yes, dear, but we don't know for certain when Mr. Forrest was ... attacked. Brand thinks it was during the night."

She was thinking of something else Brand had told her. He'd been to John Forrest's cottage and found the coat that the button had been torn from. There was no doubt in Brand's mind that Forrest was behind the attacks on her, not only in Longbury but in London as well.

She couldn't get her mind around it. He'd seemed so gentlemanly and reserved. And who would have wanted to kill him, and why?

There was a cold-blooded killer loose, said Brand, and until they unmasked him, she should trust no one.

Emily was called away at that moment, and Marion gave Clarice her handkerchief to wipe away her tears.

Between sniffs, Clarice got out, "I hate this place. It has a bad odor. I was never happy here, not even as a child." She patted Marion's knee. "You were the only friend I ever had, and that was only for a few weeks one summer."

Marion hardly knew what to say. She'd never seen Clarice like this. She had to say something. "But you and Oswald are happy together. Anyone can tell that you're in love."

Clarice smiled through her tears. "He saw something in me that no one else did. I was a lump of a girl ... well ... hardly a girl. I was twenty-five when he came into the area to look for Saxon relics. He found another relic he decided to collect: me. And the last two years have been the happiest of my life."

After a moment or two of silence, Marion said, "If you hate this place so much, why don't you leave it? You and Oswald could live somewhere else."

Clarice shrugged. "Who would look after my grandmother? Not Miss Cutter. And they're both too old to set down roots somewhere else. You saw my grandmother tonight, how frail she is becoming." Clarice stopped to blow her nose. "I don't let her know that she's all that keeps me here. She would be the first to tell me to go."

A long silence went by as Marion digested this. Finally, she said, "What about Lord Robert and Theodora? They're here. They could look after Her Grace."

Clarice's lips flattened. "Theodora is too taken with herself to spare a thought for anyone else. One has only to see the care she expends on Flora to know what she values. Only herself. You would never know that she was that poor child's aunt. Robert shows the girl more affection than Theo does. He has more time for her—"

She bit down on her lip, and gave Marion a shame-faced look. "I shouldn't be talking like this. Theodora has sorrows to bear that would crush most women. That's what Oswald says." She brightened considerably. "He's a dear, isn't he?"

Marion smiled. "I believe he is."

Clarice said, "I shouldn't complain. I'm not so lonely with your family close by. And when you're married to Brand and a member of the family, it will be even better. Your children and my children will be cousins."

This was an avenue Marion did not want to go down. What could she say? That she was afraid to marry Brand if he won a seat in Parliament? That she was delaying until she was quite sure she would not turn out to be a millstone around his neck? And when would that be?

Everything was in such a muddle. She did not know whether she was coming or going. And Brand was no help. He would not press her, he said; he would not push her. The decision must be hers and hers alone.

Clarice said, "Flora and Phoebe are as close as sisters, not unlike we were at their age."

"Only not quite as adventurous. Leastways, I hope not."

Clarice smiled. "I can't believe what we got up to, and so young, too. We were lucky we were never found out."

A thought flashed into Marion's head, and before de-bating the wisdom of what she was doing, she rushed into speech. "We *were* found out. Not long before that dreadful accident that took my aunt's life, someone told her that I was out that night. It upset her very much."

"Slow down," said Clarice. Her brow was puckered. "Who told your aunt that you were out? And what night do you mean?"

Marion took a long, slow breath. "I don't know who told her, but it was the night we lay in wait for the Priory ghost. Someone saw me and told my aunt, quite recently. That was the same night that my other aunt, Hannah, eloped. Edwina thought that I might have been the last person to speak to Hannah. You see, she never heard from Hannah again, and she always regretted that they'd parted after a quarrel. It was all in a letter she wrote."

"That's sad," said Clarice, "but not unusual. Oswald had an aunt who eloped, and her family cut her off. No one was allowed to mention her name. She might as well have been dead, Oswald said."

"Yes, but Edwina wasn't like that. She wanted to find out where Hannah was. Think carefully, Clarice. Did you see Hannah? Or anything that looked out of place? Did you see anyone else? Someone else was there. I wish I knew who it was."

Clarice was shaking her head. "It must have been whoever we mistook for the ghost. I saw no one else, and the only odd thing I can recall was the dog whining and barking."

"What dog?"

"I told you before. When I heard that animal moaning, I thought it was a ghostly dog. Isn't that what made us panic?"

"You didn't say it was a dog."

"What else could it have been? Theodora's dog was always running wild. She had no control over it. I think, now, that it must have been Snowball."

The door opened and a footman entered. "Lady Clarice," he intoned, "Sir Basil will see you now."

When Clarice got up, Marion restrained her with a hand on her wrist. "We'll talk about this later, Clarice, but don't mention this conversation to anyone else, all right?"

Her warning seemed to startle Clarice, but she nodded before she followed the footman out.

Marion got up and went to one of the windows. The light was beginning to fade, making her gloomy thoughts all the more gloomy. For the first time, as she and Clarice talked, it came to her that the witness had not mentioned that Clarice was out that night, too, or her aunt would have mentioned it in her letter to Brand.

Who saw her, and where were they hiding when she passed by? She knew what she ought to do. She should go to the stone pulpit and reenact what happened that night, just as the locals re-enacted the battle between Roundheads and Cavaliers every year.

Just thinking about it made her spirits plummet. What was it Clarice had said? *This place has a bad odor.* She'd felt it herself. Since coming to Longbury, she'd only once taken the shortcut past the refectory pulpit to Yew Cottage, and that was the night of the fête, the night she'd been attacked by John Forrest. And that night, as she'd made her way down hill in the half-light, she'd felt her skin begin to prickle.

Something hovered at the edge of her mind, but she couldn't bring it into focus, something she saw or didn't see as she ran down that hill. What was it?

She turned when the door opened, expecting to see the footman, but it was Clarice who entered. "Yes," said

Clarice, "the magistrate is ready to see you now. And you need not worry. He's not asking questions so much as taking statements. I just wanted to let you know that I'm going to relieve Mrs. Ludlow and take care of the girls, and Cook and her helpers are serving sandwiches and cold meats in the breakfast room."

"Where are the others?" asked Marion.

"Brand and Andrew have gone out looking for Robert." Her face crumpled. "It's Robert we are all worried about. He hasn't been home for the last two nights, and Sir Basil is acting as though Robert is his prime suspect."

# Chapter Twenty-three

They didn't take horses, since Longbury was a small town and Brand knew they would need to hire some sort of vehicle to take Robert home, supposing they found him. As they trooped from one tavern to the next, Brand cursed all the while, complaining about the proliferation of taverns in a small place like Longbury.

"What's the matter with the people here?" he demanded. "Why do they need a tavern on every corner? Are they all drunkards?"

Brand knew why he was so cantankerous. Fear was at the bottom of it. On just such a night as this, he'd gone looking for his father when he'd been missing from the Priory for several days. Robert had roused him from his grandfather's house, and they had searched together. They'd found his father, but he'd drunk himself insensate and choked to death on his own vomit.

They found Robert in the White Horse, a hostelry on the western edge of the town. There were a few vehicles in the stable yard, but the inn was hardly bustling.

Evidently it had seen better days. The furnishings were shabby, as were its few patrons and the landlord. He directed them to a room one floor up and they quickly mounted the stairs.

Brand entered first.

Robert was lying on the bed in a state of complete disarray. It wasn't the smell of brandy that sent a jolt through Brand but the stench of vomit. He was at Robert's side in two strides.

"Quick, he's choking to death."

His urgent words froze Andrew to the spot. "What?"

"He's trying to clear the vomit from his lungs. Move, Andrew! Help me!"

They turned Robert facedown over the bed, and the movement must have dislodged the vomit because a stream of vile-smelling bile spouted from Robert's mouth onto the floor, and he lay gasping for air. His lips were blue, his eyes were closed, but he was breathing.

"Oh, Robert!" said Brand despairingly. "What are you doing to yourself?"

Those blue lips lifted a little, and Robert looked up at Brand through half-closed lids. "Rest easy, Brand," he said hoarsely. "I'm not nearly as drunk as I look. I won't die on you like your father did. I could have managed on my own."

Brand turned to Andrew. "Coffee," he said, "and lots of it."

Andrew was rooted to the spot. "What did he mean, he won't die on you like our father did?"

"Just what you think he meant! Now make yourself useful and get that coffee."

An hour later found them in Brand's chamber in his grandfather's house. Brand wanted to avoid the Priory, suspecting that there would be an officer of the law waiting there for his uncle to return, and he wanted to spare Robert the indignity of being seen in the state he was in. He was also impatient to put his own questions to Robert, not to entrap him, but to get to the truth about Hannah. When that became known, then they would be closer to finding Forrest's murderer and Marion would be safe.

Manley was given the task of letting the family know, discreetly, where they were and that they'd found Robert none the worse for wear, but not a word was Manley to let slip to the authorities.

"What's this about?" asked Robert wearily. "Why have you brought me here? I know something is up, Brand. What is it?"

Having bathed, he was wearing one of Brand's nightshirts and a woolen dressing robe. His hair was combed, but he was still white-faced and blue about the lips. The fire had been lit because he'd begun to shiver, and he was sitting in a huge horsehair chair pulled close to the blaze.

Brand cast a swift glance at Andrew. He'd refused to return to the Priory with Manley, and was sitting off to one side, with strict instructions not to say a word. Brand admired this new steel in Andrew but, at the same time, he found it unsettling. His brother was only eighteen. He knew nothing of the seamier side of life.

Brand sighed. It seemed that his protection was no longer wanted or necessary.

He pulled his chair closer to Robert's. "Last night, John Forrest was brutally murdered," he began baldly.

Robert seemed genuinely shocked, though not grief-stricken. He fired off a barrage of questions, and Brand told him as much as he knew.

He ended with, "No one knows where you have been these last two nights."

Robert smiled. "Ah. Do I have an alibi is what you mean. I've been visiting all the watering holes in Longbury, tipsy for the most part. I'm not sure if that will serve as an alibi. I suppose I could have slipped away at some point and done the dread deed, but why would I?"

Without preamble, Brand said coolly, "To cover another murder, one that took place almost twenty years ago. You know whose murder I mean. Hannah Gunn's."

Brand had wanted to shock his uncle and he could see that he'd succeeded. Robert's hands clenched. The little color that was in his face drained out of it. He shook his head.

His voice was barely audible. "Have they found Hannah's remains, then?"

Brand steeled himself not to be moved by his uncle's distress. He'd been circumspect until now and it had got him nowhere. It was time for a different approach.

"Did you murder Hannah? Did you kill her in a jealous rage because she refused to elope with you?"

Robert stared then gave a mirthless laugh. "You've got that backwards. Hannah Gunn was a troubled young woman who hunted me as any predator hunts its prey. It's because of her that my marriage failed. She told my wife that we were going away together and that she had letters from me that proved I loved her. In fact, it was the other way round. She wrote me letters that I burned as soon as I read them. They were the ravings of a demented woman."

This came as no surprise to Brand. Hannah wasn't normal. It also explained Forrest's involvement. These were surely the letters he'd been after. If they had come to light, Robert would have been suspected of murdering Hannah. Forrest wasn't loyal to Robert, but to Theodora. He would do anything to save her embarrassment or pain.

Robert passed a hand over his eyes. "What does any of this have to do with John Forrest?"

Brand leaned forward, hands loosely clasped. "I think—no, I have proof—that Forrest was the man who broke into Marion's cottage. Everyone knows of the attack. What they don't know is that he held a gun to Marion's head and demanded that she hand over Hannah's letters. I think he wanted the letters he believed you had sent her."

"But there were no letters!"

"I believe you, but how long do you think it will be before the authorities make the connection between you and Forrest and the letters he was desperate to get hold of? They'll think you put him up to it to protect yourself, then you had a falling-out. They will want to know what happened to Hannah all those years ago." He paused, then went on in a more moderate tone, "*I* want to know what happened to Hannah. Her disappearance has cast a long shadow and it's time to exorcise it."

A silence fell. The coals in the grate hissed and flared. Somewhere in the house, a clock struck the hour.

"Robert?" prompted Brand gently.

His uncle blinked and focused his gaze on Brand.

Brand said, "Tell me about Hannah. She told Theo you had written her passionate love letters. Did she show Theo the letters?"

"No. How could she? There were none."

"Go on. You said that your marriage failed. There must have been more to it than the letters. What else did Hannah do?"

Robert shrugged. "I told you. She stalked me like a

hunter. I could never turn around but I was falling over her. At first, it was amusing, then irritating. But when she stole Theo's dog and swore that I had given it to her as a gift, I came to see that she was dangerous."

There was only one dog: Theo's dog. Brand had suspected as much, but it raised a question in his mind. "Did Hannah return the dog?"

"No. She wouldn't admit that it was Theo's dog." A faintly cynical smile touched Robert's lips. "The dog was the last straw as far as Theo was concerned. You see, she believed Hannah, not me. I think you know why, Brand."

When Brand nodded briefly, Robert said, "Yes, your father and I were both wild young men in our time, with nothing on our minds but pleasure. All that changed when we met the women of our dreams. For your father, it was your mother. For me, it was Theo. I was luckier than your father, or so I thought. It took a great deal of persuasion, but Theo finally agreed to marry me. We were happy for a time, but she never completely trusted me." His voice changed color, became bitter. "You can imagine the damage Hannah did. Theo never forgave me."

He shrugged. "I suppose we might have reconciled in time, but I would not confess to infidelity or change my story. And that was that. I took up my old ways, just like your father before me. Drinking, whoring. One good thing came of it: I had a daughter. But I think you know that."

"Flora," murmured Brand.

A strangled sound came from Andrew's direction. Brand ignored it. Robert did not seem to hear. He was staring at the coals in the fire, lost in his memories. Brand doubted that his uncle remembered why they were having this conversation.

Finally, Robert stirred. "I miss my brother." He looked at Brand. "He was eight years older than I, but we were always close. He understood me as no one else did."

This time, Andrew would not be silenced. He stood up. "Why do you do this to yourself?" He made a slashing motion with one hand. "Why did my father? You're drinking yourself to death."

"Melancholy," Robert replied simply. "Or boredom. I haven't made up my mind which it is."

"Andrew," began Brand, but Andrew would not be silenced.

"You have a daughter! Doesn't that mean something?"

"She doesn't know I'm her father."

"Surely Theo would forgive you if you told her about the child—"

Robert waved him to silence. "My dear boy, Theo knows that Flora is my daughter. It is she who suggested that the child spend half the year with us after her mother died. I'd hoped . . . well, it doesn't matter what I hoped. Flora was better off with her aunt—I mean her mother's sister. Theo ignores the child, and I am in no state to take charge of anyone. Just look at me. What good would I be to my daughter?"

Brand's voice cut across Andrew's next words. "Andrew, I'd be obliged if you would ask one of the servants to make up sandwiches for us, and a bowl of thin gruel for Robert."

"But we had sandwiches when we arrived."

"I'm still hungry."

Andrew made a fulminating sound, but the look in his brother's eye brooked no debate, and he quietly left the room.

When the door closed, Brand turned back to his

uncle. In fact, he felt much as Andrew did. Robert was throwing his life away for no good reason. Brand did not consider Theo a good reason. He held his tongue because he was older and wiser than Andrew. He'd learned that people changed when they had a powerful reason to change, and not before.

Robert was eyeing him with interest. "Tell me something, Brand," he said. "I promise I won't take offence. Do you like me? I mean, in spite of my faults?"

Liking was too tepid a word. Love was too womanish. "I'm very fond of you, Robert, as I'm sure you know."

Robert nodded. "And I of you. But it has always puzzled me why you judge your father so harshly. There is not much to choose between him and me."

Brand had no ready answer to this profound statement, so he brushed it off. "We were talking about Hannah," he said. "What did you do to make her stop pestering you?"

Robert breathed out a sigh. After a considering silence, he said, "I arranged to meet Hannah at the conservatory late one night when everyone was in bed. Naturally, I didn't want Theo to see us, or to hear from someone else that I'd met Hannah alone. You might say that I read Hannah the riot act, told her that if she set foot in the Priory grounds again, I would have her arrested and charged with trespassing. She . . ." He drew in a long breath. "She went to pieces, begged me not to break it off. She couldn't seem to get it through her head that there was nothing to break off. Then she tried a little blackmail. She had nowhere to go, she said. She'd quarreled with her sisters and told them she was having an affair with a married man and she was going away with him. She couldn't go back now. I didn't believe her.

God help me, I was so angry, I turned and left her. And that's the last time I saw her."

Brand nodded absently. So this is what the women had quarreled about at Yew Cottage that night, the quarrel Marion had overheard but not understood.

He leaned toward Robert, his arm braced on his knees. "But you must have wondered what happened to her? You must have known that she hadn't eloped?"

Robert looked down at his hands. "At first, I suspected that she'd thrown herself into the river. It's the only thing I could think of. She was distraught when I left her. But as time went by, I heard murmurs that Hannah had many strings to her bow and I came to believe, or I hoped, that she'd turned to someone else when I failed her. It suited me, I suppose, to take the easy way out. That's the story of my life."

Robert reached for something to drink and saw nothing but a cup of tepid coffee. He made a face and folded his arms across his chest.

Sighing, Brand got up, went to a small sideboard, and returned a moment later with a glass of pink liquid which he handed to Robert.

"Thank you," said Robert. "What is it?"

Brand sat down. "A little wine mixed with water. Sip it, don't gulp it."

Robert chuckled and looked at Brand with a smile that was warm and intimate. "You should have been the duke, Brand. Your father always regretted that you would never inherit his title. He said you were the best of the FitzAlans. That's why he made you the sole trustee of Andrew's affairs. He loved you, though you were very hard to love."

This was another profound statement to which Brand

had no ready answer. All the same, he was oddly affected. It was true; he had been very hard to love.

Robert's smile slipped and became edged with sadness. "Your father and I made a mull of our lives, and the family suffered. I think you and Andrew will do a much better job than we did."

Andrew returned and, soon after, the sandwiches arrived with more coffee. Robert would take only the glass of wine mixed with water. When his eyes started to glaze over, they put him to bed. Brand and Andrew sat close to the fire, eating their sandwiches in companionable silence, glancing at the bed from time to time.

Brand did not consider himself a sentimental man, but he felt more of a FitzAlan in that moment than he'd ever felt before, and he realized that the people in that room were as dear to him as his own life. He would have given anything to have his father there, even if they only talked about cricket. And for once, when he talked to his father, he wouldn't be difficult or defiant. He wouldn't be hard to love.

Andrew's quietly spoken words cut across Brand's thoughts. "How did you know that Flora was Robert's child?"

Brand smiled faintly. "Have you seen her ride? She's a FitzAlan, all right. It's more than that, though. Robert's smile is different when his gaze comes to rest on the girl. It's warm, intimate, and very sweet."

"But her coloring? Red hair? Green eyes?"

"I expect she got that from her mother's side of the family."

Andrew was still puzzled. "I thought she lived with Theo's sister for half the year."

"Evidently not. I suppose that explanation was to save Theodora's pride."

A long silence followed, then Andrew said, "What happens now?"

Brand dragged his thoughts back to Andrew. "We have to let the magistrate know that Robert is here. His alibi is convincing. I think Sir Basil will accept it."

"What about Hannah? What are you going to tell Sir Basil about her?"

"Nothing. I'm not going to do the magistrate's job for him. I've told him all that I'm going to tell him, at least for the moment."

Andrew nodded and looked away. His voice was so low, Brand had to lean forward to catch his words. "Do you think Theo killed Hannah? She truly believed Robert had betrayed her."

"The thought had occurred to me. But I can't see her murdering John Forrest."

"Neither can I, unless John Forrest betrayed her in some way that we know nothing about. There's something about Theo that gives me the shudders."

"She knows how to hate," Brand said.

His mind shifted to Marion. Marion knew how to love. *I love you.* Emotion tightened his throat.

Andrew let out a sigh. "Now tell me about our father, Brand. Tell me about the night he died."

Brand chose his words with care. He didn't want Andrew to despise their father. There was nothing to despise, but so much to regret. "Robert and I found him," he said slowly. "We couldn't bring him round."

"He was drunk?"

"He'd been drinking" was all Brand would allow. "He just slipped away from us." He looked at Andrew. "You might say that his heart gave out."

Brand left Andrew looking after their uncle, while he walked the short distance from his grandfather's house to the Priory. There were no constables or officers of the law that he could see, but he took precautions not to be seen. The key to the coal cellar was under a stone urn. He used it to gain access not only to the cellar but also to the door that gave onto the servants' staircase. Though there were no candles lit, he knew every nook and cranny in the Priory, and he reached Marion's room in less than a minute.

She'd left a candle burning on the stone hearth, and it was beginning to drown in its own wax. She was in bed, breathing softly in sleep, the coverlet thrown off and her white lawn nightgown open at the throat. He could see her pulse beating out a slow, comforting measure.

One hand was tucked under her cheek; the other rested on her pillow. Small, fragile, feminine hands that gave no hint of how ferocious they could become when she had to defend herself or those she loved. He was thinking of how she'd tried to wrest John Forrest's gun from him the night she was attacked.

He wasn't tempted to waken her. He hadn't come to her room to make love to her. He was in a contemplative frame of mind and was content to sit in the chair by the fire, watching her, feeling the same emotion he had experienced earlier with Andrew, when they'd sat quietly by the fire with their uncle sleeping close by.

Six months ago, he'd thought his life was full. Now he saw how empty it had been. If he had only one hour to live, he wouldn't waste it on advancing his political career or selling more newspapers. He'd want to spend it with the people who meant most to him, the people who knew how to love.

He didn't stay long. He didn't kiss her good-bye, but

put his fingers close to her lips without touching them, then brought the warmth from her breath to his own lips.

After locking the cellar door, he made to put the key back where he had found it, but a thought occurred to him and he slipped it into his pocket. From now on, the coalmen would have to get the key from the butler. And just to quell a nasty suspicion that kept running through his mind, he'd put Manley on to watching Theodora.

# Chapter Twenty-four

The next morning, Marion awakened feeling rested and refreshed. She smiled up at the bed canopy through half-lowered lashes, trying to remember her dream. The details were hazy, but she knew Brand was in it, and she felt steeped in happiness.

Her euphoria vanished as reality swept in. Yesterday, they'd found John Forrest's body. He'd been brutally murdered the night before. Lord Robert was the prime suspect. Even now, he was wanted for questioning. The dowager would be beside herself with grief, and Brand would be devastated. As for Theo—she would be grieving for John Forrest. Who knew what she would think of Robert?

Sighing, she pushed back the covers and got up. She had sisters who needed her, and Flora, too. Somebody had to be there for them to soothe their fears. But who was there for her? Brand, she knew, was at the Grange with Lord Robert, and would not leave his side until the magistrate had talked to him.

*This place has a bad odor.* She could feel it seeping into her. If she didn't start moving, she would expire from an attack of nerves.

Her toilette took her no more than fifteen minutes, and a few minutes after that, she entered the breakfast room. The only occupants were Emily and Miss Cutter. They both looked as despondent as she felt, though Emily did manage a smile.

"We're the laggards," said Emily. "Everyone else has breakfasted and gone about their business. The eggs are cold, but the tea is fresh and hot."

"Where are the girls?"

"They've gone off with Clarice and Oswald to see the sea. It's only six miles from here, so I gave my permission. They'll have a lovely time there, Marion, and I thought they would be better off there than here."

Marion nodded. A trip to the seaside was something that she'd promised Phoebe before they set off from the Lake District. How was it they'd never got around to it?

She looked at Miss Cutter. The poor dear was sunk in silence; this was not like her at all. This business with Lord Robert was taking its toll. As Marion remembered, Lord Robert was Miss Cutter's favorite.

Marion impulsively reached for Miss Cutter's hand and squeezed gently. "Brand is with Lord Robert," she said. "He won't let any harm come to him."

A spark kindled in those old, dull eyes, and Miss Cutter smiled. "You are so kind, my dear, but I'm not worried about Robert. Andrew was just here with a message from Brand. He says that Robert has a perfectly good explanation for his absence from the Priory. No. It's Her Grace that worries me. She has taken it so hard. I don't know how everything could have gone so wrong."

She got up. "Sit yourself down, Marion, and I'll pour you a cup of tea."

"I can manage—"

"No, no. It's no trouble."

Marion sat, reached for a piece of toast, and began to munch on it. "Andrew was here?"

Emily nodded. "He is with his grandmother now, and as soon as Robert talks to the magistrate and clears himself of suspicion, they'll all come on here."

"I see." Marion would have felt better had the message arrived after the magistrate had talked to Robert. Until that happened, Andrew's message was nothing more than an empty reassurance, much like hers had been with Miss Cutter.

"Thank you," she said when Miss Cutter set her teacup and saucer on the table.

Emily said, "There was a message from Brand to you, but it doesn't make sense."

"What is it?"

"Read my mind?"

To cover her ridiculous smile, Marion reached for her cup of tea and swallowed a mouthful before she realized how hot it was. She coughed and gasped till tears started to her eyes. "I burned my tongue," she rasped out.

Miss Cutter quickly tipped up the milk jug into the cup to cool Marion's tea. "Try that," she said.

Marion took another long swallow. The tea was now tepid and not to her liking, but Miss Cutter looked so pleased with herself that she hadn't the heart to ask for a fresh cup.

"That's better," she said, and took another sip. A thought occurred to her. "Does Theodora know that Robert has been found?"

Through thinned lips, Emily said, "She was here

when Andrew arrived. Her only comment was that she wanted to look over the contents of John Forrest's desk, to make sure that everything was in order. She's there now with the constable and Mr. Manley."

Miss Cutter clicked her tongue. A pall settled over the table. Marion sighed, reached for the dish of marmalade, and dropped a spoonful on her plate beside her slice of toast.

"I suppose Mr. Manley will advise her about her stables?" When no one answered, she tried again. "What are your plans for this morning, Emily?"

"I haven't any." Emily swallowed and looked down at the uneaten slice of toast on her plate. "I feel awful. I still can't believe that this has happened. It's like a nightmare."

Marion dragged herself from her own doldrums. "All the more reason," she said, "to find something to get your mind off these horrendous events. You should have gone to the seaside with Clarice and Oswald. Since you didn't, I suggest you get Andrew to take you to your friend Ginny's. Go shopping with her, or go calling on other friends. Do whatever young girls your age are supposed to do."

Emily brightened a little. "Why don't you come with me?"

Marion shook her head. She had her own plans for this morning. "I don't have the energy," she said. "I thought I'd read a book and keep Miss Cutter company." She looked at Miss Cutter.

Miss Cutter nodded. "Or go for a walk? I'd like to show you my herb garden."

"Why not?" said Marion.

Miss Cutter beamed. "Just give me a moment and I'll let Her Grace know where I shall be."

When she hurried away, Emily said, "I think you have made her day."

"Yes, she is too much alone. The dowager isn't much company for her, is she?" Marion took another sip of tea and screwed up her face. "If there's anything I hate it's tepid tea."

When Miss Cutter returned, the offensive tea had been removed by a servant and Marion was sipping from a fresh cup.

Miss Cutter was all in a flutter. If she'd been strangely quiet before, now her tongue rattled on like a galloping horse. It was such an honor. Young people nowadays had no time for older people. They didn't go walking just for the pleasure of it, but to go shopping or visiting. They were always in carriages. And so it went on.

Marion made what she hoped were suitable responses, but her mind was focused on the path they were on. This was the way Clarice would have come the night she bolted after seeing the monk's ghost.

They had just passed the conservatory on their right, where the refectory had stood in a bygone era. The shed where Forrest's body was found was there, too, though hidden by a thicket of shrubbery. The sun was hot and high overhead. The swallows were performing their dives like acrobats, and on the flowering plants, bees and butterflies danced around each other in perfect harmony.

It was hard to believe that in this little paradise lurked so much evil.

A few steps down the path, everything changed. Dense trees filtered the rays of the sun, dappling the shrubbery in shadow. There were no swallows, no bees or butterflies. Spiders spun their webs to entrap their unwary victims. Foxes lurked in the shadows. Feral wild cats swished their tails, their muscles bunching before they pounced to make a kill.

Marion gave a shaken laugh. This was how she and Clarice had struck terror into each other. What horrid children they must have been.

When they came to a fork in the path, Miss Cutter balked. "This is the way to the herb garden," she said.

The way she pointed to was well laid out with paving stones. The way to Yew Cottage was overgrown with thistles and nettles.

Marion said, "I thought we'd take in the refectory pulpit. It's only a short walk away. And it's where Clarice and I used to play as children."

"I'm not sure that I can manage the steep slope." Miss Cutter's face brightened. "Why don't I go along to my herbarium and get things ready. When you've looked around, you can join me. It shouldn't take you long. There's not much to see."

Marion wasn't sure they should separate.

As though reading her mind, Miss Cutter said, "If I shout, you'll hear me. And there are gardeners close by. Now, don't be long."

On that confident note, she took the path to the herb garden.

The refectory pulpit was beside the ruins of what had once been the abbot's house and the dormitories for visiting guests. The latter building had vanished without a trace under the encroaching brush and the depredations of succeeding generations of villagers who had carried off the stone walls for their own use. It was only when the Priory passed into FitzAlan hands that trespassers were warned off and the depredations ceased.

The pulpit was largely untouched. Marion guessed that the locals had regarded this relic as too holy to demolish, that and the sculpture of the abbot that marked the spot where his former residence had once stood. The trees did not encroach here, and Marion had a clear view of the pulpit as she entered the clearing.

The pulpit was much bigger than she remembered, and to a child it must have seemed like a tower. She mounted the stone steps and counted twelve—probably a sacred number, each step representing one of the apostles. From this vantage point, the lector would have looked down on the heads of the silent monks as they took their meals. Anyone who suffered from vertigo must have hung on to the stone ledge, as she was doing now.

When she and Clarice lay in wait for their ghost, everything would have been cloaked in darkness, so that they hadn't the sense to realize how far they would fall if they missed a step. Or maybe she was bolder back then. Maybe she'd climbed the steps during the daylight hours and vertigo had held no fears for her. She could not remember. That was the trouble. No shattering revelation came to her so that she could cry *"Eureka!"*

She'd come here to reenact the scene, and though she thought that the exercise would be futile, at least it was worth a try. Breathing deeply, she closed her eyes and cast her mind back to the night she'd waited in Yew Cottage for the quarrel to be over so that she could slip away to be with Clarice.

So Hannah left the house. The next thing Marion remembered was climbing the path to the pulpit. She knew that she was late and wondered if Clarice would have waited for her. On the way, she passed the sculpture of the first abbot and made the sign of the cross. Not that she was Catholic. It was a ritual, a mark of reverence that she and Clarice had devised in this make-believe world they inhabited from time to time.

How could she have forgotten that?

It was a great relief when she saw the light in the pulpit, swinging from side to side. Clarice had waited for her. She counted the steps as she mounted them. Whispered greetings, then Clarice blew out the lantern and they hunched down to await events.

She had no idea how much time passed, or whether she or Clarice heard it first. A dog was whining, then barking. They slowly raised themselves and peered over the edge of the pulpit. Lights were floating in the air, moving toward them, and a ghostly sound followed, as though some spirit was calling to the dog.

That's when Clarice bolted.

Marion remembered sinking down and shutting her eyes. She was frozen in terror. The ghost of the abbot was coming to get her, and not only the abbot, but his dog as well.

What happened next?

She remembered the dog licking her face. He'd found her in the pulpit. She could have wept with relief. Not the abbot's dog, then, but Scruff, Hannah's dog. That meant there were no ghosts. It was only Hannah, looking for her dog. Scruff was a wanderer, always getting lost.

So she left the pulpit and ran toward the lights, calling Hannah's name. Scruff started to whine, and Hannah didn't answer. Frightened now, she retreated a step, then she turned and fled. Scruff did not follow her.

What did she see?

Two lights. Two people. But Hannah was not there, or she would have answered Marion.

She opened her eyes. From her perch in the pulpit, she had an unimpeded view of the herb garden. She gazed at it for a long time, then shifted her gaze to where the abbot's house once stood, and the breath rushed out of her lungs. She had a good idea of what had happened to Hannah all those years ago, and knew, without a doubt, where she had found an unholy resting place.

Descending the steps of the pulpit was much harder than going up them. She felt a wave of dizziness, and gripped the stone ledge as she eased herself down. She frowned when she saw that Miss Cutter was waiting for her, but another wave of dizziness made her glad that someone was there to help her.

"I wondered what had happened to you," said Miss Cutter, "so I thought I'd come and find out."

"I feel faint," said Marion. "It's all been too much for me."

"Take my arm, my dear," said Miss Cutter, then she laughed, a soft, intimate laugh that, oddly enough, brought a shiver to Marion's spine. "That's right, lean on me, and I'll take care of you. I'm not as feeble as I look."

Brand saw the magistrate off the premises and returned to the library, where Robert and Andrew were drinking coffee. He'd taken them both into his confidence, telling them as much as he knew about Hannah and Edwina's letter, and felt lighter in his own mind for sharing the burden. Robert looked a little brighter after a night's sleep, and more like himself now that he was wearing his own clothes. Andrew had fetched them from the Priory earlier, but there were no messages from Theodora.

"I think that went rather well," said Andrew.

Robert gave a short laugh. "If you can call a broad hint not to leave the neighborhood going 'rather well.'" A pensive look came over his face.

"Look on the bright side," said Brand. "Sir Basil doesn't know anything about ancient history. He doesn't know about Hannah and your involvement . . ." A look from Robert made him amend what he was about to say. " . . . your troubles with her."

"You're right, of course," said Robert, and gulped a mouthful of coffee. "I wasn't thinking of Sir Basil, though, I was thinking of . . . "

"Theo?" supplied Andrew when Robert hesitated.

"No. My mother."

"Grandmama?" Andrew looked puzzled.

Robert took another gulp of coffee. "I always wondered if she knew about Hannah. I think she must have done. I think she believed that I was having an affair with her." He gave a helpless shrug. "I can't put my finger on it, but I sometimes catch a look on my mother's face that makes me feel conscience-stricken." There was a troubled look in his eyes. "Could she possibly think that I had something to do with Hannah's disappearance?"

"No," said Andrew firmly. "But you should feel conscience-stricken. Grandmama worries about you and wishes you would pull yourself together. We all worry about you."

Robert gave him one of his sweet smiles.

Brand's thoughts took a sharp turn. He was remembering his first day back in Longbury, when he visited the Priory. He'd been asking questions about Hannah, and his grandmother had seemed ill at ease. Oh, yes, he thought. The dowager had known about the bogus affair and had her suspicions, too. She wouldn't want old history to be revived or suspicion to fall on Robert. How she must have suffered all these years.

Brand sat down, but a moment later he was on his feet again.

After watching him prowl for a moment or two, Robert said, "You're very restless. What's the matter?"

"Nothing. I've been cooped up in here too long."

He sat down again, crossed one leg over the other, then changed position.

"You're worse than restless," said Robert. "What is it, Brand?"

Brand shrugged. "Small things keep nagging at me, and I don't know whether they mean anything or not."

"What, for instance?"

"I was thinking of the dog." Brand thought for a moment. "When you told me that you met Hannah that night, you didn't mention a dog."

"Theo's dog," said Robert, and nodded. "Not that he cared who he belonged to. His name should have been Casanova. He was always off exploring, and would attach himself to any pretty lady who took his fancy. That's how Hannah got hold of him in the first place. And I didn't mention him because he wasn't there. Is it important?"

"I don't know. Clarice said that she heard some poor animal whining, and Marion thinks she heard a dog barking. I don't like loose ends, that's all."

"That's easily explained. After I returned to the house, the dog got out. I was in no mood to go after him. But he was back the next day."

"Who found him, Theodora?"

"No. Miss Cutter."

"When? How?"

Robert shrugged. "I have no idea. He was forever sniffing around her herb garden, digging up her precious plants. Maybe that's where she found him."

Brand's mind was working like lightning. "What happened to the dog?" he asked.

"What? Oh, the poor beast ingested rat poison that we believe the gardeners had put out for rodents. They denied it, of course. They're not allowed to leave poison where any stray child can get to it. Don't forget, there are always hordes of children at the fête."

Brand got up. "I think," he said, "I'll go for a walk."

He was at the door before a thought struck him. "How soon after Hannah's disappearance did this happen?"

"You mean when did the dog die? Just before Christmas. That would make it six months or so. I remember because Miss Cutter wanted to give Theo a puppy for Christmas, but I had to tell her that it wasn't a good idea. Theo never wanted another dog after that."

"Thank you." Brand left the room.

Andrew said, "What was that all about?"

"I think," said Robert musingly, "Brand knows who the killer is."

# Chapter Twenty-five

They were on the path, going toward Yew Cottage.
"Why are we going to the cottage?"

Miss Cutter made a clucking sound. "Because it's downhill. I don't think I can get you up the incline to the Priory. And there's bound to be someone there. We'll send for the doctor."

Marion doubted that there would be anyone at the cottage. Since their move to the Priory had become permanent, more or less, they hadn't required the services of Mrs. Ludlow or watchmen to guard the place. She wasn't sure what the arrangements were, nor did she care. She was coming down with something—influenza, a cold? All she wanted to do was sleep. But she had something important to tell Miss Cutter. What was it?

She blinked to focus her thoughts. "I remember. I know where Hannah is buried. She's in your herb garden, Miss Cutter. That's where John Forrest buried her. He moved the sculpture of the abbot, and . . . and . . ." Her speech was becoming slurred, and she made an effort to master her tongue. "He must have been afraid that you or one of the gardeners would find her remains if ever you turned the earth over."

"Watch your step now. We don't want you scraping your knees."

"Did you hear me, Miss Cutter?"

"Yes, dear. You mentioned the abbot, I believe."

Miss Cutter was not taking her seriously, and that made her cross. If only Emily had been there when she descended the pulpit steps, she would have believed her and sent at once for the constable. This poor, confused woman was no help at all.

"We must send for the constable at once! Don't you see, Lord Robert and Mr. Forrest were in this together. If they let Lord Robert go, who knows what he'll do next?"

It was a different Miss Cutter who turned on her. "That's a wicked thing to say! Mr. Forrest, yes, but not Lord Robert. He is Her Grace's son. Have you no loyalty to the family?"

There flashed into Marion's mind that long-ago chant.

*Man-eating spiders.*
*Foxes as big as horses.*
*And cats with teeth like a shark's.*

That was Miss Cutter for a split second, then she smiled, but that gentle, vacant smile could not erase the impression in Marion's mind.

Her eyelids were drooping. Her limbs were becoming heavy. Her brain wanted to go to sleep. Marion wouldn't allow it. *Wake up, Marion! Think! What's happening to you? You were fine when you came downstairs this morning. All you had for breakfast was a slice of toast and the cup of tea Miss Cutter poured for you.*

The tea. Miss Cutter had poured her a cup of tea. Was there something in it? It didn't seem possible. Miss Cutter was an inoffensive old lady who was sinking into senility. I like her, thought Marion. No. I feel sorry for her. But now she felt afraid.

She'd taken only two mouthfuls of that tea before she'd got rid of it. It didn't seem possible that two mouthfuls of tea could make her feel so miserable.

Miss Cutter's singsong voice interrupted her thoughts. "Here we are. Edwina's cottage. This will only take a moment."

Marion staggered a little when Miss Cutter left her side. She didn't think she had the strength to move. It couldn't be influenza that was making her feel like this. She didn't have the sniffles or aches and pains. She'd been given something, and the only person who could have given it to her was the person who was standing in front of her with a vacant smile.

"Here it is." Miss Cutter had returned with a key in her hand. "Right where Edwina always kept it." She gave a self-deprecating laugh. "This is better than my herb garden. It's more private."

A chill ran up Marion's spine. Why would Miss Cutter want to be private with her?

She shuddered when they entered the cottage and stopped at the foot of the stairs. This was where Edwina's body was found.

Miss Cutter smiled into her eyes. "You look exhausted, my dear. I have only one question for you, then I'll let you go to sleep. Where are the letters that Lord Robert wrote to Hannah?"

This was the last thing Marion expected to hear, and she looked at Miss Cutter blankly.

Miss Cutter stopped smiling. "I asked you a question, Marion. Where are the letters Lord Robert wrote to Hannah? Please answer me."

"There aren't any."

"Don't lie to me! Hannah told me that Robert had written her love letters. I didn't believe her at the time, but at the fête, I overheard Phoebe telling Flora that Lord Robert's letters belonged to you and that *you* would decide what to do with them. Did you really think that I would allow you to expose him?"

It was the last remark that seemed odd to Marion. "Expose him? To whom?"

"To the world! In your family history! If it ever became known that he had an affair with Hannah, think what a stir it would cause. They'd start asking questions. They might start looking for Hannah's remains. John and I couldn't allow that to happen. Just tell me where the letters are and I'll let you go."

Marion put her hand on the newel post as she began to sway. "Is that what Mr. Forrest was looking for when he shot Brand?"

"That was bad luck. He didn't mean to hurt anyone. You were supposed to be at the Priory, not at the cottage." Miss Cutter's voice softened, became coaxing. "I've searched everywhere you were likely to hide them, and all I found was a box belonging to Hannah with keepsakes of Robert in it. You removed the letters, didn't you? Where did you hide them?"

Miss Cutter had been through her things. The thought was revolting. Bristling now, Marion said, "I told you. There are no letters."

The blow took her completely off guard. Miss

Cutter's hand lashed out and struck her across the face. Marion cowered away. This wasn't the Miss Cutter she knew. She was supposed to be a feeble old woman. Then she remembered that Miss Cutter went for long walks every day. She worked in the herb garden. She was always running and fetching for the dowager. And she was always in a flutter.

She wasn't in a flutter now. She was terrifying. Miss Cutter and her herb garden! Why hadn't she made the connection before she'd allowed this demented old woman to lead her to the cottage? If she didn't get a hold of herself, she could find herself sharing Hannah's fate. She was afraid, but her anger was stronger, and it was anger that gave her the will to beat this old woman at her own game.

Let her think she was on the point of collapse, then she'd catch her off guard and . . . and . . . Think! She had to *think*. She *was* on the point of collapse.

She gave a little whimper. "I'll tell you where the letters are if you tell me what happened the night Hannah disappeared."

"You're trying to fight it, aren't you? The sedative, I mean. I can see it in your eyes. It's quite mild, you know. You would be no good to me if you could not be wakened."

"I think," said Marion, "you misjudged the dose. I feel as though you've given me enough sedative to put a horse to sleep."

"All the more reason to tell me where the letters are."

Marion sniffed. "Not until you tell me what happened to Hannah."

It was all so childish, so sickeningly childish, thought Marion.

Miss Cutter sighed. "I think you know what happened. I killed Hannah, and John helped me bury her body in my herb garden. I couldn't leave her there for someone to find. The constable would start asking questions. He might learn that Hannah and Robert were having an affair. Robert would be the prime suspect. Think how Her Grace would feel."

"Did Edwina know about the affair?"

"Not at first. She believed that Hannah had eloped with some young man, and I was happy to promote that story. So you see, everything worked out for the best. You were right about the abbot's sculpture. John always feared that the gardeners might turn over the soil and uncover Hannah's body, so I arranged to have the statue moved to my garden."

She was waiting for Marion to tell her where the letters were, and Marion was delaying the moment when she would have to tell Miss Cutter that she had no idea.

She was becoming confused. There weren't any letters. There was no affair. She should be thinking of a way of escape. All she needed was a little time to fight the effects of the sedative she'd ingested.

She said slowly, "Is that where you killed Hannah? In the herb garden?"

Miss Cutter shook her head, smiling as though they were coconspirators. "People think I'm a nobody, poor Miss Cutter in a flutter. Oh, yes, I know what you all think of me. But it's a mistake to underestimate me, as Hannah learned to her cost." She laughed with a horrible kind of glee. "I knew about the affair, and when I saw Robert go out that night, I followed him. He met Hannah at the conservatory. I couldn't get close enough to hear what they were saying, but I could tell that they were having a lovers' tiff. When he went back to the house, Theodora's dog got out and ran straight to

Hannah. I pretended I had come to fetch it back to explain my presence there. I asked her to leave Robert alone. She laughed at me. She said that she and Robert were going to elope as soon as he screwed up his courage to tell his wife. And if he didn't tell Theodora, Hannah would show her the love letters Robert had written her. It suddenly occurred to me that if she was out of the way, she wouldn't cause any more trouble. This wicked young woman was not going to break Her Grace's heart. So I slipped into the gardener's shed beside the conservatory and found—a hammer, I think it was, then crept up behind her and whacked her on the head."

A look of revulsion crossed Marion's face and Miss Cutter said gently, "She wasn't a nice girl, Marion. Not like you. Your father knew what she was like; he said that he would never return to Yew Cottage as long as Hannah was here. And he never did, no, not even after Hannah was no longer a problem. I don't think Edwina ever forgave him for being right about Hannah."

Marion's jaw was slack. "How can you possibly know all this?"

The same gleeful laugh erupted from Miss Cutter's lips. "I read your mother's letters that Edwina had left lying around. I'm a very curious person, you know."

She was also a very voluble person, and Marion wondered if Miss Cutter was killing time until the sedative took effect and made her more pliable.

*Killing time!* What a horrible thought! But two could play at that game.

"Where was John? You said he helped you."

"Oh, I had to go to his cottage and ask for his help. He was just as glad to see the back of Hannah as I was."

Marion said slowly, "For Theodora's sake."

"Yes. John thought the world of Theodora. He would

have done anything for her. He knew that Robert would be suspected of murdering Hannah if her body was ever found, and that Theodora would be devastated. That's why I knew he would help me. I, of course, thought only of Her Grace. My one regret is that I had to poison poor little Snowball. Such a nice little dog. But he knew where Hannah was buried. He kept trying to dig her up, you see. I knew the gardeners would start to notice, and it might get back to the magistrate, so I did what I had to do."

Marion felt sick to her stomach. Had she been poisoned, too?

Miss Cutter peered into Marion's face. "How do you feel now?"

So she'd been right! thought Marion. Miss Cutter was filling in the time until the sedative took effect.

She gave a huge yawn, and looked blankly into the older woman's narrowed eyes. "What did you say?" she asked in a sleepy voice.

Miss Cutter smiled. "Tell me where the letters are, Marion."

There was no point in trying to persuade Miss Cutter that the letters did not exist. She wouldn't believe it. And, thought Marion belatedly, it might not be in her best interest anyway. What did Miss Cutter intend to do with her once she had the letters? She had a good idea.

That thought cleared some of the mist from her brain. "They're upstairs in one of the closets."

"I've already been through all the closets, Marion, and found nothing. You'll have to do better than that."

Clever Miss Cutter. "There's a loose board on the floor in my bedroom closet. Try there."

"Fine," said Miss Cutter. "We'll go together."

Marion was dismayed. She'd hoped that Miss Cutter

would go upstairs and then she could creep away. "I don't think I can manage the stairs."

"I'll help you."

No use arguing. Miss Cutter's smile was as feline as her eyes. As they slowly mounted the stairs, Marion said, "What did you put in my tea, Miss Cutter?"

"Oh, two of the powders Dr. Hardcastle prescribes to calm my nerves. I don't like them because they dull my mind, but if I don't take them, I get overexcited. I forget things or I say things out of turn that make people look at me oddly. If only I'd taken my powder that day . . . "

When the older woman's voice trailed away, Marion said, "Hannah would still be alive?"

"Heavens no, child!" Miss Cutter shook her head. "I was a younger woman then. I had no need of Dr. Hardcastle's powders. Hannah got just what she deserved. I was thinking of Edwina."

"You murdered Edwina!"

"Yes, I'm afraid she left me no choice."

A flash passed through Marion's brain. "You were the witness. You told Edwina that I was out the night Hannah disappeared."

"Yes. To my everlasting regret. I let something slip, something about Robert and Hannah. She kept asking me questions and in my confusion I told her to ask you about it, that you were there that night. If only she had left it alone, but she started asking other people questions. I had to do something, so I spread the rumor that she was becoming senile." She sounded cross, as though Edwina were to blame for what happened next. "Before that, she was so sure that Hannah had eloped that night. Now she thought that Robert might have murdered her. I had to do something, don't you see? When she went out for a walk one day, I entered the house. She always left the doors unlocked during the day. I waited upstairs, steeling myself to do the deed. I didn't want to do it. I really liked Edwina. But what choice did I have?"

Marion was leaning heavily on the older woman now, trying to convince her that she was practically helpless. It was an effort to keep up the pretense. She felt sickened by what Miss Cutter had told her and could hardly bear to touch her.

"One step more," said Miss Cutter, "and we're there. You know, Marion, I think confession must be good for the soul, because I feel so much better talking to you. It's as though a weight has been lifted from my shoulders."

Marion couldn't help giving in to her temper. "I'm not a priest, so don't look to me for absolution. Think of your victims—Hannah, Edwina, John Forrest. Mr. Forrest was your accomplice. He helped you, didn't he? First with Hannah, then with . . . with me. At Vauxhall? At the theater? Or was it you who pushed me down those stairs?"

"Of course I didn't push you! I couldn't get away from Longbury. What excuse would I give Her Grace? But John was frequently away from home. It was easy for him to slip away and find you." She shook her head. "After your chaise came to grief at the ford and Brand turned up, John was too afraid to try again."

Marion was startled. "My chaise foundered by accident!"

"No, dear. John fixed it so that it would look like an accident. We weren't going to kill you, Marion. We were hoping to frighten you off, you know, in case you recognized us again. You did see us burying Hannah, didn't you?"

"I saw two ghosts, or what I thought were ghosts. Nothing more."

"Yes, but we didn't know that. And I found a letter

Edwina was writing to you. For all I knew, she had already written to you. She wanted you to remember the events of that night, you see, and I couldn't allow that."

Marion shook her head. Either this woman was delusional—in her own way, not unlike Hannah—or she was truly wicked.

"Why John Forrest?" she asked, and her weariness wasn't all feigned. "What was his sin?"

Miss Cutter's expression turned lethal. "He said that he was worried about me, but I knew he was thinking of having me locked away. At the ball for you and Brand, I saw him talking to Dr. Hardcastle. And he gave me such a look." She shivered. "I was afraid of him, afraid that he saw me as a threat. I knew too much and I was becoming forgetful. So I killed him before he had me locked away. I told him that I had something of grave importance to say to him and that I'd meet him in the gardener's shed. When he arrived, I followed him in, and the rest you know."

*She whacked him on the head.* Marion flinched.

Miss Cutter peered into Marion's face. "Yes. Dr. Hardcastle's powders are taking effect. Why don't you lie down and have a little rest?"

She maneuvered Marion into the nearest room, which happened to be Emily's room, and helped her to the bed.

Marion didn't want to close her eyes, but her body seemed to have a will of its own. Her head sank into the pillow, her eyelids drooped, her limbs went lax. Her brain, however, had a will of its own as well. *Hannah, Edwina, John Forrest,* it told her, *and now you. And when she doesn't find the letters, maybe Phoebe will be added to the list.*

Her eyes flew open. Miss Cutter was watching her.

Marion raised her head. "I'm cold," she said. "Do you think you could light the fire?"

Miss Cutter sighed. "Don't fight it, dear. Let yourself fall asleep, and the end will be quite painless. But yes, I will light the fire if it makes you happy."

*The end?* Marion gulped. Was she going to be whacked on the head, too? Not if she had anything to do with it.

Miss Cutter walked to the fireplace, got a spark going in the tinderbox, and set it to the kindling in the grate.

Marion was amazed that Miss Cutter had agreed to her suggestion. It wasn't an innocent one. Didn't the woman realize that someone might see the smoke from the chimney? A gardener? Manley? The constable? They would know that the house was supposed to be empty. They might come and investigate. Then she'd be saved.

She sank back on the pillow and let out a sigh. This seemed to satisfy Miss Cutter, for she left the room. As soon as she was alone, Marion dragged herself from the bed and stumbled to the fireplace. Like the good housekeeper she was, Mrs. Ludlow had set the fire, ready to be lit, before she'd left Yew Cottage. The kindling was already ablaze, but it would take much longer for the coal to catch. This did not suit Marion. She wanted flames and smoke, especially smoke. Lots of it. The kindling box was right there, against the fireplace wall. She scooped some out and threw it on the fire. Sparks shot up the chimney as the kindling ignited.

She heard a step in the corridor. It was too late to get back to bed, so she collapsed into the nearest chair. A moment later, Miss Cutter entered and crossed to Marion.

Assuming a languid tone, Marion said, "I was cold in the bed. It's warmer by the fire."

Miss Cutter brought her face close to Marion's. "Are you trying to set the house on fire?" She didn't wait for an answer, but went on viciously, "There are no loose floorboards in the closets in your chamber. I'll give you one last chance. Tell me where Robert's letters are, or I swear I *will* set the house on fire, with you in it!"

She meant it. *Hannah. Edwina. Forrest. And now me. If only I wasn't sitting down but standing up, I might have a chance.*

"Try the linen closet," Marion said. "There's a loose board there." She pressed a hand to her brow. "My head aches."

Miss Cutter's eyes went wide. She twittered like a bird and hurried away.

She wasn't recovering from the sedative. She was becoming more groggy. And her head was aching. She was supposed to do something. What was it?

A shriek of outrage made Marion blink. Miss Cutter had found the cupboard bare. Marion slowly levered herself to her feet. At the same moment, a door downstairs crashed open.

"Marion!" Brand's voice. "Where are you?"

Her heart leaped to her throat. Tears of joy sprang to her eyes. She tried to shout the words but they sounded more like a ghostly whisper. "I'm upstairs."

He couldn't have heard her. She could hear his steps as he made for the kitchen.

Steadying herself with one hand on the fireplace, she picked up the poker with some idea of smashing a window to let Brand know where she was, but Miss Cutter charged into the room, eyes bulging, face twisted with fury, and Marion knew she would need that poker to defend herself.

"You'll never live to tell the tale." Miss Cutter was sucking air through her teeth. "I'll make you regret that you ever came back to Longbury."

She charged and they came together, swaying back and forth, each struggling for possession of the poker. When Miss Cutter wrested the poker out of her grasp and held it high above her head, ready to strike, Marion acted instinctively. She shoved the other woman with all her strength and sent her reeling back into the fireplace.

Miss Cutter lay there with the breath knocked out of her. In the wink of an eye, flames from the kindling licked around the folds of her gown. In another moment, she was like a fiery torch.

Screaming, shrieking, she got up and stumbled from the room. Swaying on her feet, Marion went after her.

Brand heard those bloodcurdling shrieks and his heart almost stopped beating. He raced from the scullery, through the kitchen, and into the hall. "Marion!" he yelled. "Marion!"

He stopped short, riveted by what he saw. At the top of the staircase, a small figure, engulfed in flames, paused before taking a step down. She was waving her hands, frantically trying to beat out the flames, shrieking at the top of her lungs. Brand started forward, removing his jacket as he came. Before his horrified eyes, she missed the next step and tumbled down the stairs like a Catherine wheel.

Brand used his jacket to smother the flames. Miss Cutter, her face barely recognizable, gave a rattling cough and lay still.

"Brand?"

He looked up. Marion was at the top of the stairs, and none too steady on her feet. He took the stairs two at a time and gathered her in his arms. Eyes shut tightly, he clung to her and whispered her name over and over.

After a moment, she pushed out of his arms. "Miss Cutter?"

"She's dead, I'm afraid."

She shook her head. "Don't ask me to be sorry for her, not today and not tomorrow. Maybe never."

"I won't," he soothed.

"I have something important to tell you."

"What is it, my love?"

Her face crumpled. "I think I'm going to be sick."

Twenty minutes later, she was in her chamber at the Priory, but Brand wouldn't allow her to go to bed. He forced her to drink cup after cup of bitter coffee, and when she wasn't drinking coffee, he supported her with his arm and made her walk around the room. It was only when Dr. Hardcastle arrived that she was finally allowed to lie down on the bed. She heard the two men conferring and learned that the effects of the sedative would have been much worse, though by no means fatal, if she hadn't brought up her meager breakfast after that frightful scene at the cottage.

She was restless in sleep, but every time she wakened, Brand was there, bathing her brow with a cool cloth, telling her everything would be all right. When she finally fought clear of sleep, it was to find that Brand was stretched out on the bed beside her. He looked worse than she felt.

"It's been a god-awful night," he murmured, "and an even worse start to the day. I'm glad you're awake, because we have to talk. We have to decide what we're going to tell the magistrate."

She felt as weak as a baby. Tears started to her eyes. "No one will believe how wicked Miss Cutter was," she said.

He smoothed back tendrils of hair that were stuck to

her face. "Dr. Hardcastle would, only he doesn't call Miss Cutter wicked. He says that she suffered from some sort of mental disorder that he thought they were controlling with a mild sedative. He tells me you're going to be fine."

She shuddered and snuggled closer. "Did they find Hannah's remains?"

He nodded. "Beneath the statue of the abbot, just as you said."

"We have to tell the magistrate the truth, that Miss Cutter was the killer. There's no need to mention Edwina's letter or Lord Robert. All we need say is that Miss Cutter was mad." She sniffed back tears. "But really, it's Hannah who was at the bottom of it all. She started everything. Even with my own father. That's what the estrangement between Edwina and my parents was about, and I never knew until Miss Cutter told me."

"Hush, now," he said. "I don't think you can blame Hannah for everything. Miss Cutter and Forrest had some part in this. There is nothing wrong with loyalty, but *blind* loyalty is a curse. It was that that led them astray."

They talked back and forth, each relating what had happened and what they'd learned in the hours they'd been apart. She wanted to know why he'd thought to look in Yew Cottage, and beamed at his answer.

"I saw the smoke from the chimney," he said. "I knew, in my bones, that you were telling me where you were."

There was a knock at the door and Emily poked her head in. "Is it all right if we see Marion now? Marion, the girls are beside themselves with fear and grief, worrying about you."

Brand rolled off the bed. Marion tidied her hair and

sat up. "Of course they can see me. I'm perfectly fine. Where are they?"

The door opened wide and Phoebe and Flora hastened to the bed. Emily followed after them. The tears were flowing freely. Only Marion was dry-eyed.

"Poor Miss Cutter," she said, "we must pity her."

Brand retreated a few steps and bumped into Andrew.

"Grandmother would like to see you," said Andrew, looking at Brand.

Brand turned away feeling slightly de trop. He squared his shoulders. Poor Miss Cutter, he thought, we must pity her. If Marion could carry it off, so could he. His grandmother would be devastated, but she could take some consolation in knowing that her son, Robert, was completely vindicated.

# Chapter Twenty-six

Though Brand was loath to leave Marion and the others to the gloom that blanketed the Priory, he could not delay the election, and had no option but to present himself a week later in Brighton where the main body of his constituents would cast their votes.

On his second night there, Ash Denison arrived at Brand's hotel. He had a lot of catching up to do and, as they made inroads into a bottle of claret, he listened with growing astonishment as his friend related the events of the week just past. His own errand respecting David Kerr was momentarily forgotten.

Brand said, "We could have made Miss Cutter's death look like an accident, but that would have meant that Marion would never know for sure what had happened to her aunt's body, not to mention the fact that there would always be speculation surrounding John Forrest's murder. So we told the magistrate the truth, the bare facts, I mean—that Miss Cutter admitted to murdering Forrest as well as Hannah all those years ago. She seemed to think that everyone was against her, and attacked them without warning."

"Miss Cutter!" Ash took a mouthful of wine and swallowed it. "I find that incredible. She always reminded me of my own aunt, you know, a harmless tabby cat with nothing more vicious on her mind than getting me married off."

"Well, this tabby cat had claws," responded Brand dryly.

"And the magistrate believed you?"

"Not me. He believed Dr. Hardcastle and my grandmother. They were both worried about Miss Cutter. She had always been unpredictable, but lately she'd begun to brood about things, and suspected that people were out to harm her."

His thoughts drifted to the conversation he'd had with his grandmother. She was beside herself, thinking that she was to blame for Miss Cutter's unprovoked attacks. It was his grandmother who was the first to notice her companion's growing instability, and it was she who had raised the subject with the doctor, not Mr. Forrest, as Miss Cutter suspected. But the dowager had balked at the idea of having Miss Cutter locked up. So the doctor prescribed a mild sedative. It seemed to help. But there was always trouble whenever Miss Cutter stopped taking her medicine.

Brand accepted Hardcastle's and his grandmother's assessment up to a point, but it did not explain why Miss Cutter had murdered Hannah all those years ago, before there was any question that her mind was disturbed. However, it suited his purposes to allow everyone to think that Miss Cutter was a little mad, because it kept Robert's name out of the whole sorry affair.

Ash said, "How did you come to be at the cottage at the critical moment?"

Brand smiled. "Marion had managed to trick Miss Cutter into lighting the fire. I saw the smoke from the chimney and went to investigate."

What he didn't tell Ash was that it was more like a charge of the cavalry. He'd found the Priory practically deserted, but one of the footmen had told him that Marion and Miss Cutter had gone for a walk. He'd been in the herb garden when he'd seen the smoke billowing out of the chimney stack. He thought his heart would burst when he crashed through the front door. But that was as nothing when he saw the small figure engulfed in flames at the top of the stairs. He'd feared that it was Marion. Just thinking about it made his hand shake.

"What made you decide that Miss Cutter was the villain?"

Brand smiled. "The dog was poisoned."

"What?"

"It's a long story, and I'd far rather hear how you managed to deal with David Kerr."

Ash threw a small package into Brand's lap. "David Kerr," he said, "is now on his way to Canada."

Brand opened the package and shook out the contents. Marion's emerald earrings dropped into his hand, and a ring to match.

Ash said, "Kerr told the truth. He got a pittance for them. Can you believe it, the jeweler kept the receipt he insisted Kerr write out when he sold them?"

"We're lucky the jeweler hadn't sold them to someone else."

"They were a present for his lady love. I had a devil of a time persuading him to give them up. I had to reimburse him for the funds he gave to Kerr. Then I hid the jewels in Kerr's lodgings."

He let out a rich laugh. "I wish you could have seen Kerr's face when Bow Street Runners entered his room, with me right behind them, and searched his belongings. I'd stashed the jewels in one of his dresser drawers." He paused a moment, a big smile on his face as the scene came back to him. "Then he was hauled before the magistrate in Bow Street and charged with stealing my mother's priceless heirlooms. There is nothing like a hanging offence to bring a man to his senses. I told the magistrate I would drop the charges if Mr. Kerr paid me for poor Mama's trinkets. Of course, Kerr has no money, so I accepted his promissory note instead."

"You've done well." Brand inserted his fingers into the envelope and withdrew a one-page document.

Ash's eyes gleamed with satisfaction. "In the sum of ten thousand pounds, duly signed and witnessed. He knows that if ever he should return to England and try to make trouble for Lady Marion, he'll land in debtors' prison.

"There's more." Ash took the package from Brand and withdrew two folded sheets of paper. "The parish records, as you requested. As you can see, he has torn them out of their different ledgers. I know that the bishops keep records of records, but Kerr will never be in a position to gain access to them. An unscrupulous little toad, isn't he?" He laughed. "But no more unscrupulous than we are, when the occasion merits it."

A muscle tensed in Brand's cheek. "He is beneath contempt. If I had my way, I would let him stand trial. The death sentence would most likely be commuted to transportation."

"I suppose Marion would have balked at that?"

"I didn't want to put her to the test."

He swallowed a sigh. That was the problem. He didn't want to put her to the test. Things that had seemed so simple before the events of this god-awful week were now complicated. Marion had been through so much that he was treating her with kid gloves. How could she think of him when she had just buried a long-lost aunt? They were all in mourning in the Priory, all in their blacks. If they followed convention, there could be no talk of weddings for another six months.

This did not sit well with him. Three people who were largely responsible for their own demise, three people who did not deserve respect, were being mourned by those who should despise them most.

Ash said, "How does this affect your chances of being elected, Brand?"

"What?"

Ash reached for the bottle of claret and refilled his glass. "The election," he said. "I expect all these bodies littering the Priory are all that your constituents can talk about."

Brand bit back a harsh retort. Maybe he should take a leaf out of Ash's book. Maybe there *was* something ghoulishly funny in the situation. And maybe Ash's penchant for making light of outrageous misfortune was just what he needed to jog him out of the doldrums.

He swallowed a mouthful of claret. "You're right about that," he said. "That's all they can talk about. They're not interested in what I'll do if I'm elected to Parliament, only in the gory details of Miss Cutter's murders. If this had come out before I won the nomination, well, I wouldn't have won the nomination."

"As bad as that?"

"Without a doubt."

They sipped their claret in dispirited silence.

Ash got up. "To blazes with this," he said. "If you don't get elected, it's not the end of the world. Let's go down to the taproom and crack open a bottle of brandy. It's better than moping up here. Unless, of course, your constituents would object to their member of Parliament drinking in public?"

Brand got up as well. "I'm not their member of Parliament yet and, frankly, I don't give a brass button for what my constituents think."

He gathered the bits and pieces that had been in the package Ash had given him, walked to the wardrobe, and stuffed them into a pocket of one of his coats. "By the way," he said, "how much do I owe you for getting rid of Kerr?"

Ash shifted from one foot to the other. "I had to settle his debts here in England and give him a stake to start a new life in Canada."

"How much?" Brand asked stoically.

"Three thousand," replied Ash.

"Three thousand *pounds*?" Brand was astonished.

"No. Three thousand guineas. He drives a hard bargain."

Brand stared, appalled, then shook his head. He flung an arm around Ash's shoulders. "Let's make that two bottles of brandy," he said, and laughed.

At the Priory, Marion's mood was a fair reflection of Brand's. Ever since he had left for Brighton, she'd sat through a series of dismal dinners where the diners resembled a flock of crows, and the conversation was practically nonexistent. As she climbed the stairs to her own chamber after one such dinner, she was about ready to tear out her hair. She felt like a hypocrite in her blacks, and wouldn't have dreamed of wearing them had the dowager not set the example for them all. Three far from innocent people had come to a bad end. No one was to blame but themselves. She'd had a narrow escape. How could she be sad about that?

Hannah had finally been given a decent Christian burial, but the evil she had set in motion still lived on after her. Flora had told Phoebe, who had told Marion, that Theodora was packing her boxes and was going home to live with her father. The news was not unexpected, because Theodora had shut herself up in her rooms for the last few days and Lord Robert seemed to be making a home for himself in Brand's house. Marion wished that Brand was still here or that the election had come at a different time. Without him at the helm, his family was falling apart and she didn't know how to stop it.

She sat on the edge of her bed for a long time, reviewing the last several days, going over all that Brand had told her about Robert and Theodora and Flora. It was all such a waste, and there was nothing anyone could do about it. She didn't know why it mattered so much to her, but it did.

Hannah's box was in the top drawer of her dresser. Marion wasn't impulsive by nature, but she made up her mind there and then that Theodora should know that Robert had never betrayed her with Hannah. Hannah had engineered his downfall, and her own as well.

On that thought, she got Hannah's box out of the top drawer of her dresser and left the room.

Theodora was surprised to see her, but not hostile. She opened the door and allowed Marion to enter. "This is a surprise," she said. "I was sure everyone was holding their breath until I had left."

"No," said Marion, refusing to be intimidated. "I think I'm the only one who knows you're leaving."

"Oh, they all know. Trust me. The servants are bound to have told everyone that my boxes are packed."

Marion took a chair without waiting to be invited. After a moment, Theodora sighed and sat on a small sofa. Her look was inquiring, but not particularly encouraging.

After clearing her throat, Marion said, "I liked Mr. Forrest. I know what a loss his death must be to you."

Theodora's eyes narrowed unpleasantly. "No one knows or can possibly understand what a loss John is to me. He is the one person I could always count on. If you have nothing but platitudes to offer, you might as well leave."

That was the thing about Theodora, thought Marion. She was larger than life and looked as though she might have stepped out of a Greek tragedy. As for herself, she was stubborn. She wasn't going to leave without saying her piece.

"I have something for you," she said.

Theodora had risen to her feet. She sank back again, and took the box Marion offered. "What is it?"

"Hannah's keepsakes. She was obsessed with your husband, and collected mementoes just like any love-struck girl might do. Only, Hannah made up lies, either to get what she wanted or to convince herself that she was irresistible to men. I don't suppose we shall ever know what went on in her mind. It's enough to know that Robert was blameless."

Theodora was going through the items in the box. "Where are Robert's letters to her?"

Marion shook her head. "There were no letters. Hannah was a disturbed young woman. Her last employer, Mrs. Love, lives in Brighton. She can tell you that Hannah caused havoc there, too, with the sons of her friends." Her voice dropped. "Robert was not involved with Hannah. He did not send her letters. The whole thing was a game she played, or a figment of her imagination."

She'd hardly finished speaking when Theodora shut the lid with a decided snap and thrust the box into her arms. Eyes flashing, Theodora said, "You may take that back to Robert and tell him that I am not so easily hoodwinked. He had his chance to beg my forgiveness, and now it's too late."

She stalked to the door and held it wide. Marion got up and crossed to it. She stopped on the threshold and looked into those beautiful, flashing eyes. "You must know I'm speaking the truth," she said. "Why won't you accept it?"

Theodora was as cool as ice. "I've given you my answer and have nothing more to say."

Marion shook her head. "It must be lonely being a Greek goddess." She left the room with all the dignity she could muster.

When she reached her own room, she was steaming. To think that she had wasted her sympathy on such a hard-hearted harpy. It was Robert she should have felt sorry for. He was the one who had been rejected, not Theodora. For the last twenty years, they had been together, yet apart. It was all such a waste.

Her thoughts immediately shifted to Brand. He'd been gone for two days, and already she felt hollow inside. What was keeping them apart? An accident of birth? That excuse was as flimsy as the one Theodora used to punish her husband. Was it possible that she and Theodora had something in common?

She sat on the edge of the bed, a confusion of thoughts racing through her mind. The candles burned low. The room became chilled, and still she sat there, thinking, thinking, thinking.

This was how Emily found her when she came to say good night. She looked at the candles burning low in their holders, felt the chill in the air, and quickly crossed to her sister. Sinking to her knees, she took Marion's cold hands into her warm ones. "Marion, dear," she said anxiously. "What's the matter? You're so pale."

Marion smiled fleetingly. "There is something I have been wanting to tell you for a long time." She patted the mattress. "Come, sit beside me on the bed. It's about Mama and Papa."

Late on the following afternoon, Brand was outside the tavern, close to the common where the platform had been set up for last-minute speeches before the vote was taken. He was doing what was expected of him, mixing with the locals, supplying them with beer, and smiling until his face was ready to crack.

Though it would take some time for the results to come in from outlying districts, he didn't think much of his chances. He could feel his momentum slipping away. The shocking events at the Priory had had an effect not only on electors, but also on members of his own party. They were there in force, but not standing shoulder to shoulder with him. Only a few had stepped up to the podium to endorse his candidacy.

There was nothing new in this, he told himself. He'd been making his own way in the world, without help from others, ever since he could remember. He'd always been a lone wolf. What *was* new was that he wished it didn't have to be this way.

A hand on his shoulder had him turning away from the group of men he'd been trying to win over. Ash smiled into his eyes.

"Ash! What are you doing here?" He knew that Ash had no interest in politics, and he'd left him at the Castle on the point of ordering his dinner. All the same, he was very glad to see his friend.

"I had no choice," said Ash.

Brand's gaze followed where Ash pointed. Across the common, Marion, Clarice, Emily, and his grandmother were standing on the pavement, having just descended from one of the Priory's carriages. They were smiling and nodding and waving to him. What made Brand stare was that only his grandmother was in mourning clothes. The others were dressed in all the colors of the rainbow.

The darkness inside him lifted, and a slow smile spread across his face.

There was more. Ash touched his arm and Brand turned his attention to the platform. Andrew was there and had just stepped up to the podium. Oswald was standing behind him.

"His Grace, the Duke of Shelbourne!" the chief officer called out.

There was a murmur in the crowd. Someone said, "Isn't that Lord Andrew?"

Andrew heard the comment and shot back, "Titles aren't important! What matters is a man's character and talent. I'm asking you to vote for my brother because I know he'll make an excellent trustee of whatever he takes on. If you don't believe me, take a look at the FitzAlan estates. He has been our trustee since I was a boy and we're thriving."

"Thriving, is it?" a spectator jeered. "What about John Forrest? Ask him if he's thriving."

The question threw Andrew off stride, but another bystander, Lord Robert, took up the challenge. "John Forrest," he called out, "was my employee. I paid his wages. He was in charge of my stables. If you're apportioning blame, then I should be your target, not my nephew."

Constable Hinchley was there to keep order, but he was also a voter and he, too, was stung into entering the fray. "If it hadn't been for Mr. Hamilton," he shouted above the restless murmurs of the crowd, "there would have been another murder. I can't say more, because it's official business, but me and Sir Basil knows what we knows, and I'm voting for Mr. Hamilton."

Some cheered, some jeered. It was not unlike the reenactment between Cavaliers and Roundheads at his grandmother's fête, thought Brand. And he didn't know why he was grinning.

"I have to stay to the bitter end." He looked at Ash. "This could go on for hours. Would you mind telling Marion and the others not to wait up? I'll see them at the hotel tomorrow for breakfast."

Ash stared. "The bitter end? It's like that, is it?"

"I suppose it is," said Brand, but he was still grinning when he went to speak to Robert.

Emily delayed getting into the coach to go back to the hotel. She wanted to speak to Andrew, and waved him over. When he stood before her, she grasped his hands and smiled into his eyes.

"You were magnificent!" she said. "I am so proud of you, I could kiss you!"

He cocked a brow. "What's stopping you?"

She felt a little frisson of something, not alarm, more like feminine wariness, which she instantly dismissed. This was Andrew. He was like a brother to her. She was behaving like a silly schoolgirl.

She put her hands on his shoulders, noted absently that they were broad and manly, and raised her chin. He wasn't helping, so she went on tiptoe and pressed her lips to his. That's when his arms clamped around her, bringing her hard against his full length. Her little squeal of shock was smothered by his kiss. And this young man really knew how to kiss.

The kiss was over in a moment, and he set her away from him. She was covered in blushes and didn't know where to look when she caught the knowing glint in his eye.

"What was that all about?" she asked crossly.

"Oh, just staking my claim," he replied in an odiously offhand manner. "I thought it was about time that you knew where we stand."

She let out a pent-up breath and said the first thing that came into her head. "But Andrew, don't you see, we're far too young?"

He brushed the pad of his thumb over her cheek. "Yes, my love, but we're going to get older, aren't we?"

And he sauntered off.

Only then did she notice that a crowd of people were gaping and staring. She practically threw herself into the coach and sank back against the banquette.

"What kept you?" asked Marion.

"Oh, Andrew," Emily replied, and turned her head away to hide the foolish smile that she couldn't seem to quell. "Only Andrew."

The dowager saw that smile, and the heaviness in her heart lifted a little. Her present grief faded into the background as another thought struck her. She felt that she could safely relinquish all her hopes and dreams for these difficult FitzAlans into other hands. Her time was past, but Marion and Emily were just coming into theirs.

It was a whimsical thought, but it gave her comfort. It gave her hope.

# Chapter Twenty-seven

It was the drink on his breath Marion smelled first. One moment, she was dozing in the big wing armchair beside the fireplace in Brand's chamber, the next, she was wide awake, staring into his inebriated eyes.

"You won the election!" she cried out, then huffed a little because he'd gone off carousing while she had waited up for him to hear the results.

"No. I lost it." He turned away and began to shrug out of his clothes.

Stricken, she stared, then jumped to her feet and went after him. "You lost?"

"I was trounced."

"Oh, Brand. What can I say? I'm so sorry."

He didn't look like a man who had lost his heart's desire. He looked like someone who had just won a fortune at the roulette table.

"Don't be," he said. "I won something that is far more important to me than an election. It was mine all along, only I was too blind to see it."

She was mystified. "What was?"

"You should know. Didn't you prod them into coming?"

"You mean your family? No. We all had the same idea. Though my sisters and I set off first, they caught up to us and we came on together."

"And whose idea was it to put off your blacks?"

She shook her head. "There was no collusion there, either. We all seemed to come to the same thought at the same moment, that it was ludicrous to go into mourning for three people who did so much harm. It's different for your grandmother. She has taken Miss Cutter's death, and all the circumstances leading up to it, to heart. They've been together forever."

He looped his arms around her shoulders, and suddenly his eyes didn't look so inebriated. They were intensely blue and intensely serious. "Why are you here, Marion?"

"Don't you know?"

"I'm not a mind reader, and your mind is so convoluted that it's impossible to read."

She could be flippant, she could be coy, but in that moment, when this difficult, lonely man gave her a glimpse into his soul, she felt utterly humbled. "Mr. Hamilton," she said softly, "long have I admired and loved you. Would you do me the honor, the very great honor, of accepting my hand in marriage?"

"Is this to make up for my losing the election?"

Her feelings of humility instantly vanished. "No, you idiot! Because I love you and can't live without you."

He closed his eyes and opened them wide. "I'm never going to let you forget," he said, "that you proposed to me."

She pouted. "If you're going to make fun of me—"

He held her fast. "I'm entitled to a little revenge for all the pain you've caused me. And the answer is 'Yes.' I've known you were the woman for me since . . . "

"Since?"

Humor brightened his eyes. "Since you fell down that flight of stairs and stubbed your toes." He nodded when she looked at him dubiously. "Oh, yes. I was rigid with fear until you told me to stop fussing. I love you, Marion."

She dimpled up at him. "I know. I've been reading your mind, remember? Now see if you can read mine."

She looked pointedly at the bed. With a hoot of laughter, he swept her into his arms.

A long time later, Marion stretched under the weight of Brand's arm and raised up on one elbow to look at him. "You're not going to give up politics, are you, just because you've lost one election?"

A look of surprise crossed his face. "I thought that's what you wanted, you know, a quiet life, in case the truth about your parents ever gets out?"

She winced. "I suppose I deserved that. I was trying to be noble, trying to do what was best for everyone. It doesn't work. In fact, I've come to believe that trying to be noble is a form of arrogance. What's the point in making everyone miserable?"

"Now, this is interesting." He raised on his elbow so that they were eye to eye. "Don't stop there. Tell me how you came to change your mind."

"I didn't change my mind. I think, in my heart of hearts, I always knew that I could never give you up. But Theodora made me see what a fool I had been—oh, not in so many words. Just the opposite. She gave up the man she loved for no good reason, and the longer she allowed her hurt pride to fester, the harder it became for her to admit that she had made a mistake. What a waste of two lives."

He looked amused. "I can't see Theodora ever believing that she had made a mistake."

"That's my point. If that's not arrogance, I don't know what it is." She lowered her head to the pillow. "Then there was you. You become so fixed on reaching your goals that you cut yourself off from those who are close to you, or should be close to you. You really do need a wife, and since I could not tolerate the thought of another woman taking on that role, I decided I had better do something about it. So I spoke to Emily and told her about our parents."

He said slowly, "You told Emily about your parents?"

"I felt I had to. It seemed to me that when we were married and you were prime minister—and Phoebe really believes that will happen—I would become a target for gossipmongers or hate-mongers or whatever you want to call them. So I wanted Emily to know the truth before she heard it from someone else. Did you say something?"

"No," he said hoarsely. "Just a frog in my throat." He cleared his throat. "So, how did Emily respond?"

"Oh, she shed a few tears, not for herself, but for our mother and me. But she thinks like you. She thinks that those transcripts will show that our father married our mother the first chance he got."

She shook her head. "I wish I had been like Emily. The last few years, I've guarded that secret as though the whole world would end if it ever got out." She gave him a sad smile. "That's a kind of arrogance as well. The result was, I built a shell around myself. It's lonely living inside a shell, as you should know."

He nodded. "None better."

She nodded, too. "Well, Emily isn't like us. The first thing she did after I shared our dark, family secret was run off and tell Andrew. She says that he is like a brother to her, and she felt better after she'd talked things over with him."

"A brother?" he murmured. "I wonder. That reminds me. I have something to show you."

She held him back with a hand on his wrist. Her voice was low and urgent. "Look at the time! I have to get back to my own room before the hotel staff are up and doing."

He looked at the clock. "No, don't go yet, there's still time."

"Time for what?"

He kissed the hand that restrained him, then her nose, then her mouth. David Kerr could wait.

"Read my mind," he said.

Three weeks later, after the banns were called, they were married in Longbury's parish church. Emily made a lovely bridesmaid and Phoebe and Flora were positively angelic flower girls, but it was the bride who took Brand's breath away, not because she was beautiful, but because she was radiantly happy, and her happiness made him happy, too.

Andrew stood up with him, and more than one person commented on the strong family resemblance. But it was Ash Denison who won the hearts of all the ladies present. A time or two, he was seen, surreptitiously, to dab the tears from his eyes with his handkerchief.

The reception following the service was held on the Priory lawns. The whole village was invited and they turned out in force. With Marion by his side, Brand wandered from group to group, exchanging a few words, but for the most part, he was content to let Marion do the talking while he lost himself in thought.

He was thinking of his grandfather, wondering what he would make of it all if he were here. He wanted to honor the memory of his grandfather, but not by living in the past or carrying grudges that belonged to a former generation. He was a FitzAlan as much as he was a Hamilton. The wonder of it was that it had taken him so many years to realize it.

Marion's words interrupted his thoughts. "We're making our home in the Priory," she told Sir Basil's wife, "with Brand's family. There's more than enough room, and the dowager has found the perfect tenant to take over Brand's house, General Frampton. He's of the old school and fell in love with the place the moment he clapped eyes on it."

She slid a mischievous look in Brand's direction, and he nodded at the hit. Marion had taken one look at his grandfather's house and hadn't been able to conceal her dismay. General Frampton had proved to be a godsend. He was enchanted with the dark oak paneling, the horsehair sofas and chairs and solid Jacobean furniture, and had promised that not one thing would be altered as long as he was the tenant.

He might have sold the house to the general, but Brand wasn't quite ready to give up this tie to his grandfather. Meantime, they were sure they could let Yew Cottage to, hopefully, some congenial family who were not put off by recent events at the Priory.

Sir Basil nudged Brand with his elbow. "Bad luck

about the election," he said. "I hope this doesn't mean that you're giving up politics. The timing was wrong, that's all. There will be other by-elections. I hope you'll let your name stand?"

Brand nodded and thanked the magistrate for his kind words. In truth, he hadn't made up his mind what he would do in the long run, only what he would do in the short run. He wanted a respite from his ambitions, no matter how laudable they were. He wanted a chance to get to know his family and forge bonds that could never be broken. And most of all, he wanted to spend time with his wife and lay a solid foundation for their new life together.

Marion said, "That's a lewd smile if ever I saw one. What were you thinking about just now?"

He banished the lewd thought in his mind and said easily, "I was thinking that we should name our first-born son FitzAlan Hamilton, if that's all right with you."

"That's a bit of a mouthful, isn't it?"

"Alan for short."

She nodded. "I like that." Her eyes sparkled up at him. "What if we only have girls?"

He brushed his lips over hers in a quick kiss. "We'll call her Alana."

She was laughing when she was swept away by Emily to get ready for her journey to Stratford. This was to be both a honeymoon and a pilgrimage. Brand had been right about her parents. The transcripts had duly arrived and proved that her parents were married in Stratford, most likely on the journey down to Longbury, three years before Emily was born. The transcripts meant more to Marion than his account of how he'd dealt with Kerr, though she was delighted to get back her mother's emeralds. The transcripts cleared the cloud that hung over her sisters. Nobody could shame them now.

Brand wandered onto the terrace and sipped his champagne, a little apart from his guests, but not feeling the least bit solitary. There was a difference. His eyes roamed the crush of people, coming to rest on various members of his family.

He was both gratified and humbled by how well everything was turning out. In Theodora's absence, Robert seemed to have pulled himself together. He and Andrew had plans to turn the stables into a stud, and Manley was now working for them. His grandmother had insisted on taking over the education of Flora and Phoebe until a governess could be found. There was no question of Flora spending six months with her aunt. Robert had put his foot down. Flora's aunt would always find a welcome at the Priory, but henceforth, Flora's place was with him. And last but not least, Clarice and Oswald had confided they were expecting a baby.

A new era and a new generation had begun. It was fitting.

The dowager joined him and linked her arm through his. After a companionable silence, she said, "Your father would be very proud of you if he could see you now."

Once upon a time, those would have been fighting words. Brand sipped his champagne. Finally, he said, "Tell me about my father. I want to know what kind of man he was."

They were in the vestry of Holy Trinity Church in Stratford-upon-Avon, looking over the parish register for the year of 1796. The ink was fading, but still legible.

Marion's finger trailed along the page as she read the entry she wanted: *George Dane, widower, and Diana Gunn, spinster, by Special License.*

Marion's smile was radiant when she looked up at Brand. "I remember my father in the coach with us on the way to Longbury, but I knew he wasn't at the cottage. Well, of course, now we know why he wasn't. He was avoiding Hannah!"

She looked at the entry for one last time and shut the book firmly. "No more looking back," she said, "at least not with regret. I have so much happiness inside me, I think I could drown in it."

After returning the register to the curate, they left the church and stopped on the steps to give their eyes time to adjust to the light.

Brand said, "No more fears that your murky past will overtake you?"

She shook her head. "I was never afraid for myself. You know that. Besides, I'm taking you for my model."

"What does that mean?"

"It means that I'm immune to the spite of people who aren't fit to lick my boots."

A laugh was startled out of him. "Is that supposed to be a compliment?"

She thought for a moment. "Not really. It's a statement of fact, the unvarnished truth. It's one of your most endearing qualities."

When she was silent, he said, "What are you thinking?"

She chuckled. "The best people sometimes rise from what appear to be the worst circumstances. That's you, Brand FitzAlan Hamilton, and I wouldn't change you for the world. Did you say something?"

He rubbed his throat. "No. It's that damned frog again."

"Are you coming down with a cold?"

"On my honeymoon? I am more manly than that."

She laughed. "Stratford!" she said. "Shakespeare's birthplace. There is so much to do and see here that I hardly know where to begin."

When she looked up at him with a query in her eyes, he replied, "True. But this is the first day of our honeymoon." He shrugged casually. "The attractions that Stratford has to offer will still be here tomorrow."

"You're reading my mind again," she said, and she started down the path, leaving him staring.

She turned on her heel to look at him. "Well, what are you waiting for? Let's go back to our hotel room and shut the door on the world."

He was beside her in two strides. Laughing, arm in arm, they ran down the path to the waiting carriage.